SCEPTRE

Also by Catherine Feeny

The Dancing Stones

Musical Chairs

CATHERINE FEENY

SCEPTRE

First published in the UK in 1996 by Hodder and Stoughton
First published in paperback in 1997 by Hodder and Stoughton
A division of Hodder Headline PLC
A Sceptre Paperback

The right of Catherine Feeny to be identified as the Author of
the Work has been asserted by her in accordance with the
Copyright, Designs and Patents Act 1988.

10 9 8 7 6 5 4 3 2 1

British Library Cataloguing in Publication Data

Feeny, Catherine
    Musical chairs
    1. English fiction – 20th century
    I. Title
    823.9'14 [F]

    ISBN 0 340 64960 7

Typeset by Palimpsest Book Production Limited,
Polmont, Stirlingshire
Printed and bound in Great Britain by
Cox and Wyman Ltd, Reading, Berkshire
Mackays of Chatham PLC, Chatham, Kent

Hodder and Stoughton
A division of Hodder Headline PLC
338 Euston Road
London NW1 3BH

To Raymond ffoulkes, with love.

Acknowledgements ∫

I would like to thank my editor, Carolyn Mays, and my agent, Sara Menguc, for their invaluable insight and guidance. Thanks, too, to my friend, Shaun Theobald, who, with great good humour, advised me on all the ornithological aspects of this book, including what could and could not be expected of Parus minor and who wrote to inform me that he had made what is, to the best of my knowledge, its only recorded sighting. Thanks to Graeme Duncan for help with the manuscript; Felicity-Ann Hall for reading the novel as I wrote it; Sarah Taylor-Moore for legal information and Karen Eastman for medical.

Most of all, I wish to thank Raymond ffoulkes, to whom the novel is dedicated, for playing a part in every aspect of its creation from discussing the ideas to preparing the manuscript and reading it back to me, chapter by chapter. The sound of his voice is always there in my words. They are the better for it.

The country gentry of old time lived in a rarefied social air: dotted apart on their stations up the mountain they looked down with imperfect discrimination on the belts of thicker life below.

George Eliot, *Middlemarch*

Birchwatching

Birdwatching

On a sunny day in April, Osbert Sway MP died in London and Bob Adams admitted to himself the truth about the lesser tit. These two seemingly unconnected events were to have far-reaching consequences for the seaside town of Ebbing.

About three quarters of an hour after Sway's, as yet unannounced, death, Bob was looking at Ebbing from the cliffs, spanning it with his binoculars in search of different species. The low wall he leaned against belonged to the garden of Lesley Sway, Obsert's wife. Had he been listening for such things, Bob would have been able to hear the chirrup of the telephone in the front bedroom, the call that brought the news to Lesley that her husband was no more.

Bob was on the very edge of his area of study. This was the wealthy part of Ebbing with the best views: at the ends of the gardens were scrubland and woodland, ash, elder and hawthorn, clearings of short grass running down to the cliffs where the greens and browns plunged into blues and greys, radiant or misty depending on the weather. Up here were magpies, kestrels and goldfinches. Up here were the mansions built by Victorian industrialists when the train from London came to Ebbing. The most spectacular of these, perched where it could survey not just the sea and the cliffs but also the river valley of the Ebb, was that which now belonged to the Frogwells: an inebriated mass of twirls and frills of monstrously solid construction – solidity, of course, being the main point of the building, which all that decoration attempted, rather unsuccessfully, to embellish. Bob did not know the Frogwells, though he had once been introduced to Eustace Frogwell at an official event. Frogwell himself would have been unlikely to recognise the primary school teacher.

Dotted along the cliff were various other approximations to such magnificence, including some rather more restrained Edwardian efforts, such as the one below which Bob was standing. Their red brick contrasted oddly with the chill fondant colours – the strawberries, lemons, municipal greens – and the sinuous curves of the Odeon-style buildings, placed among them in the twenties and thirties, decades which liked their sea and sky large and flat.

But these houses, and their accompanying gardens, were not within the boundaries of Bob's tetrad, which included an area of clifftop, part of the river valley, and the town of Ebbing itself, which was why he was studying it through his binoculars as it started up the business of its day, unrepresented at Westminster. Or rather, he was not looking at the town, he was looking above it, for he thought he had spotted, over the roof of Cinderella's Bridal Gowns, a red-footed falcon. No, it was just a common hobby. He lowered his bins disappointedly. Unmagnified, Ebbing seemed small and far away, though it was only about fifteen minutes' walk down the cliff path. The Seaway ferry from France, Bob noted, had docked on time, a fact that he would have taken some satisfaction in, had he not been thinking about the lesser tit. Cars with unfamiliar number-plates were queued up to cross the narrow bridge over the Ebb. The bus for the station was filling up with tourists. Two students with rucksacks, unmistakably French, were disappearing into the Beach Caff at the foot of the cliff, followed by somebody Bob thought he recognised. He raised the bins. Yes, Carmen Fitch, in clay-covered jeans and a sort of smock thing dabbed with paint, sending up into the air a greater black-backed gull, which he followed with his binoculars away from Carmen, over the pubs and tourist shops surrounding the Old Fish Market car park, onto the roof of Harry's Chippy in the High Street, outside which somebody, probably Harry, if there really was a Harry, was unloading a delivery of frozen cod from London.

Bob checked his watch. If he set off home now he would have time to buy some bread from the Health Food Shop, which he could have with some of that nice tahini, while he listened to *Ship Ahoy*, before setting off to school. He'd just have a quick pan round and then see if there were any herons in the river valley.

Restored wooden fishermen's cottages, dilapidated ones with posters and hanging crystals in the windows and bicycles in the yards, neat villas with fake half-timbers and caravans nestling in front of their garages, shot through his lenses. Nothing of interest. He stilled his binoculars on the valley of the Ebb where he was struck, as ever, by the richness of the habitat. In the gardens of the renovated oast-houses, cottages and barns, thrushes tapped snails on stones among the daisies and buttercups, swallows and martins swooped and dipped. Above the thick, olive river Bob caught a rose and azure glimpse of a kingfisher.

He sighed. It would have been a perfect morning, had it not been for the lesser tit. Bob was a birder who took pleasure in the undisturbed patterns of what could ordinarily be expected, and rarely ventured outside his own particular territory. This was perhaps why, when he glanced behind him, up at the bay window, he did not notice Lesley Sway standing there, a widow for less than an hour.

2

The Widow

It was ironic that, in death, Osbert Sway did something which he had founded his political life on utterly avoiding: he rocked the boat.

The concise, impeccably polite voice of Dick Winters, Osbert's colleague and friend since university days, had a slight edge to it as he was breaking the news. You simply did not expect apparently healthy men in their mid-forties to go and die on you, especially not when Tory popularity was alarmingly low and a by-election was the last thing on earth you needed. It was hard not to feel a certain amount of resentment towards Osbert.

This was a little unfair. Given a choice in the matter, Sway would doubtless have done all he could to die at a better moment – a fact which Dick Winters might have considered, if it were not for the extremely unfortunate circumstances of the death, an area in which Sway had had some control. A car crash or, better still, a terrorist bomb, would have guaranteed a wave of public sympathy. This, on the other hand . . . All that could be done was to hope that the papers didn't get wind of it, best achieved by informing very few of the ins-and-outs of the situation, these not to include Lesley Sway.

So when Lesley asked, 'Do they know what caused the death?' Winters replied, reverently and a bit maliciously, 'A heart attack, almost certainly due to emotional stress.' For this he must be forgiven: a distraught widow can do much in such circumstances; Lesley Sway, he knew, would be dignified, compliant, but not distraught.

Dick Winters replaced the receiver and turned back to the interesting affairs of life (after a final reiteration of sincere condolences) with a last, inward curse on Osbert's timing and the consoling thought that things might have been worse. It could have been a marginal. Ebbing had been voting Tory ever since there had been a Tory party to vote for. Unfortunately, however, he was unaware of quite how bad Osbert's timing had been – had he gone to meet his reward an hour or so earlier, someone might have got round to thinking of alerting the Department of Transport. As it was, in blissful ignorance of the passing of the incumbent, at nine o'clock precisely, the Department unveiled its plans for Ebbing to a summoned media.

Lesley Sway opened the window and leaned out. There was real warmth in the April sunshine. The horizon was a neatly ruled line. It was going to be a beautiful day.

The radio alarm clicked into life. Lesley was not naturally an early riser, a defect which she had always had to remedy with some kind of artificial wakening device. She hoped that she had managed to keep the sleep out of her voice while speaking to Dick Winters. She went into the bathroom adjoining the bedroom and put the water on for a bath, then spent some moments at the wardrobe choosing a suitable outfit for what was likely to be a busy day. Dick Winters had already informed Primrose and Tim; they would be over as soon as possible. Susie Took, Lesley's secretary, was due at nine-fifteen.

Lesley lowered herself into the water and washed briskly, listening to the shipping forecast. As she got out of the bath the forecast came to an end. 'And now,' said the announcer, 'we make today's first visit to Shrimping-on-Sea, where Luke Barnacle is still feared drowned and Captain Skate is having trouble with his lobster pots.' Lesley hastily put the radio off so she wouldn't have to hear the theme tune. 'Widow,' she thought, as she sat at her dressing-table and made up. Another situation to rise to.

She was whizzing up her breakfast in the liquidiser when she heard the key in the lock.

'Aunt Lellie,' called Susie Took. 'Aunt Lellie, Mummy's here too. It was on the news, after *Ship Ahoy*. Oh gosh.' Lesley was Susie's godmother and she had called Lesley 'Aunt Lellie' ever since she was a baby. As far as Lesley was concerned the appellation should have ceased as soon as the correct pronunciation was mastered, but it had not, perhaps due to Winifred Took's continued use of it when speaking of her to Susie.

'I'm in the kitchen,' said Lesley. She decanted the foaming mixture into a tall glass and took a quick sip. The phone rang and she heard Susie bound into the office and answer it. Lesley had taken Susie on as a secretary after she had done a sort of course up in London. The course had lasted for six months and had been designed to show its participants how to exploit whatever attributes they had that might attract the more desirable sort of man into marriage, and to teach them how to type and speed-write should that event fail to materialise. In Susie's case neither aspect of the training had been conspicuously successful. Lesley employed her out of loyalty to Winifred; Susie had only a smattering of typing. Though Winifred dreamt of a wonderful marriage for her daughter – with such optimism that she was even prone to getting excited when royal relationships foundered – and lived in hope of letting her choose whichever dress she best liked, and could fit into, from Cinderella's Bridal Gowns, Winifred's own shop, Susie persisted in being what is termed 'a big girl', with no sense of style. A more serious consideration of the career option might have been advisable. Nevertheless, Susie wasn't too bad on the telephone, had a sweet nature and was game for anything. She lived for fun and was a mainstay of the Young Conservatives, the one who organised venues, drove the minibus, made the picnics. If only she had been a little more tactful.

'Lesley. Oh you poor poor poor poor thing.' Winifred Took, Susie's mother, Lesley's oldest friend, entered now, and with her a strong smell of mint and face-powder. Her cheeks were a livid orangey-pink and her eyelids aquamarine above and puffy red below. Her mascara was running. She carried a box of opalescent Kleenex. 'Tissies,' she said, putting the box on the kitchen table.

'It is sad,' said Lesley. 'I'm just having breakfast. Would you like me to make you some tea?' She patted Winifred's heavily-ringed fingers. Once she had got over the initial shock they would consult on how the situation should be handled, as they always had done and always would do.

It was a long-standing friendship, one that needed no thinking about. They had been together through school, then university. Winifred's marriage, at twenty-one, had quickly followed Lesley's, at twenty. They were each other's bridesmaids. Susie and Primrose were, the two women liked to think, best friends, which was perhaps what had caused Susie and Primrose to think so, too. Susie had – with some protests from Primrose, of which Winifred must never know – been Primrose's bridesmaid. In due course, as Winifred never tired of saying, the perfect parallel would be maintained by Primrose doing likewise for Susie. Winifred and Lance's divorce occurred not long after Osbert and Lesley's unofficial separation. Winifred had been awarded the house on the front, where she lived with Susie, and enough money to set up Cinderella's. Lesley occupied this, the family home, where she had grown up and which she had inherited from her parents, alone, except for when Osbert's career required that he should visit his constituency. She and Osbert had continued to make public appearances together and the media seemed to be ignorant of, or uninterested in, their separation.

Lesley was not surprised that Winifred had been weeping so copiously. In the friendship, Winifred was the emotional one and she was the calm one. Just as, at university, Winifred was the pretty one and she was the beautiful one – this being Winifred's definition, not hers. Loyalty was one of the bedrocks of Lesley's character and beauty being, to her way of thinking, more desirable than prettiness, she would have bestowed it upon Winifred if she could. The other bedrock was honesty. If she could not say the truth as she saw it, she did not speak. The latter virtue, of course, had to be mainly a private one. In public, loyalty and its concomitant demands must be uppermost. In her kitchen, however, Lesley would not say what she did not believe to be true or pretend to emotions that she did not feel.

Emotional excess and prettiness sit more happily on twenty

years than on forty-five. Affection less robust than Lesley's might have, at times, found Winifred rather ridiculous. Fortunately, Winifred had several attributes which wore somewhat better. While Lesley was practical, Winifred was astute and could pin-point the socially correct with unerring accuracy. If, on occasion, the bridesmaids' mothers left Cinderella's more content than the brides', this was not the coincidence it might be assumed to be. Winifred already had something in mauve chiffon picked out for Primrose for when Susie celebrated her nuptials. So now, while, in the office, Susie's voice rose and fell, with its customary great enthusiasm, Winifred wiped her eyes on an emerald tissue, took the cup of tea that Lesley held out to her and said, 'You must talk to people yourself dear.'

'Do you think so?' Lesley took another sip of her breakfast and emptied the rest down the sink. 'Wouldn't it be more appropriate not to?'

'Understandable, but not necessarily appropriate. It will be appreciated if you do, which will be better, in the long run, for the party. Think of Jackie Kennedy dear.'

'Osbert was hardly John F. Kennedy. Nor was he assassinated.' But she noted the advice. For Winifred, Toryism was something you did. For Lesley, it was something you were; it required a specific sort of behaviour, participation in certain social rituals, shared assumptions, but, to Lesley, the kind of fine-tuning that made up the new breed of Conservative did not come naturally. She relied on her friend for that. Lesley believed the things she believed because they were moral and normal, and because everyone she knew believed them; but she did not think about them much, unlike Winifred. At times in her marriage it had sometimes occurred to Lesley that, with Winifred, Osbert might have been at the cutting edge.

'No, he was not, but he could have been,' said Winifred, taking up her point about John F. Kennedy. 'With you and Jackie, though, the analogy holds very nicely.'

Instinctively, Lesley glanced into the nearest reflecting object. Her face met her on the oven door: large eyes, soft, light-brown hair. 'Do I look like a widow should?' she asked.

'The right colours, but too calm,' said Winifred, with a sniff. 'Never mind dear, it must be the shock.'

'Any tea in the pot?' Susie Took walked in. She was wearing a big, fawn-coloured sweater, with the sleeves rolled up, and a pair of jeans. Her shortish blonde hair was loose. 'Don't worry Aunt Lellie, I'll pour myself some. That was *The Times*. Said they're sorry and all that. Awfully sorry too, Aunt Lellie.' She sloshed some tea into a mug with 'Susie' written on it and grabbed an open packet of chocolate digestives from one of the shelves. 'What next?'

'Organisation of the funeral,' said Lesley.

'Susie,' said Winifred, 'you don't need biccies after that big brekkie.'

'Oh gloom,' said Susie, munching on a biscuit anyway. 'I've just had a thought: does this mean we're going to have to cancel the Conservative barbecue?'

'I don't know,' said Lesley, looking enquiringly at Winifred.

'It's going to be such a laugh,' said Susie, 'and I've bought about a billion saus.'

'In the light of a by-election,' said Winifred, in measured tones, 'I don't think anyone could criticise if the widow of the late MP is brave enough to allow the party to use her garden for the barbecue. Though I don't think you yourself should do any barbecuing, dear.' Apart from other considerations, the yearly event was rich ground for marital partners for Susie.

'Good-oh,' said Susie. 'It's such a perfect spot.'

'It has so long been the traditional venue,' said Winifred.

'It's the loveliest place on earth,' said Lesley.

'I've closed Cinderella's, as a mark of respect,' said Winifred. 'Susie and me will be with you all day, to help ease the load. A bit later I'll make some pâté sandies and we can have them on the lawn.'

'Oh yum,' said Susie.

The phone rang.

'I'll get it,' said Lesley.

Leaving Susie and Winifred in the kitchen, she went into the office and lifted the receiver. 'Lesley Sway here.'

'Mrs Sway? Ricky Brown of the *Times* here.'

Lesley was puzzled. 'I thought you had just spoken to my secretary.'

'The, um, *Ebbing Times*, Mrs Sway.' Ricky Brown sounded

slightly crestfallen. He had evidently expected her to recognise his name.

'What can I do for you, Mr Brown?'

The voice rallied. 'Well, I wondered what your feelings were.'

Through the open window Lesley looked out at the slightly sloping lawn, its young grass so green and tender that one might imagine it capable of bruising. It would not be long before the lilac came into blossom. The carefully-pruned roses, in borders which ran the length of either side of the garden, criss-crossed with paths, were already showing the beginnings of shiny, reddish leaves. On the air was the marzipan smell of spring, combined with the coarser tang of the sea. An immense sadness assailed her, but it was not for Osbert. In fact, she was at a loss to know exactly what it was for. Perhaps it was a premonition.

'Of course I am deeply distressed,' she said.

'But you realise it is necessary?'

Lesley was puzzled. 'I'm sorry?'

'The road scheme, Mrs Sway, you realise it is necessary?'

'What road scheme?'

'The Department of Transport. They've just unveiled their plans for Ebbing. But surely you knew, Mrs Sway? Surely your husband . . .?' The voice trailed off, incredulous.

'My husband is dead.'

'Dead? Does anyone know?'

'I believe it has been announced on the news. But what are you trying to tell me about a road?'

'There's to be a four-lane dual carriageway, cutting up the cliff from the ferry terminal, across your garden, among others – lots of the houses and gardens along the cliff are going to be affected. The Frogwell Mansion will be completely demolished. A flyover will take the traffic over the Ebb valley, then the road will skirt the top of the town – there'll be a link-road off it to the station – and it'll join the London motorway further on. The *Times* would be interested to hear your comments, Mrs Sway. The scheme was approved by your husband, of course.'

Lesley said nothing. She was experiencing a wave of nausea. In front of her eyes she could see wide, grey tarmac, painted with dirty yellow and dirty white lines, coming towards her garden, destroying everything in its path, the beauty of her outlook ruined. And Osbert had intended to permit this to happen. Why? Though they led separate lives, had she not been loyal to him? Even now that he was dead, was she not already planning a life patterned by the knowledge that she was his widow? Had he, in spite of the apparent civility between them, harboured some skulking malice towards her that was using this opportunity to take its revenge?

'Are you there, Mrs Sway?'

Lesley took a deep breath. The grass was still outside the window, she could still smell the tangled scents of sea and trees and flowers. There was, she realised suddenly, no need to dredge around in the muddy waters of motivation. Osbert had, quite simply, as usual, done what he was told. It was just that it had never affected her before. She was not a consideration.

'Yes,' Lesley said, 'I'm here.'

'Can you give me a reaction?'

Lesley had spent twenty-five years of marriage listening to political discourse which, whatever else it might lack, tended towards the fluent. She undid the top button of her blouse and loosened the silly ribbon thing around her neck. Yes, she could give him a reaction.

'I think it might have been wiser dear,' said Winifred, 'to have got a clearer idea about what is actually planned before issuing a statement to the press.'

It was late afternoon. They were sitting in deckchairs on the lawn, waiting for Primrose to arrive. From the study came the hesitant sound of Susie on the word-processor.

'It struck me as very clear,' said Lesley, but she felt discomfited. She had thought that, when told the news about the road, Winifred would be horrified too. In fact, it had been received with utter calm. Winifred's house, by the sea wall, would be totally unaffected, of course. Nevertheless, Lesley had expected a degree of empathy that was evidently not forthcoming. So untroubled was Winifred that Lesley had begun to wonder if she hadn't, maybe, overreacted on the telephone. But now, as she looked out at the hazy sea – the horizon wavering in an unseasonal warmth – Ebbing's rooftops, yellow with sun, the light shining off the cobbles of the Old Fish Market car park, she felt that perhaps Winifred was a little lacking in fellow-feeling. This ungenerous sentiment she managed to push to the back of her mind by reflecting upon Winifred's kindness regarding the loss of Osbert – though it wasn't a loss really, since you could only lose something you possessed in the first place – and that this, and not the road, must be what was dominating Winifred's thoughts.

She couldn't help experiencing an unfamiliar sense of isolation, though. Did understanding what the potential loss of her childhood home meant to her really require such a massive effort of the imagination?

Lesley was just old enough to remember when there were fishing boats in the harbour at Ebbing. At night, small lights would make their way to the harbour mouth, with a rocking-horse motion in choppy weather, and thence out to sea, tiny in the massive, thick darkness. Men still drowned. In the mornings you could buy sticky wet fish out of bloody plastic boxes. That was all gone now.

The pebbly beach, the trees and clearings on the top of the cliff brought memories of a time when discovery was still possible. She had watched storms from every upper window of the house. The white wake of the ferry was the wavering hand that measured her hours. Here she had made a haven and a life, away from the chill touch of her failed marriage.

These thoughts made Lesley look forward to seeing Primrose, though the anticipation of Primrose was, she admitted, almost always better than the reality. Somehow Primrose managed to leave behind her an aura of sweetness and light but to disappoint while she was present.

A self-styled Bohemian intellectual, Primrose was now in the process of completing a book about a woman named Clover Deal who had, like Primrose herself, spent a lifetime making lovely pictures. In the case of Clover Deal, a Bloomsbury acolyte, these pictures had been on walls, cupboards and lampshades – never on canvases, which could have been hung up somewhere and given critical appraisal – for she liked to have beauty about her. Sometimes she illustrated her friends' sitting-rooms in the early morn, while they still slept, which must, Lesley thought, have been rather trying. Primrose's pictures were more a form of performance art. Inexorably fertile, she had given birth to five children in as many years of marriage: first Tansy and Sorrel, the twins, then the boys, Robin and Seth; the current baby was a girl, Jonquil. She dressed them in smocks and pinafores, clad herself in peasant clothes bought at Harrods and had always a child at her breast or by her side, or several, grouped around her, making daisy chains. She lived a life of lovely whimsy, which Lesley, because she loved her, tried to believe was, in some way, useful. Five children did seem rather a lot, however, especially as they spent most of their time with Helen, Primrose's young housekeeper. Clover Deal had already – incredibly – had a good dozen books devoted to her. Did she really merit any more?

Primrose had never made any secret of the fact that she did not like Lesley's house. She and Tim lived in a renovated chapel, that had been built in the 1890s. It was in a small meadow with a stream, which flowed into the Ebb, and had a William Morris style stained-glass window. It was reached by a cart-track. Lesley was sure, however, that Primrose, who made Helen use special washing-up liquid and who only ever wore natural fabrics, would sympathise with her mother's horror at the desecration of her own garden.

There was the sound of hooves on grass and the gentle creaking of wooden wheels. The blue and red painted caravan appeared round the side of the house, pulled by Cherry, the cob mare, and led by Primrose, who was wearing a long skirt, hand-embroidered cotton shirt, patchwork jerkin and an antique shawl. A bright scarf was casually knotted around her long hair. The typing stopped and Susie Took came out to the garden.

'Mummy!' Primrose dropped Cherry's bridle and ran lightly across the grass, like a ballerina about to make a spectacular leap. Cherry, startled, shook her mane. Susie grabbed the bridle. The door at the back of the caravan opened and a little flight of wooden steps, daubed with yellow and white painted flowers, was lowered. The children emerged, Jonquil asleep in a woven rush basket, held at either end by Tansy and Sorrel.

Primrose sobbed in Lesley's arms for about two and a half minutes, then in Winifred's for a bit less. Winifred sobbed too, and so did Susie. Lesley, dry-eyed, feeling somewhat excluded from the event, took the teetering basket from the twins and put it on the rug, then went into the house for plastic cups and orange juice. It did not strike her as particularly appropriate for Primrose to have brought the children with her. By the time she emerged with a tray, emotion had been dispensed with. Primrose had arranged herself on the rug beside her sleeping child, Winifred was back in her deckchair, pouring tea, and Susie was eating a jam doughnut which she had rushed into Ebbing to buy after lunch. Primrose sent the older children off to gather Lesley's lily-of-the-valley.

'What can I say to them?' she asked. 'How can I explain to them that he's gone?'

'They never saw a whole lot of him,' said Susie. 'I'd be surprised if they notice.'

'Tell them that he lives on in our thoughts,' said Winifred, giving her daughter a look. 'And in Heaven, of course,' she added.

'Mummy,' said Primrose, 'I've made you some bread. Or rather Helen has. It's in the caravan. Don't let me forget to give it to you.'

'I take it you have heard about the road?' Lesley's voice was grim. Primrose looked startled, and a little displeased by the change of subject. She had obviously been looking forward to a gentle session of wistful reminiscence. She frequently complained to Susie Took that she found Lesley stern and emotionless.

'Oh yes,' she replied carefully, 'but you see, where we are, at the bottom of the hill, away from the valley, we won't even hear it, let alone see it. And besides, fingers on lips' – she placed a slim white finger, tipped by a perfectly oval pink nail, over her two, rosebud lips for a moment – 'we couldn't object, even if we wanted to, because Tim – it's not confirmed yet – looks to be,' she whispered the last two words, 'Conservative candidate.'

'Primrose! How fitting!' exclaimed Winifred.

'Good-oh,' said Susie.

But Lesley did not speak. This was, of course, what she should have expected – what, if she was honest with herself, she had expected. If it wasn't happening to Primrose, then it didn't matter. She felt a quick stab of anger. Her daughter was quite happy to watch someone destroying the country, as long as it wasn't her bit of it.

The silence was broken by the sound of a car pulling up in the drive and a car door opening. Primrose leapt to her feet. 'Children, it's Daddy.'

As Tim Babcock came round the side of the house his wife and babies ran to meet him. Primrose returned to the group with an arm around her husband's waist. Tim carried Seth. The others tugged at their mother's skirt and played with her shawl.

'Lesley.' Tim had a cultivated accent and the bleached good looks of a First World War poet. In ten years he would be paunchy. 'I'm terribly sorry.' Primrose re-positioned herself on the rug. The children ran off to play at rolling down the slope of the lawn. 'Are all the necessary arrangements made?' He sat down on one of the wrought-iron garden chairs.

'I think so,' said Lesley.

'Good.'

'Timmy,' said Susie, 'would you like a cup?'

Tim always looked at Susie Took as if he could not quite believe that she had the gall to address him. 'No thanks, a gin.'

'One gin, coming up,' said Susie. She strode into the house.

There was a pause then, 'Tim wanted to talk to you about the *Times*, Mummy,' said Primrose.

All eyes turned on Lesley, who immediately guessed which *Times* was being referred to.

'Look Lesley,' said Tim, attempting to imbue his voice with a diffidence he almost certainly did not feel, 'I'm sorry to have to bring this up now, but I'm afraid I'm going to have to ask you to get back on to the local rag and explain to them that you were upset about Osbert and you didn't mean what you said. They've led with a front-page article about what you think of the road which is, frankly, horribly damaging with an election coming up. Especially since it looks like I will be Conservative candidate – Primrose has told you that, I expect. The plan is to announce it at the barbecue.'

'And you, I take it, are in favour of the road?'

Susie came out of the house with Tim's glass. She handed it to him. He took a sip before replying. 'Yes, I am.'

'Why?'

Tim shrugged. 'Same reason as Osbert was. Party line.'

'In the circumstances, Mummy, it would be silly to draw attention to yourself,' said Primrose.

'What do you think, Win?' In all the years they had known each other Lesley and Winifred had never disagreed about anything. How could they, inhabiting, as they did, exactly the same place in the scheme of things? It would be like disagreeing that the sea was blue.

Winifred smiled reassuringly. 'I think, dear, that people will appreciate that you spoke under considerable stress and that you didn't really mean what you said.'

'Do you think I didn't mean what I said?'

Primrose raised her eyes to heaven. Tim Babcock threw his arms in the air and gave an exasperated sigh. 'Lesley. Really. This is nit-picking. What you meant is neither here nor there.'

'Oh golly,' said Susie Took, 'this is getting beyond me.'

'Of course I know you meant it dear,' said Winifred. 'Personally, that is. But we are discussing politics and Tim and Primmie's future. You would not want to be external to that.'

Lesley looked at her friend's face. There was a smear of lipstick at the edge of Winifred's mouth. The cheeks were shiny with foundation. Her head was bent to one side, a gesture she had cultivated when she was a girl. The limits of the known world were there. 'External' was a big and frightening word. Winifred had chosen it with care. 'Very well,' she began. The phone rang. She stood up. 'It's all right Susie, I'll go.'

Behind her she felt the tension dispersing. As she entered the house she heard Winifred saying 'she's always been sensible about things.'

Lesley picked up the receiver. 'Hallo.'

There was the sound of the phone being dropped at the other end of the line. 'Oh sodit. Bloody thing on the edge of the table. Are you still there?' The voice sounded as if it had been soaked in whisky.

'Who is this?'

'Darryl Younger.'

'Have we met? I don't remember your name but I think I recognise your voice.'

'*Ship Ahoy*. Luke Barnacle.'

'Still feared drowned,' said Lesley, automatically.

'Negotiating the renewal of my contract with the prat of a producer.'

Lesley suddenly remembered something about an actor relative of Tim's. 'Were you at Primrose's wedding?' she asked.

'At the reception, until some thug chums of my cousin's chucked me out, which is why we haven't met. Anyway, that's not what I've called about. Listen, I'll tell you where I live. Tiny little place, about to fall down, but it belongs to me. Bought it in happier times. Ebb at the bottom of the garden. Old, unpruned apple trees, that sort of thing. If that sodding road goes through it will be bang slap under the flyover. I read what you said in the papers and I thought it was bloody terrific, and there'll be others who think the same.' There was a scrabbling sound. 'Oh Christ. Look, got to go. Catch the train to London. Keep me posted.'

He put the phone down. Lesley stood motionless, the receiver still in her hand, the dialling tone buzzing. Her mind was racing. Darryl Younger was absolutely right. Of course there would be others. They couldn't be the only Conservatives who objected to the road. Many Tory-voters lived in houses that were going to be affected. They would agree with her, just as Darryl Younger did. She shouldn't recant: on the contrary. It wasn't long until the Conservative barbecue. There was no time to be lost.

Lesley discovered that she was smiling. It was the first time in her life that she had spoken to an actor.

3

Anna Seale

In a house that was always full of other people, long and luckily rented, Anna was considering the sea. She had worked all morning, been painting all afternoon and knew nothing of any of the news that was now the talk of Ebbing. She had bare feet and was wearing a pair of baggy, faded dungarees and a loose, grey t-shirt. Her face, twisted in concentration, was an attractive and open face, forthright. It belonged to a person who would speak her mind – perhaps too easily – who was quick in judgment, given to large feelings and fearless emotions. She had strong, milkmaid's arms, pale hair the brown side of auburn. Her hands were covered in thin cuts from oyster shells. She smelled of oysters, turpentine, coffee and tobacco. A roll-up hung out of the side of her mouth. She occupied a solid space.

The canvas in front of her was as large as the room allowed: five by six (too big to be really tempting, according to Carmen). Not the right time of day to be painting – if you could choose. Not the right light (according to Carmen). On the bare floorboards, stood on sheets torn from *Spare Rib*, the *Morning Star*, *Socialist Worker*, the *New Statesman* were pots of paint. People crashing sometimes knocked them over in the night on their way to the bog. Anna was considering the sea and so the pots nearest to her were all the possibilities of green, grey and blue. Outside, the sun was setting over the pebbles and the waves, spilling its own paint among Anna's colours. Maybe if you could get the right names, she thought, then you could put them on the canvas accurately. Lilac, sapphire, lavender, bottle-green, oyster-grey, mussel-shell blue.

Anna was surrounded by the remains of events. Spag bol plates, a bowl of parmesan, a twist of lettuce in olive oil from last night, and Jay, who'd fallen asleep on the sofa, woken when Anna came back from work, rolled a joint and then another, and lay there still, eyes bloodshot, plum lips curved into a smile, dreadlocks singed with russet powder-paint that he'd looked at and talked about before he went to sleep. The morning's, oh so necessary, black coffee and hunk of toast and marmalade dregs in a mug and crumbs on the floor. A pile of shiny leaflets and Carmen Fitch, her smock artfully painty, her raddled, mannish face, puffing on a fag and saying 'I really must go', (for the umpteenth time since her arrival at two) in a raspy, husky voice: residue of a conversation about those leaflets, publicity for the forthcoming exhibition, which Anna was going to help distribute for cash. One day, Carmen had again hinted, there might even be the possibility of an exhibition for Anna, if she seemed to be developing in the right direction, which Carmen, with a distant art school background and her own small gallery or 'Space', as she called it, in the High Street, was qualified to judge, in a way Anna herself might find hard. Carmen was not afraid to be ruthless. Thank God for such tutors.

To do the sea justice, Anna knew, was impossible. You would have to dip your heavy brush in brine, crust it with salt, scatter the canvas with a million years of pounded sand. You would have to make the viewer seethe with a fierce, hungry, insatiable love for every mood of weather, every change of light: distil the ocean, like an oyster does. Which, of course, Carmen was right, was a speck of sail on a distant horizon. Far off, if ever. To dare to take yourself seriously, that great leap of art, is even harder if you are self-taught and work part-time in a crab and oyster bar. Confidence, that comes so easily to the amateur, unaware of the size of what they are attempting, was but a flashing light to Anna. She bent and poured some red wine from the end of a litre bottle into a thick tumbler, took a swig.

'"Anger II",' rasped Carmen, tapping hard on the pile of leaf-lets, 'a rage comprising the rejection of a gender-based concept of the emotion. An anger that is quintessentially female.'

'Why two?' asked Jay.

'The first was largely on the weaker more, in quotes,' Carmen scratched at the air with two fingers, '"feminine" medium of canvas. Now we are exploring the rigidity of sculpture.'

'So how come you're covered in paint? You flick it over yourself, or what?'

'Oh gawd, spare me from stoned black men.'

The door opened on Bob Adams.

'Do you want a coffee, Bob?' asked Carmen, more than at home in Anna's house.

'No, thanks ever so, Carmen,' said Bob. 'I've just dropped by to tell you some rather sad news about the lesser tit.' He had hurried to the clifftop again after school to confirm his findings, walked, unseeing, past the headline of the local paper outside Flint's Newsagent's.

Jay subsided into sniggers. Bob sat down on the sofa beside Jay's massive feet.

'Let me guess, small, brown and dull, nests in Arndale Centres and lives on a diet of cheese and onion crisps,' said Anna, not looking away from her painting. These, as Bob had unwisely explained one night, being the preferred food and habitat of most birds, given half a chance; the call of the wild rather more lively in the fancy of the lay-person than in the observation of the ornithologist.

'Small and mostly brown but by no means dull,' Bob replied, good-naturedly, thereby illustrating that birdwatching, as other passions, gravitates towards the subjective: most people would have considered the lesser tit (*Parus minor*) a very dull bird indeed.

For one thing, it was not even startlingly lesser; just a bit less. It lacked aesthetic appeal, was dun-coloured with grey cheeks. During the mating season the male's plumage turned from pale mouse-brown to mouse brown. The female's remained the same. The lesser tit laid extensive numbers of eggs but few of them hatched. Of those that did, the young seldom flourished. Hardly surprisingly, it was rare and threatened (which, as Bob now explained, was partly what made it interesting). Millions of years ago its ancestors were barely viable dinosaurs. Had Darwin ever observed the lesser tit – which had somehow persisted throughout history while other, more lively and resourceful birds, with more thoughtfully constructed nests, had fallen by the wayside – he might have felt inclined to jettison his theory, or perhaps to admit a place in it for the plain luck of the draw. Its song and call were unremarkable.

This, with certain omissions, was what Bob told his listeners, attempting to imbue them with some of his enthusiasm for the bird before breaking the terrible news that this year its nesting sites were drastically reduced. Bob had left it as long as possible before admitting this to himself but today he had decided there was no denying it any longer. Last year there were ten sites; this year there were only four. The lesser tit was a bird easily prone to despair. Next year there might be none at all.

'Wow,' said Jay, his voice hushed with the enormity of the prospect.

The two women were not so impressed. 'Sounds like a runty little thing to me,' said Carmen. 'Serve it right.'

'I don't think you would be saying that if it was a leopard, say, Carmen' said Bob, 'or something exotic like that.'

'I've torn down the fence at Greenham,' said Anna, taking a large gulp of her wine, spilling some, and speaking rather more loudly than was necessary. 'I've demonstrated for peace, whales and dolphins, the end of apartheid. I'm thirty-six and shell oysters for a pittance. Am I now expected to mobilise for a fucking tit, when all I want is to be able to paint?'

'Practice is the only way you'll get any good at it,' said Carmen, lighting another fag.

'A pittance?' said Meg Hughes, walking in. She wore jeans and a rectangular canvas top, had cheeks the faded rose of old, hand-coloured photos and a tanned, weathered look about her. She owned the Crab and Oyster Bar in the High Street and was Anna's employer.

'Oh hi, Meg. You know what I mean. Dishing out saucers of jellied eels to Cockneys on holiday wasn't exactly what I dreamt of in my girlish fancies. You neither, I bet.'

'Well what I propose,' said Bob, for birdwatchers learn tenacity, 'is a sort of round-the-clock tit watch. Our Bird Group will organise it and anybody interested can join in. The Ecologists are bound to want to lend a hand: I must make a note to speak to Adrian Dapple. It would be awful, with their numbers so dwindled, if anybody stole the eggs.'

'All right, put me down for a couple of hours then,' said Anna, 'and I'll sketch the fucking creature.'

'What colour are its eggs man?' asked Jay.

'A very nice shade of white, Jay, as a matter of fact.'

'There are worse ways of spending your life than shelling oysters and making crab sandwiches and putting jellied eels on saucers,' said Meg Hughes comfortably. 'Which reminds me: a customer told me that Osbert Sway died this morning. Something else seems to have happened as well, but I don't know what it is.'

'That must have been sudden,' said Bob. 'I saw him once. He can't have been very old.'

'Good,' said Anna. 'Him and his bitch of a wife.'

'Here's some leaflets for you to put on the counter, Meg,' said Carmen, handing her a wad of them.

'Are you exhibiting this time, Carmen?' asked Meg, looking at the black-and-white leaflets without comment.

'Gawd no, nothing ready at the moment. Too many ideas. Bitten off too much.'

'Is Anna?'

'It's primarily sculpture and, anyway, it represents a group project.'

'I'd still like to see how people reacted to Anna's lovely paintings.'

'"Lovely?"' squawked Carmen, snorting smoke out of her nose and mouth as she doubled up in a hoarse chuckle. 'Wherever do people get the idea art should be lovely?' There was a pause. 'Anna,' said Carmen, 'the light's going. Anything you do now you'll have to do over. You're out of wine. Who's for the Mermaid?'

'Christ, am I? Well I'm out of cash too, unless there's any by the ashtray.'

'I'll buy,' said Carmen.

Anna stuck her brush in a jar of turps. 'You lot coming?'

They piled out of the house. Anna kicked the door shut. It was quiet. The waves curled, splashed and pulled, curled, splashed and pulled, the pebbles raked back, raked back. Anna thought she could hear the silence around objects that the sea had thrown onto the shingle and could not withdraw again. She was drunk and planned on getting drunker. Harbour Street, where Anna lived – really a narrow alleyway which emerged onto the Old Fish Market Square – was lined with lurching, wind-battered houses and workshops: some with hanging boards; others shiny with new paint, ships in bottles in their porthole windows. Telescopes pointed from those attic rooms that could spy the sea among the rooftops of the buildings opposite, which were on the sea wall and looked out across the bay. The sky was clear and milky with moonlight. Gas flames, Anna thought; paper round oranges.

The sad sound of a foghorn: a dying animal out at sea. Though it was not foggy. There was a thin mist, just becoming silver with the light. The cliffs were chalk-white, with pearly shadows in their crevices. The grey sheet of water was so flat you could imagine walking across it; past the back of the Mermaid, over the chocolate brine of the harbour, to the pebby shingle where the Beach Caff was, the oval stones littered with tossed shawls of rubbery seaweed.

As she watched the dawn, it seemed strange to Anna that none of them had found out about the government's plans for Ebbing until they walked through the door of the Mermaid, into the murky, smoky half-light and heavy metal.

Up till then everything had been as it normally was: a salmon pink bridesmaid's dress in Cinderella's; plaster fishermen with sou'westers and nets in the windows of the tourist shops. The Woodcutter Inn, one of the chain, had a banner draped across the glass and plastic frontage which had been imposed upon another, older building. It read 'All-U-Can-Eat Garden Salad Bar'. There was a herd of shiny cars outside the Jolly Roger and a steamy, slightly fishy smell coming from its kitchens; the Anchor's maroon curtains were, as always, emphatically shut.

Quiet, subtle things event horizons.

Carmen had spotted some of her artists sitting with Mary Janet, most forceful facilitator of the Ebbing Lesbian Separatists' group, and Mary Janet's girlfriend, who had changed her name by deed-poll to Ruth Ellis. She plunged through the crowd to join them. Mary Janet had hair down to well below her waist. Today she wore it up. As Carmen approached her from behind, she swung round in the hopeful expectation of being insulted by a man, only to be disappointed.

There was a scraping of chairs and several people, attempting nonchalance, made their way towards Jay with the hopeful expressions of those who have been smoking seeds all day. He nodded in the direction of the battered purple door that led to the men's toilets.

Bob spied some of his birdwatching friends, in intense conversation with Adrian Dapple and his partner Gilda. Adrian, mild, thin and mournful, had his hand on the head of his mongrel bitch, Carrot, whose dejected stance and expression echoed those of her male human house-mate. Adrian had a clean-shaven, young face and was still convalescing from the nervous breakdown he had had when he had failed to win as Ecology candidate for Ebbing in the last general election. Gilda, who had cut her political teeth in the Green Party of her native Germany, was a tougher prospect altogether. Her cheeks were the colour of radishes. Adrian leant on her emotionally, psychologically and, sometimes, when it was all too much and even his stream-of-consciousness diary failed to comfort him, physically. And so did Carrot. The Bird Group, men and women in cords and Marks & Spencer sweaters, lace-up boots, each and every one of them drinking half-pints of bitter, had the strenuous, alert and yet vulnerable expressions of teachers in charge of sixth-form outings.

Meg bought herself and Anna pints of cider. They looked round for somewhere to sit. There were two places beside Rolf Watt, Chairperson of the Ebbing Marxists. The spilt beer on the rickety table reflected the nude colours of a string of fairy-lights, tacked there by a previous landlord in an attempt at jollity, perhaps the same one who'd put the decorative circles of cork on the walls. Rolf Watt was looking about as cheerful as you'd expect someone to look who campaigned for Marxist revolution in Southern England.

'There used to be a fishing industry,' he said as they sat down. 'There used to be factories all up the coast.' He stuck his tongue out from among his beard and quickly ran it along a thin roll-up. 'Now the basis of the British economy is selling Beefeater dolls to American tourists and scrolled copies of *Desiderata*, and even that they're taking from us. Know what they'll find when they dredge the sea over what once was Ebbing? A load of tarmac and a ton of signs that read "We aim to please. Can you aim too please?"'

Rolf always spoke like this, which explained why there were two places free beside him.

'Tarmac?' asked Anna. 'Why tarmac?'

'You haven't heard? No, too busy donating your sweated labour to the capitalist cause.' Meg Hughes gave a little sigh. 'It's all very well for Dapple over there.' He cast a glance in Adrian's direction; Adrian was putting an ashtray of water down for Carrot, who started to lick at it resignedly, as if she had hoped it was something else. 'Him and those twitching types with their bourgeois ecology and their birds. Elitist luxuries. What about the people?'

'Well I'm not setting foot in the Methodist Hall, not after what happened last time. Not for Miles Starey. Not for anyone,' said Nick Parker, a gay Trotskyist, stealing a chair that had been vacated by someone who had gone into the toilets to do some buying off Jay, and sitting down beside them.

'Heard what?' asked Meg Hughes.

'Miles Starey?' said Anna. 'Is Miles back in Ebbing?'

'Why?' asked Nick. 'Do you know him? Well he's thorough, I have to say that, to have got flyers around already. Here's one, if you want to see it.'

A Labour Party discussion of the topic of the new road scheme. Speaker: Miles Starey, Labour candidate for Ebbing.

'A road scheme?' said Anna. 'Where?'

Rolf told her. 'We'll have to back Labour on this one,' he finished. 'There's no alternative. Though voting for those queasy prats sticks in my gullet.'

'I might vote for them but I won't set foot in the Methodist

Hall. Nothing will make me. That's my final word on it,' said Nick, picking at a nail. 'What's to discuss anyway?'

'Gives an illusion of democratic freedom,' said Rolf gloomily. 'Big charade. The perfect image of the electoral choice handed out to the British people is the Boat Race. And yet they all go out and cheer it. Sold down the fucking river. They'd sign up to build their own gas-chambers if you gave them a free Sainsbury's voucher.'

Anna was silent.

Bob left Adrian and Gilda and the other birdwatchers and came and stood beside their table.

'That was very satisfactory. Very satisfactory indeed,' Anna heard him saying. 'The road scheme is even more bad news for the lesser tit, as if that were needed, but we're going to join Miles Starey's election campaign and we hope to mobilise other environmental pressure groups. We're not going to rest until the lesser tit's nesting sites are completely out of danger.'

'Fuck the bloody tit.' Anna thumped her fist on the table. The liquid in the glasses rocked wildly. An empty bottle fell over and smashed on the lino. No one turned round. A lot of things got smashed in the Mermaid one way and another. She stood up. 'I'm going home. I've got to do some painting.'

'But Anna,' said Carmen, appearing at that moment, 'it's much too late. There's no light whatsoever. And I haven't bought you a drink yet.'

'I'll walk with you,' said Bob, his lips pressed tightly together.

'It's not just about your one little issue, can't you see that Bob?' Anna asked as they stepped out into the Old Fish Market Square. Bob opened his mouth to reply but then Anna noticed a couple of women outside the kitchen of the Jolly Roger, having a loud conversation about some fucking barbecue.

'Tory bitches,' she yelled.

The younger of the two, a strapping great thing with a carrier bag under each arm, turned to look at her. The other, presumably the proprietor, glanced at Anna then continued to speak, but at a higher pitch. 'No, I'll supervise all the catering, and provide plates and cutlery. There really wasn't any need for you to bother yourself with the sausages.' A chef popped his head out of the kitchen window. 'Was there something?' asked the proprietor. He popped it back in again.

'Bob,' said Anna, 'let's get something heavy off the beach and smash one of their windows.'

'Come on Anna,' he replied. 'I've got to work in the morning.'

Now, sitting on a breaker in her old, unravelled sweater, it occurred to Anna that she would probably have to apologise to him.

Once she had got home she'd sobered up on black coffee and painted all night, turning anger into colour. Aubergine storm-clouds. Great boiling, whirling seas, the green of the edges of broken windows. Icy gulls, hammered by the wind. Waves that puckered and spat, their curves as sharp as scythes. Whenever she looked out of her window in the direction of the clifftop, which was just a darker mass in the darkness, she could see one point of light. It came from Osbert Sway's mansion. Anna grew feverish in her loathing of it. Was Lesley Sway afraid of being in the dark, now that she was alone; a coward, sheltered by money and legislation?

When the first seagulls had started crying and she was parched and exhausted she put her brushes in turpentine and went into the kitchen, where she managed to find a last slug in a bottle of whisky, which she drank to wind herself down, along with a mug of tea, while she ate corned beef and fried eggs with a doorstep of bread and butter. Then she'd come outside to watch the dawn, as she often did. Even the sea seemed quieter at this hour, a vast engine, just ticking over. The light was still burning. It had been on all night.

It was time to don the old combat gear and, yet again, go into battle. Not for the lesser tit but for Miles Starey.

Miles Starey, who she hadn't seen for seven years or so, not since he'd left Ebbing. An intellectual, committed to left-wing ideals; good in bed, especially if you wanted sex but not love, as Anna had decided she did; by that time she had had enough of those pained expressions with which men indicated that they felt you should be making more room for them. Why should love be any different from friendship? For friends it was enough if you swept a few things out of the way with your elbow to make a space for them to sit down in or eat off, and fuck the alternative. Miles understood and respected that.

Miles had been teaching Economics at Pitsbury Poly, a bit inland, when Anna knew him. That was in the mid-eighties. He didn't run in the last election – at least not for Ebbing – so he must have returned since then. He'd been greatly involved in CND, at the committee level. The demonstrating side he'd called 'the ground offensive'. He walked into rooms and chucked secondhand paperbacks in brown paper bags onto tables. He wore tight jeans and a tan leather jacket. His hair was shoulder-length. He owned his own house. It was always full of ambitious young left-wingers like himself.

Anna felt a tingle of desire in the pit of her stomach. She'd learnt a lot from Miles. His body and, more, his mind had dazzled her. To fight together for the clifftop. To take up where they had left off. To tear sheets and clothes and government plans . . .

The sun rose and flooded everything with light. The waves seemed to pick up a faster tempo; unfolding rolls of icy green, shot with lines of gold. On the clifftop the light in Osbert Sway's mansion abruptly went off.

What kind of person, Anna Seale wondered, could consent to the destruction of their own garden?

Across the bay a strip light came on in the Beach Caff.

4

The Anchor

Jack Fryer put the plastic ketchup, brown sauce and mustard pots on the formica tables. He placed a tablespoon in the sugar bowl on the counter, poured himself a mug of tea from the gallon pot, added milk from a carton and helped himself to sugar. He took a swallow of his tea and then a bite of his bacon sandwich.

This was the quiet part of the day, when the cloth draped over the tap was still dry; the part of the day before sand, he always thought of it as. Not that he minded the sand. And not much good if he did anyway. It came in on the boots of the first freight drivers who, in ten minutes or so, would be occupying the tables, leaving curled, close-smoked stubs in the ashtrays, fuelling themselves on breakfasts of eggs, bacon, sausages, black pudding and fried bread. It came in on the wetsuits of the wind-surfers, unpeeled to show tanned shoulders while they drank Cokes and 7-Ups; on the bare feet of children, their backs smooth crescents, their little swimming trunks drooping masses of crinkled material low on their hips, their faces concentrated on their 99s. It was blown in by the wind. Not much good minding sand if you live by the sea, but this was the part of the day before sand, the quiet part.

Through the large windows Jack assessed the weather. Leave it a couple of hours and then he would put some chairs and tables out, and the sunshades. People could eat in the open air if they wanted. Today's specials were steak and kidney pie with spuds and cabbage and treacle pud with cream or custard. He finished his sandwich and lit a cigarette, which he smoked pinched tight between thumb and forefinger. His body was strong and tall. His hair was long and dark. He was thirty-seven, a man given to keeping his counsel who knew many secrets which he reckoned were not his, or anyone else's, business. There were cargoes that came in which were better not known about; there were deals struck that wouldn't bear much examination. It was in the nature of a port to be like that.

The tourists and the wind-surfers adored only the sun. The drivers marginally preferred it. But Jack Fryer loved all weathers, though the sea could be vicious. He remembered the night of the terrible storm, when a ship went down further along the coast and when sea and sky had seemed to be colliding. In the morning the harbour was full: a Russian trawler, a Spanish fishing boat, numerous French and British pleasure craft (bloody morons). He'd organised coffee and sandwiches. It was the least he could do.

All set. He flicked the radio on with his thumb.

'. . . and later this morning, on *Ship Ahoy*' said the announcer, 'Sally Mackerel thinks she's spotted Luke Barnacle's boat through her telescope. But is she right? You'll have to wait until 8.45 to find out. In the meantime . . .'

Jack hoped Sally Mackerel was right. It would mean Darryl had got his contract sorted out. Perhaps then he might pay Jack some of what he owed him on tab. Jack grinned. Some chance! He poured himself another mug. It had been a late session at the Anchor. Seemed like everyone had been there last night. Pity it had ended so nasty.

Some of the waiters from the Woodcutter Inn were propping up the bar, still in the uniform of long tails and dickey the Woodcutter made them wear. When they were taken on they got sent on a Woodcutter Inn training course in Margate. At the end of the week they received a certificate. Mainly, they told Jack, they learnt how to serve vegetables with a spoon and fork and to impress the customers without scaring them off. Silver service, that was called. But there was quite a lot of sex too.

'Quiet night?' Jack asked.

They nodded.

'Coupla French tourists, had the salad bar as starter then two duck with cherry sauce and potato croquettes. Finished with Black Forest gateau from the dessert trolley,' said one of them.

'It wasn't busy at the Jolly Roger either,' said Bianca Pickle, who Jack remembered as a baby, but who was now eighteen and twiddled her varnished, ringed fingers round a menthol cigarette. She sat with Harry Smack, her boyfriend. He ran the Chippy and was old enough to be Bianca's father. His ex-wife and kids lived in London. Not exactly made in heaven, thought Jack. When Bianca spoke she drew all eyes. She sipped on her snowball and broke off from time to time to rummage in the large cotton bag, all beads and mirrors, that she kept on the table. From it she brought little notebooks, diaries, lipsticks, perfumes.

'And Veronica Tarrant was dead pissed-off about the sausages that fat girl, Susie Took, brought in,' Bianca continued, in her slightly nasal voice. Her habit was to relate what happened with no undertone of comment or judgement. The words and actions of others had little or no effect on her, so she presumed the same to be true of her own actions upon others. Veronica Tarrant, who owned the Jolly Roger, was Bianca's employer. '"They're not even proper *butcher's* sausages" she kept saying till I got sick of it. The ones she gets Chef to make are stuffed with chicken and spinach. We have to cut them in slices and put them on a bed of puréed garlic. But I can't eat them, because I'm allergict. Then someone called her a Tory bitch.'

'Who was it who shouted so loudly?' asked Hortense Smith, who ran the Dolphin guest house – though people would persist in calling it a bed-and-breakfast. Miss Smith had seen a dolphin once, when she went to Tampa with her sister-in-law in 1975, and she had warmed to it.

'That was Anna Seale,' said Jack. He knew her voice.

'It was all go down the Chippy,' said Harry. 'Though how long that'll last now the road's coming through . . .'

'It will be the death of the hotel trade,' said Hortense Smith, treating the latter word with the respect it deserved, and making it sound as if she were a central part of a vast network of commerce, rather than the proprietor of a thin building, approached by a short path, which was separated from the pocket-handkerchiefs of lawn on either side by neat lavender bushes.

Ebbing was dotted with many such establishments. They all smelled vaguely of damp and toast, and were invariably run by ladies who emanated an air of bewildered gentility and gave the impression of having been scattered there by other centuries, whose expectations of conduct were somewhat more exacting than those of the one in progress. This impression was not, however, reflected in their prices. The Beach Hotel, almost directly opposite the Anchor, was the largest of them. Run, untypically, by a husband and wife, the Beach Hotel had somehow just managed to persist in the face of the package holiday. It called itself a 'family hotel' in its tangential advertising and appealed to those who could not cope with the idea that the nineteen-fifties were over. Its main source of custom, however, was those who had been so sick on the ferry that they could not face the thought of pushing on to London, or who were so exhausted by delays and missed connections that they could be tempted by a cleanish room and Florida Cocktail followed by Breaded Fillet of Plaice and chipped or creamed potatoes then Assorted Ices. It was unique in that it served an evening meal other than by prior arrangement.

'Why the hurry? What are we hurrying for?' asked Hortense Smith. She gazed around the bar in unspecific accusation – except when her eyes rested upon Bianca; though Bianca, as her employer could have attested, was not particularly guilty in this respect.

Jack Fryer looked around the bar also but, instead of potential hurriers, he saw people tired out after their working days, glued over their drinks, glum and passive; resigned to whatever was decided on their behalf. They didn't want the road, most of them, but whoever asked them what they wanted? It would be the death blow for many of the High Street shops, already beaten to a pulp by the supermarkets. It would take away the tourists and finish off the tea-rooms and sandwich shops, along with the hotels and B & B's. The Beach Caff would struggle on but life certainly wouldn't get any easier. Ebbing: a place that got left behind. And none of those faces believed there was a sodding thing they could do about it. Poor bloody buggers.

Jack could understand why people might shout in the street, like Anna Seale had done. Quite a woman, Anna Seale, though he knew her only by sight. Of course she never came into the Anchor but she and her friends sometimes ate in the Caff. She drank black coffee and had a loud laugh that made you want to laugh with it. She liked vinegar and ketchup on her chip butty. Her hands were covered in thin cuts from oyster shells.

Jack's thoughts were interrupted by the arrival of William Flint of Flint's Newsagent's. Flint came to the bar and ordered a pint of mild in a straight glass. He was a shortish, pallid man with thin strands of hair pasted across the top of his head. His forehead was banded with bulgy wrinkles. He had a habitual half-grin.

'And what is your opinion of this road, Mr Flint?' asked Hortense Smith.

Flint took a sip of his drink. A narrow thread of foam remained on his upper lip. 'What I'd like to know is what Her Majesty must be thinking,' he replied, portentously.

A ripple of interest passed around the bar. More drinks were ordered on the strength of it. People took gulps and sips and leant back in their chairs expectantly.

'She must be a very oopset lady. A very oopset lady indeed, seeing her country filling up with you-know-who. You know what I mean. If you're like me you won't love them.' He tapped the side of his nose with a stubby finger, blackened by newsprint.

There was a silence while everyone contemplated his meaning. Flint was the centre of attention. Jack shifted uneasily.

'Seems to me it won't make any difference to that, Mr Flint,' said Harry Smack, cautiously. Jack said nothing. He was a man who preferred listening to talking. He sometimes saw the young waiters from the Taj Mahal going into the Chippy just before it closed, and Harry having a joke with them. One night there was some kind of incident in the Taj Mahal and a police car pulled up. A couple of coppers went inside. Jack didn't know what happened after that.

'Ooh it will. Mark my words it will. A better road will bring more of them in, and quicker. They'll take our jobs and bring us diseases. Don't you read the newspapers? If you get bitten by a dog that has rabies they inject you in the guts six times daily.'

Jack glanced round. Ideas were forming in people's faces. Harry Smack looked as if he were revising his opinions. The waiters from the Woodcutter Inn studied the ceiling thoughtfully. One undid a button under his bow-tie. People took cogitative sips of their drinks and held them in their mouths. The room was filled with a sudden sense of reassurance. Flint had given their dissatisfaction a focus.

'I have nothing against them as such,' said Hortense Smith, slowly, 'but I have had them request croissants for breakfast, instead of the full English, and they do sometimes object to paying extra for cruet, though salt and pepper don't grow on trees, and they know that as well as we do.'

'The Frenchies are just the tip of the iceberg. There's more where they came from,' said Flint, nodding.

The atmosphere cranked up a notch. People were getting excited.

'You'll have seen that big black man with the hair,' Flint continued. 'What I'd like to know is how a nig-nog gets to own a house next to the Woodcutter Inn. That's what I'd like to know.'

'Their hair gets like that because they don't wash it,' said Harry Smack, as if to compensate for his earlier remark. Bianca Pickle said nothing. She clicked her little cigarette-lighter.

Still Jack remained silent. He knew how Jay made a living. Not all the boats that came into Ebbing felt a need to announce their presence.

'Know what I'd like to see happen?' asked Flint. His voice dropped to a conspiratorial whisper. People leant forward in their chairs in thrilled anticipation of what he was going to say next. Jack put his glass down loudly, in an attempt to break the spell. In the hush the pub door opened and all heads turned, hostile at the interruption. The two who entered stood on the threshold uncertainly. Jack recognised them. They'd come into the Caff off the early morning ferry.

'See what I mean. Enough said.' Flint's half-grin twitched. He tapped his nose again with his finger.

The French people sat at an unoccupied table. The woman,

short-haired and attractive, took a postcard from her handbag and started writing on the back of it. The man looked at the landlord expectantly. The landlord concentrated on wiping a glass with a tea-towel.

'You have to go up and order,' said Flint. 'That's how we do things here.'

The man looked blank. Sly smiles went from person to person.

'You. Bar,' said Flint. He made a motion with a hand in order to indicate the movement. Someone didn't make much effort to stifle a laugh. Flint's eyes did a circuit of the room, triumphant. The Frenchman suddenly latched on to what was being said and went up to the bar.

'Wine please.'

'What?'

'Pardon?'

'He wants wine,' said Jack.

The landlord threw down his tea-towel and poured a couple of glasses from an open bottle of red. The Frenchman returned to his table.

'The thing I've heard about the French,' said William Flint, giving a companionable smile in the direction of the two foreigners, 'is that they don't wash as much as we do.' He lifted his glass in a mocking toast. The French people smiled back, uncertainly. The man raised his glass. Harry Smack let out a chuckle.

It was out of control. It was as if they were up to their necks in syrup and taking great, sticky, sickly mouthfuls of it. One animal with dozens of limbs and orifices, gorging itself. Jack didn't have words at his disposal. Jack's was a nuts-and-bolts sort of English. It got things done and you could pass the time of day with it, but it couldn't reach into nothing and make things happen, or stop things from happening. He thought of films on telly when someone spoke and everyone listened and agreed that they had been wrong and decided to be better people in the future.

The French woman put away her postcard. She and the man were drinking their wine with quick sips.

'No, it's good to have a chat with our foreign friends over

there,' went on William Flint, relentlessly. He raised his glass at them again. They smiled unhappily.

Bull in a china shop; all Jack was up to was throwing a bloody great spanner in the works and hoping they'd seize up.

'Mr Flint,' he said, loud enough for everyone to hear it. 'How many newspapers can you put through your average letterbox?'

'What?' Flint turned to him wildly. The French people knocked back the last of their glasses and left. In the silence that followed Jack's question, he could feel opinions dividing again, the sharp focus dissolving into various viewpoints.

Then, 'Time, ladies and gentlemen please,' shouted the landlord, in case there was a copper outside.

'You mark my words.' William Flint looked at Jack. The room had started to buzz with separate conversations. 'It's not over. There isn't just one of me, you see. There's lots of people think the way I do.' He took a breath. Jack could hear his nostrils whistling. 'They live in nice houses with garages and crazy-paving,' he continued. 'They eat off tablecloths and go abroad in the summer. You should read the newspapers, Mr Fryer. A lot of nice people who've had enough and aren't afraid of saying so. You should read the *Ebbing Property Gazette*. People aren't happy. They don't reckon they're getting what's due to them, and they know why they aren't. Like that Mrs Sway. There's a lady knows what's what and I'm going to talk to her. Don't ask me if I'm troubled, because I'm not.'

He drank up and left. The landlord locked the front door and took their orders.

What was all that about? Jack wondered. And what did Mrs Sway have to do with it?

In daylight it was difficult to believe that any of it had happened. Flint was just the grumpy little man who sold copies of the *Sun* and cigarettes and suspected the kids of shoplifting. Last night the same person had been a terrible danger: averted, or was it only postponed? In spite of the sunshine, Jack suddenly felt a sense of foreboding. If those French people came to the Caff this morning, he'd give them each an extra slice of fried bread. Or, if they came at lunchtime and had the special pud, he'd give them cream *and* custard, and not draw it to their attention.

Perhaps Anna Seale would be along with her friends today. There was a voice to make mincemeat of ugliness.

And the road? All Jack could do was think about it very carefully. Now, through the windows, he saw the first freight-drivers coming towards the Caff, kicking at lumps of chalk in the Caff's small car-park with their sandy boots.

5

The Funeral

Lesley was unused to being unpopular with her family. It troubled her and yet, at the same time, she found it oddly bracing, as if something tight and constricting had suddenly loosened. She had never thought of herself as pathologically unselfish, like some women, but now she realised that, in a sense, she was – or had been. You could, she discovered, lead an energetic life of self-denial; it need not be the passive state she had assumed it to be. Especially if it had never occurred to you to ask yourself what exactly you wanted in the first place. The extent of your self-denial appeared to be calculable by the upset that was caused when you dispensed with it.

And upset had been caused; that much was certain. Though when Lesley had returned to the garden, after her phone call with Darryl Younger, and told Tim and Primrose and Winifred that she had no intention of going back on what she had said to the *Ebbing Times* – though refraining from mentioning the reason for this decision – their main reaction was one of surprise. It became clear to Lesley that her trusting in their judgement and complying with their wishes must have seemed to them a foregone conclusion. Discussion was a pretext, a matter of form – like a parliamentary debate where a motion was argued and then everyone voted exactly as they would have done if nobody had said a word. And, to be fair, it was not unreasonable of them

– in Parliament or in Lesley Sway's garden – to imagine that the structure of things was not likely to change at the drop of a hat. How odd it would be if, one day, in the House of Commons, Labour members started saying 'What a good idea,' to points made by Conservatives, or vice versa: if decisions were made on the strength of logical argument. How correspondingly odd it was if Lesley Sway, at forty-five, suddenly based her actions on the facts before her and not on a predetermined behaviour pattern. Yet, for the first time, it struck her as extremely strange that one should find it normal to do otherwise. Was not this lack of behavioural determinism a major factor in distinguishing one from an animal or a machine?

Her declaration had been met with a raw little silence.

'Well,' said Primrose who, like God, could think of no greater punishment than depriving someone of her presence, 'we'd better get back. Helen will be wanting to put you to bed, won't she, Treasures?'

It was meant to hurt, and it did, for Lesley believed in the family as a structure, even when some of its parts were on the wafty side. It would be inappropriate if Primrose departed now, as if the day of her father's death were just like any other day and she had simply dropped in for tea. The family unit, with whatever affections it might contain, was surely more resilient than political disagreements? At the thought that it might not be, the world gave a sudden lurch.

'We'll leave Cherry and the caravan here, if that's all right, Lesley,' said Tim, standing. 'The kids are tired out.' He pointed to them playing 'he' on the lawn. 'And Primrose has had a bloody day, one way and another. There's a tethering peg in the caravan.'

'Where is it? I'll go,' said Susie Took, who might have noticed a murdered corpse on her sitting-room sofa, if it had been bleeding copiously enough.

Lesley did not particularly want a horse on her lawn but there was no objection she could raise that would not sound callous in the extreme in the light of what Primrose was supposedly going through. With a sense of invasion she watched Susie unhitch Cherry from the caravan and bash the peg into the grass with a wooden mallet.

'Does it need water or hay?' asked Susie.

'Oh I 'spect so,' said Primrose. 'I think Helen usually gives her a bucket of something.'

When the car had driven off Lesley discovered that Winifred's way of handling the situation was also to be by absenting herself. Winifred's justification was to think that Lesley was ill. This was not without an element of kindness. Incarceration of the politically deviant within mental asylums is probably, more often than supposed, the result of a genuine belief that only the sick could oppose the status quo; a viewpoint which does not go unexpressed even in such a benign country as Britain. So Winifred believed – or pretended to believe – that only stress so great as to cause illness could have led her friend to her error. Much was made of paleness, confusion, lying down, eau-de-cologne and being better in the morning. Implicit was the idea that this improvement in health might manifest itself in a call to the *Ebbing Times*.

Lesley, uncharacteristically consenting to the charade, was relieved when Winifred and Susie were gone also. Caution was unnecessary around Susie, but she sensed that her plans must be utterly secret from Winifred. The more of Winifred she saw, the harder silence would be to maintain. And it must be maintained, for Winifred, something told her, could not be relied upon to act neutrally. The idea was unsettling. A sense of isolation returned.

Bleakly, she watched the sunset through the window. The painted caravan on her lawn, she found obtrusive. Cherry was grazing, with difficulty, on a large section of Lesley's carefully-tended grass, in spite of the torn-up pieces of bread Susie had scattered for her. She had kicked over the water bucket Susie had put out. It would need re-filling. Lesley got up and put the bedroom light on. She was hungry, so she went down to the kitchen and made herself a lemon tea and cheese and biscuits, which she brought upstairs, along with paper and a fountain pen. She had had a look, in all the likely places, for a map of Ebbing but her methodical system of storing information with appropriate labels in appropriate drawers or files had long since been thrown into disarray by Susie Took's habit of stuffing things wherever they would fit at that particular moment. For want of anything better, Lesley took down from the bedroom wall a framed map of Ebbing, dated 1895, which had belonged to her father.

It was rather a fanciful depiction of the town and its surroundings – the sea was stuffed with spurting whales; two little cherubs blew east and west winds across it – but it did, at least, give a general impression of the shape of the land. Though even here, the outline of the clifftop did not seem entirely accurate.

Since it was the best she could do, however, Lesley transcribed Ebbing onto her own sheet of paper and drew a line where, from what she had been told, the road was supposed to go. Then she walked the route in her mind, jotting down the names of those whose houses would be affected. Many of the people who lived in the path of the road she already knew. Those she didn't, mainly comprising the ones in the Ebb valley, she would have to go and visit once the funeral was over. Including Darryl Younger.

Loneliness fell away and a quite new excitement and concentration of purpose overcame her. In her absorption, Lesley forgot about the tea and cheese and biscuits, did not hear the clock chiming in the sitting-room. She decided to write a list of arguments against the road scheme but this proved difficult because there was only one really: it would destroy the houses and gardens – and the environment, but that was really part and parcel of the same thing. So instead she wrote a list of people to contact. She did not look up until the seagulls started crying. Then she went to the window and opened it and sniffed the air, cold from the night, with a faint odour of rust upon it. The buildings of Ebbing were blue and grey shadows, their sleeping windows milky. Only in one little house was a light burning. Somebody who started work early. The sun came up and, after a moment, Lesley slipped out of her clothes, leaving them where they fell, not her usual custom, and got into bed. She put the light out, since it was no longer necessary, and reached a hand to set the radio alarm clock. But then it occurred to her that there was no reason to get up particularly early, so she changed the setting to 8.45. It was the theme tune to *Ship Ahoy* that woke her. She listened to the programme while she got dressed.

*   *   *

Osbert's funeral took place three days later. A good opportunity to make appointments to visit people, since Ebbing's Tories would be out in force and the senior among them – that is to say, the more affluent, many of whose properties would be affected – would attend the tea that was to be provided afterwards. This tea was not Lesley's idea but that of Veronica Tarrant, who had acquired the Jolly Roger when she came to Ebbing following a divorce, but who already owned several, similar establishments in picturesque small towns and villages in the Home Counties. Veronica offered her catering services because, as she explained to Lesley, she liked to be noticed in the right places.

'What do you think Winifred?' asked Lesley, the afternoon before the funeral. For Winifred was around still, though with a pained expression. Lesley had adopted a tactic of avoiding discussion of the road scheme by concentrating all attention on the minutiae of Osbert's funeral. Primrose had phoned once, just to say that she was too busy to pick up Cherry and the caravan.

'Tea is a perfect compromise meal,' replied Winifred, with the rather pointed implication that compromise might be wanted in other quarters also.

'What a good idea. Meringues, eclairs, sandies. Scrummy,' said Susie. 'Veronica's a brilliant cook. Should be a lovely spread.'

'She says it will be an Anglo-Indian tea,' said Lesley. 'I must admit I don't know what they had for tea in Anglo-India.'

'Same as us, I expect,' said Susie. 'I'll give a ring and see if I can give a hand with anything.'

The weather turned slightly. It rained overnight. On the afternoon of the funeral the church was black with moisture. There were white, puffy clouds. All light would drain away and then, suddenly, the sun would come out and the foliage would leap into a vivid green. Flowers arrived from the Prime Minister, who was not to attend but would be represented by the Minister of Transport. A not very sizeable group of people lined the pavement outside the church, the same group that was accustomed to watching weddings, plus a few others.

Tim Babcock, the very picture of a concerned and dutiful son-in-law, took Lesley's arm outside the church and escorted her up the aisle to her pew. They were followed by Primrose and her two eldest; Primrose in a charcoal grey dress with matching coat and an antique hat, with a veil and maroon and plum cloth roses, just a fraction faded. The twins were in black and white striped frocks, with sailor collars.

Susie Took showed people to their places and gave out service sheets and hymn books. Lesley had asked Winifred to choose the hymns and they were to sing, among others, 'For Those In Peril On The Sea'. Not because Osbert had ever found himself in this position – unless you counted the time in Crete when he'd hired a boat and gone out too far – but as a tribute to the people of Ebbing, who used to be. An address was given by Dick Winters, Osbert's friend, who had broken the news to Lesley. Impeccably turned out in a grey pin-stripe, Dick exploited to the full his well-honed powers of invention as he described the achievements of Osbert Sway's political career.

Winifred, to Lesley's surprise, spent the entirety of the service weeping into a sodden lace handkerchief. Though Lesley had expected emotion, she had not anticipated such an amount of it, now that the initial shock was over. Only once before had she witnessed Winifred in such a state and that was at the end of *Born Free*, when they saw it at the cinema together in 1965.

Others were more staunch in their grief. Lesley studied as much of the congregation as she was able to without turning her head too noticeably. She mentally ticked off all those whose presence she had noted as she walked up the aisle. Everyone was there. There were no exceptions. Perhaps even Darryl Younger was part of the congregation, since she had no idea what he looked like.

Lesley's nerve failed her somewhat. It had not struck her as wise to commence any exploration of Conservative opinion about the road before Osbert was dealt with – it might be deemed unseemly and put people off – but, until today, it had not occurred to her that Darryl Younger could be anything other than correct: that there would be those who felt every bit as angry and eager to act as she did. Now, as a solid mass in the Victorian church of St Christopher, there was an air of utter unity. Maybe true Tories thought little of the party ploughing up their land and demolishing their houses for the greater good. At this idea, however, Lesley felt a bit more confident; 'the greater good' sounded more of a Marxist notion than a Conservative one. She imagined them feeling that way in China.

On the other hand . . . In the parallel pew were the Frogwells, Maud and Eustace – singing for all he was worth; his face blue and red and fattish and marbled with little veins, his neck bulging where his collar sliced into it. Maud Frogwell was wearing a black twin-set; her hair was grey and white and showed that not all of the previous Prime Minister's influences on Conservative fashions had been fortunate ones. Maud's great passion in life was breeding long-haired dachshunds. Could dissent lurk in such stolid breasts?

Or in those of Trouncy and Desmond Lollop, who wintered in the Canaries and looked as if they were made of leather? Trouncy was slim and blonde. Beside the pool of their thirties' villa she wore a sarong. She claimed to be considerably younger than Desmond, who was a retired Harley Street dentist.

Glamour is a suspect quality and rumours about Trouncy Lollop abounded. Most weekends during the summer, youthful friends arrived in lipstick-coloured cars at the Lollops' villa. Some evenings they went in a pack to the Jolly Roger, arriving in the Fish Market car park with much hooting of horns. People said that, after gin-soaked evenings, the visitors spent the days nursing hangovers on recliners round the pool, that Desmond Lollop *knew* that Trouncy had lovers. Few were generous enough to concede that, were the gossip true, Trouncy could hardly be blamed – if one discounted his possible discretion, the most interesting thing about Desmond was his bank balance.

More certain ground, perhaps, was Veronica Tarrant who had, indeed, mentioned seeing Lesley's comments in the *Ebbing Times* when she'd phoned to discuss the tea, though nothing more than that. She was seated beside an architect, who Lesley knew only by sight, but who lived in a restored windmill on the clifftop and owned a piece of private conservation land, which he would surely be loath to see crossed by four lanes of tarmac.

'. . . devoted husband, father and, indeed, grandfather . . .' said the vicar of Osbert; inaccurate on three counts. Which gave Lesley hope. Look at them seated here: herself, Winifred, Tim, Primrose, the twins and Susie (wearing, poor thing, a trouser suit; the jacket cut not quite low enough to hide her bottom). Who could possibly guess the rifts, large and small, which separated them? There was the major disagreement about the road between herself and Tim and Primrose; a division, on the same subject, between herself and Winifred. There was the disdain Tim barely concealed for Susie Took, because she was plump and hearty; memories in Lesley's mind, if not Primrose's, of the terrible tantrum Primrose had thrown at having Susie for a bridesmaid because she would 'look like a mobile home and spoil everything'. Then, of course, there was the glossed-over separation between herself and Osbert. But maybe an onlooker, viewing Lesley Sway amid her friends and family, would only be struck by an impressive image of harmony – an image that was, to all intents and purposes, largely erroneous. This was what she had to bank on.

A tear or two might have been in order, though Winifred was providing ample, but Lesley could not bring herself to weep. It was not until the service was over, and they stood at the graveside, that she realised what a terrible and absolute thing it was to be dead. Then she thought of Osbert, not as the pompous fool he had become, but as a young man at Cambridge in the early seventies.

'Thought Lassie was some sort of dog,' said Eustace Frogwell, to Bianca Pickle, who, since she worked at the Jolly Roger, had been made to give up her afternoon off to waitress at a funeral.

'It's yoghurt and water with salt and spices or sugar and orange blossom water. But there's tea as well, though you aren't supposed to have milk in it,' said Bianca sullenly. Things had been going okay but then everyone had arrived and a whole pile of women with posh voices had invaded the kitchen, saying they wanted to help, and snatched up plates which weren't supposed to go out yet, then plonked themselves down in there and not in the rooms where they were supposed to be. And guess who Veronica had taken it out on.

'It's not too bad if you have lots of sugar in it,' said Susie Took.

'I like to see girls eating up,' said Eustace Frogwell. 'Some of those ones on the television, well they look like Biafrans to me.'

'Haven't had lassi since Independence,' said a retired colonel.

'What is in these luscious scones?' breathed Trouncy Lollop, who had put on a pair of sunglasses and removed her jacket and, thought Bianca Pickle, looked a bit like a film star. Which was not desperately wide of the mark. Trouncy had started out as a chorus-girl, working in Spanish night-clubs. Her first husband was a matador.

'Clotted cream and rose petals,' said Bianca.

'I hope they haven't been sprayed,' said Veronica Tarrant's architect.

'Not that I know of,' said Bianca.

She flounced back to the kitchen, a curvy, compact little body that no uniform, however maidenly, was power against.

'I've done a ton up the motorway in my father's car. That's when I was home in the hols. I go to Harrow. That's my grandmother over there.' The boy pointed to the other side of the room where a thin, long old lady, with snow-white hair, was sitting at the kitchen table with a cluster of teenagers, an 'I-prefer-to-be-with-the-young-people' expression on her face. 'I'm Rory St John,' the boy continued, shoving his hands in his pockets.

'Oh yeah?' Bianca gave him the look of one who did not have to spend a lot of her life listening to people who bored her. She opened a cake tin and started to slap lime tarts onto a plate.

'Those are my people.' Rory indicated a man and a woman talking to a fat, huffy-puffy young accountant-type, who looked like he might explode. 'They're awfully dull.'

Bianca glanced over at them. Rory's father had a long oval face, he was bald on top, with a beard. The mother was wiry. 'Yeah,' she said, 'they look it.'

'We live in a big house which I'll inherit when Pater pops off. It's called "The Four Winds". Do you know it?'

'Yeah,' said Bianca. She walked past it sometimes, though she hadn't known who lived there. The plate was full. She picked it up.

'I could take you to the cinema, if you like,' said Rory.

'No thanks,' said Bianca.

'Oh, well, listen: I want you to do something for me. Grandma's got a message for Mrs Sway, but she doesn't want to give it in person. Reckon she's going a bit loopy in her dotage. Well I don't want to give it, make an arse of myself, but she's bound to ask if I have.'

'So what's in it for me?' asked Bianca. She faced the sink, picked up a lime tart and stuffed it into her mouth in one.

'I could take you for lunch somewhere, I suppose. I get a whopping allowance.'

Bianca cogitated. She preferred men to boys, and this one was a pillock, but why not, if he was buying? Bianca was between boyfriends. She and Harry Smack had split up after their evening in the Anchor. Bianca had been really irritated that Harry had gone along with that bad-mouthing of foreigners when, only two days before, he'd been all friendly with the blokes from the Taj Mahal. About the only thing that Bianca noticed, and couldn't tolerate, was people behaving illogically. Now she didn't give a toss about Harry but she did miss the free saveloys that he had given her down the Chippy.

'What's the message?'

'That she'll follow the lead of Eustace Frogwell. Like I say,' Rory made a circling motion with his finger in front of his face, 'bats.'

'The Woodcutter Inn, with sweets trolley and coffee?'

'Never been there. But all right.'

'You'll have to tell me which one Mrs Sway is. And I can't do anything until I've finished serving.'

Lesley sat on a chair in the garden.

Susie had brought out the croquet things and got a game going for some of the children; others were playing 'house' in the caravan. Susie had moved Cherry further down the lawn earlier in the day, lest the horse should, in some way, perturb the mourners; she had also – no indication having been made on Primrose or Tim's part as to when they intended to reclaim the creature – driven to the Ironmonger's in Ebbing and bought a sturdier, alarmingly permanent-looking bucket, to replace the one Cherry kept kicking over, and phoned Primrose's housekeeper, Helen, to discuss feed. You could see, on the grass, quite clearly now, the area where Cherry had grazed.

Small clusters of young women discussed their jobs in law

and finance, with half an eye on their offspring. Primrose emerged from the house with another of her bridesmaids; one of more acceptable proportions. The young woman had just left university and was asking Primrose whether she thought she should opt for journalism or for a position with one of the auction houses. Her fiancé was a television producer, who worked in current affairs. He was in earnest conversation with Tim Babcock.

'Can I get you anything Lesley? I can probably source a gin, if it's all getting a bit too nursery tea for you.'

It was Penny St John, Rory's Pre-Raphaelite sister. She lived with the sculptor, Steven Toe, great grand-nephew of Matthew Toe (who had designed the famous Art Nouveau portals at the Carr Mansion – of Carr's Vacuum Cleaners – near Beaconsfield).

'No, thank you Penny.' Lesley felt a brief guilt at the thought of throwing into disarray the plans of all this gilded youth. Then it occurred to her that in the light – or rather shadow – of death, attempts at happiness had a tendency to gain a poignancy that was not intrinsic to them. 'How's the Slade?' she asked.

'Oh. Dull. Interesting. Not too bad if you look upon it as a stage to be passed through. But listen. If you want a real laugh, Lesley, do go to Fitch's Gallery and have a look at the latest exhibition. "Anger II", it's called. The most frightful rubbish. Bits of this that and the other, mainly bicycle parts, welded together and painted black. I've no idea where the anger comes into it. Perhaps the person whose bicycle it was. Steven's showing in Stockholm till tomorrow, then I'm just going to have to drag him along to it. My theory is that Fitch chooses such awful stuff so that her own occasional efforts look good in comparison. Look, why don't we go down there together? Sometime before it closes? Do a girls' lunch at the Jolly Roger too?'

'That would be lovely, Penny,' said Lesley, vaguely. Maud Frogwell was heading towards them.

'Oh God,' said Penny, noticing. 'I just have to avoid Maud. All that puppy talk makes me feel sick.' She slipped away with a graceful smile in Maud's direction and a gesture that indicated some sort of errand.

'Lesley.' Maud sat down and, leaning forward, took one of Lesley's hands and cupped it between hers. 'How *are* you?'

'Well . . .' said Lesley.

'What can I say in this time of . . . distress? Spring follows winter. Birth follows death. Banjo whelped yesterday morning. I was expecting it, of course, because I had been taking her temperature twice a day, so I was there, ready to break the membranes if necessary. As it was, I only had to cut the cords, because she was biting them too close. Five lovely little puppies. Three dogs and a couple of bitches.' She paused and looked up at the figure who had just approached them. 'Nothing to eat, thank you, but could you bring a jug of milk and some Hermesetas?'

'Nothing for me,' said Lesley.

'Mrs Tarrant isn't letting anyone have milk. People have been asking. Anyway, I've started washing up now 'cos I get off in half an hour. It's a message for Mrs Sway.'

'Yes?' Lesley stared at the girl, puzzled.

'Rory St John's gran says she'll follow Eustace Frogwell.' With that the girl turned tail and trotted back towards the house.

There was a pause. The sound of a ball being hit with a mallet.

Lesley raised her eyes to Maud Frogwell's face. 'Can you imagine what that can have been about?' she asked.

The fingers, still cupped around her own, closed a little tighter.

'Why don't you come round tomorrow?' Maud replied. 'It would be nice for you to see the puppies.'

6

A Discussion

It proved easier than Lesley had expected to keep her plans secret from Winifred. After the excitement of the funeral there was the Conservative barbecue to prepare for. Any crevices of silence could be stuffed with discussion about costume and climate, the placing of tables, charcoal. Perhaps it had always been so. Certainly Winifred noticed no difference.

The weather was warm. The days were growing longer. In the early evenings Lesley took to going for walks and dropping in on people. She visited the Frogwells and drank sherry with Rory and Penny St John's grandmother. Now, on the eve of the barbecue, with her house and garden full of people, it was quite understandable that she should wish to go out on her own for an hour.

She set off on foot for the Ebb valley. Darryl Younger might be at the barbecue anyway, but she couldn't bank on it; he hadn't come to the funeral. He was back on *Ship Ahoy* now, though the character he played, Luke Barnacle, had a hare-brained scheme for buying a fishing boat cheaply, even though Captain Skate advised him that it wasn't safe, so maybe contract negotiations were only in brief abeyance.

Lesley now listened to the programme every morning. She was also aware of it being listened to around Ebbing, in shops and through open windows. It was on several times a day.

Shrimping-on-Sea was rather like her father's framed map of Ebbing (which Lesley had grown rather attached to and had, in fact, brought down to the office that afternoon and placed on the desk, in case she needed to refer to it). There was a lively fishing industry. Everyone knew the ways of the sea – when storms were heading in, where there were rocks hidden underwater, unsafe bits of cliff, dangerous currents – except for Luke Barnacle. Captain Skate watched the horizon through his telescope. He had a parrot and had been in the Indies in his youth. The women spent much time gathering mussels and boiling up lobsters. Everyone pulled together. Virtually nothing ever happened at Shrimping-on-Sea but, what little did, the inhabitants made a tremendous fuss about. Whole episodes were devoted to whether or not to use the village hall for a bring-and-buy sale or who should be president of the Women's Institute.

It was hard to tell where *Ship Ahoy* was supposed to be set because everyone had different accents. Some days Lesley felt it must be Cornwall, then she decided that it had to be nearer to London because of the preponderance of a form of Cockney. One or two of the characters appeared to have originated in Birmingham. Anyway, she began to derive reassurance from their voices. In particular that of Luke Barnacle, which was rich and mellow and suffused with a charm which one did not usually associate with fishermen.

'Looks like rain,' said Captain Skate as Lesley left the house. Veronica Tarrant had the radio on in the kitchen. She was overseeing the making of a chilled Vichyssoise. Penny St John was chopping the leeks and Susie Took was peeling the potatoes. Penny's lover, Steven Toe, returned from Stockholm with raves, was plaiting his beard on the sitting-room sofa. 'Yes, it does that,' said Sally Mackerel. 'P'rhaps I shouldn't have put my washing on the line.' 'I told you not to,' said Mrs Haddock, the village know-all.

Darryl Younger's description of his house proved to be a mixture of accuracy and exaggeration which, though Lesley did not know this, tends to be the way with actors. It was set well back from the lovely lane that ran along the floor of the Ebb valley and was reached through a rickety – though not awfully rickety – gate in a hedge made up of honeysuckle and brambles and wild roses. The front lawn was lush and thick and crammed with daisies. But the house was not 'tiny', as Darryl had said. In fact it was medium-sized. Nor was it 'about to fall down', so far as Lesley could judge – though it did give the impression that, if that was what pleased you, you were free to fancy that it was.

Lesley knocked on the wooden door and heard the silence of the interior of the building. It was clear, beyond any doubt, that he was not at home. She decided to check round the back, however, in case he was in the garden. Yes, there was the Ebb, as he had told her, quite shallow at this point, and the apple trees: unpruned, but not too unpruned, under one of them a wooden garden seat. A clock inside the house struck seven. Lesley went to the window and, shading her eyes against the reflections, looked in.

Usually she was not a curious person, but Darryl Younger interested her. A disembodied voice on the telephone, and on the radio, she wanted to know what he looked like almost as much as she wanted his support at the Conservative barbecue. She hoped for a framed photograph, such as she imagined actors placed on grand pianos, and prepared to be disappointed. He would be squat with thick glasses and looking rather pathetically delighted as he shook hands with somebody like Princess Margaret. But there was no photograph. And no grand piano either. Instead, a cheerful room, full of books. An enormous marmalade cat, asleep on a sofa. Scripts, presumably, on a low table. An expensive-looking sound system and several rows of compact discs. And, over the fireplace, a stunning seascape: the cliff above Ebbing – Lesley's house, the Frogwell Mansion, the chalk, the trees, distant shapes on the edge of a bucking, reeling, swallowing ocean. A painting which burst with love and passion. Loud and unafraid and utterly unselfconscious. What she was fighting for encapsulated.

Whose sensual nature was she looking at? Partly her own, Lesley admitted.

Interest and curiosity spontaneously vanished, to be replaced by a startlingly intense desire to meet the man with the gorgeous voice who had bought such a painting. Surely this year he would be at the barbecue. It was the event that all of Ebbing's

Conservatives came to, if they possibly could. He was not away; that much was evident. The house had an occupied feeling. Where was he? Out walking, perhaps. He could return at any minute.

Lesley went and sat on the seat under the apple tree. It was a lovely place to be anyway, and what was there to rush back for?

The Labour building in Ebbing High Street was constructed in 1946, in a spirit of hope and optimism, tempered by weariness. There was a celebratory tea there for the children on the day it was declared open, with jam sandwiches and jelly and lemon squash. The mothers saved up their coupons and made a cake with powdered eggs. There were speeches. Some people in Ebbing still remembered it.

Over the years, however, the building had been neglected; little or no maintenance done; necessary repairs put off or botched. The result being that, in 1995, when Miles Starey, Labour candidate for Ebbing, needed a venue for his discussion of the new road scheme, he had to rent their hall from the Methodists who, in spite of corrugated iron, evidently thought in the long term.

The discussion was due to begin at seven o'clock.

By six-thirty, a picket of Trotskyists was assembled outside. Few were sure quite why and the leaflets explaining their position, which they gave out to anyone who was willing to take them, though not lacking in fervour, were somewhat short on elucidation. The mystery was compounded by the fact that Carmen Fitch had decided that this was an ideal occasion to publicise 'Anger II' and her artists, tougher-looking than most of the Trots, were being conspicuously successful at inflicting their leaflets on people. Thus many came away with the idea that the Trotskyists objected to the Methodist Hall as setting for the Labour Party discussion because they felt now was the time for a 'clitoro-centred understanding of aggression'. Or, conversely, that 'Anger II' was an exhibition about the necessity that the (imminent) fall of Western Capitalism should be dissociated from the fate of the Soviet Union.

Inside the hall, the Lesbian Separatists had penned off a section of the seating for women and children, which Mary Janet, her hair loose today, was policing. Her girlfriend, Ruth Ellis, who was wearing a t-shirt which said 'Support a Male Curfew', and a couple of other battle-hardened Separatists, were setting up an 'Abuse Crisis' table in a corner of the room for anyone (female) who wished to talk about their abuses, real or imagined. They were looking daggers at the Non-Separatist Feminists, with their plaits and clogs and papooses or their mobile phones and brief-cases, depending on the angle from which their views emanated.

At the back of the room was a cluster of men from the Anchor. Old, mainstream Labour mainly; unemployed, many of them. Bottles of Newquay Brown dangled from their yellowed fingers. They cast furtive and threatening glances in the direction of a group of gays, who were dusting the rostrum.

Single Mothers For A Zebra Crossing Outside The School formed a barrier of pushchairs along the front row. Their offspring wailed and wept, dropped plastic cups with spouts, puked spontaneously and filled their nappies. The men and women of the Free Lois Zimble campaign wore t-shirts picturing Lois with her machine gun. Adrian Dapple and Gilda and the other Ecologists tacked posters of animal experiments on the wall, which were ripped down by an enraged single mother as disturbing to children. Gilda pointed out that the posters were meant to be disturbing. Bob and some of the Save The Lesser Tit campaigners suggested replacing them with the photographs that they had brought of the lesser tit doing some of the few things it ever did do. Rolf Watt and his Marxist comrades exchanged bitter comments with the Anarchists, who were scattered about the room. Jay and the other members of the Legalise Marijuana And Jesus Was A Black Man group, lolled in their seats and talked to each other about the texture of the paintwork.

Anna was exhilarated; in the thick of what she knew best: political activity – an area beyond self-doubt, a world away from the fragile, tenuous joys of her attempts at painting. She and Carmen cracked a six-pack. The beer was cold. Her head surged with optimism. Soon she would see Miles again. What a turn-out for him.

The hall filled up and became smoky. All the seats were taken. There was a little outcry from some of the Non-Separatist Feminists at the discovery that a pregnant woman was standing. There was a scuffle and a young man was turfed off his chair. His gay friends, affronted, pointed out he had a septic foot, which qualified him as handicapped. They cast reproachful looks at the men from the Anchor, obviously in goodish health and not volunteering to shift themselves. The man with the septic foot had to sit on someone's lap.

Still the audience kept growing.

A large group of new people entered the room, ones Anna didn't recognise. They pushed their way to the front and stationed themselves against the walls, parallel to the rostrum: a proliferation of skirts and blouses, shirts and neat trousers, suits. They greeted one another formally, looking sideways at the mob already in occupation.

'Well it swells the numbers, I suppose,' Anna heard one of the women say to another. 'And I imagine Miles knows how to speak to them.'

'Hey,' said Jay, in the seat behind her, 'an invasion of Munchkins.'

'Jesus H. Christ,' muttered Rolf Watt. 'New bloody Labour. The insipid face of the fucking future.'

Similar mutterings resonated around the room. St Christopher's clock struck a quarter to seven. The various components of the Ebbing Left Wing regarded one another with suspicion and hostility.

Mary Janet tried to make an announcement from her place in the middle of the pen of Lesbian Separatists. With her hair loose she had the slightly wild look of a normally-repressed individual who is taking part in an amateur dramatics production. Her heavies yelled for silence.

'Can you shut up at the back there?' shouted Ruth Ellis at some men in cloth caps.

The majority of the talking ceased.

'Before the meeting begins,' said Mary Janet, 'I propose a vote about smoking. Are we going to allow women and children be made to undergo the violation of ingesting other people's excreted toxins?'

New Labour exchanged amused glances and raised their eyes to heaven.

One of the Non-Separatist Feminists, a doctor named Rosalind Farrow, stood up quickly. She and Mary Janet were at logger-heads because Dr Farrow made no secret of being in favour of epidurals.

'In the light of the known damage that can be done by passive smoking,' said Rosalind, 'I would suggest that the issue is not debatable. I propose a vote first about whether we should vote about whether we should permit smoking.'

Anna lit a fag while it was being decided whether or not she had the right to smoke it.

A heated discussion started up.

There were those who argued that everyone, including children, should be allowed to vote on the issue – or issues – and there were those who disagreed with them. One of the Single Mothers For A Zebra Crossing Outside The School maintained that certain minorities should be allocated two or more votes, in proportion to how greatly they were under-represented in the macrocosm. Eventually, as St Christopher's struck seven, the second vote was counted. Most cigarettes were extinguished. A small fire had to be dealt with when one, not properly stubbed out, set light to a couple of crisp packets.

While all this was going on, quietly, from among the new-comers, emerged Miles Starey. He awaited his moment, until all the fuss had subsided, then made his way to the rostrum and stood there smiling.

At first Anna didn't recognise him, assuming it must be some-body from the Party headquarters, there to introduce him. The group Miles had issued from burst into spontaneous clapping, the fact that he was wearing a suit apparently not striking *them* as strange or excessive: a dark blue suit, expensively cut – the kind he used to rail about when Anna knew him. Under it, a crisp white cotton shirt and a loose red tie. He had a butterscotch suntan. His hair was shorter than it used to be, but he had a small pony-tail. It was the look of a stylish young man from one of the more expensive public schools, who is soon to go to his chosen university.

The room fell silent.

'Hi,' said Miles, making eye-contact. There was another ripple of applause from the group of New Labour, as if it were a lovely surprise to them that their candidate was able to enunciate. Horrified, Anna studied the face for familiar expressions. She saw nothing but changes.

Miles lifted a hand, as if afraid that the clapping might continue indefinitely.

'Links between people,' he began, without preamble. 'West and East united. Jobs. These are what the road will result in.'

There was yet another shower of joyous applause from New Labour. Around the rest of the hall there was a shocked hush; people were incredulous.

'What road?' shouted one of the Marxists.

Miles Starey looked surprised, and slightly affronted, at the interruption. 'The new road scheme along the clifftop. The subject of this meeting.'

There was a murmur of disbelief.

'Why?' shouted someone else, uncertainly.

'Why?' repeated Miles, meeting the question with more confidence than he would have done had he not, earlier in the day, anonymously phoned the Tory campaign headquarters and spoken to a plummy-voiced young woman, who had read him a prepared statement about the benefits of the road and suggested that she send him information about Conservative policy in general; an offer which, though torn, Miles had, for obvious reasons, declined.

Now, without confiding his source to his listeners, he parroted, with feeling, the Tory reasons – or at least most of them; there were some that even the young woman was not privy to – for the road scheme. His voice reached a crescendo and he banged a fist on the rostrum.

Anna, dumbfounded, watched with incomprehension. Did Miles seriously believe the shit he was spouting? He couldn't possibly. But, if it was purely expedient, could she now trust that he had meant what he used to say either? In her own bed, had he lied to her when he read out wodges of Left-wing theory and expatiated on their wisdom? Or was he lying now because, like this bunch of simpering wets – whose slight consciences wouldn't quite allow them to vote Tory – he reckoned that only by doing as the Tories did would he get to Westminster?

It was hard to decide which of these alternatives was the more despicable.

A hot, hostile buzz, barely audible, was cranking up in the room as Starey's position sank in. He continued to speak, blithe and oblivious, twittering on about improved access to London and the face of progress. Anna stared at the floor. She could not bear to look at him. She thought of the cliffs at dawn. Rose in sunlight. Blue-lilac in rain. She thought of smudged foliage and dripping skies, the way that light darted around the slippery rocks in the shallows of the Ebb: worked herself into a rage of shattered trust and spoiled memory then, standing, launched in Miles's direction a pyrogenic of spat language – obscene, political, personal – soon only one among a chorus of different voices, each with their own particular betrayals. A fraction of a second and they were all at it, but she was the first. In such divisions of time our lives change direction.

'"Some have greatness thrust upon them."'

'You were there then?'

'For the whole thing. At the back. I've found your tequila. Do you want one?'

'Coffee.' Anna went into the bathroom and turned the taps on. She picked up a handful of emerald bath-salts and chucked them into the water. 'My campaign manager and chief financial contributor is on his way.' She pulled off her clothes and got into the bath. Darryl entered with her coffee and another tequila for himself. He put down the loo seat and sat on it.

'Was that the answerphone?' Anna asked.

'Bob. Something about tits and the Conservative barbecue. And congratulations, of course. Did you get badly spattered?'

'In the cross-fire. Who brought the tomatoes?'

'The Anarchists, I expect. They probably never travel without them.'

'Why the fuck did they get in a fight with the Trots after their walk-out?'

'God knows. Perhaps they don't believe in a clitoro-centred understanding of aggression.'

Anna reached for the mug and took a warm gulp of coffee. The room was sweet-smelling and steamy. She experienced a rich inner satisfaction at the memory of Miles and his cohorts legging it out of the hall, the look on Miles's face when he saw her – the past rearing up at him. Then she felt a rush of angry sorrow.

'That storm painting you're working on,' said Darryl: 'it's bloody amazing.'

'What do you know about it? You're just a third-rate actor.' Then she realised that it wasn't Darryl she wanted to lash out at.

'Second-rate. And I know enough to trust what my eyes tell me and not what some art-school dyke has to say on the matter.'

'It's not just a question of what's in front of you, Darryl.' Anna soaped a sponge fiercely.

'What is it a question of then, Anna?'

To see something and to try to convey it with passion and honesty was a starting point, Carmen always admitted; a finishing point, indeed, if you were happy to be a naif, like Rousseau.

'The expression of an intellectual vision.'

Darryl threw his hands to the ceiling in the gesture of one of the more put-upon patriarchs in a Biblical epic.

'Whose, for heaven's sake? You screwed that prat Miles because he had an intellectual vision – and a pretty bum, admittedly. An hour ago you were on your feet yelling that he'd sold out. I agree with you. But the fact that he took, what he claimed, was an intellectual approach to things never guaranteed he had any integrity.'

Anna was silent for a moment.

'Carmen knows about art.'

'And Miles knew about politics.' Darryl made another expansive gesture. 'If you ask me, you're using Carmen Fitch's warped view of your creations to protect yourself from having to risk getting other, professional, assessments. The devil you know, and all that. Easier to march for causes and paint on the quiet.'

Anna stood up.

'You're a shit Darryl. Pass me a towel.'

He handed one to her. She rubbed herself dry, then picked some track-suit trousers and a t-shirt off the floor and put them on.

'But I've never sold out, have I?' Darryl took a gulp of tequila.

'Only because no one was buying. And marching for a cause isn't easy. You've never had the pigs do you over.'

Darryl was silent. Anna pulled the plug out. They went back into the studio.

'Lend us a fiver, would you Anna?'

'Don't they pay you for that crap programme?'

'Not as fast as I spend it.'

Anna pointed at her patchwork shoulder-bag. 'Look in there. There probably isn't as much as a fiver, but whatever there is, take half of it.' She slumped onto the sofa. Darryl found the money and came and sat beside her.

'There was nothing Miles said that couldn't have been agreed with by a fucking Tory.' Anna sighed loudly.

'That's the whole point of it. New Labour obviously reckons that if Babcock's lot think a new road is going to get Babcock to Westminster, or at least not prevent him from getting there, then the most sensible thing to do is make their policy exactly the same. Ape the Tories, win the election.'

'Why bother?' Anna picked up Darryl's glass and drank a mouthful of tequila.

'Couldn't agree more. "Preserve your motivation": that was what one of the instructors used to say at RADA. Done some bit-roles in *Crossroads*. "There was once a sultan" – while we all stood round in our tights and jock-straps – "whose wife died and, for love of her, he decided to make a beautiful mausoleum." Like the Taj, I suppose. Anyway: "for years artists and architects worked on it and all the time the sultan kept saying to embellish it further." Never good enough for him. You get the picture. Then, one day, as he was wandering round the building, admiring all the magnificence and what-not, he told the chief architect that he was pretty nearly happy with it. "What I want to know, though, is what that little oblong thing in the middle is. It spoils everything."'

As he told his story, Darryl was sultan, teacher, shivering

drama student, artist and architect: a Protean display; a magical ability – more appealing in actors than in most of its other manifestations.

Neither of them spoke for a minute. There was the sound of the quiet waves on the shingle.

'You know you've got a problem, Anna?'

'I know I've got dozens. Which one are we talking about?'

'There aren't enough of us. Pure and simple. The Anarchists and Trots have gone off on their own tack already. So have Single Mothers and Free Lois Zimble . . .'

'And what's left could bicker itself out of existence at a moment's notice. Yeah, I know. So you got any bright ideas, Darryl?'

'Inklings. Only inklings.'

There was a hammering at the door that made them both jump.

'Open up! Police!'

The door opened.

'Jesus Jay,' said Anna, 'I wish you wouldn't do that.'

Sometimes Jack Fryer went for a night-time walk around Ebbing after the Anchor closed. He knew who slept well and who didn't. He noticed changing habits. Lesley Sway's, for instance, and William Flint's – a jaundiced light burned late in his flat above the newsagent's, which squatted at the Fish Market end of Harbour Street.

Darryl Younger, a confirmed night-owl, walked past on the opposite pavement; he raised a hand in greeting. He was slightly drunk.

'I owe you money, Jack. I owe everyone money.'

'Night, Darryl.'

Jack watched him down the street, thinking.

Bloody mess that whole meeting, but at least they'd picked the right leader. Though you weren't supposed to call her that. She was only allowed to be referred to as 'the people's candidate'. The decision over what to call the party itself had taken even longer. Anna's Rasta friend wanted '. . . and Legalise Marijuana And Jesus Was A Black Man' tacked onto the end of it; that was when the Single Mothers left. (Old staunch Labour, Jack's nodding acquaintances from the Anchor, had left already with Starey. They'd vote for him whatever. Most of the Anchor's customers hadn't thought it worth their while coming.) Eventually Anna's Rasta friend agreed to the Preserve The Ebbing Clifftop And Jesus Was A Black Man Party: it didn't exactly trip off the tongue, but it kept them all happy, and he was, after all, putting up the money. Though what the arguing came down to Jack was buggered if he knew since, at the end of the day, it seemed to him that, broadly speaking, they agreed with each other.

Well if anyone could pull them into some kind of shape, Anna Seale could. She knew a bit of language, that woman. Her hips were curved and spacious. They made Jack think of sweet, creamy things, eaten fearlessly. Was she the person he should talk to about what he was beginning to suspect about the clifftop, or should he bide his time and wait to see who would make best use of it?

7 ∫

The Barbecue

Nobody knew why it was Conservative tradition to have an annual barbecue. Certainly they were not very good at them. Those who were unaware of Veronica Tarrant's usurpation of the proceedings expected what was usually on offer: a small glass of warm white wine, a long long wait and, eventually, a sausage, thickly crusted with carbon on the outside, raw within. Food poisoning was not uncommon. Maybe deeper, more complex motives were at work then, since enjoyment, and even nutrition, did not appear to be uppermost. An atavistic desire to be the ones who controlled fire perhaps; the wish to show that Conservatives could have every bit as much fun as anyone else – without having to resort to sex or drugs or violence on television – and thereby appeal to the more discerning youthful voter. Though the battle for the minds of youth had really been fought and won by 1995, as witnessed by the large number of under-twenties, some of whose, less resourceful, parents remained at home, indulging in all or some of the forementioned unhealthy versions of enjoyment. Or it could just have been that, by happy chance, the candidates and senior members of Ebbing's Tories invariably possessed beautiful houses with large and even more beautiful gardens.

Such is the love of habit that it is reluctant to exchange what it is used to, even for something indisputably better. When they were met, on arriving at Lesley Sway's, not by an overriding smell of methylated spirits and a few sad bowls of peanuts, but by orange coals, little porcelain cups of chilled Vichyssoise and puffed pastries – to take the edge off the appetite – the sight of skewers of marinated monkfish, sate, mushrooms and peppers (for the vegetarians) and a dripping ice-sculpture of a seagull, many felt discomfited. To enjoy yourself too much or, in some cases, at all, struck them as somehow disloyal to their principles. This tendency of the human psyche goes quite some way to explaining almost all of the political systems on the planet.

The sensation was particularly acute among a section of the Conservative voters who were accustomed to being at the bottom of the pecking-order and to compensating for their lowly status by a particular ardour: namely the lower-middle classes. Peanuts, meths and sausages they were at home with; they gave them a sense of belonging. Here was an, essentially unwise, glimpse of the fact that they did not necessarily partake of all the privileges which they voted in favour of. The changes that Veronica had worked came dangerously close to evoking the same emotions which were evoked by Sarah Ferguson – the royal who guaranteed the end of monarchy simply by failing to pretend that she was not having an absolute ball. They sipped their chilled cremant in cardies, white shoes and pastel skirts with threads dangling from the hems, in awkward and vaguely resentful clusters.

It was a truly glorious evening. Proof, to those who thought in this way, of whose side God was on. As the sun dropped over the simmering horizon, Primrose Babcock flitted beneath the trees, lighting the lanterns that were hanging from them; too girlish – as she heard chorused from person to person – too young to be the wife of a political candidate. She wore a sleeveless, drop-waisted dress of peach-coloured cheesecloth, and an Art Nouveau slave-bangle – a witty reference to one worn by Clover Deal, the subject of Primrose's oeuvre, commissioned from a friend of Penny St John and Steven Toe who worked in metals.

'Veronica, you lovely thing,' she said, when she had finished, coming over to where Veronica Tarrant was superintending the cooking of the brochettes and squeezing her about the waist, 'what a beautiful display.' Her voice dropped to a murmur. 'And an absolutely perfect change of image.'

'Phew,' said Susie Took, approaching with two greasy carrier bags in one hand and a white plastic pudding-basin in the other. 'Thank goodness I remembered them. What would we have done with ten dozen bangers?'

'Yes, what a relief,' said Veronica, 'though there really isn't any room for them at present. What are those things?'

'Marshmallows,' said Susie. 'For later. They're super fun. You hold them over the coals on sticks and they go all gooey.'

Primrose and Veronica exchanged quick glances. 'There are some people looking awfully lost and forlorn,' said Primrose. 'Give me the marshmallows, Susie, and the sausages, and why don't you get the Young Conservatives to do some mingling?'

'Oh golly, are there?' said Susie. 'Can't have that.'

Lesley watched it all from her bedroom window. The light was off, so she could remain unobserved. People kept tripping over Cherry's tethering-rope, but it was preferable that the horse should be there, if the caravan had to be. Without it, it might be thought that the caravan was a decoration, like those old ploughs, with clumps of flowers planted around them, that graced the gardens of a fair number of individuals in Ebbing who, otherwise, cared to know little of tilling the sod. Lesley was loath to descend until just before the candidate was to be announced, the lateness of her presence being, in the circumstances, quite excusable.

'Nobody expects much of you tomorrow, dear,' said Winifred, the previous morning.

Lesley smiled grimly. No, most of them probably didn't. Though when she had returned, disappointed, from Darryl Younger's house, she had found Winifred and Primrose in the office, studying the framed map of Ebbing. They had both looked at her sharply when she entered and Winifred had opened her mouth to say something. But then Susie, hearing Lesley's footsteps, had bounded in.

'Guess what, Aunt Lellie, oh guess what! Primmie and Tim are going to Bermuda.'

Primrose coloured crossly. 'Nothing's decided yet, Susie.'

'But I thought I heard you tell Mummy . . .'

'I'm going to have a bath and change,' said Lesley, and slipped away, angry with herself for having stayed out so long.

Well, soon the subterfuge would be over. Which was good because it went against all Lesley's instincts. Winifred would understand, wouldn't she?

There was a soft knock and, as if Lesley's thoughts had summoned her, Winifred's head popped around the door.

'Can I come in, dear?' She entered, without waiting for Lesley's reply, and put the light on. 'There's a nasty little man who keeps asking to speak to you. The newsagent. William Flint, his name is, though I didn't know it till this evening. I've managed to fend him off but you'll probably have to see him eventually.'

'Whatever can that be about?' said Lesley.

'Oh, planning permission; a barking dog; something of that nature, I imagine.' Winifred perched on the bed. Lesley sat at her dressing-table and, picking up a hair-brush, started to brush her hair self-consciously. 'But that's not what I wanted to talk to you about,' Winifred continued. The old friends' eyes met in the mirror; Lesley looked down. 'I'm here on behalf of Primrose, really.'

'On behalf of Primrose, Winifred?'

'Yes, well, she thought I might have more influence on you than she would.'

Lesley was irritated. 'Primrose is my daughter.'

'And the wife of the new candidate. Jealousy is only to be expected, dear. We felt it would be easier for just you and me to talk about it.'

Their eyes met again and, in that instant, Lesley knew that, due to her carelessness the previous evening, Winifred had now guessed that she was planning something. She knew also that, whatever Primrose might think (and she quite likely did think that Lesley was jealous of her; for being young, pretty, married to Tim Babcock, on the brink of having a coffee-table book published; in short, for simply being Primrose: cause enough for any amount of envy) that Winifred did not believe for half a second that Lesley was jealous of her daughter. It was a bluff of the most Machiavellian shrewdness: this was what people were going to think, Winifred was telling her; this (was it possible?)

was what Winifred and Primrose would tell them. They were gambling on her pride. Wrong move, thought Lesley, bitterly. How much of that sort of pride did they think could remain to the wife of a dead politician, one of whose final acts had been to betray her?

'There are things about which one does not have choices,' she said levelly.

'Loyalty, I would have thought,' said Winifred, 'would be one of them.'

There was a silence.

'You know,' said Winifred, 'what killed Osbert?' She paused for effect. 'It was the stress of the separation.'

Patently ridiculous. Osbert Sway was as bereft of sentiment as his pretty daughter. The only external event that would have had the power to despatch him would have been a financial one. But Winifred's face, with its orange lipstick and beige foundation, told a story that was altogether more wounding. Hitherto, Lesley had been of the belief that her passing thoughts as to Winifred's superiority to herself as a wife for Osbert were shared by no one. Now she saw that they were most profoundly shared by Winifred herself. It occurred to her, for the first time, that it was no coincidence that Winifred's life had imitated her own – that marriage had followed marriage, child followed child, divorce followed separation. In each case, Winifred's lot had been disappointment; a disappointment that Winifred must regard as utterly inappropriate. Winifred had got the wrong husband and the wrong daughter; maybe there had even been an inexplicably unsuccessful attempt to hijack Osbert. Why not? What a politician she would have made of him; and how she would have rejoiced in Primrose. They were three of a kind, after all: experts in the social virtues. At some level, Winifred must feel that Susie was more what Lesley deserved in a daughter. Tactlessness was only the uncut form of honesty.

Lesley felt as if she were in a lift that was plummeting down twenty storeys. Her best friend loathed her. A sad state of affairs though not, unfortunately, terribly unusual.

There was a sharp rap on the door.

'Come in,' said Lesley.

Bianca Pickle entered, a little lace apron tight around her even tighter black skirt. 'Mrs Tarrant wants you in the garden. The speeches are about to begin and she's got the champagne ready.'

Lesley stood up in silence and followed Bianca down the stairs, dimly aware that Winifred was walking behind her.

Rory St John was at the entrance to the garden. On impulse, and unnoticed by anyone else, other than Steven Toe – whose sexual preferences did not stop at art-school sophisticates – Bianca stuck her tongue out at him. Rory got that sensation you get when you're in a swimming pool and one of the other fellows dives down and grabs your foot and pulls you underwater. He and Bianca had had their lunch at the Woodcutter Inn now and Bianca had eaten more than he'd believed a girl capable of. He was in love, he decided, and so he'd hang around the anti-road lot with Penny and Grandma, whatever Mater and Pater thought about it, since it looked like that would be his best chance of seeing more of Bianca given that her employer, Mrs Tarrant, did catering for Lesley Sway. Steven Toe made a modified version of the same decision and conceived a longing for wet clay and nudity.

Everyone was assembled in a polite horse-shoe around Dick Winters and Primrose and Tim Babcock. They held champagne glasses. Various people with bottles stood among them, ready to pop the corks at the appropriate moment. Lesley felt like Macbeth rushing out to meet Duncan, Judas pulling up his chair for the last supper, Geoffrey Howe: all those imaginative individuals who make history, fiction and myth so interesting and eventful. There was a pleasure in not being good any longer. Though, when all was said and done, the territory within the pale was quite acceptably extensive and it need not stop her remaining a Tory.

If one can imbue applause with pity and compassion, mixed with admiration, the assembled crowd, at the sight of Lesley Sway, attempted to do so. Led, of course, by Tim Babcock. Looking out at the faces, Lesley had the not altogether pleasant sensation that what she was really being clapped for was not being dead also. But more was afoot; there were knowing glances. Maud Frogwell crushed her face into a proud smile.

Trouncy Lollop, wearing something tight and short, rather drunk, blew a kiss onto the palm of her hand and puffed it in Lesley's direction.

Dick Winters led Lesley into their midst and clapped near to her chin a couple of times to show how heartfelt was his appreciation. When there was silence he began speaking.

'This is a time of new ventures and great excitement,' he began. Then, the voice plunging gracefully into regret, 'And, of course, of great sorrow.' The faces of the crowd contorted, sypathetically, in an endeavour to convey these two conflicting emotions. Dick continued. Great sorrow was, predictably, due to the absence of Osbert. The excitement was provided by Tim Babcock. It was the funeral speech, rehashed and with the announcement of Tim as official candidate tacked onto it. Dick Winters had quite enough speeches – of more national distribution – to work on without going to the bother of thinking up a whole lot of new things to say about Osbert. What little originality there was in the discourse had Tim as its topic. Dick expatiated on all the ways in which Tim was a wonderful person: the rock he had been to Lesley in her grief; the respect he felt for the example that Osbert had set him and which he intended to build upon. 'And now, without more ado . . .'

The cork-poppers prepared themselves but, at that precise moment, Lesley raised a hand. 'There's something I would like to say, Dick. If I may?'

'Lesley, of course.' Dick Winters looked decidedly miffed, and so did Tim, who had been all set to launch into his speech about the road – an awfully similar one to that which Miles Starey had delivered the previous evening – and, that over with, on to the champagne, and perhaps Primrose could be prevailed upon to drink one too many and indulge in a bit of intercourse for purposes other than procreational for once.

That life might be sensible: this had been Lesley's constant wish. But slip the last four letters off that word, replace them with another three, change 'wish' to 'desire', consider that one sometimes seeks in foliage and flowers, in the buffeting wind and the threshing waves that which you dare not look for in other quarters and you have an aspect of Lesley Sway – intact and untouched, virgin even – which she herself was only aware of in translation: Lesley was sensual. In spite of her tightly-wrapped life. In spite of her liquid breakfasts. Which was why she watched storms, could sleep deeply for hour upon hour, and responded to sexy voices. Which was why nothing but honesty would do, and had learnt only painfully to defer to caution – honesty is a sensual attribute; a most self-indulgent virtue. It was, in a sense, her body and all its untended demands that she was defending. Which is not what is generally expected of widows.

It was a short speech, and it lacked polish compared with Dick Winters'. But it got its idea across. Only once did Lesley falter and that was when she looked at Primrose's face and saw a curtain closing; when she looked from her to Winifred and saw a door being shut that she knew would never again open, that – saddest of all – she did not even want to.

The birth of 'Independent Conservatives Against The Road' coincided with the death of friendship and family commitment, or perhaps the recognition that they had never truly existed.

Susie Took, who had been listening with only half an ear, partly because she never much listened to the speech bit of these occasions, and partly because her attention had been distracted by something going on in the undergrowth beyond the garden wall, noted the hysterical applause – but not that it came from only a portion of the spectators – and popped the cork of the magnum which she was holding. Bianca, who'd been getting bored, followed suit and, taking it as their cue, so did all the others. Glasses were filled. Some were drunk from. Some were not. There were those to whom it was clear beyond any doubt what must be their course of action. There were others who were now forced into the horrifying realisation that they needed to do some pretty damn swift thinking.

It was hardest for the lower-middle classes, so squeamish about their position, so aware that it could just possibly be only their voting tendencies that kept them from being *the one below*. A sip of that delicious, icy, sparkling liquid – the real thing and not the Asti-Spumante that pretended to be it at the only weddings they got to go to – and – bingo! – alliance with what might be the flagship of the new order or merely an obscure craft which would, in due course, sink without trace. Those who were surer of their social position – and not in the know – had only to consult their own specific wants and opinions and not to juggle options. Rory St John's parents, for instance, their house, 'The Four Winds', well out of the way of the road scheme, had no great problem in deciding which tack to take. Winifred Took: foregone conclusion. Penny St John, however, something of an ecologist, and not overly prepossessed with Primrose – seeing in her airy postures, perhaps, something not a million miles from her own comportment – had already opted for Lesley. Veronica Tarrant, whose pub-cum-restaurant might suffer if the road went through, but with an eye to some political bread-buttering, now decided that she would run with the hare and course with the hounds – at least until it became apparent who was winning.

Most of those whose houses would be affected, and who Lesley had spoken to, had already made the decision to be part of the breakaway party. Most, though not all, of the lower-middle classes came to the conclusion that the status-quo was their best bet and, regretfully, put their glasses asunder.

And then there was Susie Took who – in as much as she considered it – would stick with her pal Primmie (though awfully sorry about it to Aunt Lellie), or go along with whatever Mummy thought, and, her magnum now empty, went into the kitchen for another bottle. The bin was overflowing so she replaced the black bag and took the full one out to the dustbin where, on lifting the lid, she saw . . . her two carriers of sausages; her marshmallows. For a moment she thought it must be another mistake. Then she knew it wasn't.

Tragedy is so much a part of the human condition that it adheres as easily to sausages as to kingships. Susie didn't cry, though her eyes watered. She didn't lose her trust in humanity, just a bit of it.

She left the bags where they were and went and got another bottle of champagne. She walked out to the lawn and started replenishing glasses.

Primrose and Tim were white to the lips with rage. Whatever Primrose had suspected, it was obviously nothing of this enormity. Lesley's behaviour had crossed all the traditional boundaries. Worse, it had divided the Conservative vote.

'How could you Mummy? How could you?' she whispered as Dick Winters hastily announced Tim as 'official' Conservative candidate and made a graciously condescending off-the-cuff speech about 'the best man winning'. 'Don't you feel any loyalty to Daddy? Not any?'

Lesley did not reply, though the answer was, quite frankly, that she didn't. Why should she blindly follow against her own self-interest? Though Primrose could be forgiven for expecting otherwise. She had grown up with Lesley as her example. She was, and probably always would be, the wife to Tim that Lesley had been to Osbert; perhaps he wouldn't betray her: mostly they managed not to. Yes, Lesley forgave her. There was no one better qualified to do so.

'You will regret this, Lesley. By God and how you will regret it,' muttered Tim Babcock from between clenched teeth, as the applause for his candidacy drained away into a puzzled silence, for the rustlings in the bushes, which Susie had noted earlier, now grew louder and everyone was suddenly conscious of them. With a rare loss of control he pointed at the end of the garden and cried 'There it is, Lesley, and I hope you're pleased with it. There is what you are allying yourself with: anarchy!'

All eyes followed Tim's gesture. Beyond the garden wall a group of perhaps twenty individuals had emerged from the undergrowth, all of much the same size, shape and attire. Beneath the startled eyes of the assembled Tories, they quietly unfolded a banner, on which was written 'Save The Lesser Tit'.

Anarchy indeed it was – and here Tim Babcock had shown a greater understanding of the term than is common, even among anarchists themselves – though, looking at it, it did not strike Lesley Sway as particularly undesirable or alarming; she even went so far as to think to herself that this group of people (apparently opposed to the road scheme) could join them, if they wanted to.

The birdwatchers, in their turn, were well pleased with the effect of their sudden appearance. They had been in the bushes for hours – long before Susie Took first heard them – and could have stayed there almost indefinitely, the situation being far from unfamiliar to them. There had even been little excitements which, along with the opening of a couple of thermoses and the distribution of some fruit and nut, accounted for the rustlings: Bob had spotted a black redstart and everyone had grabbed at their binoculars at the same moment to get a sight of its beautiful underbelly; then a woman named Pamela, who worked at the Nat West in Pitsbury, had drawn their attention to a couple of dunnocks. All in all it had been a pleasant place to be and no hardship to wait until what felt like the right moment to come out. Which was after the champagne corks had started popping, though their appearance was delayed by the banner getting caught on a bush. They had thought of making it a candlelit vigil but there was a danger that the lesser tits might see the flames, get frightened and die.

Unfortunately, very soon after the beginning of this dignified demonstration, and though the merrymaking some years went on as late as eleven-thirty, those who had not allied themselves with the forces of disorder started to make for their cars.

'Mrs Sway?'

Lesley turned. It must be the man Winifred had mentioned earlier, William Flint, the newsagent. 'Yes?'

'Things are turning out very nicely, Mrs Sway, very nicely indeed. In the light of present developments we should be able to make use of each other.'

The thought was vaguely repugnant. 'Well, I think, for the moment, Mr Flint . . .'

The newsagent tapped his nose with his finger. 'We understand each other, I believe, Mrs Sway. 'Nuff said. We'll touch base.'

In spite of Winifred's strong objections, Susie Took stayed on for the meeting which followed, though she gave her usual hug to Primrose and sent bundles of cuddles to the children. Lesley was her employer, after all, and politics didn't really come into it for Susie.

The proceedings were calm and orderly, the outcome predictable. Eustace Frogwell was voted candidate. Lesley Sway was voted campaign manager. A list of tasks was drawn up for the days to come, which Susie would type in the morning. People wished each other civil good nights and Lesley, declining Susie's offer of help, was left to clear up alone those things that Veronica and her employees had not already transported back to the Jolly Roger. (A task which had been performed while the meeting was in progress, thereby allowing Veronica to appear present but not necessarily implicated; though not necessarily *not* implicated either.)

Things had gone very smoothly and yet, on surveying the empty garden, the watery pool which had been the ice-sculpture, Lesley fell prey to a sense of desolation that was not entirely because, every other year, Winifred stayed on and they gossiped about the events of the evening. It just didn't seem fair, in the light of all she had done to instigate the split, that Eustace Frogwell should be chosen as candidate. And, if it couldn't be her, Maud Frogwell was, beyond any doubt, the more intelligent and the more eloquent of that couple.

This was a new sentiment. Lesley picked up a damp cloth from the trestle table. How much easier it would be if things were just normal. She put it down again. There was no rush. Let it wait until morning.

On impulse, she went into the house and got the phone book. Seated at the desk in the office, she looked up Darryl Younger's number, expecting him to be ex-directory. He wasn't. She dialled.

There were a couple of rings. Then a voice. Lesley's heart started thumping. 'Hallo . . .'

'. . . not here at the moment, unless you're offering employment or money. Anyway, leave a . . .'

She was just replacing the receiver when the message clicked off and a real voice came on the line. She raised it again quickly.

'Mr Younger?'

'Lesley!' He sounded as if he had been sitting by the phone all day awaiting nothing other than her call. She was amazed that he knew who it was. 'Darryl, for God's sake. Nineties and all that.'

Lesley realised that she didn't have the first notion of what exactly she had been wanting to say to him. Without thinking, she started on the evening from the very beginning: the terrible scene with Winifred; Dick Winters' announcement; her announcement; Tim's threat; the demonstration. At one point Darryl went off to get a gin and, realising that she had neither eaten nor drunk anything the whole evening, Lesley got herself a white wine and a couple of water biscuits. They recommenced. It was almost entirely Lesley that spoke, though Darryl interspersed what she said with the occasional short comment: 'prat'; 'terrific'; 'jealous, of course, stands out a mile'.

When she had finished there was a silence, then Darryl said something that startled her.

'Sounds like you've been having fun, luvvie.'

Lesley was too taken aback to reply. Fun? Yes, now she thought about it, that was exactly what she had been having.

'Listen,' said Darryl. 'Fractal unfolding, yin and yang coming together and all that; we've got to meet up. There's something you're going to have to do if you want to win this sodding election. But, such is life, fraught with problems. Anyway, are you free to meet up the day after tomorrow?'

'Yes, I think so.' She expected him to suggest the Jolly Roger.

'The Beach Caff. Do you know it?'

'Over the bridge, in the direction of the ferry terminal? I've never been there but . . .'

'You've got it. One suit?'

'That would be fine.'

'Better go then. Getting late. Sleep well, Lesley.'

It was only after she'd replaced the receiver that Lesley remembered that she had no way of recognising him.

She went to the kitchen and put the kettle on for a tisane; glancing at the clock, she was astounded to see that it was two a.m. She returned to the garden. The night was very dark and still. Cherry must be sleeping. There was no moon but the sky was thick with stars. Lesley gathered a handful of crumbs of olive bread from one of the tables and walked down to the end of the garden. The birdwatchers had long since departed. She threw the crumbs over the wall, for the lesser tit to find in the morning. She did not know that it was a fussy eater.

8

An Interesting Discovery

Meeting Darryl Younger – when it eventually happened – was like getting on an aeroplane that you imagined to be heading for Manchester, only to have it land in Istanbul.

Some of Lesley's practicality derived from the fact that she expected anti-climax and disappointment – not in a pessimistic way but a brisk, mature one. (It was perhaps this alone that prevented her from viewing her life as every bit as disappointing as Winifred's. Winifred did not have that kind of negative insurance, as evidenced by her hopes for her daughter and the fact that she sold bridal gowns.) Usually such an attitude stands one in good stead; it is one of the things which defines the transition from child to adult. When it doesn't, though, the resultant emotions can be profoundly unsettling. Hope was, mythologically, the last to arrive. Certainly it is the first to leave. But when it comes back ... part of you, gazing at the azure Bosphorus, might be nostalgic for the predictability of Manchester.

'Oh yum, Aunt Lellie,' said Susie Took, 'you smell like a sponge cake.'

On impulse, Lesley had used some vanilla bath oil that Primrose had given her for Christmas and that she had not yet opened. Primrose's presents were more designed to convey an impression of herself than to suit the recipient – as Lesley had known and would have remembered if she had not been feeling, well yes, excited. The vanilla, she read as she soaked, was prepared by natives, whose livelihood was threatened by artificially produced vanillin. Merely by putting some of the oil in her bath, Lesley was helping to make the world a better place, though whether the gift was designed to express Primrose's sympathy for the Third World or the fragrance of her nature, it was hard to say. Lesley wished she had stuck to White Linen.

'Have you seen *The Times*, Susie?' Lesley asked.

'Maybe it wasn't delivered,' said Susie. 'Triff get-up, Aunt Lellie. I like that sort of bluey colour.'

'Do you really like it, Susie?' It was an outfit Lesley had not worn before: cotton trousers and a matching loose top, with the sleeves rolled up. Susie nodded energetically.

'I'm going into Pitsbury, Susie. Then around lunchtime I'm meeting somebody. I expect I'll be back early afternoon-ish.'

'No sweat. I might go out for an hour or so at elevenses, if that's all right, Aunt Lellie.'

Lesley smiled. 'That's fine, Susie, but try to remember to put on the answerphone.'

Lesley drove with the windows down and her hair blowing. It was still lovely weather. The heat gave everything a kind of foreignness. The bottle-green Ebb, with its expanding circles of emerald, where a swallow had skimmed it, could have been one of those secret, leisurely rivers of rural France. Pitsbury Cathedral, with its cool, grey squares and rectangles of shadow, looked Teutonic in the sunlight. The chalky car park by the Beach Caff put Lesley in mind of the vast, boiling acres of parked cars you saw around American shopping malls.

Darryl Younger, she told herself, must be on radio rather than stage or television for a reason. One could not expect a body that would live up to that glorious voice.

The door of the Beach Caff was open. A smell of vinegar wafted out. A metal sign for ice-creams swayed a little in the sea-breeze. A couple of windsurfers emerged in wet-suits, their hair an absurd, Nordic blond. Lesley entered. There were stifled giggles. As her eyes adjusted to the light, Lesley found herself staring at a table of adolescents; the girls sharply animated, poised at that moment before anaemia and push-chairs, the boys with gaping faces. She wondered why young men voluntarily had their hair like that. She scanned the room for likely candidates to be Darryl Younger. It wasn't just the adolescents that were looking at her; everyone was. Perhaps her new outfit was quite startlingly inappropriate.

'Over here, Lesley.'

The voice came from a table by the door. Lesley turned. Istanbul. Darryl Younger.

To say he was handsome would not have been to do him justice, for the first thing that struck her about his face was its enormous expressiveness; they were features that were utterly suffused with warmth and humour. Then there was the delightful ease of posture, the complete relaxation in his body, as if it were some comfortable clothes he had just slipped on.

Darryl leapt to his feet. He was about six feet tall; around Lesley's age, she guessed. He wore a sweatshirt and faded jeans. He held out his hand and, with it, it seemed, the suggestion that life could be exciting and the assertion that, in the end, charm was the only thing that really mattered.

'Why aren't you on television?' Lesley blurted, then could have kicked herself for the gaucheness of the remark.

But Darryl treated it quite matter-of-factly.

'Have been from time to time, though not in anything you'd have been likely to see. Most recent was one episode of a terrible series about a policeman on an island somewhere. Policemen are so inherently dull, when they're not being brutal, that the Beeb couples them with an island in an attempt to make them interesting. Damp squib, of course, since they're too bloody mean to make it an exotic island. Place we went to was like Essex surrounded by water. Stayed in a piss-awful hotel with a bar that closed at ten o'clock. I played a drug-dealer and insisted on wearing a suit. The producer let me. Well he got through a couple of grams of coke a night – which he wasn't buying from old hippies on street corners. But sit down and I'll get us something. What would you like?'

'Whatever you're having,' Lesley replied, thinking in terms of tea or coffee.

'Right. Back in a minute.' Darryl went to the counter. 'Two

special fry-ups, Jack, and your pud of the day, and a couple of mugs of tea.' He turned round. 'Do you want sugar, Les?'

'No, thank you.'

Darryl returned with the mugs and sat down. 'Jack'll bring the food over when it's ready.' The tea was almost black. Lesley drank some. It made her think of basic virtues.

'How are the contract negotiations?' she asked, unaccustomedly shy all of a sudden, Darryl was looking at her with such rapt attention.

'Oh, that boat I've acquired gets leakier by the day. "Those are pearls that were his eyes" for me, I fear. Need the dough, of course, but they're an awful bunch really. Can't act for toffee, most of them; couldn't hold down a job in the theatre because they'd never remember the lines. Captain Skate's twice been done for cottageing . . .'

'Cottageing?'

'Picking up men in public loos, Les. All well and good, but there's loos and loos and some of them are fuller of pigs than the bloody cop-shop which, public eye and all that, is worth researching. Occasionally we get to tackle a "controversial issue", like whether a million tons of raw sewage should be dumped next to the toddlers' pool but, other than that, it's just the daily grind, duller than life itself.' Though 'life itself' did not seem dull to Lesley at that moment and she suspected it rarely did to Darryl Younger.

'Good morning Mrs Sway.' It was the man from behind the counter, whom Darryl had called 'Jack'. He put down a plate in front of each of them. 'I'll just get your cutlery.' Lesley stared at her plate in something akin to fascination. Two eggs. Baked beans. Black pudding. Bacon. A sausage. A great mound of chips, and a triangle of fried bread. The cutlery arrived.

'Just what I needed. Tuck in,' said Darryl, cheerfully, helping himself to ketchup and shaking malt vinegar over the chips.

Lesley cut into the tight, shiny skin of the black pudding and took a mouthful. They ate in silence for a few minutes.

'When did you first get interested in politics?' she asked.

'Sixties, of course. Vietnam. Did the old overland to India thing in the early seventies. Bit of a maverick though. Bloody-minded lot, actors. I've always preferred to fight the wrongs in front of my nose than to theorise. Took part in a big charity show for anti-apartheid in the early eighties – amateur night really Les, but it got lots of publicity. Not a party man, except for a brush with WRP.'

'Which was why you weren't at the Conservative barbecue?' Lesley was beginning to be puzzled.

Darryl put down his knife and fork. A hand shot to his mouth in a gesture that blended incredulity, apology and amusement. It crossed Lesley's mind that, for Darryl, the combination of expressions required by Dick Winters' speech about Tim and Osbert would have been effortless. Probably two conflicting emotions had been mastered well before the end of his first year at drama school.

'Oh Christ! You think I'm a Tory!'

Lesley was embarrassed. 'Of course you're not. I should have realised. It's just . . . everyone seems to be.'

Darryl nodded. 'Out of the woodwork, Les.'

'But in that case, why did you phone me?'

'Like I say, maverick. And anyway, we're talking right or wrong in the end, aren't we?'

'Well, I suppose so.' This struck her as a bit too simple.

'Shall I take your plate, Mrs Sway?'

Lesley looked down. It was empty. The puddings arrived. Marmalade roly-poly with custard.

'That's what we've got to talk about,' said Darryl, 'this sodding road. Bloody disaster, whichever way you look at it.'

'Yes,' said Lesley, though she had forgotten the road momentarily, and would rather not have thought that this meeting had a specific purpose that was nothing to do with her or Darryl.

'The problem is numbers,' Darryl continued. 'There just aren't enough of you in your breakaway party. You haven't got a look in, quite frankly.' He leant back in his seat and grasped his hands behind his neck. 'What you need to do is form a coalition.'

There was a silence.

Then, 'With the Liberal Democrats, do you mean?' asked Lesley.

'Oh what would be the point? No one knows what they think. No one's sure what they're called. No one is completely certain they exist. A bit like God, when you consider it.'

'You don't mean Labour?'

'That would have been a possibility, but their candidate, Miles Starey, is running after your lot's vote. In favour of the road. I used to know Miles, back in the eighties. All mouth and trousers. "Sell out" should have been written across his t-shirt. These trendier-than-thou types never stay the course. No,' Darryl paused. 'You're going to have to ally yourself with the Alternative Left – the Far Left, if you like.' He spoke casually, as if this were the most normal thing imaginable.

Lesley was astounded.

'Ally ourselves with the Far Left?'

Darryl shrugged. 'Well you and I have managed to establish a rapport, and there's ample historical precedent: Communists and Fascists and all that.'

'The Ebbing Conservatives are not Fascists.'

'Well the Ebbing Alternatives are not Communists – or most of them aren't. Christ knows what they are really. But they are against the road scheme, and that's what matters.'

'I have every confidence,' said Lesley – her voice taking on a warning edge – 'that we can succeed without resorting to that kind of measure in order to swell the numbers.'

Darryl shrugged again. 'Well you're going to have to resort to something, Les. You've seen the papers. You know how ruthless they're planning on being.'

'The papers?'

There was a pause and then, to her surprise, Darryl pushed the empty bowls out of the way and scooped both her hands into his. 'Oh Lord. You haven't seen the papers today, have you? About your husband?'

'No.' The marmalade roly-poly suddenly felt very heavy in her stomach. 'Tell me what they're saying.'

Lesley gave a brief knock on the chapel door, which was open anyway.

'Come in,' called a cheerful voice.

Lesley entered the kitchen, a tall room with copper pots and dried flowers hanging from various bits of it. There was a heavy oak table. The floor was the original flagstone and, Primrose's pride and joy, there was a turn-of-the-century brass – a memorial to a young poet, who had died before achieving anything, depicting him as a knight; this had been brought from elsewhere, in numbered sections. Helen, Primrose's housekeeper, was helping Tansy cut scones from some dough. Jonquil was asleep in her basket. Robin and Seth were colouring at the table. Sorrel was curled up on a rug on the floor, sucking her thumb.

'My goodness, children, it's all go today. Coffee and scones, Mrs Sway? There's a batch due out in a minute. Or there's some parkin we had for elevenses.'

'No thank you, Helen. But they do look lovely. So you're helping, Tansy. Aren't you clever!' She glanced at Sorrel, who was breathing loudly. 'Asthma bad again?'

Helen nodded. 'Got a bit much for her yesterday, and Mrs Babcock's been so busy. She's a sensitive little thing.' She raised her voice. 'But we've been helping up to ten minutes ago, haven't we, my lovely? Just needed a little nap now.'

'So Mrs Babcock's not at home?'

'Oh yes. She's in the studio.'

The studio was the former belfry; all exposed wood and sunbeams. A bell, of course, though not the original, alas, which had been recklessly sold to Americans. This was actually a ship's bell, bought from the flea market in Paris. Primrose was at her escritoire, considering illustrations for her work on Clover Deal: the lovely honeysuckle that Clover had executed above the mantelpiece of the country cottage of her (good) friend, the writer, Heather Mood; the lampshades she had done that summer at Splatters, in spite of her unhappy love affair with the diarist, Dixon Wander, who had eventually deserted her and gone to live on Kos with his sister, the socialite, Cleopatra Vaunt (whose husband was Marmaduke Vaunt, the flautist); Primrose believed that you could see an indication of Clover's turbulent emotions in the hues of these lampshades, and the fact that they mainly depicted the more sombre and fleshy members of the fruit family. She looked far from pleased to be interrupted. Especially by Lesley, who she had not seen since the Conservative barbecue.

'Mummy!'

One could either recline on a hammock covered with ethnic cushions or squat on Primrose's *yuruk*. Lesley chose to remain standing.

'Primrose, I know that things are a bit strained at the moment, but I do think that we must have a family . . . position in relation to the things they are saying in the papers about Daddy. Perhaps you and Tim and me . . .'

There was a small, thumping sound on the wooden stairs.

'Oh bother,' said Primrose. 'Will it never end? Helen knows they're not supposed to disturb me when I'm in the studio.'

Tansy entered with a scone on a plate. 'I made this, Mummy.'

'Tansy, Cherub, you know you aren't allowed to be a pain when I'm working.'

Tansy said nothing. She turned to Lesley. 'Daddy and Uncle Dick shouted, then they made important telephones.'

Primrose took a quick breath inwards, looking furious. A small patch of peach-pink appeared on her fair cheeks. It rendered her startlingly lovely. She glanced nervously at Lesley. Lesley's mouth dropped open.

There was the sound of other, heavier footsteps.

'Oh there you are, mischief. Sorry Mrs Babcock. I was just giving Sorrel her inhaler and she slipped out while my back was turned. Let's go and see if we've got any jam and butter to put on that, shall we?' Helen gathered up Tansy, plate and scone and left the room.

Lesley recalled Primrose, on the day of Osbert's death, in the garden; her icy little sentence as she sat on the rug: 'In the circumstances Mummy, it would be silly to draw attention to yourself.' Tim's threat at the barbecue. How had they dared upbraid her with loyalty and tradition when they themselves – aided and abetted, extraordinarily, by Dick Winters – had tossed all that aside as soon as it was no longer useful?

Primrose gave a pout. 'You were dividing the vote, Mummy. You were ruining Tim's chances.' She paused. 'It's what Daddy would have wanted.'

'If you believe that, Primrose,' said Lesley, acidly, 'you evidently have a rather different image of your father from my own. Even for the furtherance of western capitalism, I doubt Osbert Sway would have liked it known that he died wearing plastic rompers, in the company of a woman who went by the professional name of Nanny Enema – and who, incidentally, appears to have had the good sense, lacking in both yourself and, I presume, your husband, to have kept her mouth shut about the matter.'

'We only did it to discredit you,' said Primrose, appearing to regard this as an extenuating factor.

'I am not the one discredited by this.' And Lesley was not referring to Osbert.

She left the house and drove straight to Flint's Newsagent's. Mercifully, Mr Flint was not there. She was served by a vicious-faced adolescent in a Union Jack t-shirt. Lesley bought every newspaper except for *The Times* which, sure enough, she found in the waste paper basket in the office.

Lesley spread the papers out on the desk and looked at them, one after the other. It wasn't hard to find the articles. In all but two of the newspapers the circumstances of Osbert's death made the front page, though the treatment of the topic varied. Lesley read every single one from 'Thanks For The Mammaries' through to 'Backbencher Dies In Company Of Prostitute'. The *Express* had a picture of 'Nanny Enema', who increasingly struck Lesley as a sensible and businesslike woman – one perhaps not wholly unfamiliar with the more conventionally acceptable inner workings of the Conservative Party. 'Nanny Enema' was smiling placidly against a background of floral wallpaper. You felt that, when she was not engaged in her professional activities, she probably enjoyed entering competitions that involved sending in can labels and completing a slogan.

By the time she had finished, Lesley felt that she had a pretty clear picture of what had happened.

There was a grim humour in how wrong Winifred had been about what had killed Osbert; certainly not stress, at least not the emotional kind. Maybe, it occurred to her suddenly, it was Nanny Enema who was responsible for preventing the realisation of whatever hopes Winifred might have harboured about ousting Lesley and making of Osbert the politician he should have been. There was no doubt in Lesley's mind that, whatever else Primrose had confided in Winifred, it had not included this; Winifred would never have been party to such revelations – perhaps, at last, her Conservatism, too, was becoming tame and old-fashioned; over-scrupulous. Poor Osbert. Lesley found she rather preferred her husband in death to how she had known him in life. It was all so sadly human. If that, and things like that, were the missing elements that would have made for a happy marriage, couldn't he have asked her . . .?

No, of course he couldn't. But, for the first time, she was able to allow herself to believe that her marriage might have failed, in part, due to forces that were beyond the control of either of them: little shames; ingrained assumptions; expectations about behaviour and emotion (what would horrify, what repel), so that the adults they became had only little spaces within which they dared meet one another. You do not entertain guests in your bathroom.

Lesley even felt rather grateful to Nanny Enema. Who, she guessed, had phoned Conservative Central Office – perhaps some special number – as soon as it became clear that Osbert's body and soul had parted company. The whole affair was somehow hushed up and few were allowed to know about it, not including her. Though why not? God knew, she wouldn't have gone round blabbing to the papers. Because she was a woman, she supposed, after a minute's consideration, and it was assumed by Tory men that women couldn't keep secrets.

Hah! Lesley almost snarled. If all the things women kept to themselves were revealed, they'd have to re-write the history books.

It was that idiot Tim who insisted on telling, of course. Primrose went along with it and Dick Winters, realising that Tim was adamant, did his best to inject a note of subtlety and to focus the attack on Lesley. She could even distinguish his handiwork from Tim's. Tim had gone straight to the gutter press and laid the facts before them. Dick, on the other hand, had supplemented the basic details with a certain amount of interpretation, which some of the more lazy journalists had written down verbatim. Much was made of the Sways' separation. Lesley had, the *Telegraph* softly, almost sympathetically, suggested, known about Nanny Enema; hence the estrangement from her husband and hence too – poor, misguided, over-emotional creature – her hysterical posthumous revenge. The tone, the ideas, were horribly familiar. Lesley blinked. Had Dick derived them from Primrose?

What Lesley couldn't fathom was what all this was meant to achieve. That Primrose saw discrediting her as an extenuating circumstance suggested the deeper motivation was even worse. Would people really change their mind about the road scheme because of Osbert's sexual proclivities? There was ample reason to assume that they would rally round – that they might, just possibly, see her as the injured party.

It was done to frighten her off.

Lesley reached for the phone and dialled Darryl's number. She was pretty damn sick of being under-estimated.

'Darryl?'

'Lesley. Look, I'm awfully sorry about what happened at the Caff. Financial blip. Thought I'd got enough cash on me.'

Lesley had immediately wanted to make a speedy exit. Darryl had gone to pay but been unable to. Lesley had looked in her handbag and hadn't had quite enough money either, due to her shopping in Pitsbury, but it was not until she counted out the contents of her purse that she was able to ascertain this. Jack said it didn't matter, they could pay him when they were next in. Lesley wrote a cheque. Then Jack detained Lesley with questions about the Independent Party. He said he had a suggestion to make to them. She managed to brush him off, politely, by telling him to phone her and then, at last, she was able to escape. Everybody watched the whole proceedings.

'It seems at the moment,' Lesley observed drily, 'that there is no situation in which I find myself that is sufficiently distressing or embarrassing that extra distress or embarrassment cannot be heaped upon it. But I am phoning to talk about what you said earlier. I am willing to do anything, absolutely anything it takes to win this election. If it involves talking Eustace Frogwell into a coalition, then I will do so. Give me the phone number of the man in charge of the Alternative Left, or whatever, and I'll contact him.'

'It's not a man. It's a woman, a friend of mine. Her name is Anna Seale. And, though she is in charge, as much as anyone can be, they call her "the people's candidate".'

'Oh, well give me the number then and I'll have a word with her. Or perhaps you would like to?'

'I'd love to do that, Les, but she won't go along with the idea unless you speak to her in person. That I'm sure of. And, even so, you should be aware that it's a long shot. She may refuse to talk to you at all.'

Lesley gave an exasperated sigh. Nothing in Darryl's tone had suggested it was a long shot when they were in the Caff.

'Why is that?' she asked.

'Because she hates you.'

Lesley was astounded. 'You mean in the abstract, I take it?' she said, after a pause. She was beginning to be intensely irritated by this Anna Seale.

'No Les, quite literally.'

'But I've never even met the woman.'

'Yes you have, though you probably don't remember it.'

'I cause a person to hate me and I don't remember it?' The idea was overwhelming. Did she have some strange other life, with its own activities and consequences, of which she was completely unaware?

Darryl spoke and Lesley listened, her expression becoming progressively more serious. It was going to be very difficult indeed to phone Anna Seale.

Lesley felt completely at sea. She needed time to think. She needed time to consider. She needed Winifred, and Winifred's wonderful certainties; Tim and Osbert and Dick, a suited shield against vagary and ambiguity; Primrose. What was she doing, what on earth was she doing, discussing how to court the good will of some wild woman, with a feckless actor whose friends, or at least colleagues, (it was easier to comprehend the import of what he had said, now that his gorgeous eyes were not smiling at her) took cocaine and picked up men in lavatories? What business did a person like Lesley Sway have in Beach Caffs, exposed to ridicule and forced to eat plates of food that could do your heart permanent damage? Would it not be best to carry on as things were: do as well as they could in the election and tell Darryl Younger to take a running jump?

Unbidden and wretchedly she imagined Darryl running to a cliff edge, across a swoop of powdery green grass, his arms exposed, his sweatshirt blown backwards by the wind. But he did not plunge and fall. He had a hang-glider, like the ones you saw further along the coast. He soared into the sunlight.

She ended the call on a note of cool uncommitment.

Barely had she replaced the receiver when it gave a furious bellow and Eustace Frogwell came on the line with ten minutes of bluster, that was intended to reassure but was actually mildly insulting. The gist of it was that nobody blamed Lesley (or Osbert) but that everyone blamed what he referred to as 'the young lady'. Eustace, rightly, suspected conspiracy, though Lesley did not see fit to confirm his assumptions. 'Never fear, my dear, they will find this has completely backfired,' he concluded eventually.

Other calls followed, all along the same lines. By consensus it was agreed that to cheat on your wife with a prostitute did not come into the same category of misbehaviour as, by carelessness or design, to draw the attention of the general public to such a matter. Lesley was glad to be able to give her sincere agreement, albeit for private reasons.

Eventually the telephone stopped ringing and Lesley changed out of her, now sweaty, new outfit and threw herself onto the bed to make some big decisions.

At least, she thought, the repercussions of Nanny Enema were over and done with.

But here Lesley made a mistake and one which, in the light of the day's other revelations, she should have avoided: Nanny Enema's effect on things was far from over. In fact, her most profound implications were only just beginning to be felt.

9

Friends

The room was cool. The window was open. A mild, salty breeze tugged at the curtains. Lesley made no big decisions.

When she woke, the sun was setting. Grey helium balloons of cumulus hung above the horizon. Somebody was having a massive bonfire below the level of the world. Susie Took was standing at the bedroom door.

'Oh Aunt Lellie,' she said, 'I knew hiding the paper wouldn't make it go away. It was just so beastly I needed to do something.'

Lesley thought of Primrose's pretty face; her handsome son-in-law; their act of treachery. It was beastly. Something did need doing.

'Suppose, Susie,' she said, sitting up, 'that, from now on, you called me "Lesley".'

'Lesley.' Susie tried it out and, instantly, they were on a different footing; it was clear why Winifred had preferred the nickname. 'I've brought sausages and marshmallows, oh and some parkin. I thought it might cheer you up to have a *proper* barbecue. If you like.'

'Sausages,' said Lesley.

When she came out to the garden, blue and mauve flames were flickering among the charcoal, but Susie had put the sausages on anyway. Way across the bay, on the pebbles, burning people, fire children, were gathering driftwood. Little etched birdwatchers, far out on the polished sand, raised their binoculars to watch black gulls.

'I can see why you want to keep this,' said Susie.

'Can you?' said Lesley. Then, after a pause, 'Do you think charm is worth anything, Susie?'

'I should say so,' Susie replied. 'But it's more sort of grand than charming.'

'I mean, in people.'

'Boys?'

'So to speak.' Lesley hesitated. 'It's just, I wonder if it isn't, somehow, rather manipulative.'

'P'raps,' said Susie, doubtfully. 'But at least it shows someone bothers. Do you remember that man at Primrose's wedding? The one who nearly went off with Christie Marks's younger sister, who there was all the hoo-hah about?'

Lesley shook her head. 'I remember there was an upset, and that Tim was furious about something, but I was rather preoccupied.'

'He was charming. I suppose Uncle ... um ... Osbert was charming originally?'

'Not really.'

Lesley wondered what 'originally' signified for Susie (though her reply would, in any case, have been the same). Did she imagine some point at which a person was as good as they were ever likely to get? And if she had to home in on one such given moment, which would she choose?

Certainly none to do with Osbert – or Primrose either, for that matter. Even Primrose's birth had been one of a number of predictable events (a follow-on to marriage, a prelude to ... what?), wonderful, of course, but lacking the originality that would make it unique to the texture of her life, Lesley Sway's, and nobody else's. Those linked to Osbert were the same, only more so. He and Lesley had assumed their way into going out together, getting engaged, getting married. Nothing had involved any inspiration or effort. She had lived her life as if it were someone else's; and as if it would continue indefinitely.

Susie was right: there was something to be said for bothering.

'Drunk though,' said Susie. 'Really ripped. But I got tiddly too, and so did Mummy, I reckon. She kept on and on about how you and her were like me and Primmie and how, on your wedding day, you'd aimed the bouquet at her and how Primrose would do the same for me.' She fell silent.

'I expect Winifred would rather you didn't work for me any more?' said Lesley quietly.

'Nothing's as much fun once you drag politics into it,' said Susie. 'I mean, once you've got politics involved, oh gloom, people go off on their own. I like to stay chums with everyone.' She paused. 'But that reminds me. Guess what? There's some big media event coming up in a few weeks' time.'

'You mean for Tim?'

'Yes. Something rather special's going to happen, I think. I don't know what. It's terribly hush hush. I expect I'll hear all about it though. Crumbs!' She leapt to her feet. 'Saus need turning.' She began piercing them with a fork. Fat ran onto the coals. Flames surged upwards. One of the sausages caught fire. In the light of the burning sausage, both women became aware at once of a man standing beyond the garden wall.

'Goodness,' said Susie. 'Whatever's he up to?'

They were silent, studying him for a moment.

'I think,' said Lesley, 'he might be a birdwatcher.'

'Do you think he's been there since the barbecue?'

'I don't imagine so,' said Lesley, not wholly convinced.

'I suppose it's owls he's watching. Most birds sleep at night, don't they?'

'Nightingales,' said Lesley, vaguely.

The sausage went out.

'Well, we know that one's cooked,' said Susie. 'I've an idea, Lesley.' And, before Lesley could do anything to stop her, she stabbed the sausage and waved it in the direction of the birdwatcher. 'Would you like to join us for a sausage?' she yelled.

The man's reply was barely audible.

'What?' bellowed Susie.

There was no reply. Instead, the birdwatcher scrambled over the wall and hurried across the lawn towards them; followed, to their surprise, by another. Cherry gave a startled whinny.

'Golly,' said Susie, as the second man approached, 'you're black!'

'Oh Susie!' said Lesley.

'As the ace of spades,' Jay replied, untroubled.

'Take a pew, do.' Susie indicated the chairs. The men sat. 'Why on earth were you muttering?' she asked the first one.

'Well the lesser tit is nesting in those bushes, and it's inclined to panic if it's startled.'

'Oh gloom! I must have scared it to death then,' Susie wailed, still rather loudly. She grabbed a plate off the table and piled it with sausages.

'I expect everything's all right.' But the man looked rather uneasy. So that was why he had accepted Susie's invitation with such alacrity. 'Please, gentlemen, do help yourselves to some sausages,' said Lesley, in the awkward silence that followed; then it occurred to her that they might be vegetarians and, in an attempt to save the bizarre situation that Susie had got them into, 'Susie, why don't you go and choose some of Osbert's wine, and bring out some glasses?'

'Right ho,' said Susie.

'That lady is bad,' said Jay, appreciatively, surveying Susie's rump disappearing into the house.

'Oh no,' said Lesley, hurriedly, 'just a bit tactless sometimes.'

Wine was one of Osbert's few indulgences – or so Lesley had believed. He bought it mainly for investment purposes. They seldom actually opened a bottle and then only with a view to impress somebody important. Susie, unwittingly, brought out a couple of bottles of claret at the very peak of their perfection, worth a king's ransom, such as to make angels weep that they had not been made mortal.

She poured. They sipped. The atmosphere lightened.

Bob, reassured, now that everyone was speaking more quietly, ate a sausage out of politeness. He described the habits of the lesser tit, talked about its rarity and the importance of preserving its environment. There had been a nasty occurrence, vis-à-vis the tit, earlier this evening, when Bob had discovered that somebody might have been trying to poison it, with something disguised as bread, though, fortunately, the tit's intelligence had led it to reject the offering, or perhaps it simply didn't like the taste.

'Are you going to report the matter to the police?' asked Lesley, nervously.

'I don't really think the evidence is sufficiently conclusive,' Bob replied. 'Unfortunately. And the police aren't always very sympathetic to the concerns of birdwatchers.'

'People are utterly rotten!' said Susie.

'Yes,' said Lesley, faintly.

Jay told them about the trip to Montego Bay he was planning.

An hour went by, and then another. They ate the parkin and marshmallows with a Sauternes.

At the end of the evening, Susie gave the men a lift home in her old banger. Lesley sat on in the garden. Her sleep earlier had left her wakeful. She watched the stars appearing.

Darryl's caveats now seemed alarmist and her fears ridiculous.

If this was the Alternative Left, Lesley reflected, then handling them was unlikely to present any problems. They might have their obsessions, but they were mild enough about them. As for Anna Seale, well, if she called herself 'the people's candidate', and if these were the people she was representing, whatever her own sentiments, she must necessarily bow to their wishes. As Darryl himself had pointed out to her, the two of them had managed to establish a rapport; she had just spent a perfectly civilised evening with a birdwatcher and a Rastafarian. It was purely a question of everyone being grown-up and sensible and focussing upon what they wanted to achieve rather than on their ideological differences. Lesley and her friends could take what they needed from the relationship. The rest, they could ignore.

For that same reason, her own reactions to Darryl Younger were of very minimal importance. He had fulfilled his function, as far as she was concerned, and they were unlikely to need to have any but the slightest contact in the future.

Carmen Fitch was in a seething temper but pretending to be gratified. She lolled on Anna's sofa in a strange position, slopped coffee, dropped fag-ash.

From the beach came the sound of Gilda, playing the guitar, and singing a Joni Mitchell song about the awfulness of the life of a successful rock musician. The fire was low; scarlet cinders, inspired into cream-coloured flames when gusted by a burst of breeze. A joint was going round and a flagon of scrumpy.

'Lois Zimble,' someone was shouting, 'was a victim of racism.'

'Nonsense,' returned Ruth Ellis. 'It was because she was a woman. She was threatening the fucking patriarchy.'

'She was threatening big business and the banks,' said Rolf Watt.

'Which is why I can't see how the Free Lois Zimble Campaign can dissociate itself from environmental issues,' said Adrian Dapple.

'It was because her skin was the wrong colour. Period.'

'But everyone's skin is that colour where she comes from,' said Rolf Watt.

The conversation had been in this vein for the past forty-five minutes.

'Don't you want to join them?' Carmen asked several times. Then, always receiving a negative, 'Toe came in today,' she said.

'Toe?'

'Steven Toe. Gawd, Anna! Sculptor. Extraoooordinary work. His "Young Girl Exploring" is in the Tate. The *Guardian* wet themselves over his Stockholm exhib. He's keenly interested in the avant-garde, of course, though he tends towards the more "literal".' She ringed the last word in quotation marks. 'Fascinated by what we're achieving.'

Or that was one way his visit could have been interpreted. What Carmen refrained from adding was that Toe had been accompanied by Penny St John, with whom Carmen had a nodding acquaintance that was only just on the right side of cordial. The sculptor and his young mistress made a striking combination: he tall, with a long white beard, she slim and sophisticated, with masses of barely-restrained auburn curls. The thirty years or so age difference gave them an air of eroticism.

The two had wandered around the gallery, Penny drawing Toe's attention to things. They studied, for some time, Mabel Birch's broken bicycle pump entitled 'Phallus Surrenders'. Carmen pretended to be busy.

'Carmen,' said Penny eventually, 'you aren't exhibiting?'

'Gawd, no,' Carmen replied. 'Working on an experimental project.' And she launched into a description of the project – that had yet to advance beyond the 'concept stage' – while Penny listened with massive interest, sympathised and agreed and Toe, perhaps getting tired of their conversation, kept turning his back and surveying the sculptures.

It was not until they were gone that Carmen realised that they had been laughing at her.

Ebbing was, for the most part, too intellectually unsure of itself to pass judgement. London was not.

Which accounted for Carmen's mood. She was angry, rather than devastated, because the raison d'etre of her art was actually not creative expression; it existed simply in order for Carmen to be able to call herself an artist. This, as long as she never ventured beyond Ebbing, she could do indefinitely. It was galling, nevertheless, when someone broke her cover. It was galling too, to watch the real thing being created in front of her nose, with grace and abandon and the minimum of language. Carmen's jealousy was the very worst kind: it was not of what she desperately wanted, but of what she would quite like to have.

'When you see the work of someone like Toe,' she now said, 'you wonder why you even try.'

But she, at this moment, was drinking coffee. It was Anna who, after an exhausting day in the Crab and Oyster Bar and then a meeting to discuss the political campaign, was trying.

'Oh do leave off, Carmen,' she said, unaccustomedly unnerved by the woman's presence and mentally cursing Darryl Younger. On the night of the Labour Party discussion, Darryl hadn't come up with anything that he hadn't said before, but it had been given an unsettling edge in the light of her patent wrongness about Miles. Miles was a fake and a sell-out. For the first time, she was forced to wonder if Darryl might possibly be right about Carmen. For the first time, Carmen's comments rankled.

Anna hated having her assumptions thrown into question. Because she made them quickly, it happened fairly often. One of her responses was to hang on to the original judgement for dear life. For that reason, the news that Bob had brought after the Tory barbecue had also been unwelcome.

Or rather, the news he had mentioned in passing. For what he had actually come to tell her about was the success of the demonstration in terms of pinpointing the lesser tit as one of the electoral issues. As he spoke, however, he'd started to get a little worried that the sudden, unfamiliar noises of the event might have made the lesser tits abandon their eggs. Worse still, he wouldn't be able to set his mind at rest until the day after tomorrow, due to an early staff meeting and a parent-teacher evening, followed by a day's in-service training module in Pitsbury.

'If they have fucked off,' said Anna, 'you being there to see it sooner rather than later isn't going to make any difference.'

'No, I suppose not,' Bob replied, though she could tell, in his heart of hearts, he didn't believe it.

'So what were the unfamiliar noises?'

'Champagne corks,' said Bob, absently.

'What was that in aid of? Or was it all they were drinking?'

'Goodness, well I hadn't thought about it really,' said Bob. 'I suppose it was for the announcement of the breakaway party.'

Further probing had revealed the whole story. Lesley Sway had done something irritatingly impressive.

Now Carmen picked up a copy of the paper and started to chortle.

'How, in the name of reason, can a woman know so little about a man she's been screwing?'

'What?' snapped Anna.

'Lesley Sway. Nanny Enema.'

'Oh.' She returned to her canvas.

'Men are so transparent. Wouldn't you know what was really happening?'

'Not if I was blinded by . . . emotion or something. Or if part of me didn't want to.'

'Oh come on! "Blinded?" Pull the other one. Just plain stupid, if you ask me.'

Anna put some paint in the wrong place. She threw down her brush in disgust.

'What do you know about it, Carmen? You never lived with a man in your whole fucking life.'

Carmen's fag had gone out. She lit it again before replying, with maddening calm, 'I see, so a true erotic relationship can only be heterosexual, is that it? Believe me, Anna, if you were to explore the full . . .'

Anna was bored before the sentence was even half over.

'I'm just saying that I can understand the fucking woman,' she interrupted crossly.

'Because you're all heterosexuals together?'

In reply, Anna picked up a palette and chucked it at the door. It spattered the colours in interesting patterns. But Carmen who, like most proselytisers, believed any reaction to be better than none at all continued, unrattled. 'I think you should ask yourself, Anna, why, at this moment . . .'

The phone rang twice while Carmen was speaking. The answerphone picked it up.

'Hello, this is Lesley Sway, with a message for Anna Seale. I wonder if we could meet, maybe tomorrow? Perhaps you could get back to me? I'll give you my number . . .'

There was a surprised silence. Then Carmen said, 'Oh I see,' with bitter satisfaction, and started to gather up her fags and her lighter and her other accoutrements and to stuff them into the shoe-bag sort of thing she carried round with her.

Anna watched.

'What the fuck are you talking about, Carmen? What do you see?'

'Well you're buddies already, aren't you? That's why you're bending over backwards to stick up for her. What I wish, Anna, is that you'd figure out who your real friends are, rather than siding with any heterosexual rather than a lesbian.'

There were various neat and trenchant arguments that Anna could have advanced at this point. Instead she yelled, 'Fuck your lesbian paranoia! And how dare you monitor who I'm friends with?'

10

An Attempt to Seduce

It was a restless night, full of voices and the still, heavy heat that presages thunder. The phone kept ringing and, when it stopped, the speech that followed seemed to come from not quite real people – the kind who, in nightgowns or shorts, might phone late-night radio stations from silent kitchens. Words came and went, with varying distinctness. Usually the telephone was inaudible from Lesley's bedroom; tonight the thick, conductive air, the motionless sea, had conspired so that everything should have access to her. Raving, there was definitely raving. Then it stopped and a voice from the day's muddle of occurrences, or maybe only from her dreams, was telling her to go and walk on the clifftop and consider things there. Lesley turned and the sheets tangled around her. She was on the clifftop already: her part of it. Why on earth should she go walking? There was another voice, a woman's, and then silence.

She jumped into wakefulness. It was raining.

'I don't care what-all they told you,' said Captain Skate, 'that craft ain't seaworthy.'

Lesley's head was aching. Captain Skate! You imagined some-one with a beard and a cap and a navy-blue blazer. But probably he had a shorn head and an earring, and wore a sleeveless t-shirt. Maybe he went on gay pride marches.

Ship Ahoy's signature tune bounced into merry life. She must have slept through almost the entire programme.

Lesley put on the first clothes that came to hand. In the kitchen she poured herself a coffee from a pot that Susie must have made and went into the office, feeling rather nauseous. Susie was seated at the desk, eating a doughnut.

'Any news, Susie?'

'Oh yes, lots. That media do of Tim's I mentioned? Do you remember about it?' Lesley nodded. 'Well, it's in about four weeks' time, June 16th, in the Woodcutter Inn's Harvest Room. There's going to be artists' impressions of what the cliff will look like with the new road all landscaped in.'

Lesley imagined it: the road an incidental, narrow line amid frolicking rabbits and meadows awash with wild flowers; happy families in clean cars driving purposefully towards London and looking well-pleased that the time they were saving would allow them to stop off at a motorway service station. It was all so slick, so thorough.

A thought occurred to her. 'Primrose phoned for me then Susie?'

'No,' said Susie, 'actually I phoned her. But I haven't told you the biggest news. I know what the hush hush thing is now. They're keeping it as a big surprise, sort of for added impact.'

Lesley listened. The news, that Susie found so thrilling, only depressed her further.

'Nothing on the answerphone?' she asked, remembering the night's voices.

'Yes. Awfully odd stuff some of it. Listen.'

After a moment's search, she found the 'on' switch. The first message was from William Flint. It was lengthy, disconnected and nasty. Nanny Enema and her repulsiveness, and that of all women like her, was dwelt on in loving detail. Then Flint launched into a racist diatribe, followed by the reassurance that there was a rising army of right-thinking people getting ready to combat invasion and sexual indecency.

'Bonkers,' said Susie. 'The next one is nutty too. It's all about walking on the cliff. Do you want to hear it?'

'No,' said Lesley.

'Then there's a girl. She says she'll meet you this evening at

'. . . um . . .' Susie peered at the notepad where she erratically recorded messages in her round handwriting with the little stars, instead of dots, above the 'i's. 'Oh, here it is.'

'Not the Beach Caff?' asked Lesley, faintly.

'No, the Old Fish Market car park, at seven-thirty. And Mr Frogwell phoned about twenty minutes ago. I told him you were still in bed and he said he'd call back.' The phone rang. 'That's him now probably.'

Lesley would have rather Susie had not said this to Eustace. She picked up the receiver, trying to sound alert.

'Morning Lesley. Up at last.'

'Eustace, good morning.'

'Listen, Lesley, I'll tellyer what I've been thinking. What you need is a profile of me to give the kind of personal whatnot that the voter can latch onto. Like that Labour chappie did. Whatsisname?'

'Kinnock?' said Lesley. 'But it wasn't awfully successful.'

'Times change. Can't open a paper without their current fellow beaming out at you. It's what the public wants now. Charisma.'

In Eustace's case, this seemed even less achievable. 'How did you have in mind presenting this material, Eustace?'

'Your business Lesley. You just be a good girl and write down the details and then think of some way of putting them over. Got a pencil and paper?'

'Yes,' said Lesley, feeling annoyed and patronised. And why on earth did it have to be her who did the writing? Did he believe it to be beyond the capabilities of Susie? As Eustace spoke she looked out of the window. The rain had stopped. A white, watery sun was emerging, the clouds splitting, and frayed patches of blue beginning to show. She caught a glimpse of anorak beyond the garden wall. Bob's head turned towards the building. No, above the building. He followed whatever it was with his binoculars. Lesley suddenly felt guilty that she had so few bird names at her disposal. But what was he doing out there at this time of day? He had said he was a teacher. Then she realised that it was a Saturday. In which case, why was Susie in the office?

Eustace had now got beyond his third in Law and was on to the beginnings of his career in banking. What he said started to register. His major dealings had been with Chile and South Africa, though his strenuous efforts on behalf of his employers had not prevented him from having a wide range of leisure activities. He shot pheasant and grouse and had been a Master of Foxhounds (the avenue which had led him to Maud). In his early forties he became – and still was – a magistrate. He was on the boards of governors of two schools and one detention centre. In recognition of his devotion to his nation, on his retirement he had been made a member of the Ancient Order of the Hogweed (established 1827; motto: *Beati monoculi in regione caecorum*). But even now, in his latter years, he had not ceased in his tireless desire to better society. His lifelong interest in legal justice had recently led him to make up part of a committee which was looking into prison ships and the tagging of first-time offenders . . .

Lesley listened, not with her own ears, but with those of Anna Seale. Eustace Frogwell had always been a fact of life; a strong supporter of Osbert; a harmless old buffer; she was utterly unprepared to discover that there were so many things that Anna would find appalling, not the least of them being Eustace's utter unawareness that his activities were in any way controversial. As the recital drew to a close, Eustace's voice took on a somewhat reproachful tone and Lesley realised that he had expected appreciative noises. Ecstatic congratulations at the end would have made amends, but she was able to do no more than mutter something about getting the profile typed up as soon as possible.

'Bring it over after church tomorrow,' said Eustace. 'Have a sherry.'

The phone rang again immediately Lesley put it down.

'Can you get it, Susie? Whoever it is, I'm not here.'

Susie lifted the receiver. 'No, she's not,' she said. 'All right. Hang on a mo.' She grabbed the notepad and wrote 'Darril Youngor'.

'Oh, if it's him, I suppose I'd better take it,' said Lesley. She took the receiver. 'Hallo Darryl, I didn't want to talk to anyone but you . . .' No, that wasn't what she meant. 'I mean, I didn't sleep well, so I've been making myself unavailable.'

'Hallo Les. Phoned to find out if you'd made contact with Anna.'

'Yes I have. But I was just about to call her and cancel. I have had Eustace Frogwell on the line and I cannot believe that anything is likely to induce the young lady to wish to ally herself with him. I'd always thought Eustace was normal enough, but now it transpires that he's spent most of his life harrying poor people, exploiting the Third World and killing animals.'

'And in that respect he is unique among Tories?' Darryl asked.

'I'm afraid I fail to see the humour in the situation. In ten hours or so I have to convince a violent . . .'

'Not violent, supposedly abusive or disorderly or something, and even that they thought better of trying to charge her with.'

'. . . woman to ally her party with one led by a man who would like to bring back birching. I cannot go through with this. I simply cannot go through with this. I mean, Captain Skate is bad enough.'

'Captain Skate? What's he got to do with it?'

'He's Alternative, isn't he?'

'Not that I know of. Camp as a row of tents, but not Alternative. Staunch Thatcherite, to the best of my knowledge. The original idea was to offer Anna numbers.'

'That I can do but, from what you've told me about her, I can't believe it's going to be enough.'

'It's a lovely day,' said Darryl. 'Why don't you come over and we'll go for a walk by the Ebb?'

Lesley looked out of the window. Only a few puffy little clouds now; light and shadow: it was a lovely day. How had that happened?

Darryl opened the door doing up the button on a pair of cut-off jeans. He was wearing a faded t-shirt. His feet were bare. His hair was wet.

'Come in. I'll put the kettle on.'

The kitchen was small and rectangular, mid-way between tidy and untidy. It smelled of spices. There were jars of beans and pasta. There was a spider-plant and a busy Lizzie. There was washing-up in the sink and on the table. Darryl unhooked a couple of large mugs from a row beside the cooker.

'Tea or coffee Les?'

'I'm dying of thirst. Do you have any orange juice?'

Darryl opened a cupboard and got out a thick, rectangular glass. He looked in the fridge. 'Apple do?'

Lesley nodded. He poured some for her. 'I think I've got a hangover,' she said.

'Really? I didn't put you down for a drinker. You should get on with Anna then.'

'I'm not "a drinker". It was just we – my secretary and I – invited some people, a birdwatcher and a Rastafarian, to visit and I thought some wine would break the ice.'

'Jay and Bob?'

'Yes.'

'Well that's a start. You don't waste time, do you?'

'It was purely by chance.' She took a sip of apple juice. 'Anna drinks, did you say?'

'Like a fish.'

They took a footpath beside the river, damp and dotted with puddles from the recent rain. A million shades of green, a million gradations of fluttering light. Eventually, even the occasional lovely houses disappeared and, with them, the mossy stone walls, the hedges and fences, and they were walking on the edge of fields. They sat on a stile.

'I wish I could spend more time here,' said Darryl.

'Why can't you?'

'I have to go where the work is. At this stage in my career, I need to be constantly available.'

'So you could leave at any moment?' Of course. It was only to be expected.

'If something good came up. There's a big role I'm hoping to read for at the moment actually. Waiting to hear from my agent.'

A duck landed on the water, back-pedalling madly.

'I feel the same as you do about this place,' Darryl continued. 'The cliffs, the river valley. And there's my house. It's not just the value of it – though it's all my capital and I haven't got any liquid; hopeless with money – I've had some bloody marvellous times here. Kelly Davis used to sleep on my floor when she was broke, before she made it. Used to wander around starkers, except for a candlewick dressing-gown with holes in it. Put up lots of people. Lived on dahl. Christ, I remember Dee Frazer, when she was doing panto at Pitsbury Rep – before they pulled it down – weeping at the breakfast table because she had such a hangover and had to go on in a couple of hours – the good fairy and the wicked witch, doubling. We had a party one time where everyone had to come as their favourite deadly sin.'

'Which did you come as?' asked Lesley.

'Lust,' said Darryl.

A glistening dragonfly darted over the shallows.

'How well do you know Tim Babcock?' Lesley asked.

'Seen him at family do's over the years. That's about it. His mother is my mother's sister. We're from the black sheep side but they're still pretty close. It's through my stepfather that I got interested in the Business: theatrical entrepreneur; angel.'

'Angel?'

'Backer. Stumps up the cash.'

'And Primrose, have you met her?'

'Once or twice. She didn't want me at the wedding, you know. It was the mothers who insisted. Hate those events. Only thing to do is to drink your way through them.'

A lark started to sing. Some heavy creature plopped into the water from the opposite bank.

'It was Primrose and Tim, and an old friend of my husband's, who gave the story to the newspapers,' said Lesley. She swallowed. 'I feel betrayed. I know I shouldn't. I'm the one who set the bad example.'

In the silence that followed, Darryl rested his arm nonchalantly, comfortably, on her shoulder. Then he leapt off the stile. 'Would you like some birthday cake?'

Lesley followed him. 'Is it your birthday?'

'Sally Mackerel's, the day before yesterday. Fifty-two.'

'Fifty-two? But she's just discovered she's pregnant.'

'That's what you get for screwing the scriptwriter, Les. Eternal fertility. Anyway, she gave me a big hunk to bring home with me. White icing. Dolphins. A big jolly boat.'

'Where exactly is *Ship Ahoy* set?' asked Lesley, as they started walking.

'Mummerset,' said Darryl.

Back at the house he cut them a piece of cake each and made some more coffee. Lesley told him about Tim's secret media event. 'They just seem so much in control,' she finished, gathering up the crumbs and bits of icing left on her plate with a finger. 'I don't know how we can compete with them.'

She looked up. Darryl was watching her intently.

'My secretary, Susie, told me about it. She was at the wedding, so you may have met. She's terribly good-natured and, really, all this conflict washes over her. I don't think she sees it as in any way inappropriate to be working for me and maintaining a friendship with Primrose and Tim, or any of that group of people, for that matter.'

A thought stirred in her mind but, before she had time to formulate it, Darryl said: 'Would you like to go to bed with me, Lesley?'

White doves flying out of a silk handkerchief. A tablecloth, pulled away, leaving the china quivering but intact. A sudden sense of being an adult woman and the word 'adult' having only an erotic meaning. A fizzy bunch of cheerleaders, in the pit of her stomach, cried 'Yes! Yes! Yes!' Darryl had a way of making whatever he suggested sound delightfully simple. As simple, for example, as taking her clothes off and being embraced by that easy body.

Which could leave at any time: an uncertain investment. Investment! What was she talking about? Such scenes as the one in the Beach Caff were, doubtless, far from infrequent. Hopeless with money, he said so himself. And all the ease was, it turned out, illusory. Witness the long-shot that was Anna Seale and her cohorts. Witness the arguments with the producer, the leaky boat; witness the charm that had enmeshed her in a situation and only then mentioned the catches. Deadly sins. Drinking. Semi-naked actresses.

'I think you have misjudged the kind of person I am,' said Lesley. 'I view our relationship as . . . professional.'

'God, do you? Well let's change it, shall we?'

'Yes! Yes! Yes!' cried the cheerleaders. A minute, no half a minute from smelling the masculine smell of that chest, of touching the contours of muscles.

'I saw you at the wedding and I thought you were bloody gorgeous,' said Darryl. 'I was going to introduce myself but . . .'

Realisation hit. 'You got drunk and tried to seduce Christie Marks's younger sister. You were the one all the upset was about. Tim was furious. Why,' Lesley worked it out, 'Primrose mentioned recently that she and Tim were invited to the girl's twentieth. She can only have been . . .'

'Fifteen, going on forty. Ann Bancroft was less sophisticated in *The Graduate*. Look, Les, I didn't mean to shock you. You said you'd had affairs, like your husband. I'd just adore to be one of your conquests.'

'Affairs?'

'On our walk you said you were the one who had set a bad example. That's marvellous. I'm all for bad examples.'

'I meant to my daughter, to Primrose. That hideous loyalty – to Tim; to the Party – which made her willing to tell the press about her father, to try to sully my reputation, without any thought at all of pure and simple human considerations.' A sob erupted. 'I cannot, unequivocally, say I wouldn't have done the same for Osbert, who I didn't even love. Love? For God's sake, after the first year or so I didn't even like him. I haven't ever had sex with anyone other than Osbert and the last time we did that was on election night, 1979. At least Primrose loves Tim, or appears to.'

There was a silence. Lesley took out a handkerchief and blew her nose.

Darryl said, 'Lord, Lesley. I'm sorry. Bloody hamfisted. I assumed that you and Osbert had had rather a passionate time of it. I mean, it's understandable: Nanny Enema shows a fair amount of sexual imagination . . .'

Lesley's tears dried almost instantaneously. She rose to her feet.

'Are you telling me that you thought that I and my husband . . .?'

'Well, it wouldn't have mattered, would it?'

'Good-bye Darryl. Do not contact me again please.'

Self-righteousness has a short half-life. By the time Lesley got home, it was in need of sharing if it was to be maintained. But Susie had gone and there was absolutely no one else to talk to. No Winifred. No Primrose. And now, of course, no Darryl either. Any possibility of any kind of relationship with him whatsoever was over. She would never see him again. Never. True friendship, as she had known and allowed herself to forget, was only possible with another woman. But all the other women she knew were merely acquaintances. Confidences would shock them. Susie was the only one who remained and she was sweet but inadequate. Indignation dwindled into profound loneliness.

At a loose end, with no idea quite what to do with herself, she wandered from room to room, finding no reason to be in one rather than another. There were various things she supposed she should do: have a bath and change, phone Anna Seale to cancel, think about a way of making Eustace Frogwell look charismatic or, at least, not morally dubious. She did none of them.

Instead, eventually, she put up a deckchair and sat in the garden, staring out, beyond the grazing Cherry, beyond the edge of the cliff, where Bob was sitting, eating a sandwich, to the warm, hazy sea. The ferry was approaching the harbour, white and lovely in the sunlight.

Primrose's wedding reception had taken place in this garden. Lesley had worn a brown silk shirt-dress, with a string of amber beads, a matching straw hat and shoes. No one had told her she looked gorgeous. They had told her that she looked too young to be the mother of a bride, which had, paradoxically, made her feel old all of a sudden. Well, if you lived your life in terms of the role you played in other people's, they could nudge you into middle-age by getting married.

Something fluttered on the wrought iron table. A note, placed there by Susie, and weighed down with a crumbly piece of chalk. Susie had a habit of putting messages where she thought you were most likely to find them, as opposed to in one fixed place where you would always know to look. It just said 'See you Monday. Hugs, S.'

And now the thought that had been emerging to do with Susie, which she had not had a chance to pursue before Darryl propositioned her, came back to Lesley. She sat, considering, for perhaps twenty minutes. Then she made a decision: she would keep the appointment with Anna Seale. There was nothing to be lost by doing so, especially now that she had come up with something, in addition to numbers, that she could bargain with: something that, if she read Anna correctly, she would find hard to resist.

II

Dinner With Anna

Ebbing was nostalgic about its Fish Market: there were sepia postcards of herring gutters and mussel-sellers in the souvenir shops which really were reprints of old photographs. Not so nostalgic, however, as to prevent the County Council from making it into a car park, at about the same time as it was granting planning permission, in Pitsbury, to flatten the kitchen garden of a medieval convent in order to make more parking spaces for one of the new supermarkets. All part of a sort of parking incentive.

Not even Ebbing's oldest resident, Olive Ford (98), who had lost husbands in both world wars – one to a bullet, one to a bomb – remembered the Market though. Had the residents of Ebbing done so it might have tempered their nostalgia a little, or occasioned them to define more precisely what exactly it was they were nostalgic for.

Certainly not fish. The vast majority of the catch netted by the dwindling fleet along that coast ended up on the more animated side of the Channel, where it was eaten off large white plates by appreciative tourists. Meg Hughes's Crab and Oyster Bar – now being closed by Anna – also catered mainly to tourists and day-trippers, the overspill from Pitsbury, tired of admiring the cathedral and finding nothing else to admire, or making a hasty exit at the onset of evensong. Fish, as served by Harry Smack at the Chippy, was, by mental dispensation, considered to be an honorary meat; just as Jay was considered, by some of Ebbing's well-meaning liberals, not really to be black. Others, of a less charitable disposition, sought explanations in Jay's colour for the really deplorable blot upon the Old Fish Market Square that was Jay's house. Right next door to the tastefully in-keeping façade of the Woodcutter Inn and yet every window filled with stickers advocating dubious causes and depictions of Bob Marley on red, green and yellow scarves.

That must be Jay's house, Lesley thought to herself now, as she stood outside the Jolly Roger, waiting for Anna. The window of Cinderella's Bridal Gowns was full of a crinoline. Jack entered the Square, from the direction of the Beach Caff and, seeing Lesley, approached her.

'Mrs Sway.'

'Good evening.' She shook his outstretched hand.

'You got my message?'

'Yes,' said Lesley.

'And?'

'I am very grateful and will be looking into it.' That was what Osbert would have said. She could see that such formulae had their uses.

'Oh.' He stood, awkwardly.

A thought occurred to Lesley. 'I am waiting for a young lady. Anna Seale. We've never met before, not properly. You know her perhaps? I'm worried I won't recognise her. I don't even know the direction she's coming from.'

Jack looked around, eagerly. Then, 'There she is.' He nodded towards the High Street, nonchalantly enough, but his face leapt into an animation that made it really quite handsome. Lesley turned in the direction Jack had indicated and barely noticed him disappearing from her side and into the Anchor. Momentarily, she was surprised that Anna was walking so unerringly towards her. But, of course, she would have seen Lesley's face often enough in the newspapers, and might remember her from their last, and only other, encounter. Though there was nothing about Anna that was familiar to Lesley.

As Anna came closer, Lesley wished that she had indicated

what might be suitable clothing for the evening. But when she had left her message she had yet to decide what exactly they were going to do; and, anyway, when she had played this scene over in her mind, it had been a form of Primrose who had walked towards her, or of Penny St John, maybe – wearing their embroideries, their Central American colours and patterns; she had imagined their slim arms and silver bracelets. But Anna was large, in bleached jeans with holes in them, a pair of flip-flops, a faded khaki, sleeveless top which exposed her unshaven armpits and a tattoo on her left shoulder. She was older than Lesley had expected; in her mid-thirties. She was preceded by a smell of fish and vinegar.

Veronica Tarrant was not going to be happy.

'Ms Sway,' said Anna. A statement of fact, not a question, the 'Ms' calculated to irritate, though it didn't. Rather, it sounded quite pleasant, unbound a cord that had fastened her to Osbert. Even if it had upset her, though, Lesley was practised, as a politician's wife, at not reacting until later. She was also skilled at gauging moods and psychological intentions, with a view to pussyfooting around them: another legacy of her marriage to Osbert. (Which did not mean that Anna Seale had infinite leeway: it was the necessity for such behaviour that had caused the separation.) She was also used to dealing with the graceful petulance of Primrose.

'Ms Seale.' And Lesley Sway gave a brief, purely formal, smile. Anna, accustomed to assessing people for strength rather than beauty, noted the shrewdness of the face and decided that it was not, as it might have been, merely a question of how quickly the woman would frighten.

'I thought the Jolly Roger,' said Lesley.

'The Jolly Roger?' Anna shrugged. 'Why not? If we're drinking.'

'We're drinking,' said Lesley.

The Jolly Roger was all knots, nets and starfish, shells and scrimshaw. The menus were as large as newspapers. Many of the offerings were sold by weight or by the dozen, and all of them, ostensibly, depended on the weather. There was a bubbling tank full of things waiting to be eaten. Conversation was conducted at a diffident volume. It ceased. All eyes fixed on Anna.

'We'll sit over here, shall we?' said Lesley. Her voice, in the silence of the room, sounded high and overly animated. In her desire to impose her own context on the occasion, she had ignored the fact that Anna would stick out like a sore thumb in this enclave of Ebbing's Tory middle and upper-middle classes; who, it being Saturday night, were there in large numbers, in suits and summer dresses.

'Lesley,' called Penny St John, who was sitting with Steven Toe and her brother, Rory, 'Come and join us, do. We're celebrating. The old boat-builder's workshop is, as of now, an artist's studio. The renovation's completely finished. We moved our materials in today.' She smiled and raised her eyebrows and pulled a wry face which suggested she imagined Anna's presence to be something beyond Lesley's control.

'Oh,' said Lesley. But Steven Toe had leapt up and was – perhaps seeing a chance to underline his Bohemian credentials – getting chairs for each of them. Rory stood, automatically, until they were seated, his eyes on the dining-room, where Bianca Pickle was resentfully writing down an order. He'd like to see if she'd let him take her bra off.

Steven Toe, but with the bait of Art at his disposal, had the same project in mind. Hence his suggestion that he and Penny celebrate at the Jolly Roger, whereupon Penny's brother had asked if he could join them.

'What can I get you, ladies?' he asked, redolent of old-world courtesy.

'A pint of cider,' said Anna.

There was a silence.

'The same,' said Lesley.

'You do smell awfully of fish,' said Rory to Anna. Toe returned with the drinks and, reseated, picked up his clay pipe from the ashtray and lit it.

Anna made herself a roll-up. She stuck it into the corner of her mouth and took a couple of puffs. 'That's because I've been fucking all afternoon,' she replied. Toe choked. Penny St John gave a little snort of laughter. Rory blushed crimson. Lesley was torn between embarrassment, sympathy for Rory and the feeling that this sort of treatment, if anything, was what it would take to stop the boy from turning out like Tim Babcock. Things were not going smoothly.

'I think you're a friend of Carmen Fitch's, aren't you?' said Penny to Anna. 'We were in her gallery yesterday. Steven's a sculptor.'

'I strive to be,' said Steven.

'Toe,' said Anna.

'The same, for my sins.'

'She really does need to get some good stuff in there,' said Penny. 'I mean, I'm sure it's all awfully worthy, and all that, but it is the most utter rubbish.'

Bad-mouthing one's friends is a closely-guarded privilege, though Anna rarely spoke behind people's backs.

'Carmen,' she observed, 'sees art as something other than a harmless pastime for the leisured middle-classes.'

'Touché,' said Toe, valiantly, and dodged the epicentre of Penny's look by gesturing to Bianca for the menu.

'If you mean me,' Penny replied, too brightly, 'I am not leisured. I am studying at the Slade.'

'That must be exhausting,' said Anna.

'Shall we order?' said Lesley, passing Anna a menu in the hope of distracting her attention away from conversation.

'Order what?' asked Anna.

'The special of the day's steamed monkfish on a bed of mung beans,' said Bianca.

Steven Toe got a mild erection.

'I thought we could talk over dinner,' said Lesley.

Anna glanced at the menu and snapped it shut. Her voice thickened. 'I can't eat here,' she said.

There was another silence

Then, 'I'm so sorry,' said Lesley, tentatively, 'I should have thought. So many people are allergic to seafood.'

'There's steak and there's the vegetarian option,' said Bianca, with one of her rare bursts of helpfulness. They occurred when the answer to a problem struck her as obvious.

'A meal here costs more than half what I earn a week,' said Anna. 'I can't afford it.'

'Perhaps,' said Lesley, 'you would let me . . .' she did not finish the sentence. The expression on Anna's face told her that, if she did, there would be no coalition. Though really, what point was there in continuing this ghastly evening? Things had already gone as badly as they possibly could. Or so she thought, not having noticed that Veronica Tarrant had just approached their table.

'It was you, I think,' said Veronica to Anna, without preamble, 'who shouted "Tory bitch" at me.'

'"Bitches",' said Anna. She took a drag on her roll-up. 'I said "bitches". There were two of you.'

'Lesley,' said Veronica, 'I do not wish to distress you, but there are limits. I'm afraid I cannot serve this person.'

'She doesn't want to eat, anyway,' said Bianca, who had decided Anna was all right. 'She says it's too expensive.'

'Too expensive?' Veronica turned her enraged face back to Anna. 'Do you have any idea of the cost of seafood?'

'Yes I do,' said Anna. 'I work in the Crab and Oyster Bar and you're making a fucking killing.'

'So it wasn't sex,' burst out Rory.

'We have a table booked.' Everyone turned. A picture of loveliness: Primrose, in an Indian cotton smock, and an ankle-length dirndl in lavender, her hair twisted round a burgundy silk scarf. She was accompanied by Winifred and Susie Took.

'Hallo Lesley,' said Susie.

'Mummy.' Primrose gave a stiff little nod, but treated Veronica to a quizzical raise of the eyebrows, and a sideways look at Anna. Winifred said nothing, but inclined her head slightly. One role she had not been able to steal from Lesley; the other, she had. She laid a reassuring hand upon Primrose's shoulder, presumably in recognition of the turmoil of emotions that Primrose must be experiencing. A well-hidden turmoil, thought Lesley, cussedly. And if Winifred was so damn sensitive, she could possibly have exerted that faculty upon a consideration of what it would be like to have a road running straight through your garden. Winifred looked at Anna Seale as if she were an organism that lived in a water-butt.

'Primrose. Of course,' said Veronica, deciding, for the moment, that to be in favour of the road scheme was the most sensible –

and, certainly, satisfying – political position. She turned her back on Lesley, who rose to her feet.

Had Primrose and Winifred not made an appearance, she would have been inclined to leave without Anna and let whatever scene would, ensue. But how sorry they would have been able to feel for her then. As well, the sight of Primrose, feigning delicacy, and Winifred, smug, brought out a rather adolescent desire to irritate. And what could be more irritating than Lesley having a new – and even interesting – life, and therefore no cause to miss them? There was also the suddenly pleasing thought that Anna represented a real challenge, as opposed to the passive ones which Lesley was more used to, and which mainly emanated from her family: how to bite her tongue each time Primrose announced yet another pregnancy; how to contrive a liking for Tim; how to endure a social occasion with Osbert.

'Well then,' she said. 'We shall eat elsewhere.' And she started for the door, without looking to see if Anna was following.

Standing in the Square, waiting to see if she would, Lesley did some quick thinking. There was no room for the pretence of civility in any relations she might have with Anna Seale. Persisted in, it would lead Anna to despise her. The only way forward was plain-speaking.

So, when Anna appeared, she said, 'All right, you've had your fun. You've embarrassed me in front of my acquaintances . . .'

'Do you think I wasn't embarrassed? Do you think I like telling strangers how hard up I am? Do you think I like snobby adolescents saying that I smell?'

'You didn't have to smell. It was quite deliberate. There was no reason you couldn't have set a later time to meet and had a shower.'

'I don't have a shower.'

'A bath then. You could have taken a bath. You have a bath, I imagine?'

'How did I know we were going anywhere together? We could have been going to sit in the Square, for all I knew about it.'

'Oh be honest, Anna, for God's sake. You set me up. You set all of us up.'

'That bitch with Toe insulted one of my friends.'

'You didn't have to respond.'

'But why shouldn't I? Why should I keep quiet if I don't like what I'm hearing?'

The face was filled with self-righteous fury; such a naked emotion that Lesley stopped short. Why indeed? A thought crossed her mind: 'Without Osbert, might I have been a little like Anna Seale?'

They glared at one another. The level of antipathy demanded that they separate: it was the appropriate action; the only one available if pride was to remain intact. Both, however, were unwilling to do so.

Anna, in her turn, had become intensely curious about Lesley Sway. How would Lesley respond if Anna told her what she had been put through because of her? Evidently Lesley knew nothing of it, or she would never have had the gall to telephone. And what exactly had gone wrong between Lesley and her daughter? Demonstrativeness was not to be expected, but aversion, love, pain, bitterness, confusion: all those sharp emotions had been on plain show, in a brittle casing of civility. How bizarre to view convention as something to fall back upon, rather than to bash your head against. Had Lesley known about Nanny Enema all along and merely operated some social code that indicated how to pigeonhole such knowledge?

A horn sounded. The two women, instinctively, looked to the horizon. The ferry, its white sides rosy with the sunset, bringing its usual air of expectancy and busyness: 'I won't be here long. There are other places I must be, shortly.' But then both faces took on expressions of wonder. Another ship, altogether more intricate, floated upon the absolute margin of sea and sky, where the water was cobalt. A clipper, maybe; anyway with mother-of-pearl sails, melting into mauve shadows, thin, lilac rigging, twisty ropes, twirled carvings: a beautiful, rainbow thing, almost translucent, almost capable of being believed to be purely a trick of light and water. It paused, dwindled, and was gone.

'I'll cook us something,' said Anna. 'If you want.'

Lesley followed Anna through the open door.

'Oh my goodness,' she exclaimed. 'What a terrible thing to have happened.' She gazed around the room. The thieves had made an appalling mess of the place: upturned china, strewn papers, pots of paint on their sides, their contents bleeding onto the wood floor and spattered over one of the walls; a cracked palette, food, smeared clothes. 'Don't touch anything until you've phoned the police,' she said. 'There might be fingerprints.' She froze. A stony calm dropped upon her. 'Anna,' she said, 'there's a body on the sofa.'

'It's Jay,' said Anna. 'He's a friend.'

'Yes, I've met him. Is he dead?' The thought made her awfully sad. He had seemed so genial and harmless.

Anna stomped over to the sofa and gave Jay a shake. He stirred a little. 'Comatose, but not dead,' she said. She went into the kitchen and put a light on.

Jay's eyes opened. He spotted Lesley. 'Hey! The she-friend of my queen.'

'He's raving,' said Lesley. 'Perhaps they hit him on the head.'

Anna looked out of the kitchen. 'He's been asleep. He often kips down here. He works nights.'

'Works nights? What does he do?'

'Importer,' said Jay.

This struck Lesley as highly improbable.

'Anna, I really think you should get in touch with the police. Even if Jay is all right . . .'

Something started to sizzle in a frying-pan. Anna came out of the kitchen, a fish-slice in her hand.

'Home sweet home, right?' she said, crossly. 'This is the way I live. And you can push off, Jay.'

'What time is it?'

'Fuck knows. But you can push off anyway. What do you want to drink, Lesley?'

Lesley, horribly embarrassed, said 'A gin and tonic,' without thinking.

'There's beer or red wine.'

'Red wine would be lovely.'

Anna poured them about half a pint of wine each into two tumblers from a screw-top bottle. She took a large swig.

Lesley took a sip of wine, aghast. Nobody she had ever met had lived in such chaos. Her mistake had been quite understandable, so an apology would look ridiculous. If you wished to be charitable you could say that it was artless, and that this was refreshing if you compared it with the deliberateness of Primrose's kitchen say, or Winifred's sitting-room, where the heavy rugs and the Chinese pottery screamed good taste a little too shrilly. Yes, you could say it was refreshing but, in truth, the room indicated a careless nature in which the desire for order was completely absent. Only the view from the window – the fading beach, the darkening sky – gave any sense of the world as a place in which harmony could sensibly be desired. Anna could see her house, she noticed, and the Frogwell Mansion.

Jay stood up, yawning. Checked his pockets. 'Later,' he said, and was gone.

From the kitchen came a rattling sound, as Anna emptied a bag of mussels into the pan. Lesley saw the canvas. She put down her glass. The silhouettes, the gleaming sand, the plum-coloured clouds, the amber sky: last night – unfinished, but recognisable.

'Did you do this?' she asked.

'Yeah,' said Anna. She gave the pan a shake.

'And the one at Darryl Younger's house: you did that too?'

'Yeah.' Anna grabbed a couple of large, chipped bowls from the washing-up rack and filled them with mussels. She came into the sitting-room and gave the food to Lesley, who had sat down on the sofa. Anna plonked onto the floor and started to scoff, hungrily. All Lesley had eaten that day was birthday cake.

'They're stunning,' she said, after a moment.

'What are?'

'The paintings. They are absolutely lovely.'

'Yeah yeah. Lovely.' Anna sighed. 'You know Darryl then?' she asked.

'Not well,' said Lesley. She wondered whether Anna knew about the events of the afternoon. 'Have you seen him recently?' she asked.

'A few days ago. He came by cadging money.'

Lesley's indignation flared up again; along with it, a satisfaction that she had judged Darryl correctly. 'It was Darryl Younger,' she said, seeing an opening, and feeling that the subject should be addressed sooner rather than later, 'who told me about the unfortunate event which I may have played some part in.'

There was a silence. Anna put down her bowl.

'You knew about it?' she asked, slowly.

'Not at the time, but, now that I do, I want you to know that I regret it.'

'Oh, so you "regret it"? Do you want to know something? It never occurred to me that anyone who was aware they'd done that to me would have the nerve to . . .'

Lesley put down her bowl also. 'Firstly,' she said, her voice rising, 'I did nothing to you. The behaviour of the police, I have said, I am sorry about. Secondly, don't you think, anyway, that you are making rather a fuss?'

'Fuss? It's a concession even to speak to you. A massive bloody concession.'

'Now wait a moment . . .' Lesley paused. 'Sounds like you've been having fun, luvvie,' a voice inside her head said to her. Her conscience was stabbed. Yes, at this awful, decisive instant she was actually enjoying herself. After years and years of Primrose's peevishness and Osbert's sulks, there was much to be said for shouting. 'If we are talking about concessions,' she continued, 'you, in any alliance with me, only have to move in the direction of normality.'

'Normality? You destroy jobs, you tear down trees and habitats, you pollute the fucking skies, and you call that normal?'

'At least,' said Lesley, haughtily, 'we take baths and eat up to table.'

'And this is to be a consolation when the bombs start falling?' The door swung open.

'Having a tiff?' said Carmen Fitch.

'What do you want, Carmen?' said Anna, her rancour less than it would have been if she hadn't defended the woman an hour or so earlier, and if they hadn't, anyway, argued and called a truce many times before.

'Well I was going to ask you down the Mermaid.' Carmen's eyes swept over Anna's canvas. 'Mad colours,' she observed.

There was a silence.

Then, 'But it was like that,' burst out Lesley, astounded, the emotions evoked by Anna undissipated from her voice, injecting into it an unaccustomed vehemence. The other two women looked at her. 'Last night – it is last night, isn't it?' Anna nodded.

'There *was* a feeling that everything was . . . exaggerated: surreal, almost.'

'Surreal!' Carmen aped posh.

Lesley ignored her. 'Which is your gallery?' she asked Anna. 'I would love to see your portfolio. I know one can't compare painting and sculpture, but it seems to me that your work is every bit as good as Steven's.'

Anna did not speak. It was like the blow of the Zen Master that whams you violently into a new level of consciousness: she was being taken seriously, for a reason other than friendship.

Carmen said, 'Steven Toe, you mean?' She shrugged, dismissively. Toe had, apparently, taken a nose-dive in her estimation since the night before. Anna remained silent. 'Well anyway,' said Carmen, with an appraising look at her, 'I'll be in the Mermaid, Anna, when you two have finished your tête-à-tête.'

She left. Anna reached for her tobacco. Lesley, though not knowing why Anna's resentment had subsided, seized the opportunity.

'We might disagree politically, Anna. Socially, we have nothing in common. There is one area only in which we are in accord: we want to save the clifftop. Listen: this is what I can offer you. Numbers, of course, but something else as well: I have access to information about Tim Babcock's campaign – classified information. Working together, we can pre-empt them at every turn.'

Anna did not look up from her cigarette paper. 'And where does the information come from?' she asked, softly, her voice sounding subdued, now that there was no rage in it.

'Are you with me?'

'I could be.'

'The information comes from my secretary, Susie Took. She's a close friend of Primrose and Tim. You saw her with Primrose this evening, if you need proof of that. She is also still working for me. I am not going to use Susie. That is to say, I will not ask for information, but I will exploit absolutely any she volunteers. And she will volunteer it, believe me. Already I know, for instance, secret details about an extremely important event that Tim is organising.'

'What's that then?'

'Are you with me?'

'I could be.'

'I'm afraid that's not good enough.'

Now Anna looked at Lesley. 'And my word is?'

Lesley returned her gaze, levelly. She raised her eyebrows. 'Shouldn't it be?'

'I'm usually honest,' said Anna.

'That,' said Lesley, 'is something we have in common.'

12 ∫

Walking on the Clifftop

The next task was to talk Eustace Frogwell into agreeing to a coalition. St Christopher's struck eleven as Lesley walked back along Harbour Street to the Old Fish Market, where she had left her car. When she got home she would have to start work on Eustace's profile. It was unreasonable of him to expect it to be done so quickly but it was worth having it ready for the following morning: if it was flattering enough, it might put him into an accommodating frame of mind; perhaps she could even present Eustace with an image of himself that would persuade him that he was quite liberal and open to new ideas. A pre-lunch sherry after church on a Sunday was, moreover, the perfect occasion for calm discussion: a time at which no Frogwell could doubt that, whatever expediency might temporarily demand, the shape of things would remain the same forever.

The pubs were closing and the atmosphere was hostile. Animal sounds came from the High Street, where louts were piling into Harry's Chippy and the Taj Mahal: an army of discontented youth, subdued during the days and week nights – dutifully pumping petrol, mending cars, rodding drains – but which erupted, each weekend, into resentments, unfocussed or wide of the mark. Sunday morning, all that remained were the traces of its rampage. Greasy white chip papers tumbled down the streets, blew against the legs of day-trippers and were shaken away. There were pools of vomit, shattered windows, smashed flower-pots, trampled flowers. Ebbing woke to a peal of burglar alarms.

Now Lesley heard the sound of breaking glass, almost exactly parallel to where she was walking, a split second of silence, and then running feet. She remained unperturbed: the action was two streets away – though, even had it not been, she sensed that she could have walked past it untouched. Their business was not with her.

Lesley paused outside Flint's Newsagent's to get her car keys out of her handbag. Should her arrival at the car coincide with Primrose and Winifred's leaving the Jolly Roger, she wished for no delay to her departure which would demand the exchange of unfelt civilities. She found the keys and was about to continue walking when, in the window of the shop, two eyes met hers. It was a poster of a man with an identikit face, wanted for the armed robbery of a post office in a suburb of London.

Lesley stared at it. Like most identikit faces, this one resembled everybody and nobody. It was flat and lifeless, had no thoughts or sensations. It was like a dummy upon which you might test the efficacy of seat-belts or learn artificial resuscitation. The only thing that particularised it – at least in Ebbing – was that the face was not white, though what exactly the man's race was, it was impossible to say. Anyway, unless the man were subnormal and, again like all such faces, he gave the impression that he might have been, this would be an unlikely spot for him to seek to hide himself. In the light of the hideous telephone message William Flint had left on Lesley's answerphone, it was impossible to doubt the motivation behind the poster's presence.

'Mrs Sway?'

Lesley turned, and instinctively recoiled.

'Opportunity knocks,' said William Flint. 'I've been wanting a chance to natter. But, first of all, Mrs Sway, let me repeat my very sincere, very sincere regrets that your family life and your memories of your hubby have been besmirched by . . .'

Before Flint could start on another gloating denunciation of Nanny Enema, Lesley interrupted. Clearly, for this odious individual, Nanny Enema represented an excuse to voice what he would have liked to say about women in general – with the possible exception of a few mothers, grandmothers and less publicised members of the royal family. Lesley would not have described herself as a feminist but she felt an increasing camaraderie with Nanny Enema.

'Mr Flint,' she said, 'I received your message on my answerphone and it convinces me that we have absolutely nothing to say to one another.'

'But that's where you're wrong, Mrs Sway, that's where you're wrong.' The newsagent's grin twitched. He laid a hand on Lesley's arm. She looked at it. He removed it. 'We have things to talk about to do with politics, to do with your breakaway party.'

'It is not my party, Mr Flint, it is led by Eustace Frogwell. I am merely campaign manager.'

'The power behind the throne, Mrs Sway.'

The man appeared to believe he was being gallant.

'Mr Flint, I believe I have made myself perfectly clear. If you wish to discuss politics, you must speak to Eustace Frogwell.' Other considerations apart, if Lesley was going to have to spend her nights performing tasks that Eustace had set her, he could be the one to get rid of people like William Flint.

Flint's eyes filled with anger. He might have spoken again but, at that moment, a window opened above the shop and an adolescent leaned out. Lesley recognised him. He was the one with the Union Jack t-shirt, from whom she had bought the newspapers.

'Done?' he asked. Flint shook his head slightly, his eyes indicating Lesley's presence. The boy now noticed her, muttered 'Fuck', put his head back in and slammed the window shut.

'A relative,' remarked Flint. 'Staying with me temporarily.'

There was the sound of a police siren in the High Street.

When she reached home, Lesley poured herself a glass of mineral water and, seated at the kitchen table, tried to settle down to Eustace's profile. After ten minutes, however, she stopped in despair. How could one doctor such raw material to make the man appear even likeable, let alone open and broad-minded?

The frustrating thing was that she knew it could be done, because they had done it with Osbert. Dick Winters could have told her how; even now he was probably seated at his desk, doing the job on Tim Babcock, who had the additional advantage of being young and good-looking. Or maybe, considering the hour, Dick was sleeping the peaceful sleep of the totally in control, press releases already distributed to a delighted media.

Lesley sighed. There was no doubt, either, that photographs of Tim and Primrose, surrounded by their adorable offspring, would have considerably more appeal to picture editors than Maud and Eustace, surrounded by Maud's long-haired dachshunds. There was a grown-up daughter, called Ursula, somewhere, but the last Lesley remembered of her was when she left home, at seventeen, to be lead singer in a punk rock band called Eat Shit And Die. Since then she had not been mentioned. Of course, the girl might have blossomed but, lacking confirmation of this, she could not be considered an asset.

Lesley decided to seek inspiration in a walk along the clifftop. She put on a cardigan and went out of the back door, walked down the lawn, stopping to give Cherry a pat, and slipped over the low wall at the bottom of the garden. There she chose a path that took her to the very edge of the cliff, where you could either turn left for Ebbing or follow the path to the right which, after about an hour, brought you to the little village of Cove, where Lesley used to take Primrose for tea when she was a child; or you could, as Lesley did now, simply stand and regard what lay before you.

There was a big, icy white moon, drowning out the stars. The rooftops of Ebbing glistened. Lesley picked out the yellow lights of Anna's house across the bay. What was she doing with this night, Lesley wondered. Nobody who loved paint and the sea and Ebbing could fail to be recording it; the curves of light on the fidgeting waters, the sense of almost absolute silence, the calm.

'Excuse me.'

Lesley jumped out of her skin. She looked all around. There was no one to be seen anywhere.

'Excuse me,' the voice repeated.

It seemed to be coming from below the edge of the cliff. Lesley walked as near to the edge as she dared, then lowered herself onto her stomach and gingerly pulled her body forwards until she was able to see over.

'Oh hallo Mrs Sway,' said Bob. 'I seem to have got myself into a slightly difficult situation.' He was sitting on a not very wide ledge about ten feet below.

'What happened?' asked Lesley.

'I was watching an oyster catcher and the cliff crumbled away,' Bob replied. Lesley moved backwards a little. 'Fortunately I'd hung my binoculars around my neck,' he continued, 'otherwise I would have lost them. I don't always do that, so it was a stroke of good fortune.'

'And how long have you been here?'

'Since seven fifty-three. You're the first person to go past. There was no point trying to make signals across the bay because, though I might be visible, no one would be able to see me clearly enough, unless they were looking through binoculars, which would have been possible most weekends but, as chance would have it, all the other birders have gone on a trip to Sheppey today and the minibus isn't expected back until late. They thought they might stop off at a couple of pubs that specialise in real ale on the way back. I volunteered to stay behind and keep an eye on the lesser tit. I tried waving at the ferry but everyone just waved back. I suppose they thought I was on a footpath. I haven't broken anything and, generally speaking, it's not been unpleasant; I've counted fourteen varieties of wild flower and moss on this ledge alone. I would rather it were known I was here though.'

'Known you were here?' Lesley was astounded. 'I scarcely think that will do. You must be rescued.'

Bob's face took on a nervous expression.

'There's no need. Really. It's dark now and it would be a shame to disturb anyone. I'll probably have a doze later.'

'Have a doze? Whatever are you talking about? Suppose you roll off?'

'I don't believe that happens, Mrs Sway. If you read about animals, they never inadvertently roll on their offspring in the night. There's a sort of sixth sense that governs their movements, even when they're asleep. Well the lesser tit does occasionally smother its brood by accident, but that's probably not by rolling on them.'

'We cannot,' said Lesley, 'rely on sixth sense and animal instinct. Besides, what if a violent wind blows up?'

'Oh I don't think it will,' said Bob, scanning the horizon. 'Really, Mrs Sway, just send somebody along with a winch in the morning.'

'That,' said Lesley, 'my conscience will not permit. I am going to go back to the house and phone Air Sea Rescue.' She made to move away.

'Don't do that,' cried Bob. 'I beg of you, don't do that.'

Lesley stopped. 'Whyever not?'

'Have you seen *Apocalypse Now*?' asked Bob.

'*Apocalypse Now*? No, I don't believe I have.'

'But you've seen the clips. You must have done. Everyone has. The helicopters. The noise. *The March of the Valkyries*. Think of the effect on the lesser tit. It would never survive that kind of upset.'

Lesley was beginning to lose patience. Ecology was all well and good but hardly worth risking your life for.

'The lesser tit will just have to take its chances,' she said briskly. 'If it's any consolation, I seriously doubt there will be more than one helicopter, and I am certain there will be no musical accompaniment.'

'Even so,' said Bob who, at times, lacked a sense of humour, 'it would be mad to risk it.'

'It would be mad not to.' Again Lesley began to shuffle backwards.

'Mrs Sway.' Bob's voice was stern. 'Unless you give me a solemn undertaking not to phone Air Sea Rescue I will, right this minute, attempt to climb back up the cliff.'

'But you'll fall.'

'And the lesser tit will fly free. Or flutter free, to be strictly accurate. It can fly, but it's not awfully good at it, so mainly it prefers to flutter.'

There was a pause. Lesley contemplated the face of Bob Adams in the moonlight. He appeared to be in deadly earnest. She wondered if all birdwatchers were so stubborn.

'So there is no choice,' she said eventually: 'I shall just have to stay here with you. If you look like you are falling asleep I will keep you awake. If, however, a wind does blow up, I will have to phone Air Sea Rescue, and you must assure me that you will allow me to – you have already told me you are convinced that it will not, so that shouldn't present a problem. Are we agreed?'

'I don't want to put you to any trouble,' said Bob.

'Believe me, Bob, you and your kind have put me to a considerable amount of trouble today and I have no intention of reassuring you otherwise. The last thing I desire is to spend a night on the edge of an unstable bit of cliff lying on my stomach watching a birdwatcher.' Bob looked sheepish. 'Have you eaten or drunk anything?'

'The remains of my sandwiches were the only casualty. And a banana. I managed to keep hold of my thermos.'

'If the situation remains unchanged I shall go and make you some more sandwiches a bit later. I will phone somebody about a winch as soon as appropriate.' Though who that 'somebody' might be she could not possibly imagine.

They fell into silence.

After ten minutes Bob said, 'You can see the lights of my friend Anna's house from here.'

'I met your friend Anna today,' said Lesley. 'I also met Carmen – Carmen Fitch, I take it. You know her, I imagine?'

'Yes, I know Carmen.'

'And?'

There was a pause.

'Without wanting to be uncharitable – and, it has to be said, Carmen has given tremendous support to quite a number of . . . more experimental artists, who are probably her main area of interest – I don't think Carmen has been very good news for Anna.'

'You mean Carmen Fitch has discouraged her out of jealousy?'

The baldness of the statement obviously unsettled Bob. 'Well I wouldn't go quite so far as to say that. We must remember, it hasn't been easy for Carmen.'

'What hasn't?'

'Her affections for Anna not being reciprocated. Or being reciprocated but not in the way Carmen would like.'

Lesley digested the information. All became clear. Bob was somebody who balked at speaking ill of anyone but, reading between the lines, Carmen Fitch was systematically discouraging Anna, both out of jealousy of her abilities and as a kind of revenge for her not becoming Carmen's lover. The thought was not a pretty one.

'Is Anna a les . . . er . . . gay?' she asked.

'Oh no. Well, that is to say, no more than anyone is. Like all of us, she's probably tried it, but her main orientation, I would say, is towards heterosexuality.'

Lesley had always assumed that sexual proclivity was a clear cut matter. She gave an inward sigh: the Alternative Left did make rather a meal of things.

'Can't Anna see how good her paintings are?' she asked. 'Doesn't anybody tell her?'

'We tell her all the time,' Bob replied. 'Carmen, however, thinks there is lots of room for progress.'

'But she's only one person.'

'Mrs Sway,' said Bob, 'before I became a primary school teacher I worked in adult education up North. Before that I taught at a technical college. The authority the uneducated give to the supposed "expert" is invariably quite out of proportion to what is deserved.'

'One doesn't think of Anna as "uneducated".'

'I agree, one doesn't. It would perhaps be better to describe her as self-educated. But she trusts Carmen because Carmen went to art school, rather than me, or her friend Darryl Younger, or Meg – Meg Hughes, that is; she runs the Crab and Oyster Bar.'

'Darryl Younger encourages her?'

'You know him too? Yes, he does. Probably more than anybody.'

The rustling of leaves broke the ensuing silence.

'That may well be the tit,' Bob whispered. 'If you don't mind, Mrs Sway, we'd better not talk any more. It would be ironic if our chatting were to scare it.'

'Wouldn't it?' said Lesley drily. Twenty minutes passed. Lesley became increasingly aware of the ridiculousness of the situation. In the garden, Cherry gave a soft whinny.

'I suppose,' Lesley whispered, irritably, 'the lesser tit won't like that noise either.'

'It's interesting you say that, Mrs Sway,' Bob whispered back. 'And, of course, you may be quite correct, but most people who have observed the lesser tit have noticed that it is unexpected sounds – Champagne corks, helicopters, human voices – that upset it, rather than the sorts of things it might expect in a pastoral setting.'

There was a pause.

'I will be back in twenty minutes.' said Lesley

'Are you going to make sandwiches?' asked Bob.

'No, I'm going to get the horse.'

Less than an hour later, Lesley and Bob were sitting at Lesley's kitchen table, Cherry was back in the garden, and Lesley was experiencing an intense fondness for the creature, who had behaved with that bemused obligingness that the nicer of animals display when disturbed unexpectedly.

Cherry had allowed Lesley to put the round, padded thing, that the reins were usually attached to, and which Susie had, fortunately, left in the caravan, around her neck without protest. On either side of it were two convenient loops. Lesley unfastened Cherry's tethering rope at both ends, with some difficulty in the case of the end tied round the peg – Susie was a dab hand with knots and mallets. She threaded it through the loops, over the horse's neck. Cherry permitted Lesley to lead her, the ends of the rope trailing behind, around the side of the house and then along the footpath that Lesley had taken earlier.

The horse's flanks were silver in the moonlight. Its placidity was reassuring. Its hooves made an agreeable sound. It would be pleasant, Lesley found herself thinking, to ride on a horse such as Cherry through woodlands on a night such as this one, or through a thin film of waves on the sand. She forgave her for kicking over her water bucket.

Bob, evidently regretting having mentioned that there might be an area in which the lesser tit showed a touch of sangfroid, was standing on the ledge, looking worried, when Lesley crawled to the cliff edge and looked over.

'I'm going to get Cherry to back towards the edge,' she told him. 'I've had an inspection and the ground seems firm but, in view of your experience, I only want to get her as near to it as is absolutely necessary, so shout as soon as you think you've got enough of both ends of rope to loop properly around yourself.'

'Could I whistle rather than shout?'

'Oh all right, whistle,' Lesley replied, exasperated.

Cherry consented to walk backwards, only twitching her ears a little. Had the moment been appropriate, Lesley would have been sorely tempted to draw some pertinent comparisons between the cooperative nature of the horse and the uncooperative nature of the lesser tit, which was not even being asked to help out, merely to continue to exist. Eventually, there was a whistle and Lesley walked Cherry forward. Bob's face and then his entire body appeared on the clifftop. A largish shower of chalk and small rocks fell away behind him. They heard the fragments bouncing off the side of the cliff.

'The appropriate drink for occasions such as these is brandy, I suppose,' said Lesley now. 'But I personally would prefer wine. Would you object to that? There's some bread and cheese we could have it with.'

'Wine would be lovely. I don't think I'm in a state of shock,' Bob replied.

Lesley went to Osbert's cellar. She had never felt a great interest in Osbert's wines in the past, but after the delightful experience of the claret and Sauternes of the previous evening, which had, for some reason, tasted better than she remembered any of Osbert's wines ever tasting before, she was inclined to explore the collection's possibilities further. She chose, at random, a 1985 Gevrey-Chambertin to go with the cheese and three bottles of white to put in the fridge, in case of visitors.

'What are you writing, Mrs Sway?' Bob asked when she returned to the kitchen.

Lesley groaned. 'Eustace's profile! I'd completely forgotten about it.' She looked at the clock. It was two a.m. She poured the wine, put out the food, then flopped into a chair. Over their first glass, she told Bob about the coalition. Over their second and the cheese, she swore him to secrecy and showed him the notes she had made about the career and interests of Eustace Frogwell. She poured them a third glass.

'It is not going to be easy to sell the idea of a coalition to Eustace,' she said. 'Any more than it was to Anna . . .'

'I think the birders will be amenable to it, Mrs Sway,' said Bob, 'in the light of your agreeing not to phone Air Sea Rescue for the sake of the lesser tit.'

'Please, do call me Lesley. That's good. Anna seems to think she can find a way to get the assent of her party to the idea. But, of course, it will all come to nothing unless Eustace agrees too. If I can flatter him and, if possible, in such a way that he believes that he and the Alternative Left have . . . oh I don't know . . . something in common, then maybe, by the time he gets round to remembering our very profound differences, he will already be committed.'

There was a pause.

'Well if that is your problem, it looks as if things have turned out rather fortunately,' said Bob. 'That is, if you are willing to let me help you. You see, this is an area in which I have a certain – albeit limited – expertise.'

13

The Frogwell Mansion

The Frogwell Mansion smelled of wet dog, puppies, straw, mildew and dog biscuits. Today being Sunday, there was the additional aroma of cabbage water, gravy and burning meat from the basement kitchen. It was full of large, murky pictures of stags (at bay and otherwise), bowls of fruit and Highland scenery. There were also numerous photographs of Maud and her dachshunds, with and without trophies. The rooms were dark and rather grubby, illuminated by small, twisted light-bulbs covered with maroon lampshades, half of which didn't work. The furniture was upholstered with a tight, shiny fabric that always seemed to be damp; it was dotted with patches of what Lesley fervently hoped were grease stains. Here and there the wallpaper sagged from the walls. On the long mantelpiece above the fireplace where, in winter, a few coals smouldered, an enormous clock, on a pink veined marble base, told the wrong time.

'Not at church this morning?' Eustace greeted Lesley in blazer and cravat.

'No,' Lesley replied. The wine had sent her into a deep, luxurious sleep, from which she had woken only forty minutes earlier.

'Well, come in anyway.' Eustace evidently viewed Sunday lunchtime drinks as a sort of privilege, to be earned by attending divine service. To have the drinks without undergoing church apparently struck him as cheating; though whether others would have seen a glass of cooking sherry and a savoury biscuit, from a tin left over from Christmas, as adequate recompense for sitting through one of the vicar's rambling sermons was debatable.

Eustace opened the sitting-room door and a flotilla of long-haired dachshunds leapt off the sofa, where they had been sitting with Maud, and ran at Lesley, barking. One of them made a quick dart forward and bit her on the ankle.

'No, Rummy, that's naughty,' said Maud, with a fond smile at the creature. 'Forgive me if I don't get up, Lesley. I don't want to disturb Tinder, I had to squeeze her stuffed glands this morning.'

'I quite understand,' said Lesley, sitting, and surreptitiously examining her ankle to see if the skin was broken.

'Sherry,' said Eustace, handing her a glass.

'Have a biscuit,' said Maud, picking up the tin. Lesley took one. It was spherical, the exterior had the texture of an ice-cream wafer. When you bit into it, it was filled with a cheese-flavoured powder.

'I've done some work on your profile, Eustace,' Lesley said hastily, lest she should be offered another. 'Let me read it to you and you can give me your reaction.'

'Go ahead then,' said Eustace, gruffly.

'Lesley! How *efficient* you've been,' exclaimed Maud.

'I did have some help,' said Lesley. She read.

Bob, it turned out, had displayed considerable modesty when he had said that his expertise in such matters was 'limited'. Lesley had been amazed to see with what efficiency the teacher had been able to produce an image of Eustace that, while wholly accurate, gave a likeable, caring slant to a personality that was a touch on the short side when it came to those attributes. Years of writing school reports and references for jobs, Bob explained, rendered one practised in this regard. Compared with some of the cases that had passed through his hands – particularly those he referred to as having 'learning difficulties' – the material that Eustace Frogwell provided was rich in possibility.

Under Bob's hands Eustace's questionable activities in Chile and South Africa became 'extensive experience in the developing world'. His hunting and shooting were transformed into 'an interest in wildlife'. Bob, truthfully, noted that Frogwell wanted to see 'reforms in the prison system', without going into unnecessary detail as to the precise direction these reforms would take. Frogwell, he rightly claimed, had never attempted to stand in the way of his wife's 'vocation' and had, in fact, allowed it to be the dominant factor in the organisation of their home life – it was not specified that this vocation was breeding dachshunds and that their presence in his household had never been allowed to inconvenience Eustace for a fraction of a second; those who fancied it meant that Eustace was content to play second fiddle to a high-flying partner had only their imaginations to blame. The honours system, Bob informed Lesley, was not overly popular in Alternative circles. Frogwell's reception into the Order of the Hogweed needed a bit of thinking about since, if the primary purpose of the piece was to flatter the man, it clearly could not be omitted. After a few minutes, inspiration struck: Eustace 'took part in ancient rites'.

There was a silence when Lesley had finished. Then, 'Well I think that about says it all,' said Eustace, attempting to conceal his delight. 'Come over as a decent sort of chap. Down to earth but open to new ideas. Sensible type, but not too much of a stick-in-the-mud.'

'Absolutely,' said Maud.

Lesley struck. 'It occurs to me, Eustace,' she said, 'that a person like yourself has wider appeal than we have given you credit for; that your interests speak to a larger spectrum of the electorate than we originally thought. Maybe we have underestimated you.' She took a sip of her sherry, allowing this to sink in.

'That could be,' said Frogwell, thoughtfully.

'In which case, shouldn't we be seeking to trawl in those who might not have thought to look in your direction?'

'Of *course* we should,' said Maud.

Lesley permitted a silence for both Frogwells to wonder how this could be brought about.

'There have been indications,' she said presently, 'that another political party in Ebbing would be interested in forming a coalition with you; in spite of this party's concerns being somewhat tangential, it does command a sufficient portion of the vote to, quite possibly, give us an overall lead. Without this party, I fear our numbers may be lacking. It would mean that you would have to have a joint candidate . . .'

'What party is it?' asked Maud.

'Labour?' questioned Eustace, darkly.

'No, indeed not Labour.' Lesley injected into her voice a note of reproach. 'They are a breakaway group, like ourselves; their candidate is a woman, named Anna Seale. They are called the Preserve The Ebbing Clifftop And Jesus Was A Black Man Party.' Lesley had vowed she would not rush over the latter part of the name, since it must be faced up to sooner or later, but, in the end, she could not prevent herself from doing so: it came out muttered.

'Jesus was a what?' exclaimed Frogwell. Both he and his wife looked deeply shocked.

'A black man,' said Lesley.

'But Lesley,' said Maud, 'Jesus was white. Like us.'

'He may have been olive-skinned,' said Lesley, bravely, remembering university debates that tested how well you could argue for things that you did not believe. 'He was a Jew.'

This did not go down at all well.

'Always thought of Him as a Christian myself,' said Frogwell.

'Even allowing that He spent a lot of time out in the sun,' said Maud, making the Deity sound like a keen gardener, 'that would only make Him a light brown man. Certainly not *black*.'

'Maybe,' said Lesley, beginning to be irritated, 'they felt that the Jesus Was A Light Brown Man Party did not have the same ring to it.'

'Nevertheless,' said Maud.

There was a pause.

'But this is a side issue,' said Lesley. 'What is important is that these people wish to preserve the clifftop and that they bring crucial votes with them. Eustace has already shown himself to have broad enough popular appeal for his party to take in any number of floating voters, without sacrificing its Conservative essence.'

Both Frogwells brightened.

'And, of course, we would discard them and their candidate after the election,' said Maud.

'Let me get this straight then Lesley,' said Eustace. 'This bunch of people – call them what you will – wants to join us because they like the cut of my jib and they want to stop the road scheme. That it? We take on whoever they want to be my joint candidate, promise them that, after the election, when the road has been knocked on its head, we'll go along with implementing their . . . whatnots – like one does. Then, once the election's won, lo and behold, no can do. Back to base camp and no hard feelings. All's fair etcetera. Like the sound of it?'

No, she did not. Lesley was silent for a moment. Then, 'I think a coalition is our only chance,' she said, coolly.

There was a pause.

'What *I* cannot understand,' said Maud, 'is why these people are so eager to help us to save our houses. You must admit, Eustace, it is perfectly sweet of them.'

It was early evening. Lesley sat on a deckchair in the garden, watching a grey cocoon of cloud gathering on the horizon. Jay's head appeared among the bushes beyond the garden wall. Lesley waved. It disappeared again. He must be doing a session guarding the lesser tit, Lesley supposed. In the aftermath of her visit to the Frogwells, this struck her as altruistic and noble – not to mention somewhat unexpected: she had not put Jay down as a birdwatcher; certainly he had said nothing to indicate that he was when Bob had been waxing lyrical about the joys of ornithology.

Bob. Yes, he struck her as altruistic too. Giving up a perfectly good Saturday to crouch in the comfortless undergrowth with only a thermos and a picnic (Lesley was not to know that this represented the crux of the birdwatching experience); willing to risk his life to protect another living thing from extinction. How egotistical the Frogwells were, in comparison. And how patronising she herself had been when she had looked out upon the birdwatchers' little demonstration and thought how they could join her party if they wanted to – as if all offshoots of political thought must draw nourishment from the same undercurrent of selfishness. Guiltily, she remembered her abortive list of arguments against the road scheme. She had run out of ideas after the first and only one: it didn't suit her.

Though the Frogwells had urged her to stay to dine, having secured Eustace's agreement, Lesley had made a swift getaway, lest he should change his mind, or say any more things that she would find distasteful. The Frogwell Mansion, where everything was warped, dilapidated, shabby or dysfunctional, oppressed her in a way Anna Seale's house – chaotic though it was – had not. The smell of Maud's gravy seemed to encapsulate all that was worst about British society at the end of a pretty horrendous century and in the death throes of a millennium that wasn't much to write home about either.

In such a state of mind Lesley was unable to face the radishes, cottage cheese and Ryvita she had earmarked for her lunch. Having escaped Maud's roast beef (which, from past experience, you could have made walking boots out of) she felt she deserved better. She ate a ham sandwich, with tomato pickle, listening to *Ship Ahoy*. Luke Barnacle was arguing the merits of the craft he had purchased, with considerably less conviction than Darryl Younger would have carried, had he been doing the same thing. A leaky ship that he maintained would float: the perfect metaphor for Darryl Younger and all he represented.

And yet she missed him. Sitting there now, watching the storm gather, she almost craved him, as if he were an addictive indulgence – profiteroles with hot chocolate sauce, fresh cotton bed linen, a wonderful novel on a velvet sofa. It would have been wrong, completely wrong. Risks at living must not be taken. Men were, at the best of times, chancy, it had proved: look at Osbert, on the surface the most dependable of mortals. Though even the pretence to be trustworthy was absent in the case of Darryl Younger.

It is scarcely original to observe that sexual attraction is difficult, if not impossible, to reason yourself out of – or into, for that matter – but emotions lack originality; the best they can do is to give the illusion of uniqueness. Lesley's psyche was rubbed as raw as if she were the first person ever to attempt to inform their sentiments (not to mention other, more corporeal components of their being) that they were not going to be permitted to rule the roost. She was angry, agitated, resentful of feeling out of control and when, as if in answer to her desire, the phone rang in the house, it made her furious to feel her heart start to thump painfully, with a gallumphing rhythm that filled her chest and made her ribs ache.

It will not be him, she told herself as she went inside to answer it; the nature of life is disappointment.

'Lesley?'

An effervescent surge of excitement at the sound of his voice was too much to tolerate.

'I don't wish to speak to you Darryl. I said so.'

'Lesley, how many times can I apologise?'

Lesley did not reply to the question. Instead, absurdly, she was overcome by a desire to make Darryl lose his temper – and his poise – in order to punish him. Though for what? His breezy, carefree existence that was not, ultimately, any of her business?

'You are a womaniser,' she said, taking herself by surprise.

'Oh not that bloody bridesmaid again. Anyway, Les, you can hardly expect fidelity in retrospect.'

'I have never expected fidelity,' said Lesley. 'Only discretion. You drink,' she continued, the compulsion which had inspired her first statement gathering crazy momentum. He would be the one to go away this time, and she wouldn't have to be strong any longer. 'Your friends take drugs,' she went on. 'So do you, I imagine.'

'Lesley, is any of this greatly important?'

'I am drawing these facts to your attention in order to under-line that we have nothing, absolutely nothing in common. You are a . . . Socialist, Anarchist, I don't know, but not a Tory. I am a Conservative. It's what I always have been . . .' It seemed to need stressing that she belonged to the world of the Frogwells, which was really not such a bad one, or so dull either. It had its own artists, such as Steven Toe, its own touches of glamour in the form of Penny St John and Trouncy Lollop. Best of all, it was completely stable. Well, actually, no it wasn't. But it was unstable in ways that she was at home with.

'Oh come on, Les, you're not a Conservative . . . We're two of a kind, good-for-nothing sensualists, greedy for whatever fun there is going. That's not such an awful thing to be, so why not admit to it? At least it fetches you up on the right side, for some reason.'

There was a pause. 'You are a terrible, disgraceful scrounger,' said Lesley. 'You even borrow money from Anna Seale who, God knows, has little enough to spare.'

The job was done. There was an appalling silence, then Darryl began to speak again, slowly. He had not lost his poise. Maybe actors never did. Outside, Lesley noted, the garden had plunged into shadow.

'Anna and I have a lot of history, I am hopeless with money . . .'

'It isn't charming, you know.' Her voice sounded pettish. Almost, even, like Primrose's.

'You're not in a very strong position, Les, championing the rights of Anna Seale.'

'As far as I'm concerned, Anna made a foolish decision,' said Lesley. 'Not that I don't regret what happened afterwards, but she didn't have to harangue me about Osbert's stance on nuclear weapons – as if I had anything to do with it.'

'Well, if you didn't have anything to do with it, Lesley, who in God's name did? Anna saw a chance to be heard and took it. She'd have felt it was the only possible course of action. Why didn't you just listen to her?'

'I have no recollection of the event, if you remember. Probably I was alarmed. You will admit the girl can be alarming.'

'You didn't have to call the filth.'

'I did not "call the filth". I asked a policeman for assistance.'

'Oh don't come the language. Look how it ended up. And, incidentally, I'd avoid getting on your high horse about my scrounging the odd bob or two off Anna, when your son-in-law's raking it in like nobody's business.'

Lesley was startled. There was a moment of silence. 'You mean political hand-outs?' she asked.

'Got it in one.'

'I assure you, I am not conscious . . .'

'Then you aren't looking very hard.'

Mechanically, Lesley replaced the receiver. Darryl must be right; he was Tim's cousin and would know all the family gossip and there was absolutely nothing about Tim Babcock to indicate a nicety of conscience that would make such an accusation unlikely to be true. She sat down, weakly. Her first thought was that, if this were made public, it could win them the election. Her second was that, certainly, there would be nothing specific that one could point to. Gifts, meals paid for, favours done, advice given: all these political treats and rewards were insubstantial, abstract even. And anyway when, in recent years, they had been so clumsily handled as to come to public notice, somehow it had not made any difference to the outcome of the elections. Which was not right, when you considered it.

But Primrose: did Primrose know?

Without being sure of what she hoped to achieve, Lesley dialled Primrose's private number.

> Here with a Loaf of Bread beneath the Bough,
> A Flask of Wine, a Book of Verse – and Thou
> Beside me singing in the Wilderness –
> And Wilderness is Paradise enow

Recited Primrose's voice, to a background of plain-chant. Lesley wondered how she had managed to produce a daughter with such scant self-knowledge. Then: 'I would so like to have talked to you that I wish I hadn't gone out. Please please please leave me your message.' Lesley was putting the phone down when it was answered by the housekeeper.

'Oh hallo Helen, it's Mrs Sway. Mrs Babcock isn't there, I take it?'

'Hallo Mrs Sway. No, she and Mr Babcock have gone to Splatters for a festival of dance and mime in the yellow garden. They're staying on for dinner with the Wanders, so they won't be back until late. But if you're not in a hurry there's someone here who wants to say hallo.'

'Sorrel was sick,' said Tansy, 'and I found a grasshopper. Mummy and Daddy are going to Bermuda, where it's always sunny. Bye bye.'

'Bye bye,' said Lesley.

She put the phone down and sat, motionless, staring into space. 'Mummy and Daddy are going to Bermuda': she had the answer to her question.

Before her eyes was a terrible vision: Primrose after Primrose, stretching to the crack of doom. Tansy grown up. Sorrel grown up. Jonquil grown up. Each with her own Tim Babcock. Each relentlessly giving birth to their own Primroses. Robin and Seth marrying Primroses and begetting yet more Primroses. Just as Primrose's supposed artist, Clover Deal, and her Bloomsbury cohorts had managed to spawn interminable offspring, who spawned more offspring, who grew up and wrote for the Sunday supplements, became interior designers, film stars, models and photographers, published books, produced television programmes, entered the Cabinet, lectured at Oxford. Oh God, England had a plague of egocentric elfin beings, who did not know how to change a car tyre or a nappy, and Lesley was implicated.

She had to get the hell out. She must, right this minute, make contact with something earthbound and practical. Above the garden the sky was boiling. The sea wore a shocked aspect.

Lesley went outside. The air was humid.

'Jay,' she called.

Jay's arms, then his face appeared above the wall. He had evidently been sleeping. He clambered to his feet.

'Hey lovely lady!'

'I'm going out, but do shelter in the house if the storm breaks. I'll leave it open.'

Jay grinned. He looked more grateful than the offer really merited.

'Got you,' he said. To Lesley's surprise, he produced from his jacket a pink mobile telephone and wandered into the undergrowth, dialling. Perhaps it was something to do with the lesser tit, a change of shift, maybe, or a kind of update on its progress.

Lesley went into the house and got her car keys and, on impulse, a bottle of the white wine from the fridge. She hurried out to the car and switched on the ignition.

She was driving too fast, but so was Susie Took, which was why the accident happened.

14

Different Territory

Mandy, Susie's old banger, had recently had a tune-up, so she was going like a bomb. Susie gave her one from time to time; the chap she'd bought Mandy off – a sort of ex-boyfriend, actually – had shown her how. There was a wonderful little short-cut that Susie used when she was in a rush, and she was in a rush now: a hard right down Oyster Alley, left into the High Street opposite Fitch's Gallery, then you wiggled around a bit and, before you knew it, you were on your way up the cliff road.

At the end of Oyster Alley Susie glanced in both directions, checked the fuchsia lipstick she'd borrowed off Mummy's dressing-table in Mandy's rear-view mirror, and accelerated into the High Street, just at the moment that Olive Ford, Ebbing's oldest resident, chose to step out into the road, on her way home from the Crab and Oyster Bar after her customary Sunday evening treat of a saucerful of jellied eels with bread and butter. Swerving to miss her (Mrs Ford's eyesight was not up to much these days) forced Susie into the opposite lane, whereupon, perceiving the car coming towards her on that side of the road was going too fast to stop in time, she made a desperate attempt to pull up on the pavement, which would have come off too, had it not been for the presence of Fitch's Gallery. Mandy came to a juddering stop, her front bumper wedged under Carmen's bay window, in which Carmen placed what she considered to be the most important sculptures, with small white cards beneath them with title and date in understated font (price on request).

By slamming her foot on the brake, Lesley managed merely to put a small dent in Mandy's rear door and to smash her own left headlight. Olive Ford, who had not noticed the event – being more occupied with considering the seagulls and her jellied eels and how the colour of the world was fading and her wireless growing quieter – assumed that Lesley was badly parked and walked around the back of her.

The High Street filled with people. Out of the Taj Mahal, with its boarded-up broken window, came the waiters. The scent of curry wafted behind them. Harry Smack came out of his Chippy. Hortense Smith emerged from the Dolphin guest house, followed by two of her guests, a sad little couple, who had been eating their high tea. The vicar appeared from round the back of St Christopher's, hoping there would be no need to do anything too Catholic.

In the distance, there was the sound of thunder.

'Lesley!' said Susie.

'Susie,' said Lesley. 'Are you all right?'

'Oh yes,' said Susie. 'Are you?'

'Yes,' said Lesley.

'No harm done then. I'll just back Mandy up.'

Anna came out of the Crab and Oyster Bar.

'Anna,' said Lesley, 'I was coming to see you.'

'Well you certainly know how to make an entrance.'

'I say,' said Susie, 'I know who you are now. It was you who called me a Tory bitch.'

'Sorry,' said Anna.

'That's all right. Nothing behind?' Susie put Mandy into reverse and shot backwards. The frontage of Fitch's Gallery collapsed. Glass shattered, wood splintered, masonry crumbled. The important sculptures toppled into the road. Quite a bit of the front part of Mandy was ripped away. Susie had been more firmly wedged beneath Carmen's bay window than she had realised.

'Oh gloom!' Susie jumped out of the car. She stood in the road, surveying the damage. Anna and Lesley came to join her. Most of the bystanders remained a distance away from the accident, presumably in order to avoid the contamination of ill fortune.

Bicycle pumps, hammered metal, bits of brick, broken mirrors, the handle of something.

'It's going to be frightfully difficult to work out which bits are art and which bits are Mandy,' said Susie.

A horrified gasp went up from those bystanders whose view was obscured.

'Mandy is the car,' explained Lesley to Anna.

Anna said nothing, she was looking at the mess on the pavement and road: Susie was right, it would be hard to tell the difference. And suddenly she realised that this should not be true of art, however Modernist.

Carmen Fitch had reassessed Steven Toe as soon as Lesley Sway had mentioned him in the same breath as Anna. Lesley had, unprompted, given the same verdict on Anna's painting as Darryl always did. Carmen Fitch did not know what she was talking about. A stage in Anna's artistic development was over.

When searching for a culprit and given among our choices a person we dislike already, it is human to assume that they are the guilty party. The blame for the accident should really have been shared three ways, though Carmen, arriving in her black car, with 'Fitch's Gallery' written on it in lettering designed to give the impression that it was one of a fleet, was not to know that: Olive Ford, who lived in a tiny house on the High Street, was now seated beside her wireless, listening to the day's last broadcast of *Ship Ahoy*. Still, that did leave two candidates for Carmen's wrath, with Susie Took the more obvious one. Maybe Carmen would have been fairer if Susie had not just had a good idea and bounded over to see if the ironmonger – who'd been awfully nice about Cherry's new bucket, saying they could have it on approval, provided Cherry didn't dent it – was in and could lend them a big broom. The idea was to sweep everything, car, art and bits of building, into a pile and then decide what was what.

'You've destroyed my Space and the most pivotal exhibits in "Anger II",' Carmen squawked at Lesley, inspecting the damage grimly.

'I am awfully sorry, but I imagine the insurance will sort things out to everyone's satisfaction,' said Lesley.

'Don't talk to me about insurance,' retorted Carmen, spitting out the word as if it were the most extreme of affectations. 'Talk to me about the silencing of women's voices.'

Anna, who was experiencing those emotions one does upon discovering that one's guru is, at best, fallible, now entered the discussion.

'For fuck's sake, Carmen, Lesley was just coming to see me, right? You make it sound like it was done on purpose.'

Susie returned. 'He's lent me a broom.' She looked at Carmen. 'I'll sweep away and anything you see that looks like a bit of a sculpture, grab it and put it on one side, then tomorrow we can glue them back together. I'm in rather a hurry now.'

There was a wave of amusement among the section of the onlookers which did not know the intellectual (and social) risks one ran in viewing art with anything other than reverence.

'That looks like a bit of sculpture to me,' yelled Harry Smack, pointing at a lamppost.

'Here's some,' shouted another working-class type, raising the front wheel of his old bicycle.

An adolescent, with a bristly, shaven head and a Union Jack t-shirt spat onto the pavement.

The lower middle-class element in the crowd, distracted by the accident from their evening strolls, or en-route to profit from the Woodcutter Inn's 'Sunday Nite Special – Kids Half Price! (under 12's only, one reduction per family)', remained silent; though Hortense Smith drew the attention of her guests to the rendition of bison hanging on their bedroom wall.

'Priceless. These pieces are priceless,' shrieked Carmen, furious.

'How many of them have you sold then, Carmen?' Anna asked loudly.

'I'll give you a bob for the bicycle pump,' suggested someone.

'For your information Anna, there's been tremendous interest from the investment market. But woman's right to self-expression transcends "monetary" value. Even the insurance company admitted that.'

'So how come the sculptures are priceless?'

'Are these people bothering you, Mrs Sway?'

Lesley turned. It was a young policeman. He was most specifically looking at Anna.

'Bothering me? No. No, of course not. There's been a small accident.'

'Nobody injured?'

'No, nobody.'

'Make sure the highway is cleared as soon as possible please.'

The man sauntered away.

'Oh good point,' said Susie, looking up the High Street in the direction of the harbour. A coach full of trippers from Bromley had come to a standstill, blocked by the cars and the debris. One of the trippers was being sick into a paper bag with 'Seaway: The Way To Travel' written on it.

In the end Harry Smack got one of his mates, who was a builder, out of the Anchor. At a price, seeing as it was a Sunday, he managed to organise a skip from his brother-in-law, who lived on the outskirts of Cove. His brother-in-law's lad shovelled the rubbish into the skip and put a couple of lamps and a few witches' hats around it.

Mandy still worked. Susie shot off in the direction of the cliff. Carmen, scorning offers of help to tidy up, disappeared into the interior of her gallery. Rain started to fall. Lesley took the bottle of wine from the back of her, now neatly parked, car and entered the Crab and Oyster Bar for the first time in over twenty-five years.

A grey-eyed woman – Meg Hughes, presumably – stood behind the counter opening oysters.

Like all places from long ago, the Bar was smaller than Lesley remembered. In fact, it was tiny. The stools were the only seating. The people queuing had to stand behind the eaters. The counter itself was about two feet wide and half the width of it was occupied with plates and bowls: silvery blue eels in clear jelly; a coral slab of smoked salmon; prawns in their shells; anchovies curled round olives; oysters. There was a plastic bag of sliced bread and a net of lemons. On the floor behind the counter was a large sack of mussels and a bucket of oysters. On shelves were bottles of orange soupe de poisson from France, jars of fish paste, tins of sardines. Outside the rain thickened. On the swimming-pool green walls the remaining light floated, luminous; the room felt as if it was in slow orbit. It smelled of brine and lemon juice and wet sacking.

The last time Lesley had been here was long before Meg Hughes owned it. She used occasionally to come and buy smoked salmon sandwiches, to eat on the beach with boys down from Oxford. That was before she met Osbert, who did not like Ebbing and whisked her off to London most weekends.

Anna appeared from the back of the shop, carrying a plate with a dozen oysters on it. She put it down in front of a wedge-shaped woman, whose fat little feet bulged over the top of her white plastic shoes, and her hunched husband, who had a cigarette stuck behind one ear.

'Almost everyone's agreed,' she said to Lesley. 'So Eustace Frogwell and me get to be candidates together. Thank Christ for the lesser tit. Thank Christ for Nanny Enema.'

'The lesser tit?'

'*Parus minor*,' said a bespectacled, middle-aged man in khaki shorts and walking-boots, who was sitting with a woman wearing an anorak and a woolly hat. 'Proliferates in this neck of the woods. We have hopes of spotting one on our walk to the Cove Youth Hostel. Which, by the by,' looking at his watch, which abounded with information, and then at his companion, 'we must be setting off for, or it'll have closed.' Then, to Anna, 'Could you put this remaining sandwich in a doggie bag?'

'*Parus minor* does not proliferate, as a matter of fact,' said Lesley, rather irritated at being informed about the lesser tit by a know-all tourist. 'Its numbers are actually severely diminished.'

'Don't you start,' said Anna, emptying the bread onto the counter and handing the man the plastic bag. 'It's bad enough having to listen to Bob about the wretched bird.'

'You bring us bad tidings,' said the man to Lesley. 'Doesn't she, Moira?'

'Yeth,' said Moira.

'People have responded positively, then, to how last night's problems were handled?' asked Lesley, as the door closed behind the couple, remembering now that Bob had predicted her actions would go down well with the birdwatchers.

'The heroine of the clifftop. The Save The Lesser Tit Group

are on for the coalition because of what you did. So are the Ecologists.'

'So everyone's agreed?'

'Mostly, yes. The other groups were harder. That blurb on Frogwell helped cut it with some of the Feminists.'

Bob had taken a copy of the profile of Frogwell with him when he had left Lesley's house in the small hours of that morning. He had a key to the primary school and sometimes went in at the weekend to prepare projects and to do photocopying, and he'd try and get it copied up and distributed that day. Lesley, unfamiliar with the energy of birdwatchers, was amazed at Bob's efficiency.

'The Feminists liked the sound of Eustace?' she asked.

'They're interested in ancient rites too, a lot of them. Is he into the tarot?'

A thin little boy in a striped t-shirt stuck his finger into one of the oysters on the plate Anna had put down.

'Is it alive?' he asked.

'Course not,' said his mother, who was wiping the face of a toddler on her lap, who was holding a dripping Mr Whippy. 'It's a vegetable.'

'Fingers out,' said the boy's father. 'Do you have any tabasco?'

The man with the wedge-shaped wife removed the cigarette from behind his ear.

'I wish you wouldn't,' said Meg Hughes.

He popped it back again.

'Two more plates of oysters,' said Meg, 'then I'm closing.'

Anna disappeared to open the oysters, leaving Lesley to ponder the problems that might result from the image that Bob had created, or allowed people to create for themselves, of Eustace Frogwell. Did they really imagine that an elderly Tory would pass his time reading tarot cards? Did they picture him, perhaps, sitting on a prayer mat in the Frogwell Mansion, chanting a mantra? Surely they had some inkling of what kinds of behaviour could be expected in Eustace's sector of society? But then it occurred to her that Primrose had been calmed, during her second pregnancy, by regular visits to an acupuncturist in Mayfair. And, of course, there was Nancy Reagan. Maybe they could put it about that Eustace was secretive about his runic activity, which would have the advantage of verisimilitude.

The people left. Meg turned the sign on the door to 'Closed'.

'I'll lock up,' said Anna. Meg left. Anna opened Lesley's bottle of wine, a Puligny-Montrachet 1989. 'Lime green,' she said. She put out a plate of oysters and another of crab sandwiches. She and Lesley sat at the counter.

'What I fail to understand,' said Lesley, 'is how Nanny Enema can have affected your people's attitude to a coalition.'

Anna explained, between mouthfuls of sandwich and swigs of wine.

Lesley listened, surprised. By a curious sleight of hand, and without any movement on her part, her status, as viewed by the Alternative community, had changed from that of oppressor to that of victim – a role which was more highly respected in the Alternative sector than by society as a whole and even, to a rather unhealthy extent, coveted.

This is what had happened: the members of the Alternative Left had read about Osbert Sway and Lesley Sway and Nanny Enema in the newspapers and, since it was their habit to bring their own interpretations to bear upon what was written there, they had come away with rather a different picture of Lesley from the one that the majority of the papers had sought to guide them towards.

Lesley Sway was a single parent, protecting her daughter from her perverted husband, noted the earth-mother Feminists and the Lesbian Separatists. Lesley Sway knew about, and tolerated, Nanny Enema, decided the career Feminists, who had met with, and deeply respected, the Prostitutes' Union, with its claim to represent the quintessence of the relationship between men and women. For the gays, Osbert Sway's romper-suit qualified as a form of cross-dressing, and the wife of that sort of MP was okay by them. Which left only the Marxists and the Legalise Marijuana And Jesus Was A Black Man group. Rolf Watt, seeing the way the wind was blowing, glumly observed that if they had been willing to be allied with Labour they might as well be allied with the Tories, for all the difference there was between them. And Jay, well Jay said something about a sausage, which no one quite understood, but which seemed to indicate that he was in.

By prior agreement, Anna and Lesley were keeping to themselves the fact that, in Susie Took, they had a mole in Tim Babcock's camp. The plan was to make use of, but not to make known, all the information they were getting.

When Anna had finished, Lesley was quiet a moment, thinking. The contrast between the Alternative Left's interpretation of events and the newspapers' interpretation and that of Frogwell and her other fellow breakaway Tories, was striking. There was no question that it was pleasing, for once, to be seen as the wronged party. Though she didn't feel greatly wronged, in point of fact, nor had she ever considered herself a single parent. Primrose was nearly an adult when she and Osbert separated and she had never experienced anything even approaching financial hardship.

Vengeful hysteric, closet feminist, betrayed widow, saviour of the lesser tit: none of these were Lesley Sway. Though what was? Hadn't the fear of having to decide that been partly what had made her destroy her relationship with Darryl Younger?

The bottle was nearly empty. Anna drank fast. There was a clap of thunder. The sound of the rain took on an urgent aspect. Lesley was assailed by an unfamiliar sense of depression. She thought of her silent, empty house, of watching another storm from an upstairs window, of thinking about Darryl and Primrose and, eventually, for want of anything else to do, going to bed early, with all the dull rituals that that entailed, as if someone else were watching. Then putting out the light, glad of having been so sensible and brave, and remembering, in the darkness that your good sense and bravery would not be rewarded. It must have been on such nights that people had come up with the idea of God.

'Are you busy?' she asked Anna. 'I mean, how about a drink somewhere?'

And Anna agreed because she did not want to go home either, because going home would, almost certainly, mean having to face Carmen.

It was hard to imagine that an intelligent life form would willingly enter the Mermaid unless, like Lesley, they had the excuse of never having been there before. The interior was a truly horrific combination of dark and garish, fairy lights and a pinball machine providing the only illumination other than that behind the bar. The floor had plastic tiles, which were covered in pools of beer. The room was thick with cigarette smoke.

'Great,' said Anna, 'there's a free table.'

It was piled with empty crisp packets. There was an overflowing ashtray. The back of Lesley's chair had something sticky on it. As she sat down there was the sound of applause from a neighbouring table. Looking round to see what had occasioned it, Lesley found herself facing a bunch of eager smiles raising halves of bitter to her.

'I spotted you arriving,' said Bob, coming up to them. 'I can't join you, I'm afraid, because we're having a strategy meeting, but I've taken the liberty of buying you a pint of the Mermaid's scrumpy, Mrs Sway.' He put a glass down in front of her, and another in front of Anna, then went to sit with the people who had clapped.

'If you care so much, tell me what you're going to do for Lois Zimble.' The speaker had orange hair and was wearing a black beret. There was a ring through her nose with a wooden bead on it. With a sinking feeling, Lesley realised that it was she who was being addressed. She took a gulp of cider.

'Leave off,' said Anna.

'No, tell me. I want to know. Tell me what you're going to do about Lois Zimble.'

'Lois Zimble doesn't live on the fucking clifftop. We're talking about Ebbing.'

'No, Lois lives in a stinking dungeon in South America, where you don't have to think about her, where you can pretend she doesn't exist. I bet you drink coffee, don't you?' the woman asked Lesley.

'Coffee? Yes, sometimes.'

'"Sometimes". And you think that's good enough?'

Lesley wondered whether, in the woman's opinion, she should be drinking more coffee or less. She also wondered how either would help Lois Zimble, whoever Lois Zimble was; Lesley was sure she had never heard Osbert mention her.

'I couldn't bring them round,' remarked Anna. 'What they

don't realise is, if we win the election, we could do a lot for them.'

Lesley said nothing. She was thinking, guiltily, about Eustace's plan to dispense with the Alternative Left as soon as possible. She also had a nasty feeling that, in view of his business dealings in Chile, Frogwell might well know about Lois Zimble. Still, it was something of a relief that the woman with orange hair would not be involved in the coalition.

'Is there a Ladies here?' she asked Anna.

'A what? Oh, the women's bog is over there.' She pointed to a distant corner, which was in almost total darkness. The tables were so closely packed together that it took Lesley almost ten minutes to reach it. Fortunately, there was only one door, though when Lesley opened it she discovered a corridor, which opened out onto a yard full of empty crates. She stepped outside. It was just spitting with rain now. There was a snuffling sort of sound, which she thought might be rats, but which proved to be a couple of people, crouched by one of the crates, discernible only because of the light from their cigarettes. As her eyes grew accustomed to the dark, Lesley made out a sink attached to one of the walls. She guessed that this was where the lavatory was.

There was no lock but there was a light. On the door were a variety of stickers: Rape Crisis Line, AIDS Helpline, Free Lois NOW and Single Mothers For A Zebra Crossing Outside The School. The tap on the sink didn't turn. The people seemed to have vanished, though it might just have been that they had put their cigarettes out. Lesley headed back in the direction she had come from. Or thought she did.

Like everywhere in the building, the room which she opened the door of was full of smoke. There was a long table, covered in ashtrays and beer mugs. Seated around it were about fifteen women. From an adjoining room came the clamour of children playing and babies crying. A toddler momentarily appeared in the doorway, its face painted to look like a rabbit or a cat; anyway, an animal with whiskers. Someone was speaking and everyone was listening.

'Here, there's room if we all squeeze over a bit,' whispered one of the women to Lesley, indicating a small space at the edge of a bench. The woman was vast, with long, pale hair, folds of ancient sweater and no bra. She wore a wrap-around skirt. 'We've decided to all bring pushchairs, those who've got them. Have you got a pushchair?'

'No,' said Lesley.

'Well, sign the paper then. We're trying to borrow the number we need from wimmin who can't come but want to express solidarity.' She whispered and gestured up the table. A sheet of paper was passed down. The woman handed it to Lesley, along with a stump of pencil.

Lesley read what was written there. She discovered that these were the Single Mothers For A Zebra Crossing Outside The School, and they were planning a demonstration, which would involve a day of constant road-crossing. Date to be decided.

Lesley looked around the table. An argument had broken out now. There was lots of shouting and raised voices. A woman stood up and gesticulated rather madly. Another woman rose also, grabbed her waving arms and said 'It's all right to be angry.' To Lesley's surprise, the first woman burst into tears. The two embraced and sat down again, the sobs still extremely audible. Nobody seemed startled or embarrassed. Lesley wondered whether this kind of thing happened often; it was not the behaviour one encountered at Tory gatherings.

The discussion continued. The main problem, apparently, was that most of the women worked in Pitsbury and, because of the bus times, couldn't drop off or pick their children up from school. Lesley considered the tired, worn faces. So different, it struck her, from those of Primrose's girlfriends who were also, mostly, working mothers. She remembered Robin's christening.

Because Robin was Tim and Primrose's first son – and, therefore, the first baby really to count – it was not at St Christopher's but in the church where Tim himself had been baptised, near Tim's parents' home on the edge of the New Forest. The christening robe was the one Tim had worn. It was made of Honiton lace. There were lots of Primrose's friends there; all, it seemed, with babies in their arms, or expecting, or both. Robin had been put down for the Dragon School and Winchester. The fates of the other boy-children present had been similarly decided. One could fancy that, in the Babcocks' divine garden, the components of the Cabinets of the early decades of the next millennium were already assembled. There had been no talk of road crossings or public transport where these babies were concerned; the idea would not have occurred: there would always be au pairs or nannies to conduct them to and from wherever.

Lesley turned to the woman next to her. 'I've got a date for the demonstration,' she said.

'We're not discussing that yet.'

'I have to go. This is it.' Lesley wrote it down on the piece of paper. 'Really, I know. June 16th is the date you want it on. Believe me.'

'Knock that one back, I've bought you another,' said Anna, when Lesley eventually returned to the table. Some music had started up. Not a group, mercifully, though this was bad enough. A woman with a red face and a short, blunt pony-tail, clad in army-surplus, had launched into an angry sort of dirge. She had a vague accent.

Anna pointed at a thin, mournful individual, sitting at a table near to the singer, at whose feet was spread out an indeterminate sort of dog. 'That's Adrian Dapple. He ran against your husband in the last election. I'll introduce him to you at the meeting. The singer's Gilda, his companion. She knew Petra Kelly.'

'He ran against Osbert?'

'Ecology. He had a breakdown when he lost but he's getting better now, thanks to Gilda and his stream-of-consciousness diary. It might help him if you read some of it.'

'Did he really expect to win?'

'He must've.'

Lesley looked at Adrian Dapple's broken features. The Left Wing did seem to take politics awfully personally. Then something Anna had said registered.

'What meeting?'

The song finished with a clash of chords. There was, what seemed to Lesley, excessive whooping and applause. The woman launched into another, identical song.

'What meeting?'

Anna looked surprised. 'Between my lot and your lot.'

'Well, I would like to be there, and I'm sure Mr Dapple would too, but it should really just be between you and Eustace, since he's the other candidate.'

'So how come he's not done any negotiating? How come he's not sitting here?'

Lesley tried to imagine Eustace Frogwell sitting in the Mermaid with a pint of scrumpy and failed.

'No, everyone'll have to be involved,' Anna continued. 'I was wondering if here would be a good place to have it.'

'Everyone? Here? No, absolutely not.' Lesley felt near to panic. Anna seemed to envisage an encounter between the entire membership of both groups, something Lesley had never, for one moment, anticipated. She remembered the shouting and, worse, the weeping she had just witnessed among the Single Mothers. Suppose people decided to experience their anger around the Frogwells, around Penny St John and Steven Toe, around Trouncy and Desmond Lollop? And they did seem so very angry too. This terrible song that was being droned out was about a child being shot and its mother raped by soldiers. Lesley did not believe in being unrealistic, but there was something to be said for looking on the bright side.

'Why not here?' asked Anna.

Lesley thought fast and, as was her habit, came up with the truth. 'It's not neutral territory. But really, Anna, does there have to be a meeting?'

'They won't go for it otherwise.'

'I thought they had already gone for it.'

'Yes, but everyone must have a say in how the campaign's conducted.'

'Can't there just be talk about it among a small group of chosen individuals and then tasks allocated?'

Anna looked Lesley up and down. 'Not if you want a coalition.'

The song finished. Again there was enthusiastic applause.

'I was thinking about battered women the other night,' said Gilda, 'and this is what I wrote.'

There was a wave of anticipatory clapping from a distant table, accompanied by clenched fists and loud whistles.

'Who are those men?' asked Lesley.

'They're not men,' said Anna. There was a silence. Then, 'You're right about neutral territory,' she said.

Lesley tore her face away. Her eyes met Anna's. Clearly, there was no choice about this meeting. 'What do you think of the Methodists' Hall?' she asked. Perhaps a proximity to religion might tone things down a bit.

'Labour's using it.'

'The Jolly Roger?'

Anna raised her eyebrows.

'No, perhaps not,' said Lesley hastily.

'Babcock's lot've got the Woodcutter,' said Anna. 'Though we could never have afforded it anyway.'

'St Christopher's Hall?' asked Lesley, making another play for religion.

'St Christopher's is where your old man had his funeral.'

'Where did they put the people on the night of the terrible storm?' asked Lesley.

'The Anchor, I think, but we can't go there. There's the Labour building, since Labour aren't using it. It's been condemned but it's still just about standing.'

'Eustace and Maud Frogwell would not countenance the Labour building. What about the primary school?'

'The Single Mothers For A Zebra Crossing would disrupt the meeting.'

'Aren't they part of the coalition?'

'No, and they'd feel we were usurping their campaign.' There was a silence. 'When you get down to it, nowhere is neutral,' said Anna.

15

The Storm

Storms had nudged Ebbing throughout the evening but now one mighty one passed right overhead. It doused the manicured gardens of Ebbing's lower-middle classes. It hammered on the windows of their centrally lit lounges, where they leafed through copies of the *Daily Express*. Damp socks were lain out on the fireguard at the Cove Youth Hostel and walkers sipped cocoa sitting beside the flames. Adrian Dapple and Gilda dried Carrot with her special towel then went round putting saucepans in strategic places. Trouncy Lollop, in her thirties villa, on her long, thirties sofa, necked with the son of a friend of hers before a long, rectangular window where lightning flashed whitely. Carmen Fitch smoked, drank the dregs of a bottle of red wine full of sediment, and read Beatrix Campbell.

In William Flint's flat there was an army of bouncing shadows. It was a trick of the light; there were only fifteen or so assembled there. Flint was reading from a sheet that trembled in his hand.

'Sooth Africa,' he said, 'Chile.' The half-grin twitched and the wrinkles on his forehead bulged. Her Majesty, depicted from the shoulders up – a glittering chandelier, with an expression on her face as if something were biting her foot – seemed to undulate inside her frame, as though painted on water. Flint gnawed on a finger nail. A man with one eye made notes with a blunt HB.

'At least I have one eye,' his look implied; 'some people have less than that.' The glass eye rolled in its socket, the kinder and more humane of the two. Easier to gloat over the eyeless than to envy those with the full set.

'It's her car all right,' said the adolescent in the Union Jack t-shirt, who was sitting on the window-sill, looking out through the net curtain at Jay's house, the colours of which were a kind of insult. 'Saw it smashed in the High Street. It's the same car. House door's not locked again.'

Flint lowered the sheet and came to join him. People paused among their lists and plans, the coughed-out English of their arguments.

'The same one. Yes,' he said. 'Pretty lady like that you'd have thought would have no problem finding someone suitable.'

'Fat though,' said a cadaverous woman, with grey rings around her eyes, chewing on a Milky Bar.

'All the same,' said William Flint. 'All the same.'

Anna, who had refused a lift in the taxi, for the pleasure of walking home through thick black ropes of rain, watching the strip-lights of lightning illuminate the reeling waves and, soon, sinking into a hot bath with loads of bubbles and a large slug of whisky, yelled good night to Jay as he disappeared into his house.

Nothing had been decided about a location for the meeting, but Anna was used to nothing being decided. A crash of thunder shook the sky. Someone was chucking furniture around. She looked up. They had broken a window and between the clouds was a jagged bit of sky with one white, misty star. Strong stuff, that scrumpy. Anna's clothes were soaked, rain streamed from her hair. Scrumpy tasted of twigs full of sap. Lesley Sway had a better head for the booze than you would expect from a Tory, which was a criterion by which Anna Seale chose to judge people, hating, as she did, prudence and caution. She had never truly liked anyone who didn't enjoy drinking, except for Miles Starey, who, when she knew him, joylessly drank pints of bitter in order, she saw now, to be one of the people. Had the people elected tomato ketchup or meths, Miles would doubtless have drunk them instead. Probably now he drank wine.

All that happened with Lesley was that her voice gained precision, which was the way with alcohol. You gained precision or you lost it. What had they talked about? It was hard to remember. Only that Anna had become aware of a quick, sharp, rather dry intelligence. Which was a surprise. Like discovering you are being watched from an upper window.

Shocking, or attempting to shock, Lesley had lost its appeal. Probably it was possible (though Anna, whose definition of normality was generously cut, did not realise quite how possible) but Lesley made such things appear schoolgirl, silly, caused Anna to strive for her own brand of dignity – which did not exclude drinking, smoking, swearing, laughing loudly, chucking things at walls, bawling out those who looked for it, or reddening the cheeks of priggish, virginal public school sixth-formers, but did exclude pettiness and malice.

Lesley Sway was the kind of person who did not mind crossing a muddy field but saw no reason to do so without wellingtons and Anna, who would have chosen bare feet, could respect that.

Harbour Street glittered where rain shattered the reflections on the puddles. The rain roared around her. An umbrella with four legs hurried past. Two doors from Anna's home, for the first time in years, the lights were on in the boat-builder's workshop, where no boats had been built for at least three decades and where, on and off, throughout the late eighties, a 'For Sale' sign had hung, in the hope that it would be spotted by someone who possessed the imagination to see the workshop's possibilities and the affluence to realise them. Steven Toe's eventual acquisition of the workshop came too late for its elderly owner to gain much from the deal (when age and weather fought over bricks and mortar in Ebbing, weather always won). Though the builder (whose brother-in-law had provided the skip after the accident) had been greatly enriched, the town itself could only profit from such architectural metamorphoses.

Anna stood, invisible, at the enormous picture window which did indeed face North and would have provided lashings of light had the town not come between it and the sky. Still, it allowed Penny and Toe to see out and, of course, passers-by to see in. Everything was bare, functional and covered with grey clay dust.

On one wall was a large rendition of an artichoke in charcoal, exact but uninspired. Toe, in smock, jeans and Indian sandals was chipping away at a piece of bluish marble. From the stone was emerging a woman.

Let it never be forgotten that great artists can be very silly people; and, even more interestingly, vice versa.

Anna felt the scrumpy, warm in her stomach. She blinked away a hot tear. Lesley Sway believed Anna's paintings to be every bit as good as Toe's sculpture.

When Anna reached home she went through drawers and scattered papers, emptied the waste paper basket onto the floor, pulled catalogues off the shelves. She made a list of London art galleries.

'Cheeky chops,' said Harry Smack. The Anchor had exhausted the topic of the accident perhaps ten minutes before last orders. The curtains were tight shut. The rain and thunder had to slug it out with laughter and no one in the pub saw the lightning. Harry was tickling an effigy of Miles Starey, Labour, under the chin, for Starey had recently come into blossom around Ebbing – though strictly no fly-posting. Starey endeavoured to look relaxed yet alert, serious but easy-going, concerned though confident: all things to all men (and women).

'I,' said Hortense Smith who, pinkened by sherry, looked like a peg doll, 'would personally prefer a man who,' she paused, considering, 'a man who you felt would give you good directions were you to get lost in the one-way system of a sizeable town.'

People looked at Miles. Most of them came to the conclusion that he was not such a man.

'Someone as'll leave cliffs alone,' said a waiter from the Woodcutter, 'and think about the issues from our situation.' He was bushed after the Sunday-night rush.

'Those being?' asked Miss Smith tipsily.

The waiter waved a hopeless hand, thrown off balance by the question. 'Jack?' he said, as if Jack Fryer had been awaiting his turn.

'Yes, come on Jack. What say you? How are you going to win our vote?' asked Harry Smack.

'I'll put my face all round the town,' said Jack, 'and you can vote for my smile.'

'Evading the question,' said Harry.

'Babcock's teeth are shinier,' shouted someone.

'Come on Jack.'

'I'll brush them more often.'

'I have had no answer to my question,' said Hortense Smith. 'No answer at all.'

'Well, issues,' said Harry Smack, 'if you want issues there's defence, health, the economy, inflation, taxation, immigration, education.'

'Ebbing station, Pitsbury station, bus station, social station,' said the waiter, swaying a little. 'Multiplication. Multiplication of complexity until we don't know what the bugger they're on about, which is when they get you to vote for them. Wrong way round the one-way system.'

'One more last orders. Last last orders,' said the bloke behind the bar, 'then I'm chucking you out into the wind and rain.'

'Mine's a pint,' said Harry Smack. 'Any way you look at it, it's too much to handle.'

There was a silence. Then, unexpectedly, 'Call it right and wrong,' said Jack Fryer, taking a swig of his bitter, his kind, comely face suddenly serious. 'Makes it easier.'

He had seen the massed shadows in William Flint's flat and he could guess that no good would come of them. He had taken stock of the silence from Lesley Sway about the suggestion he had made that she look at the cliff properly, that she consider it carefully. He had been too abstract, was his conclusion. What he needed was solid facts, supported evidence. When he had them, he would present them to Anna Seale this time. As straightforward as two plus two equalling four. As concrete as right and wrong.

Though they voted for him anyway, the taxi-drivers of Ebbing loathed Osbert Sway, who did not tip. One who did not know the habits of taxi-drivers could have thought that the discourse they subjected him to, as they ferried him about, was their form of revenge but Lesley, who did tip, got exactly the same treatment. By the time the cab reached her house the driver was on to Jamaicans and Pakistanis. Lesley was relieved when the car pulled away. She vowed never to drink scrumpy again or anything else, for that matter, that would leave her unable to drive home.

The night was savage. The landscape was all movement. Lesley paused on the doorstep. The desperate arms of branches, their tips madly clawing at the heavens. A phalanx of stomping trees. Lesley's heart started to beat wildly. She was quite alone and it was not the weather. Someone was out there. She did the thing of fumbling to get her key in the key hole, stepped into the calm, dry building and slammed the door behind her in the face of the night and whatever it was hiding.

Her heart slowed but then quickened again as a sound came from upstairs. A light went on in the spare bedroom. As she waited to see who was up there, Lesley felt as if her whole being might just switch itself off, the way the picture on the television contracted into a thin line and vanished when she was a child. A yawning figure appeared at the top of the stairs.

'Susie!' Her pulse decelerated. The presence was Susie. Lesley had known, somehow, that her house was not empty and imposed that knowledge on the landscape.

Susie was smoothing down her jumper. When she reached the bottom of the stairs, Lesley noticed that she smelled of some unaccustomedly exotic perfume; usually she borrowed Winifred's Blue Grass.

'I fell asleep,' said Susie, vaguely.

'But what were you doing here in the first place Susie? And,' its absence suddenly occurring to Lesley, 'where's your car?'

'Oh,' said Susie, 'I lent her to someone. But it doesn't matter. I'll walk home. It's a lovely night.'

'A lovely night? Susie, it's pouring.'

'Oh, is it?' said Susie. 'Well, I suppose I mean rain can be lovely, can't it?'

'Of course it can,' said Lesley. 'That is not in dispute. But Susie, if you walked, there would be a danger of your being blown off the cliff.'

'I don't think there would,' said Susie, seeming suddenly a little more wakeful.

The phone rang. Lesley's wretched heart started up like a tom-tom again but, when she answered, it was Winifred.

'Lesley dear,' said Winifred. 'You may remember Warren and Virginia Payne? They dined here this evening, with Annabel and Victor. Annabel is to be married in the autumn and wanted my thoughts on ivory sateen. Victor has grown into a delightful lawyer with a house in Wimbledon. We had hoped for the Babcocks, but they were unable to attend.' She made Tim and Primrose sound like a particularly delicious confection. 'But where is Susie? Perhaps you can tell me?'

'Susie?' said Lesley. 'Well . . .' But Susie was shaking her head emphatically.

There was an almighty crash of thunder and a hissing bolt of lightning, the wind tore across the clifftop, scattering dead wood from old trees, bringing down the wires maybe.

Another taxi was ordered and drove Susie home.

The storm rumbled off in the direction of France.

Lesley went to bed, where she lay awake for a long time, thinking about Winifred. It appeared that Lesley had now graduated to the last stage of the British social cut: the pretence that nothing offensive has happened. Hereafter she would be treated with utter civility (there might even be conversations, where they were unavoidable); there would be acidic smiles, kisses perhaps. In that brief call, with its text and sub-text, Winifred had offered the standard modus operandi, much as one might give a tea-towel with woodland creatures on it to the neighbour who has fed your cat during your absence. And it would have been a good way of proceeding really, since it was likely that they must meet at regular intervals now, and into the future.

Except, of course, in covering for Susie, Lesley had taken on a level of involvement which such an arrangement would not permit. The result being that, if Winifred were to discover that Lesley's house was, curiously, the only one in Ebbing to lose its telephone line during the storm (and then to consider that telephones are no more likely to get cut off during awkward conversations than important letters are to get lost in the post) and if Susie was doing something of which Winifred would not approve, then Lesley, having flouted her social reprieve, might expect the consequences to herself to be concomitant with how serious a crime such defiance was considered to be.

As Lesley fell into a deep slumber, she was consoled by the thought that, fortunately, there was a limit to what kind of retribution Winifred would be able to inflict. Nothing anyone could say about Osbert had power to wound and there were no skeletons in Lesley's own closet.

She was awoken at eight-thirty by the ringing of the telephone. She grabbed the receiver, dropped it, caught it.

'Yes?'

It was only Eustace Frogwell, who seemed to class being in bed after seven in much the same category as manslaughter.

'Caught you napping?' he asked.

'What can I do for you, Eustace?'

'Wanted to know what happens next.'

In spite of her drowsy state, it occurred to Lesley that, since he was one of the candidates, this was really more for Eustace to decide. She took herself in hand, stifled a yawn and attempted to sound efficient.

'I'm afraid they want a meeting, Eustace.'

'Afraid?' Eustace laughed at the concept of fear. 'Well, probably should meet my running-mate, I suppose. Send the chappie round then.'

'It's a woman, if you remember, Eustace. Her name is Anna Seale, but it wouldn't just be her. It would be everyone. That is to say, all the supporters of both groups who wished to attend.'

There was a silence while Eustace took in the information, during which Lesley pulled herself into a sitting position and drank some stale water from a glass on her bedside table.

Then 'Splendid,' Eustace said. 'Tea here tomorrow afternoon. I'll get the girls into their pinnies and muster up some Victoria sponge sandwiches.' And he rang off before Lesley could object.

Slowly, she got out of bed, stretched and went to the window and drew back the curtains. The storm had scrubbed the sky to a raw, tender blue. A brisk wind was blowing and there were lively little waves, with foamy tips. A small yellow boat was rearing and bucking its way towards the horizon. Lesley's eyes watered in the light.

She stood there, thinking.

The Frogwell Mansion could scarcely be considered neutral territory, but it did have the advantage of being dilapidated and odd. It did not reek of privilege, like Primrose's chapel or, she had to admit, her own house; or rather, it did, but perhaps not in a way that you would spot unless you were very au fait with the habits of the gentry. Maybe the Alternative Left would think that the Frogwells were poor old people fallen on hard times, rather than positively rolling in money and choosing to indulge in a particularly subtle affectation.

Lesley made a decision and dialled Anna's number. It rang for a long time before Anna lifted the receiver.

'What the fuck is it?' was the first thing she said.

'Anna, it's Lesley. Did I wake you?'

'Of course you bloody woke me. I've had two hours' sleep. And I've got a fucking awful hangover.' There was the sound of a roll-up being lit. 'What do you want anyway?'

Lesley was not discouraged. On the contrary: strangely, what Anna had just said seemed to indicate a certain degree of friendship. She explained about Eustace's offer.

'It'll help that he's a mystic,' said Anna.

'What?'

'Frogwell: a mystic.'

'So you think people will agree?'

'It'll probably be okay. Remind him we'll need a crêche.'

There was a pause.

'Can't the children go to baby-sitters?' asked Lesley. Anna did not reply. 'Oh,' said Lesley, 'they are rather expensive, I suppose. Well I'll see what I can do but . . .'

'Fuck off Lesley,' said Anna. She put the phone down.

Lesley re-dialled the Frogwell Mansion. Tentatively, she explained the gist of the situation to Eustace, omitting the parts he might not understand.

Eustace's reaction was a surprise: 'Problem solved, Lesley. Leave it to me.'

'There will be quite a number of children, Eustace.'

'No problem, I tell you. I'll get on the blower to Nanny.'

'Nanny?' For a brief moment Lesley saw the picture of the woman in the newspaper, who had so intimately known her husband. Then realisation dawned and horror struck. 'Nanny Scot, you mean? Oh no! That is to say, isn't she a bit old now?'

'Nonsense,' cried Eustace heartily. 'She's just back from a trip to the Andes. Sent a postcard with some kind of humped thingummy on it.'

'A llama.'

'Could well be.'

'Then maybe she's tired after her holiday.'

But Lesley knew she was clutching at straws. Nanny Scot was never tired.

16

Musical Chairs

Nanny Scot had ministered to Eustace and, later, to his daughter and to various other members of the Frogwell family. In spite of offers, Lesley had always managed to decline her services for Primrose. She had come to her profession at a time when the sole indispensable qualification was a deep and utter loathing of children and, though ninety-three now and retired, there seemed to Lesley, who somehow found herself with the task of picking Nanny up from the train from Broadstairs, little evidence that she had mellowed. Nanny resided in a home for old nannies, where, Lesley gathered, she and the other residents passed their time vying over the excellence of their former charges, rejoicing in the triumph of The Nanny over the dark days of the sixties and the au pair, and striving to outlive each other. When a nanny succumbed to death those that remained feasted on ginger nuts.

Arriving at the Frogwell Mansion, Nanny Scot consented to a cup of tea, then installed herself in what was still referred to as 'the nursery', that square, musty room near to the top of the building, with the bars on the window, where Eustace and Maud's daughter had sat, year in, year out, watching the sea and dreaming of London, even before she was quite sure what London implied.

Lesley descended to the cabbagey depths of the Frogwell

Mansion kitchen in a kind of despair. Should she have mentioned face-painting and juggling workshops, peace songs, clay-modelling and the construction of giant friezes of whales and dolphins which, it transpired, according to Anna, a crèche implied? Nanny had brought no plasticine, no crayons, certainly no face-paints; only a shiny suitcase from which she had removed her black uniform and two books, one entitled *Moral Tales And Verse For Good Children*, the other, *Fairy Stories*. The majority of even Tim and Primrose's children's books now depicted a world in which Mummys went out to work and Daddies arranged flowers in vases and where almost every person in any position of responsibility was Asian or Jamaican. How much more so must this be the case in the stories that were told to the children of the Left?

In the kitchen, Susie Took was making butterfly buns and listening to Veronica Tarrant, looking so much like her normal self that Lesley decided against questioning her as to what, if anything, had been going on the other night. Lolling in the chair next to Susie's was Jay; he was licking a nutmeg.

Though the meeting was not due to begin until some time after five, people had been drifting in throughout the afternoon in a vague and rather troublesome manner, which accounted for the presence of Maud's dog, Rummy, in the larder. Adrian Dapple and his girlfriend, Gilda, had arrived with Anna soon after lunch, whereupon Rummy had immediately leapt onto Adrian's bitch, Carrot. Adrian had tried to separate them and been bitten by Rummy, leaving it to Maud to deal with things by emptying a bucket of water over the two dogs. To be on the safe side, Eustace had taken Adrian off to Pitsbury General for an anti-tetanus and a stitch. They were expected back at any moment

'The bitch must have stood for Rummy. It wouldn't have happened otherwise,' Maud remarked as the car disappeared in the direction of the hospital. Though she would have been the first to deem a union undesirable, she found it rather presumptuous of Carrot to be of the same opinion.

It was Gilda who had shut Rummy in the larder. She was engaged in making her own bean concoction, evoking dark glances from Veronica. Anna was in the sitting-room, sharing the bottle of tequila she had brought with Trouncy Lollop, who arrived soon after all the upset, wearing something tight and short and shocking pink and carrying a treacle tart.

As Susie iced and scattered hundreds and thousands, Veronica was explaining her unexpected defection from the Babcock camp. Basically, it had come to her attention that the big media event that was being organised by Tim and Primrose was going to take place at the Woodcutter Inn and not, as would have been so much more appropriate, considering Veronica's loyalty to the cause, at the Jolly Roger. As a result of Veronica's presence, Bianca Pickle was in the dining-room laying the table, helped by Steven Toe. Penny St John wasn't expected until later.

'Glad to see you girls at work,' said Eustace, entering the kitchen now, followed by Adrian Dapple and Carrot.

'We are not girls. We are women,' said Gilda.

'Nonsense!' said Eustace, thinking that Gilda was deflecting a compliment. 'Girls every last one of you.'

'And we can presume you are a boy?'

Eustace blushed with pleasure.

Adrian sank into a chair, looking rather white.

'By the by Dapple,' said Eustace, 'since we're in the frontline together, in all the kerfuffle haven't inquired what you do.'

'Do?' asked Adrian, mystified.

'Mr Dapple,' said Lesley, hastily. 'Would you like some tea?'

'Yes, what you do,' said Eustace.

'I read books and I work on my diary,' said Adrian. 'I take Carrot for walks. I consider whether I should become a fruitarian. Sometimes I just think.'

'Think?' bellowed Eustace, astounded. Clearly this was not the kind of activity he expected of a sensible person.

'In fact, Mrs Sway,' said Adrian, turning to Lesley, 'the reason I came early was because I wanted to read you a little of my diary. It might help us both to come to terms with what happened.'

'With what happened?' asked Lesley, puzzled, assuming he meant something to do with the dogs.

'With the fact that your husband won the election and I lost it. I'll begin where I first consider suicide.'

Though Osbert Sway liked, as such people do, to quote from Kipling at school prize-givings about treating triumph and disaster 'just the same', there was little doubt in Lesley's mind that, had political triumph – or at least mild success – not been as forthcoming as it was, he would have been less sanguine about disaster than he liked to think, notwithstanding the fact that his two directorships would still have provided him with useful occupation. Nevertheless, it was impossible to imagine Osbert Sway ever keeping a stream-of-consciousness diary in order to make sense of his suffering or, indeed, of suffering to this morbid extent.

Dapple was on to the joy and beauty of the world and how he would miss it and Veronica was casting her eyes to heaven and Eustace was shuffling about when Lesley, feeling that things had gone far enough and that plain-speaking was called for, interrupted. Only Susie Took, whose eyes were filled with tears, and Gilda, who looked as if she was considering putting the whole thing to music, and Jay, who found one thing pretty much as interesting as another, were disappointed that she had.

'Mr Dapple,' said Lesley briskly. Adrian looked up, dolefully. 'I do not wish, in any way, to add to your distress but, to the best of my knowledge, my husband was unaware of your existence. Why not put the past behind you and deal with the matter in hand?' Sensible words indeed and not bad as a political axiom.

Adrian Dapple burst into tears.

'Gracious!' said Nanny Scot, entering at that moment, 'A big boy like you snivelling.'

'Oh gloom!' cried Susie Took.

'Pull yourself together, old chap,' said Eustace, 'don't want people to think you're one of those nancies.'

'We don't call them that any longer,' said Anna, who had come into the kitchen just in time to hear him. 'And you'd better get that right because there's eight of them arriving any minute and if you offend them they'll fuck off.'

'Nancies? Here?' thundered Eustace.

Why oh why had Anna had to say that? Lesley had been reckoning on Eustace not noticing. Though, if he was likely to give offence anyway, the subject probably did need addressing. She handed Dapple a piece of kitchen roll.

There was a waft of musk and honey, strong enough, for a

moment, to drown out the smell of cabbage. Trouncy Lollop weaved, unsteadily, down the kitchen steps, in bare feet.

'Do you have a lime?' she questioned, with a radiant smile, looking around a little blearily. Her eyes fell upon Nanny Scot. 'So,' she breathed, 'you are the Nanny.'

'I think you might be getting confused, Trouncy,' said Lesley quickly.

Trouncy ignored her. 'Tell me,' she asked: 'How did you enter the profession?'

'I answered an advertisement in a magazine,' said Nanny.

'Under "S & M?"'

'Under "Positions Vacant".'

'And when,' Trouncy continued, fascinated, 'did you get into enemas?'

From the hall above came the sound of barking dachshunds. Car doors slammed. 'People are arriving,' cried Maud.

'When naughty little boys and girls would not eat their vegetables,' said Nanny Scot.

The billiard table had been moved out of the smoking-room and Maud, Toe and Bianca – though it was not her job – had filled the room with seating of every possible variety: three-legged milking-stools; eighteenth-century chaise longues; delicate Regency dining-chairs; monstrous, upholstered Victorian sofas and a number of scatter-cushions that had belonged to Maud and Eustace's daughter. The effect was somewhat macabre and, according to several of Carmen's artists (including those to whom Carmen had yet to break the news of the fate of their sculptures), quite obviously designed to make some kind of point. For others, it served to underline Frogwell's shamanistic credentials. Which was just as well for, at the thought of his house being overrun by homosexuals, Eustace had climbed the staircase to greet his guests with the full intention of calling the whole thing off. He was immediately questioned, however, by a tall woman in clogs and a patchwork skirt, who wanted to know all about the ancient rites he took part in. Having ascertained that she was referring to the Order of the Hogweed, Eustace launched into a description of what membership entailed, which evoked no little flattering interest: particular costumes, laden with symbolism; talismanic medals; attendance at feasts; ritualistic incantations. Lesley need not have worried that the truth about Eustace's activities in this respect would be disappointing. By the time he had finished answering questions, he was fairly resigned to the presence of the slim young men in coloured dungarees, though he didn't like it when they put their arms round each other or looked in the sandwiches.

Nanny Scot drove the children upstairs to the nursery, where, at her command, a separate tea had been laid. Upon entering the room, she was horrified to witness children as old as five embarking instantly on the food without waiting for her permission.

'I think,' she remarked, in tones so glacial as to evoke instant silence, 'that somebody has forgotten to invite Mr Manners.'

When permission was eventually given to commence the meal, Nanny was surprised to discover that, although the Marmite and tomato and cheese sandwiches were being eaten, except by the few Tory infants, the corned beef, sardine and meat paste ones were being left, along with the chipolatas. This threw her only momentarily though. Battle-hardened on behalf of The Vegetable, it required little effort on Nanny's part to switch her allegiance to Meat. That day, most of the children had their first-ever sausage. Some were corrupted for life.

'When do you think we should begin the meeting?' Lesley asked Anna. Accustomed to the dainty pecking at food that went on at Tory gatherings, she was amazed by the speed with which almost everything had been devoured. The Alternative Left stoked up whenever free food was on offer.

'Let people get to know each other first,' Anna replied. Which was precisely what Lesley hoped to avoid.

Fortunately, however, Maud was clapping her hands. 'Time for the meeting. We're about to begin.' Eustace was shouting 'Into the smoking room,' and those who were not already in there were trooping in that direction.

'You sit here, my dear,' said Eustace to Anna, when she and Lesley entered, indicating the chair next to him, and placing himself at the very centre of the table at the head of the room. 'And you on my other side, Lesley.' Anna looked at Eustace as if she were considering whether or not to punch him in the face. Lesley, realising that this was something she should have foreseen, said 'Eustace . . .' But Eustace had picked up a large bell.

'The meeting will come to order,' he roared.

'Order! Order!' echoed Maud, who had evidently heard it done on television.

At first there were gales of laughter from the Alternative Left who, used to street theatre, thought it was a pastiche. Then, on being shushed by the Tories, realisation struck that Eustace and Maud were serious. Silence fell.

'Good,' said Eustace. 'Shall we begin?'

Mary Janet leapt to her feet, her cheeks pink with rage, her forehead shiny, her hair in a knot so tight as to pull at her eyebrows. She was in the middle of a group of women, some of whom Lesley remembered from the Mermaid. She could hardly bear to imagine what was about to happen.

'The Chair recognises you, Madam,' said Eustace.

There was a gasp of horror. Lesley closed her eyes.

'I would like to know who you are,' said Mary Janet.

Now it was the turn of the Tories to be indignant.

'He is Eustace Frogwell, young lady,' boomed a retired colonel. 'And you are a guest in his mansion.'

'I am candidate,' said Eustace, dumbfounded.

'A candidate,' squawked Carmen Fitch. 'You are one of two joint candidates: you and Anna Seale. Which doesn't necessarily mean that you facilitate.'

There was a round of applause from the Left Wingers. The Right was mystified.

'Facilitate what?' inquired Rory and Penny St John's grandmother. 'What is so difficult?'

'Lord knows,' said Penny, who had only just arrived and was miffed at not being able to sit and swap comments with Steven Toe, who was right over the other side of the room, between Rory and a waitress.

Lesley leapt to her feet. 'May I suggest,' she said quickly, 'that the meeting should be chaired . . . er . . . or, if you prefer, facilitated by a . . . um . . . a minority?' She gave a desperate glance at Anna who, evidently deciding to co-operate, stood up and said 'I nominate Jay.'

'Can I nominate myself, as a white, male heterosexual?' asked a snide young stockbroker, who owned a converted barn in the Ebb Valley. This witticism went down better with one sector of the assembly than the other.

Jay proved a clever choice on Anna's part, since he was quite happy to say little but was, indisputably, in a minority. He was not female, of course, but one couldn't have everything. Barely had he been instated in Frogwell's chair at the centre of the room, however, when Frogwell rose and said, with solemn reverence, 'Shall we now commence with The Lord's Prayer?'

Oh Eustace! Lesley could scarcely credit his stupidity. An uproar broke out again.

'Neither God nor master,' yelled the Marxists.

'I will not,' cried Dr Rosalind Farrow, 'endorse a patriarchal religion in which I do not believe.'

'But we none of us *believe* in it, my dear,' said Maud Frogwell, with a puzzled smile. 'It is merely something we *do*.'

Adrian Dapple rose to his feet, still paler than his small bandage, but somewhat revived by a hummus sandwich that Gilda had made for him.

'Usually,' he said, 'we play a game.'

'Cricket?' asked the colonel.

'A game!' exclaimed the birdwatchers.

'A game sounds lovely,' said Trouncy Lollop, directing her gaze at Rolf Watt, who was seated beside her in army surplus. It takes a lot to charm a Marxist, but Trouncy was equal to the task.

'We cannot replace religion with a game,' said Frogwell.

Rolf stood up. 'A game or we're out of here.'

'Musical chairs,' said Anna.

There was a vote and the game was passed by a narrow margin, a number of the Tories, notably Steven Toe and Trouncy Lollop, but also some of the lower middle-classes, who were good at Scrabble and saw this as a chance to come into their own, voting against their whip. This was followed by a few minutes' uncertainty when it was realised that there was no music. For a while it looked as if Gilda might have to do an unaccompanied solo, but then Maud discovered in her daughter's room an old ghetto-blaster and a demo-tape by Eat Shit And Die.

Anna explained the rules. Most of the Tories didn't listen

because they thought they knew how musical chairs should be played. This was a different musical chairs from the one they knew, however. All the pieces of furniture were pushed together as usual and the music was played. When it stopped, nobody's feet must be on the floor and – herein lay the difference – it was the job of everybody to make sure that this was the case. As more and more of the furniture was taken away this became harder, people had to hold onto one another more tightly, those who looked like they were going to fall off had to be clung to.

Maud started up the tape and her daughter howled her frustrations through the Mansion, as once she had done in person. When she switched the music off the game had to be stopped, re-explained and started again: because of their failure to pay attention to Anna, many of the Tories completely ruined the spirit of the thing by scrambling for a place for themselves and pushing others off.

The game recommenced. Gradually, the amount of furniture grew smaller. When the music stopped Steven Toe clamped an arm around Bianca's waist. The old colonel helped Carrot to balance on a settee. Jay clutched Susie. Eustace Frogwell found himself supported on one side by a man with three earrings and, on the other, by Ruth Ellis. Dr Rosalind Farrow and Meg Hughes gripped Veronica Tarrant by the strings of her apron. Bob and some of the birdwatchers caught an architect who was about to fall. Trouncy Lollop could only keep from tumbling off her perch by clamping her thighs against those of Rolf Watt. Gilda and several of Carmen's artists held on to Adrian. Penny and Rory St John gripped their grandmother's elderly shoulders.

'Here Lesley,' called Anna. Lesley was on a narrow stool which was threatening to topple. She reached out a strong hand, covered in cuts from oyster shells. Lesley grasped it.

Chips of stars glittered in the oblong of sky contained in Trouncy Lollop's bedroom window.

'But why a demonstration?' asked Trouncy. 'Couldn't,' she waved a varnished finger, ' . . . someone just,' she shrugged, 'write letters or something?' She took a sip of her strawberry daiquiri.

'Yeah,' replied Rolf Watt, drawing on his joint. He blew out slowly. 'That would get them running. I mean, why didn't the peasants just write to the Tsar of Russia? Or maybe they could have sent a postcard to Louis to tell him how they felt about the Bastille.' He paused and looked down at Trouncy's gorgeous face. 'Have you ever tried a shotgun?' he asked.

'Guns as well?' Trouncy shook her head.

'No. Watch.' Rolf reversed the joint so that the burning end was in the hollow of his mouth. He bent over Trouncy's lips. She opened them to receive the joint. He blew out.

'Delicious,' said Trouncy. 'I'm all in favour of non-violence.'

'Non-violence!' said Rolf. 'You know what that means? I've been to non-violent demonstrations before. It means that, on June 16th, while Babcock parades his road-scheme in the Woodcutter Inn and does his big media show, the police will be beating us up outside. As long as we're out of camera-range, that is.'

'Do you think so?' asked Trouncy, who had only ever had pleasant encounters with policemen. 'Then why are you in favour of the demonstration?'

'Because it's all we have.'

'Couldn't we,' breathed Trouncy, 'just ask somebody to write letters?'

'The problem,' said Rolf Watt, looking out at Trouncy's private stars, feeling the touch of silk against his stiffening member, considering the softness of the white, shag-pile carpet, 'is not that *you* get to have all this but that *everybody* doesn't.'

He slid down the bed and buried his face in Trouncy's luscious thighs.

Because Penny and Steven had both come by car, it made sense that Penny should drop off Rory and meet up with Steven at home later. Toe might even just have a quick look in at the studio on his way back, as he thought he had possibly left a light on. Then it turned out that Bianca needed a ride back to Ebbing and there was nothing more logical than that Toe should take her, since it wasn't out of his way.

'I can walk you,' offered Rory. 'I could buy you a spring-roll if the Chippy's still open.'

'I'm not hungry,' said Bianca, with a toss of her head. She

was of the opinion that a larger and more refined period of her life was now beginning. She got into Toe's car and let him show her how to fasten her seat-belt.

'What is it exactly that we are going to demonstrate?' asked Rory and Penny's grandmother, as Eustace ushered her into her taxi.

'Our anger about the road,' said Anna,

'But I am not angry. I am just very very cross.'

'Nanny,' said Maud, as another cab drew up, 'here is your cheque. Your fares are included.'

'Where is Ursula?' asked Nanny. 'It was rude of her not to be here to see me. But then she always was an extremely rude little girl.'

'We don't quite know,' said Maud, with a self-deprecating smile, as if there were a certain charm in their situation.

At that moment, Susie Took hurtled off down the road in Mandy. Jay, in the passenger seat, put Eat Shit And Die's cassette into Mandy's rudimentary tape-deck. He had borrowed it to copy onto DAT. Ursula's voice screeched to the skies.

'But that is her singing,' said Maud.

'Better come round sometime soon and discuss how we go about this demonstration business,' said Eustace to Anna. 'Get a plan together. Two heads are better than one. You as well Lesley.'

'I'll walk with you to your place,' Anna said to Lesley. 'If you've got anything to drink.'

Lesley thought of Osbert's cellar. 'I have,' she said. 'We can go by the cliff, if you like. It's such a beautiful night.'

They made their way down the dark Frogwell lawn, along a slippery path between Rhododendrons and out to the clifftop through a rotting gate, fastened with metal wire. After a minute or two weaving through scrubland, they came into a grassy clearing at the end of which was the edge of the cliff.

The sky was damson. The stars had a brittle, grainy quality. Perhaps not a brush but a palette knife for them.

'Are you sure that Babcock's camp aren't going to announce their piece de resistance before the day of the media event?' Anna asked, as she and Lesley looked out over the water. 'If they do, we can reckon on the Trots and the Anarchists turning up and confusing the issue. Your lot, I suppose, would pull out altogether.'

'It won't be announced,' said Lesley. 'Very few people other than us know about it. It's supposed to be a surprise – a wonderful one.'

'I guess there are different views on wonderful,' said Anna.

There was a pause.

Lesley said, 'Perhaps I was a bit hard on Adrian Dapple. It's true though: I don't believe Osbert was aware of him any more than I was aware of . . .' She stopped.

'Me.' Anna finished her sentence.

A silence followed.

'I wonder,' said Lesley suddenly, 'whether Osbert had a nanny.' Anna glanced at her with an amused expression. 'I mean,' Lesley continued, 'it would explain some things, wouldn't it?'

Anna turned back to the sea. 'What?' she asked. A dredger had appeared on the horizon, a brick-shaped blackness with lights blinking.

'Well,' said Lesley, 'Nanny Scot was a success, wasn't she, really? The children found her a bit fierce but they did enjoy their day. They all said so. Maybe Osbert just wanted somebody to be in charge. Maybe that, in the end, was what made him happiest.'

'It's what we all think would make us happiest. That's why it's so fucking dangerous.'

They continued walking.

In the squats and flats and shared houses around Ebbing, where the children of the Alternative Left were now asleep, after their day of calm certainties their dreams were less reassuring. Nanny Scot had read them poems about boys and girls who knew they shouldn't suck their thumbs, play with matches, refuse the food they were given, and who ended up with their thumbs cut off, burnt to cinders, starved to death – all, as Nanny had pointed out, utterly avoidable. It had seemed such a controlled and automatic world that Nanny offered them that the children had instinctively loved it. It was so much more pleasant than the troubled, muddled one they were used to.

Their sleeping selves, however, were sceptical. Tattooed mothers, bi-sexual fathers, lesbian partners, orange-haired homosexuals with rings in their noses answered the cries of the small girls and boys when they woke from nightmares. They rocked them and soothed them, gave them glasses of soya milk and pieces of carob and listened to the sobbed accounts of dead, dismembered, burnt bodies, without denying that such things happened, or suggesting that they had any kind of correlation with what anyone deserved.

17

Campaigning

During the weeks that followed, election fever truly hit Ebbing. It was the arrival of the media that caused it really, their presence increasing as June 16th, the day of Babcock's big event, got nearer. Up until then, except for among those directly involved, interest had been spasmodic. Now, however, with lorries full of television equipment parked in the Old Fish Market and cameramen drinking from polystyrene cups provided by mobile catering, with national journalists downing whiskies in the Jolly Roger and TV presenters with blonde hair and brooches standing around talking to make-up, it was important to have an opinion or, better still, a viewpoint.

The hotels and bed and breakfasts and guest houses were taken over by men and women who sat up late and told stories, filling the rooms with smoke, bringing in bottles, which they drank with their chairs tipped back and their feet on the tables. They were gorgeous, the media people; bigger, somehow, than the average.

In the mornings they were monosyllabic. They sipped at black coffees and refused toast and grunted into telephones looking at their watches. Hortense Smith wiped ashtrays and opened windows.

The candidates made regular appearances.

Primrose and Tim Babcock understood the value of rationing

themselves, especially as Tim's media presentation became more imminent. Word that they were on the street resulted in a herd of running feet and the snatching up of cameras. When they appeared on television or in the newspapers they were mostly getting out of cars and going into buildings, or coming out of buildings and getting into cars. Often they were accompanied by one or more of their children. Sometimes Primrose was filmed with her pal Susie – for friendship such as theirs could never be ruined by mere politics and Primrose looked so very slim beside her plump companion – visiting Ebbing's Sunset Rest Home, for example, and squatting beside wheelchairs and nodding sympathetically at silly old people who should have been euthanased.

The only thing that marred these expressions of concern was the quite uncanny ability of the Independent Conservatives Against The Road, Preserve The Ebbing Clifftop And Jesus Was A Black Man Coalition Party to anticipate Tim and Primrose's movements. There was nowhere they could go but Marxists, frolicking homosexuals or grim-faced feminists were there also. Tim and Primrose found themselves having to grit their smiles when the coalition stole the attention, diverted the focus ever and eternally back to the road scheme and shouted questions (which just did not have simple answers) within the range of the microphones.

Bob and the other birdwatchers had meetings about the demonstration on the 16th and how they could increase public awareness as regarded the lesser tit. Mary Janet and Ruth Ellis organised a banner-making session and so did Rosalind Farrow, at another location. Anna Seale attempted to verse Eustace Frogwell in the rudiments of political protest.

There was a five minute spot about each of the candidates on *Aspect South*. Primrose and Tim were pictured in their garden, with their children and a Labrador, which they must have borrowed, looking marvellously unaffected. There was an interview about them with Winifred who stressed, lest it should not have been noticed, the intense commitment that Tim and Primrose had to their family (and to The Family) and citing loyalty as among their cardinal virtues and the one which made them so nice.

'You know, the reason I want this road,' said Tim to the interviewer (who did know, because they were old friends) 'is in order that my children will have a choice and choice, as you are aware, results in the kind of productivity which keeps inflation low and allows us to redirect vital resources to where they are most needed.'

'Such as?' asked the interviewer, with a look which implied the question was hard-hitting.

Tim was lit well. He had an easy manner. He waved a relaxed hand. 'Tax cuts,' he suggested.

Less successful was Miles Starey's appearance on the same programme. He was shown wandering round the halls and empty classrooms of what was now Pitsbury University (not to be confused with the University of Pitsbury) which, apparently, back in the days when it was Pitsbury Polytechnic had witnessed the genesis of a political consciousness that was now, from what Miles said, nothing if not catholic. He mooched along corridors speaking directly to camera in order to exploit his good looks to the utmost. What he wanted for Britain, he told those who were watching, was a caring society in which people were totally and absolutely self-reliant; he wanted low taxation so that people could learn that self-reliance by paying for their own health-care and, ideally, for a fair whack of their own education too. Socialist ideals were strictly outré, now that everyone had become so much more sensible, which did not mean that Miles Starey wasn't greatly concerned about the under-privileged, provided they showed that they were willing to fend for themselves. A new road scheme would help to allow that to happen by letting people have a choice.

The educational establishment was doubtless supposed to give Miles an artsy gloss, which was where his media advisors made their biggest mistake, not taking into account the alarm bells which are rung in the British consciousness by anything that smacks of intellectualism. Overall, the effect of the piece was to give the impression of someone who had wandered into an official building – perhaps while killing time waiting for a bus because he could not find a taxi – and got lost.

Better received was the Liberal Democrat, a moon-faced woman, with a slightly madly joyful aspect, who informed the off-camera interviewer that she was concerned about inequality and was shown in her bedsit feeding her cat.

'How about them discussing something together?' suggested the producer of *Aspect South* to Lesley, referring to Frogwell and Anna. It was an idea which Lesley, fortunately, managed to veto. In the end it was agreed that there would be shots of the cliff and the sea and of car exhausts and roadside litter. Eustace would outline the path of the road on a map (he consented to this somewhat secondary role – as Lesley had banked on him doing – because he rather liked the little pointer thing Lesley gave him to do it with) and Anna would be interviewed. No footage was included of the lesser tit and the birdwatchers were torn between regret at a wasted chance and relief that the tit had not had to be subjected to the presence of a camera crew, which (unlike the Arctic tern) it might have been disinclined to consider part of a pastoral backdrop.

Anna spoke with eloquence, common sense and passion and would have come across extremely well had it not been for the awkward edits. These, perhaps, due to the interviewer having told her, in most patronising tones, as soon as the interview was finished, that he really went for powerful women, whereupon Anna had emptied her glass of water into his lap.

To the horror of the Alternative Left and the irritation of Dick Winters, who viewed this particular political territory as a kind of Alsace – to be annexed if strictly necessary but at least to be borne in mind as an ideological hinterland which might be referred to obliquely – William Flint was announced candidate for the British Patriotic Party.

Aspect South took advice from its lawyers and made the decision not to do a piece on the BPP. Flint wasn't a newsagent for nothing. He went to the Jolly Roger and brought this flagrant censorship to the attention of the journalists there, who liked nothing better than a story which arrived on two legs and was willing to sit on a bar stool and pay for rounds of doubles. Flint got much more publicity than he would have done if *Aspect South* had permitted him coverage in the first place, especially in the gutter press, which agreed with Flint that a new road in Ebbing would bring job-hungry aliens, AIDS, mad cow disease, rabid bats, drugs, pornography, turbans in schools, non-Christian religions, fruit you didn't know the names of in the supermarkets, foreign ownership of British industries and the end of British civilisation as people knew it. Ebbing read with interest. In dens with bars and sunburst clocks, and at cloth-covered tables where cut-glass jugs of evaporated milk were poured over tinned peaches, husbands and wives observed to each other that Flint made quite a lot of sense, when you got down to it, and they felt brave, and a bit defiant.

Starey's PR people decided that Olive Ford, Ebbing's oldest resident, was an opportunity not to be missed. Their mouths positively watered at the thought of Miles, with his suntan and pony-tail so . . . they sought adjectives to give him an idea of what they were getting at . . . so 'New', so 'Contemporary' compared with the old lady, who had been born at a time which could never have dreamed that things would one day be as contemporary as they were now. The contrast would startle.

Miles knocked, then hammered on Mrs Ford's door. The photographers stood around with fags in their hands, smirking.

'Old bag's probably on the bog,' one of them suggested.

Out came Olive Ford eventually, blowing her nose because she had been listening to a particularly moving episode of *Ship Ahoy*.

'Mrs Ford,' shouted Miles, while the cameras flashed around him, 'can you tell me who you are planning on voting for in the Ebbing by-election?'

There was a pause. Mrs Ford could not make out Miles's features. All she saw was a blur which a voice came from, against another blur which was the sky.

'I shall be voting for Mr Attlee,' she said.

The photographers burst into malicious chuckles.

'But Mrs Ford,' said Miles, 'Mr Attlee is dead.'

There was another pause, during which Olive Ford wondered how long it was since she had last eaten a bloater.

'Then he won't be able to get up to any mischief, will he?' she said.

'He were a good lad, though he were headstrong,' said Sally Mackerel.

'I told 'im and I told 'im,' said Captain Skate. Which was

certainly true: whether or not Luke Barnacle would heed Captain Skate's good advice had been the note of suspense on which every episode of *Ship Ahoy* had ended for weeks now. Two days earlier, Luke Barnacle had set out in search of ling and his vessel had sunk, yesterday they had found his body (so that Younger's agent would have to accept, once and for all, that there was absolutely no possibility of renewing his bloody contract). Today was the funeral.

Lesley lay in bed, angry to find that her eyes were watering. How very much worse this felt than when Dick Winters had broken the news to her about Osbert. The little church-bell of Shrimping-on-Sea's fishermen's chapel began to toll.

'Safe journey, Luke Barnacle,' said Captain Skate. 'That craft went down like a ton of bricks, like I told 'e it would.' (This line had caused some ill-feeling. Captain Skate said it sounded silly and sulked in the Gentlemen's until lured out with tea and a Bath Oliver. Now, however, it was rendered with great conviction. Hot tears poured down Lesley's cheeks and onto her duvet.)

'Oh this is ridiculous!' Lesley leapt out of bed, washed and dressed and went downstairs and into the kitchen, where Susie Took was eating piccalilli from a jar and weeping into a handkerchief with 'S' embroidered on one of its corners.

'It's only a programme, Susie,' said Lesley, though her own throat was tightening again.

'What is?' asked Susie.

'Luke Barnacle. *Ship Ahoy.* Isn't that why you're crying?'

'No,' said Susie. 'This is real. Carmen Fitch. I tried to get her to let me help her sort the art and rubbish the day after the accident, the way I told her I would, but she said she was too busy to deal with it for the moment. Just now, when I phoned to offer again – I could be useful, I know I could; I can weld as well as glue – she slammed the phone down on me.'

Susie burst into renewed sobs. Lesley watched, with growing concern. This over-reaction was totally unlike Susie. She wondered if there was something going on that she really should get to the bottom of.

As if she read Lesley's thoughts though, Susie blew her nose, wiped her eyes and, evidently attempting to rally, said, in a muffled voice intercepted by sniffs, 'Oh, by the way, a rather dishy man knocked on the door. Jack Fryer, his name is. There was another man with him. He said they're looking into something on the cliff and might want to nip over the wall into the garden, if that was all right with you. I told them I didn't think you'd mind.'

'No, of course not, but what can they be doing?'

'Something about the lesser tit I should think.'

'Well I suppose so but . . .' Lesley stopped. Susie had sat down suddenly, swallowing and looking awfully pale. 'Are you all right Susie?'

'I feel a bit odd. Perhaps it's the piccalilli.'

Actually, Carmen had not slammed the phone down because of a reaction to anything said by Susie. It was because she had noticed two tall individuals, with long hair and big feet, going through her dustbin, which she had put out on the pavement the night before. Experiencing this as a kind of violation, she had rushed out to catch them before they had a chance to run away.

When she got outside, however, the men merely straightened up.

'Morning love,' said the older of the two. 'This your dustbin?' nodding in its direction and looking at her as if he thought she might try to deny ownership.

The younger one was more chummy. He wore a hooped earring and a pair of jeans. 'Police, love. Just checking everything's all right.'

It was then that Carmen perceived that the skip, with the bits of sculpture in it, was gone.

'My skip!' she shrieked. 'My skip! What's happened to it?'

'It's been moved on. It was a security risk,' said the older one.

'Security risk to who?'

'Ah,' said the one with the earring.

'Did you ever lecture at Pitsbury Poly?' asked the other.

'No, I didn't. Who's taken my skip away?'

'The blokes from Pitsbury Central. You'll get it returned in due course.' The older policeman now returned his attention to the dustbin.

'But I hadn't finished with it,' rasped Carmen. 'There were things I was going to take out of it, for Gawd's sake.'

'Now how could we have known that?' asked the younger policeman.

Carmen tore inside and phoned Pitsbury Central. The person who might know about the skip had gone home with a stomach-bug and wasn't expected back till the day after tomorrow at the soonest. She phoned the Chippy and got the number of Harry Smack's mate, the builder, whose brother-in-law had provided the skip. The builder wasn't there but his wife was. She gave Carmen her brother's number. She dialled it, but he hadn't seen sight nor sound of his skip since the day he provided it. He dropped heavy hints that, in the event of loss or damage to said skip, the customer was liable. Then Carmen called Anna to tell her what had happened, but only got the answerphone.

Carmen lit cigarettes with her silver lighter and puffed smoke all over the place. She made black coffees. There was a good reason why, during the weeks that the skip had been sitting on the pavement, she had not got round to sorting through it and why, when they inquired about their sculptures, she had only told the women whose works had been damaged that, in the light of the accident, they had been put into storage for safekeeping: Carmen had been much too inspired creatively to deal with other matters. Concepts, long-term projects, visual innovations and experiments: thoughts of these had been filling her hours. In the circumstances, who could have expected her to sift through masonry for bits of other women's work which had, anyway, probably had their day?

Carmen became increasingly angry; with Susie Took especially because Susie was the person she had spoken to most recently, but also with Lesley Sway and Anna. If Anna hadn't got so palsy-walsy with Lesley Sway then Lesley Sway would not have driven into Ebbing to see her. If she hadn't driven into Ebbing to see Anna, Lesley would not have had the accident with Susie Took; the sculptures wouldn't have got broken; a skip wouldn't have been necessitated and, therefore, not got taken away.

And now Anna was growing so distant, so caught up in her own concerns, so confident – over-confident, one must say – about her artistic abilities. No desire can be more self-seeking than the desire to spare one's friends from the possibility of failure. Anna must be spared, decided Carmen.

Jack Fryer and his companion parted in the Old Fish Market car park, which was being circled by a policeman with a large sniffer-dog.

'You really are certain?' asked Jack, as they shook hands.

The man nodded. 'No question about it, though it'll take me a while to get it written up for you.'

Jack hesitated. 'Wouldn't you have thought . . .? I mean, with all the trouble that it's causing . . .'

The man shrugged. 'Par for the course, I'd say.' He opened his car door. 'Not everyone's as clever as you are, Mr Fryer. Especially not politicians.' He got in the car and drove off.

Jack remained standing there, in the sunlight, struck by what had just been said to him. Was he, Jack Fryer, cleverer then, in some respects, than Tim Babcock or Miles Starey or Eustace Frogwell?

Anna Seale came out of her friend Jay's house at that moment. Jack waved at her.

He was tall, with dark hair, a sensitive, intelligent face, with a perceptive look to it that suggested a sense of humour. Anna waved back, though she only half recognised him, then disappeared in the direction of the Crab and Oyster Bar.

Two men, with posh voices, dressed in expensive suits, walked past Jack, talking. Jack looked up at the roof of one of the tourist shops. A bloke was standing on it with a pair of binoculars. Out from the High Street came an adolescent in a Union Jack t-shirt, a white paper bag in his hand, his lips greasy with chip-fat. A pair of plain-clothes coppers disappeared into the Woodcutter Inn.

Maybe it was always like this when there was going to be a big event during a by-election. Jack didn't know, but it struck him as excessive. There was an undercurrent of violence in the air; Jack could feel it cutting through the sense of excitement and he didn't like it. He knew about the demonstration of course; maybe that was what the law enforcers were getting so hot under the collar about. Anyway, he'd be glad when Babcock had shown off to the telly and papers and whatever important people he'd got invited and the demonstration was over and done with. Until then, he was going to be worrying that something might happen to Anna.

18

The Demonstration

A bright, blustery day. Seagulls sending up a chorused cry, as if by prior agreement, gliding above the choppy harbour at angles. The wind puffing insistently at the Woodcutter Inn's banner, turning it from strip of ribbon to parachute and back again until it was a pile of yellowy-white canvas on the ground. The manager of the Ebbing Woodcutter had had to phone HQ in Croydon re that: the obvious benefits to be accrued from publicity for the 'Prawns 'n' Pasta' offer versus decorum in the light of the dignitaries expected – Mayor of Pitsbury; Minister of Transport; a Bishop; Maureen Halley, 'The Girl Back Home' (who sang to the Forces and had a thirties' mansion the other side of Cove); Babcock and Mrs, of course, etc. etc. Decorum won.

In the Harvest Room waiters folded thick, white napkins into fan shapes and dusted the flower displays.

A helicopter flew overhead. The drains were full of policemen.

Though Lesley had understood quickly enough, it had taken several sessions for Anna to explain to Eustace Frogwell the right way of doing a demonstration, and even then he hadn't been totally convinced. 'Wouldn't the best thing,' he kept insisting, 'just be to show up in the Old Fish Market car park, make our feelings known and go home?'

Anna had pointed out, with ever-decreasing patience, that there was no way the police were going to let several hundred

people 'show up' in an area where a member of the Cabinet was
expected to make an appearance. And in any case, their feelings
were known already. What a demo was about was drama, force
of numbers, presenting a visual image that would make the
headlines. First you assembled, about a mile from where you
wanted to be, then you marched there, using the fact that there
were so many of you to make it impossible for the coppers to
prevent you going where you wanted. Then you shouted.

'*Must* we shout?' asked Maud, pausing in the process of
grooming a dachshund called Pepe.

The dignitaries were due to arrive at the Woodcutter from
twelve onwards. Assembly point for the demo was a large,
disused station yard. Assembly time, ten o'clock.

The Tories were the first to arrive, at ten on the dot, not
knowing that the time was chosen to allow for everybody to be
late. Frogwell marched up and down, consulted his watch every
other minute and asked Lesley, irritably, whether she was sure
this was the right place (this worry, though the Tories did not
know it, was also a customary part of the experience). Lesley,
beginning to wonder herself, reassured him that it was. Maud
took Rummy for little walks round the block.

The Tories had not been sure what one wore for a demonstration. Only Steven Toe and Penny St John were in jeans. Eustace
had opted for slacks and one of his second-best ties; Rory St
John, a younger version of the same. Maud was in tweed and
sensible lace-ups. Trouncy Lollop chose black leather trousers
and a matching jacket. Desmond Lollop sported a grey suit.
Veronica Tarrant wore a navy pinafore-dress over a sprigged
cotton blouse. Susie was in her trouser-suit.

Most of them were rather jealous when the Alternative Left
eventually showed up, festooned with badges and with messages
all over their t-shirts. Ruth Ellis, in a torn sweatshirt, with 'Keep
Your Dirty Laws Off My Body' written on it, doled out leaflets
for people to distribute. Anna, who was to be at the front of the
march with Eustace, was wearing green dungarees. Around her
hair was knotted a cheesecloth scarf covered in marijuana leaves.
She had a small metal hip-flask stuffed in her back-pocket. The
Save The Lesser Tit campaigners had laundered their banner and
re-done the lettering where it had faded.

At eleven-thirty Anna shouted, 'Right, we're ready for off. What shall we start the singing with?'

'"Jerusalem",' suggested Frogwell.

'"Four minutes to midnight. Four minutes to Armageddon",' suggested Gilda.

But Mary Janet and Carmen Fitch launched into 'Were You There When The Women Saved The World?' which was picked up by the other Feminists.

The demonstration moved away, flanked by a dozen or so police officers.

The helicopter hovered above them, aggressive and flattering. The sunlight bounced off walls and doors, rooftops, windows, parked cars, letterboxes, as if they were water. What did they look like from the air? Lesley wondered. A spreading, thinning, clumping, contracting mass of hats and hairstyles, of sudden, pale, upturned faces, weaving through the streets of Ebbing. Under the railway bridge, past the allotments and lock-ups, the blanked-out frontages of long-closed grocers, the splitting bottle-green paintwork of dead sweetshops. Through the territory of wishing-wells and crazy-paving and double-garages. Round a corner and into a Victorian street untouched, save for a few carriage-lamps. Then among larger houses, like 'The Four Winds', home of the St John parents.

They had their own momentum, their own gaiety, their own sense of purpose. They were separate from all they walked past. Lesley imagined herself as transported by a vast, invisible vehicle. She joined in the singing, once she'd picked the tunes up, overwhelmed by a feeling of comradeship: for Adrian and Gilda and Carrot; for Maud, who was striding out, with Rummy at her heels, as if across moorland; even for Eustace, who was puffing a bit; but especially for Anna, who had dragged her into a life in which things happened, though, of course, it had not just been Anna . . . Fun, this was fun; not a word she had had much call for in the past but which, if asked, she would have applied to shopping with Primrose, going to a matinee with Winifred: things which were actually not fun at all, merely pleasant. Fun, Lesley realised now, was an anarchist.

The procession reached the High Street. People came out of the shops to watch it. Groups of day-trippers, getting settled into the tea-rooms for their lunches, peered at them through bay-windows. The vicar stood on the pavement, frowning. Meg Hughes had decorated the Crab and Oyster Bar with posters of The Rainbow Warrior. Doors were open in the sunshine. Ebbing smelled of chips and vinegar.

The songs gave way to chanting:

'What do we want?'

'To save the clifftop.'

'When do we want it?'

'Now!'

There were cameras, reporters, the telly, radio, newspapers; there was scrambling, elbowing; photographers in the road, getting the demo coming towards them.

But now the parade came to a standstill. Beyond the photographers, the High Street was blocked with metal barriers. Against these barriers was a dark line of policemen.

'What's happening?' yelled people at the back. 'Why are we stopping?'

A senior officer approached Eustace.

'I'm afraid I'm going to have to ask you to tell these people to disperse, Sir,' he said, in the calm tones of one who believes himself in charge, in spite of everything. 'We cannot allow you any further for security reasons and you are, at present, obstructing the highway.'

What happened now? A roadblock was something Lesley had not anticipated. Nor, evidently, had Eustace, who had gone his own, distinctive shade of purple and was looking thoroughly uneasy. The expression on Anna's face, however, showed that she was taking it in her stride. Had she, Lesley wondered, known that something like this was pretty inevitable but chosen to keep quiet about it, lest the Conservatives should lose their nerve? Wisely, perhaps, though suddenly Lesley resented being lumped in with the rest of them.

'Tim Babcock is showing a new road scheme to the media and we want to protest against it,' said Anna. 'We demand you give us access to the Old Fish Market.'

'*Please*,' said Maud, leaving it unclear whether she was correcting Anna or seeking to persuade the policeman.

'I can't do that, love.'

There was a nastiness to the situation which was quite new to Lesley. Usually, of course, none of this activity would be known to her. She and Osbert would be in the Woodcutter Inn, shaking hands with everyone, laughing plentifully at the dignitaries' small witticisms. 'Come on Anna, it doesn't matter, let's leave it': the words welled into her mouth but remained there, unspoken. Anna was unperturbed.

'We have a right to demonstrate,' she argued.

'And you have done so.' The officer turned to Frogwell again. 'Please ask these people to disperse, Sir.'

'Could, maybe, just a *few* of us go into the Old Fish Market?' asked Maud. 'If we promised not to shout?'

'Maybe it would be best to go home now,' said Frogwell. 'Lunchtime anyway.'

'I thought I explained,' said Anna. 'We don't stop now. We use the fact that there's a lot of us to go where we want to.'

'That would be very unwise, Sir,' said the policeman to Frogwell.

'I think I have to agree with the officer,' Eustace said to Anna. 'Don't want to upset security. Didn't imagine there'd be barriers and whatnot.'

Anna looked at Lesley. Lesley looked at Anna.

Eustace was going to comply and, if he did, the Conservative contingent would give up also and, thought Lesley, the fun would be over. And though it would be easier, safer, probably wiser, and it would certainly end the nastiness, Lesley was getting pretty sick of the fun always being over. So it was not really on behalf of her house or the clifftop or the environment, or anything laudable or rational; not so much because of a decision as an impulse that Lesley – when Anna hurled herself between the bodies of two of the policemen, knocked part of the barrier over, and started running towards the Square – ran too.

Anna's scarf was whipped away by the wind. Her hair streamed out behind her. A policeman grabbed at Lesley's jacket. She pulled away, left it in his hands, discarded. The street was open, empty, except for Lesley and Anna. Lesley remembered the egg-and-spoon race at Primrose's little school and how ashamed Primrose had been of her for winning, sensing the inappropriate enticement that crashing through the straight, white tape had held for her. Any moment, there would be renewed attempts to stop her. But they wouldn't be able to. The jacket was nothing. Lesley could discard her blouse, her earrings, her shoes; limbs too, if necessary. The policemen would find themselves holding only arms, fingers, ears, locks of hair: ephemera. Lesley was pure spirit.

No more attempts were made, however, for, in a minute more, the street was thick with other people. The cordon was broken. Panting, Lesley slowed to a jogging pace alongside Anna.

'Holy shit,' said Anna, 'I'm going to have to give up smoking.'

They entered the Square, Lesley feeling as if it were the first time she had ever done so. The rest of the demonstration flooded in behind them. They came to a stop outside the Woodcutter.

Assembled there, officially, was a polite group of Babcock's Tories and numerous serious and well-behaved members of the media. A small ring of police encircled a paddock around the entrance to the Woodcutter Inn, which had been marked off with metal poles that looked like airport ashtrays, linked by thick, maroon ropes. There was a reddish carpet.

The route by which the dignitaries were to arrive became clear now; also why the High Street had been blocked at the point it was. Lesley could see another police block at its harbour end, just where the small road, which went past Jay's house, intersected it. On the other side of the High Street, that road passed the Primary School and eventually – by the kind of unlikely, circuitous route which would appeal to security people – joined up with the main London to Pitsbury. London and Pitsbury were the directions from which VIP's tended to emanate. Having failed to keep the demonstration out of the Old Fish Market Square, it was this intersecting road that the police were now endeavouring to keep open – with more success, since it was such a small one – trying to give the impression that this was how they had been planning on doing things all along.

The guard was increased around the Woodcutter Inn, on the steps of which stood Tim Babcock, Primrose, all their children, including Jonquil, and Winifred.

'Oh gosh!' said Susie Took, coming up beside Lesley.

'I'm not sure you should have been running, Susie,' said Lesley.

'It's not that,' said Susie. 'It's just it feels so sort of odd to be here and not with Prim and Mummy. In fact, Prim did invite me actually, but I prefer to be here.'

Primrose was wearing an artificially distressed straw hat and a cornflower muslin with leg-of-mutton sleeves. Winifred had pinned to her twin-set a Tory-blue rosette the size of a cauliflower. Robin and Seth were in knickerbockers and little leather jerkins; Tansy and Sorrel also wore jerkins but with full-length velvet skirts. Primrose held Jonquil in her arms, wrapped in a silk shawl that set off the cornflower to perfection. With her smiling husband and Winifred, they made the very picture of a happy family.

Lesley considered them. It did feel odd, though not unpleasant. In fact, she felt relieved, as if she had realised something just in time to prevent a disaster. What Winifred, with all her acuity, had not worked out was that anyone in the right clothes could have occupied the spot where she was standing; just as anyone appropriate could have stood in for Primrose in relation to Tim, or Tim in relation to Primrose. Or, of course, Lesley in relation to Osbert. Take one away and replace them with another, similar, and nobody would notice, like when the goldfish died that the children had won at the fair. Who among his party-loyal still mourned for Osbert?

Lesley had narrowly escaped living out her existence in the belief that her position was unique in the lives of those around her when, in reality, she was only one of an inexhaustible supply of understudies.

She turned her attention to other parts of the crowd. A little way away from her were Maud and Eustace and the rest of the Tory contingent of the coalition – self-assured again, now the way had been made clear for them. Those who were intimates of the Frogwells were keeping half an eye on their ankles; Maud was calling Rummy, who she appeared to have lost. Anna Seale cupped her hand round a match as she lit a roll-up. Bob, who'd got out his binoculars, was looking at something through them, that dun bird, probably, that was sort of hanging on the wall of Jay's house, from every window of which floated large clusters of helium balloons – red, green and yellow.

The chanting started up again. A Rolls edged down the street next to Jay's and stopped at the red carpet. Babcock's party clapped restrainedly as the porky Mayor of Pitsbury and his Lady got out of it – mayors were the Conservatives' concession to the lower middle-classes. Having deposited its burden – which shook hands with Babcock, kissed Primrose, tickled Jonquil – the car left, in the direction it had come from.

Maureen Halley, 'The Girl Back Home', arrived and looked very much as if she would have liked to give an impromptu chorus of 'If You Love England', which she performed with increasing tunelessness and everyone said she was marvellous for her age, but, unfortunately, the Minister of Transport arrived a second or two later. Halley was whisked into the Woodcutter so that the Minister could get the kind of greeting that was his due, and grasp Babcock's hand for as long as was necessary for the press to get the shots they wanted.

Eventually the Minister also went into the Woodcutter. Now there was a pause, during which nothing happened, but anticipation hung in the air. The demonstrators sang, a question mark in their voices.

Lesley looked up, away from the thick mass of bodies around her, into the unencumbered sky, where seagulls glided down invisible slides.

She lowered her eyes again. An angry shouting started up. It came from the direction of the Primary School. Lesley craned her neck and thought perhaps she glimpsed the official car. The crowd surged, parted, revealed . . . across the other side of the Square, not far from Jay's house . . . standing in the sunshine . . . Darryl Younger.

Her tears had not been for the loss of Luke Barnacle. When the explosion occurred, Lesley thought it was only inside her head.

Debris was floating around her. The crowd pulled Darryl away from her vision, swallowed him up. Or maybe the bomb had sucked him into its evil belly, to spit him back, broken. There were terrified faces, fragile bodies, pulling away, away from Jay's house, where the explosion was – though glued in the slow-motion of horror. She could have caught raw eggs, if someone had been throwing them; they would have ridden the atmosphere, like surfers. Policemen waded past her.

Then Susie began to scream. Everything shattered into fast-forward. The crowd anticked – grotesque, giant insects – in stick-figure agitation.

'No, Susie. No!'

Lesley grabbed Susie by the shoulders but Susie still struggled to run in the direction of the explosion. Lesley wrapped her arms around Susie's waist. Strange, laughable, quite absurd that, at this terrible second, she thought of dumplings and dough and pancakes, of sweet icing; that she felt a massive surge of love wash over her for Susie Took, hot and living, utterly unique, infinitely dear, never anything other than completely Susie. Who was getting away, slipping out of her grasp towards the very heart of destruction. Except that, suddenly, Lesley's arms were enmeshed with those of Anna and, together, they were hauling Susie out of the way of harm and Susie had stopped trying to resist.

Now, though, Lesley was seized by an opposite momentum and it was she who was being dragged away from Susie. She discovered that she was not ether after all – far from it. She was flesh; because her arms, clamped behind her, were bruising.

'They don't bend that way,' she tried to say to the thick blue sleeve that had got hold of her. 'Arms don't bend like that. They aren't supposed to.'

19

Inside

In thirty years of legal practice, Mr Woodruff, of Woodruff, Marrow & Pitt, had never set foot in a police station or prison. His clients moved house, died, occasionally they got divorced, the sensible among them keeping all these activities to the minimum. They did not get arrested.

Now, as he entered one of the cells of Ebbing police station, he remarked to himself that it resembled a waterless swimming-pool. He wondered how a human being could experience a need so great or a belief so fervent as to be willing to be compelled to spend any length of time in such a place. Six hours, so far, to the best of his knowledge. It crossed Mr Woodruff's mind that this was something he was probably meant to check up on.

Mrs Sway leapt to her feet. She looked untidy.

'Is there any news?' she asked, anxiously.

'Indeed there is.' Mr Woodruff made his announcement with no little excitement. 'You will be surprised to hear that it now transpires that the Prime Minister was to have been one of Mr Babcock's guests at the Woodcutter Inn. I am relieved to be able to inform you that he is completely unharmed.'

He did not add the full circumstances of the Prime Minister's escape – perhaps because he did not know them. Nor did he add that, as soon as he was certain that he was not dead, the Prime Minister had had the car turn round and hot foot it back to London. Babcock's bird had flown. The wonderful surprise, which he had kept under wraps for weeks, a visit from the Prime Minister himself – indicative of all kinds of faith and support and concern – had failed to come off.

Safe back at Number 10, the Prime Minister had phoned the Babcock residence; not, as would have been polite, to apologise, but to inquire as to why there was no zebra-crossing outside Ebbing Primary School. Babcock was at a loss. His own children's futures to be otherwise dealt with, he was only dimly aware that there was an Ebbing Primary School, let alone one with a compelling lack. The Prime Minister instructed him to look into it immediately, appending a little homily about the needs of one's constituents, which was totally unnecessary and, though Babcock did not know this, somewhat hypocritical. While they were holding up his car by crossing the road in a constant stream with toddlers and pushchairs and placards, the Prime Minister had passed some less than cordial comments on the topic of the Single Mothers. It was the realisation that the delay might have saved his skin that made him now feel so positively towards them.

Babcock was, at present, closeted in his renovated chapel, seething. Dick Winters was issuing frequent statements on his behalf, but even these were being completely upstaged.

'And?' Mrs Sway asked.

'"And", Mrs Sway?' Mr Woodruff was at a loss. Should not this be enough?

'Is anyone else hurt? Don't you know if there were any other casualties?'

'I do not,' replied Mr Woodruff.

It was with relief that he left the police station, some ten minutes later, having reassured himself, and his client, that the police were acting completely correctly and that, in the fulness of time, his client might well be allowed to return to her home.

This was the information that he relayed to the man who accosted him as he was taking his first breath of freedom. The man insisted that he had a right to know; he was a relative of Mrs Sway by marriage. Due to his testamentary work, Mr Woodruff was a great believer in relatives.

After Mr Woodruff's departure, Lesley succumbed to despair.

She had thought that her first hours in Ebbing Police Station would turn out to have been the worst part, but the continuing lack of information about Darryl was more terrible still.

If Mr Woodruff could not make them free her, at least, surely, he could have told her something that would have given her an idea as to what might have happened to Darryl. He could have agreed with her that, when they had taken her out of the police car, led her inside and put her in a room with no clock on the wall, and refused to answer her desperate questions, the police had been doing something blatantly inhuman, not simply following procedure.

Invisible, filed away deep in this building, Lesley had been seized with a terror such as she had never before experienced. She had not realised that time was a weapon; that a person with the power to take it away or control it had one of the greatest of all instruments of oppression at their disposal. To think that it was something that she had wasted – year after year fed into a marriage, and then a pretence at one, with Osbert; prize-giving after prize-giving, clapping white gloves together, listening to Osbert's speech.

When was someone going to tell her what had happened to Darryl?

Lesley reminded herself of her protectors: law, intelligence, money, social status. She reminded herself that Anna had had access to only one of these and had emerged, unscathed . . .

No, not unscathed. Anna had emerged from Ebbing Police Station enraged, afraid and humiliated.

'Don't you think that you are making rather a fuss?': Lesley's question, that first day, eating mussels. She heard it through Anna's ears now.

They had strip-searched Anna! They had strip-searched Anna and then released her without even charging her with anything.

Would they strip-search her? Why hadn't she thought to ask Mr Woodruff what rights she had in this respect? At any moment a policewoman might enter and tell Lesley to take her clothes off. The woman would be dressed and Lesley would be naked. They would be in a room into which anyone could wander. Lesley wanted to cry very hard, to bawl her body out of existence, so they couldn't do the same to her as they had done to Anna.

There flashed across her mind the knowledge of how and why one human being could find it possible to kill another.

'This is England,' she told herself. 'Everything will be all right. Everything will be all right. This is England.'

She felt a global pity for all prisoners, everywhere, guilty or innocent.

The door opened.

'Follow me, love.'

She followed the policewoman down a greenish corridor with no natural light. She was stiff, thirsty, cold but sweating. The policewoman unlocked a door.

'In there now.'

Lesley filled her lungs with air. If they touched her, she would start screaming. She would pretend to be demented. No, she would not pretend – she would not need to.

The door closed behind her.

'Anna!'

Lesley hurtled across the cell and into the arms of Anna Seale. 'Anna! I'm so so sorry,' she babbled. 'If I'd known I would never have called a policeman. Did they strip-search you this time?'

The blast across the bay had sounded like a cannon starting a yacht race; the bomb was announced on the radio not many minutes later. A race: yes, a race to get to Anna. 'She's dead,' said the clock. 'She's hurt,' said the clock. 'She's frightened.' Jack felt as if a mass of windows inside him were being thrown open and cold air was rushing in at each of them.

The Caff was jam-packed. Turfed off the ferry, trapped by the road-block, there was nowhere else for people to go. Jack had to step over rucksacks to put plates of food on tables. He'd have shut up shop if the road had been open, but they were bumper to bumper, right up to the barrier. They weren't letting anyone through on foot either. A forty-footer from Calais had broken down, to add to everything. Jack could hear sirens. Except on the topic of the Prime Minister, the radio was uninformative. And yet Jack felt as if speed was of the essence. Get them fed, get the tables wiped, get the oil hotter, make the steam whoosh out louder and time could be kicked along faster. The streets of Ebbing would unclog. Ambulances would get their freight quickly to Pitsbury General. Roads would open. Traffic would move again. He'd get in his van and hurtle towards news, be ready to go wherever she was, do whatever she needed him to.

Time slouched, hung around though. It wasn't till just under six hours later that they dismantled the barrier, gave the go-ahead to the foot-passengers, beckoned the traffic round the forty-footer.

In a phone-box on the edge of the Square was Darryl Younger. Jack stopped the van, got out and pulled the kiosk door open.

'Sodit,' said Darryl into the receiver. 'Okay, I didn't have quite enough, but how was I to know what you did at midnight? . . . I know I'd travelled with you after midnight before, but I didn't know it was after midnight . . . No, not that time either.' Now he saw Jack, looked past him, saw the van and slammed down the receiver. 'Bloody taxis! My car's been towed away. I've got to get to Seagate. They've got Les and Anna banged up and that damn-fool solicitor doesn't know shit from Shino. Leave them in there much longer, with that idiot their only representation, and it won't be long before the pigs get round to thinking Prevention of Terrorism.'

'She's all right?' asked Jack. The relief was so great that he felt suddenly exhausted.

'Who? Les? All right as you can be in the circumstances.'

'And Anna?'

'All okay, from what that fool told me. But we've got to get to Seagate. Pick up Madeline Rush. Wretched woman doesn't have a car. Bicycles everywhere, or goes by train. Needless to say, the trains aren't running. Any excuse.'

They were getting into the van now.

'Madeline Rush?'

'Old friend of mine. "The Plumpton Three".'

'Oh,' said Jack Fryer.

What bridesmaid?' asked Anna.

'At Primrose's wedding,' said Lesley.

'So when are we talking about?'

'Not long ago really.'

'How long?'

'About five years.'

'Five years! Darryl got drunk at a wedding five years ago, before he even knew you, and tried to seduce some upper-class scrubber. No wonder you're upset. What should he have done, Les: stayed pure until he met the right woman?'

'I didn't expect him to be faithful. I only expected him to be discreet.'

'Who did you expect to be discreet?'

'Osbert, of course . . .' Lesley stopped. What was she saying? 'Darryl, I mean Darryl.' She stopped again. 'I do mean Osbert, don't I?'

Anna nodded.

In the past there were days, months – years even – during which Lesley experienced little change of emotion. Now, in the space of a few weeks, an afternoon . . . Lesley burst into tears.

'I'm sorry,' she gasped. 'So much has happened: Darryl; being arrested.'

Anna patted Lesley's smooth hand with her large, coarse one, brushed a lock of hair out of Lesley's eyes and hooked it behind an ear. 'Darryl'll be okay. And you'll have to get used to being arrested, now you're one of us, you know.'

Lesley swept her knuckles across her face quickly. 'I assure you, I am not planning on making a habit of it.'

There was a pause.

'He is a scrounger,' said Lesley.

Anna shrugged. 'He can be generous. Bought one of my paintings when I was skint. He's not perfect, but who is?'

'Osbert *looked* perfect,' said Lesley. She sniffed. Her words poured out in an angry torrent. 'I didn't care about Nanny Enema. But I'd invested so much time and energy in the image of our marriage, I'd worked to maintain it and I thought Osbert would always do the same. And he didn't, did he? Then I saw Darryl – having fun, nothing mattering, getting away with God knows what. I took it out on him but, you're right, I suppose it was really Osbert I was angry with – and Primrose for being so like him, and myself, most of all, for basing my life on such a bloody rotten deal.'

Anna thought of the London galleries, her unposted letters. 'You were frightened,' she said gently. 'Darryl doesn't exactly inspire confidence. We all want guarantees and we're scared shitless when we have to face the fact that there aren't any.' She paused a moment. 'You know Miles Starey?'

'Miles Starey, the Labour candidate?'

Anna nodded. 'We had a thing going, a while back. The sexual part wasn't that important, but I trusted him politically. When he sold out, I was thrown – all right, frightened. I mean, I thought I'd known where things stood and suddenly,' Anna's voice got louder, she turned a naked, incredulous face to Lesley, 'suddenly they're not standing, they're not based on anything real either, they're just going wherever the wind blows, and trust doesn't even come into it.' She untensed, sighed. 'Still, I suppose it was partly what got us together.'

'Us?' asked Lesley.

'You, me, the coalition. Nanny Enema: I figured you hadn't known your husband had a thing going with her, any more than I'd sussed the truth about Miles. Kindred spirits. Fellow fucking idiots.' She grinned at Lesley, wryly. Lesley smiled back.

There was a pause.

'So how long have you been involved with Jack?' asked Lesley.

'Jack? Jack who?'

'The Beach Caff. He looked so pleased to see you . . .' Lesley's voice trailed off. Anna was looking astonished.

Madeline Rush, left-wing solicitor, had thick auburn hair and large eyes, had aced it at Cambridge. A star danced; after presiding over Madeline Rush it had had to rest a week.

Ms Rush entered Ebbing Police Station and seemed to raise dust.

The dear old Duty Sergeant did not look up from whatever he was doing.

'I demand the immediate release of my clients,' said Ms Rush. 'I also want an explanation from the Superintendent as to why they have been held for so long.'

'Them being, love?'

'Don't you "love" me, Sergeant.' Ms Rush seized the biro from between the dear old Duty Sergeant's fingers, thereby attracting his full attention. 'Ms Sway and Ms Seale. We are talking the following: we are talking assault; we are talking unlawful detention.'

'Mr Woodruff has been made cognisant of the charge we are considering bringing against Mrs Sway and Miss Seale,' said the Duty Sergeant, avoiding Ms Rush's lovely eyes and gazing, instead, at the furry tip of his biro.

'Mr Woodruff has been dismissed. Give me a laugh, Duty Sergeant, make *me* cognisant.'

'Failure to comply with lawful directions given by a police officer in respect of today's demonstration,' said the Sergeant. The words hung in the air like a nasty smell.

Ms Rush waited. 'Those being?' she asked.

The dear old Duty Sergeant looked as if he would have liked someone to take him down the vet and put him out of his misery. 'To disperse,' he said.

'Why?' asked Ms Rush.

'Because they were obstructing the highway?' The Sergeant made it sound like a question.

Wrong reply. Ms Rush said nothing, let the walls and counter and floor and files draw their own conclusions.

Then, 'But the highway was already obstructed, wasn't it?' she almost whispered. 'What was it obstructed by, Sergeant?'

'By a roadblock,' muttered the Sergeant.

'Speak up, Duty Sergeant, I can't hear you. It was obstructed by a roadblock, wasn't it? And what else was it obstructed by?'

'By policemen.'

'It was obstructed by policemen.'

A telephone started ringing at the back of the building. It gave the Duty Sergeant courage.

'They ran through the police barrier,' he suggested.

Ms Rush pounced. 'Thereby ceasing to obstruct the highway, which was what they had been requested to do. So I ask you once again, Sergeant: why are my clients still in custody?'

'A bomb has exploded,' said the Duty Sergeant. 'Which is a serious matter.'

'Indeed it is, no one is disputing that. But, I put it to you, Sergeant, if you had placed a bomb somewhere, would you then remain in the direct vicinity?'

'I might.' The Sergeant fidgeted with a bit of Sellotape he found stuck to his trouser leg.

Ms Rush raised her gorgeous auburn eyebrows. 'Oh really, Sergeant? Why?'

'To check it had gone off all right.'

'Even though you might lose a limb, say, in the process? Even though, if it hadn't, there was nothing you could do about it, short of entering somebody else's premises in the full view of any number of security people and police officers? Though, from what I have seen of the Ebbing police force, I agree that the latter might fail to notice.'

The dear old Duty Sergeant stood up. He was nearing retirement age now and had spent a lifetime in the Force dealing only with lawyers like Mr Woodruff. He would have liked to say 'special powers,' but did not dare to.

St Christopher's was striking ten. The streets were preternaturally quiet. Shaken by its day, Ebbing had gone to bed early. The sky was far away, shut out by the orange street-light, which lay, scummily, on the roofs of wishing-wells and miniature windmills.

Anna and Lesley were let out of a back entrance, through a metal fire-door. No explanation of their release was given.

The door clanged shut behind them. They stood, at a loss, forgetting, for the moment, that they were in Ebbing and that a bit of wandering around would restore their bearings. Each had a repertoire of prison exits at her disposal – Lesley's more secondhand than Anna's. Anna half expected a group of bouncing women in baggy sweaters, cheering and embracing. Lesley half expected someone in a dubious car, offering her a job, or a chorus of Irish accents proclaiming justice.

Instead – now she saw him – there was Darryl Younger. Not dead, not even dishevelled, though just the right amount unshaven.

'Wait till you hear the news!' he shouted. 'Bloody amazing!

Everything's played into our hands. Wait till you hear what's happened.'

Lesley began to walk towards him; then, for the second time that day, she was running – smashing through barriers, leaving bits of herself behind, discarded.

20

Aspects Of Love

Opalescent fish swam slowly around a luminous model castle. The restaurant walls were scattered with curious, decorative ovals of indented plastic, back-lit with turquoise, mauve and yellow lights. A song without beginning or end bounced along cheerfully. Behind a small bar, there was a television, switched on but with the sound off.

Anna and Darryl had fallen on the menu with confidence, ordering Bombay ducks, poppadums, raitas, breads and curries in a practised way. Lesley, who had not eaten Indian food since student days, chose cautiously. Now she sipped on a pint of lager and watched the waiter cover the table with plates of yellow and orange rice, sizzling metal bowls of chicken and beef, dishes of okra, spinach and aubergines, chutneys. Except for themselves, the Taj Mahal was deserted.

'What happened?' Darryl asked the waiter, nodding in the direction of the boarded-up window. 'You can't have caught the blast over here.'

'Blast?'

'There was a bomb in the Old Fish Market this afternoon.'

'I didn't hear of that.'

Darryl glanced at the television. 'This is it!' he said. 'Turn up the sound a minute, could you, Sunil?'

The waiter went to the little bar and turned off the music.

He switched on the volume of the television. The urgent theme tune of a news programme invaded the restaurant; on the screen, globes hurtled about among a montage of various heads of state. The theme tune shuddered to a temporary halt and a young man, with slicked-back hair, seated behind a desk, shouted the headline: 'Ebbing attempt on Prime Minister's life. So far, no one has claimed responsibility.' There was a final burst of theme tune and then the young man continued in calmer tones.

There were shots of the Prime Minister's car, close-ups of Tim and Primrose and their children, footage of the arrival of the Mayor of Pitsbury – all, presumably, designed to give an idea of how secure everything had been before the bomb had struck – followed by shouting, scuffling, the customary skewed camera angle and loss of picture. Back in the studio, the presenter explained that, happily, the bomb had gone off before the Prime Minister was scheduled to arrive. It had been placed in a house on the Square, which had been unoccupied at the time of the explosion, and although it had caused severe structural damage to the building, it had not been large enough to do damage elsewhere. An inquiry had been launched into how the terrorists could have known about the Prime Minister's visit, which had been planned with the utmost secrecy. Claims that the bomb attack had racial motives – the owner of the building was a Rastafarian – had been completely dismissed.

Anna groaned. 'We're fucked. This'll get them the sympathy vote. I thought you said things had played into our hands, Darryl.'

'Hang on a sec, Anna. Hang on a sec.'

Now the presenter's voice went into famine and air-crash mode. A few people had been treated for cuts and bruises from flying debris, he informed the viewers, one or two had been taken to Pitsbury General suffering from shock, but were discharged later. There had only been one fatality.

'A fatality!' Lesley's mind flicked through all the ghastly possibilities: Bob, Adrian Dapple, Trouncy. Onto the screen came Maud Frogwell, filmed in the sitting-room of the Frogwell Mansion, perched on the edge of one of the greasy armchairs, beside a baroque, marble table, on which were placed a large arrangement of peonies, photographs of Maud, Eustace and various dachshunds and several cups and shields. Maud was wearing an expression of extreme bravery. Lesley gasped: Eustace, killed during a demonstration; the irony was searing.

But no. Her eyes dewy with held-back tears, Maud was speaking, not of her husband, but of Rummy who, she could only surmise, had been sniffing around the front of the building when the explosion occurred and had been killed instantly when the door was blown out.

Had it indeed been Eustace who had been snatched away in this untimely manner, it was hard to imagine that Maud could have been inspired into greater eloquence. Resigned and yet stunned, grief-stricken yet determined to fight on – that Rummy's name be not forgotten and that the men of violence be not seen to triumph – Maud described, with admirable composure, Rummy's habits, how greatly he was loved by all who had encountered him, how terribly he would be missed.

The picture changed to the Old Fish Market Square and the singed structure of Jay's house. Flowers of sympathy were pouring in from well-wishers, the presenter informed the viewers, in a stricken voice. There was a mound of them in the doorway, where Rummy fell. A collection had been started for a plaque to mark the spot. Maud had been invited – and agreed – to make an honorary appearance at Crufts. (She had also, though to this the TV presenter did not appear to be privy, had some extremely tempting offers from dog-food manufacturers.)

'That woman should have gone into the Business,' remarked Darryl, tearing off a piece of warm nan. 'A total natural. She's been on the radio continuously ever since it happened. We've got the sympathy vote. We're way ahead in the polls. Things stay like this and we've won the election. And that was true even before my idiot cousin made his statement.'

Tim Babcock, when asked to comment on the nation's loss, had unwisely observed that this sort of thing was what happened when people went around demonstrating. The callousness of the remark had caused a public outcry and Primrose and Tim had received anonymous phone-calls from angry dog-lovers. Someone had thrown a can of Pal at their kitchen window. The other candidates, profiting from the example, had fallen over themselves to show how much they cared about animals in general and dogs in particular. There were a few seconds of Miles Starey on the topic of Jack Russells and the old footage of the Liberal Democrat with her cat. The Jack Russells were only in the abstract, however, and the cat was alive, so lacked the power to move. Doubtless guided by Dick Winters, Tim Babcock had, it was reported, now issued a retracting statement to the effect that his earlier remarks were caused by the shock of the situation, and pointing out that he had been shown with a Labrador on *Aspect South*. Too little, too late.

The topic switched to drought in the Home Counties. The sound was turned down, the music back on.

'Can you give me a lift, Les?' asked Darryl, when they left the Taj Mahal. 'They towed my car, the bastards.'

'I thought you said you went and fetched Maddie Rush from Seagate,' said Anna.

'I did, but we went in Jack's van. Once we knew they were letting you go he ran her to the station to see if the trains were on again. If not, he was going to drive her back to Seagate.'

'Oh.'

There was a silence.

'Can we walk you home, Anna?' asked Lesley.

'No thanks Les,' said Anna. 'Good night Darryl.' She turned, brusquely, and strode off down Oyster Alley. Lesley watched her, almost disappointed for a moment. Given the intensity of the day's shared experiences, wouldn't something more have been appropriate? But then she thought of those shopping trips to London with Primrose. Ciabatta, mozzarella and sun-dried tomatoes, in cafés with scrubbed floorboards, with Primrose's girlfriends and girlfriends' mothers. All the gnat-like kissing à la française on departure and arrival, flurry and exclamations. She remembered, with a shudder, the phase Primrose went through of giving each of her guests an arum lily when they left her dinner parties.

It was these appalling images that gave Lesley the courage to say to Darryl, 'Would you like to come back for coffee?'

'Oh Lord,' said Darryl.

Lesley blushed deeply. Maybe even Darryl had his taboos; maybe he considered it highly unseemly that a woman should issue such an invitation; maybe he hadn't yet forgiven her and was embarrassed that she had put him into a position where he would have to make that clear; maybe he no longer found her attractive.

'Doesn't have to be coffee, does it? Haven't you got anything stronger?' said Darryl.

Anna didn't go straight home. She went to the sea wall and sat on it, looking out across the bay, sipping from her hip-flask. There was a moist, vegetable smell of seaweed on the air. No moon. Slithering clouds. Tomorrow she would post the letters to the galleries and have done with it, she decided.

The brandy was hot in her throat. There were no lights on in the Beach Caff. Anna replayed the small encounter with Jack in the square. She ran her eyes appreciatively across the memory, explored the parts that were important to her in a man. It struck her as incredible that she might have inspired emotions and action in a person with whom she had only the most slight of relationships. The idea was not altogether pleasing. Anna made a roll-up and cupped her hand to light it. She took a deep puff of the sweet tobacco and a big swallow of brandy. The pleasure was almost perfect; she resented Jack's intrusion into it, the way in which he had enmeshed her single acts in invisible consequences. Anna knew love – or the potential for love – when she saw it, how quiet and patient it could be, on the sidelines, waiting its moment. There were easier ways to get your pleasures: wham, bam, thank-you Miles. She wasn't scared, like Lesley, she just didn't know that it was what she wanted.

Even so, her imagination unzipped zips, undid buttons.

What she did not need, on returning home, was to find Carmen Fitch on her sofa, reading an old copy of *Spare Rib*, smoking a menthol cigarette and eating from a bag of Twiglets.

'So you're back, are you?' Carmen remarked, without looking up.

'Yes Carmen, I've been under arrest.'

'They serve curry at the police station, do they?'

It was then that Anna noticed, on the low table where Carmen was resting her feet, on top of a leaning stack of books and magazines, six envelopes, unstamped, laid out in a neat square.

'What are those?' she asked.

'You wrote them, Anna. You tell me.'

The hip-flask was empty. Anna pulled the cork out of a half-drunk bottle of red wine and poured some into a tumbler.

'I'm not saying the time won't come, Anna, when this will be totally and absolutely the right move to make. But it isn't now. The galleries'll take one look at your letter and when they see that you haven't exhibited they'll simply bin it. They won't even bother to write back because they get that kind of letter every day. Sacks of them. Too many to bother replying to. Whether you're good enough – if you were – won't be something they have the time to look into. It would cost them thousands a year.' As she spoke, Carmen leafed through pages of the magazine. Seeming to make a decision, she threw it onto the floor. 'You know why I'm telling you this Anna, don't you?' she rasped.

Anna collapsed into an armchair.

'Enlighten me,' she said thickly, viewing Carmen slightly unsteadily, while the back of her brain told her that Carmen was right and that, however little the woman might know about art, the logistics made sense; CV's, introductions, catalogues, stuffed portfolios: those were the sorts of things the galleries would be looking for.

'It's because I love you,' said Carmen.

Anna took a swallow of wine. She started to laugh. Carmen's expression changed to horror. Nothing else would have done it; Carmen could have, as in the past, withstood any amount of ranting, swearing and insults; she could have ducked hurled objects. Laughter, however . . . Carmen was not to know that the last gasp of her power had hit its mark, that the letters would not be posted but would remain, frozen, on the table. Diminished, she stared at Anna with utter loathing.

Lesley unlocked the door. The house was dark. She reached for the light switch but Darryl's hand grabbed her wrist. Practisedly, he pulled her into his arms and kissed her in a way that she had thought only happened in films.

Urgent desire was something Lesley had never experienced before. She had not known that clothes could literally be peeled off, the thrill of running hands along clean curves of muscle, nor felt damp excitement mount exponentially: expanding circles of longing forming on the tips of her fingers, twisting down her breasts, her waist, her stomach, stopping between her thighs, recommencing, doubled, at the tips of her fingers. It was virtually unbearable – the assurance, the insistence, the ease with which he slipped her panties down her legs in order to enter her, the erotic thrill of semi-nakedness.

The circles of feeling began to form with greater and greater speed. There was not room for all of them between her legs. Lesley arched her back and gasped. Her thighs flooded with pleasure. It peaked and subsided. They fell apart and lay on the carpet, panting.

'Like I said,' said Darryl, after a few moments, 'a sensualist.'

'Why did you forgive me for criticising you?' asked Lesley.

There was a pause. Darryl rolled on his side to face her. She could make out the contours of his body. There would be times when they would be in public somewhere and she would think how she had seen him like this. She felt a ripple of renewed desire.

'Well I'd like to be able to tell you it was because I admitted to myself that you were, broadly speaking, right,' said Darryl.

'But I was.'

'Yes, I know, Lesley, but however much you Tory types are into facing up to your defects and deciding to reform, the case is rather different with actors. Most people are only as good as they have to be and actors can usually get away with behaving more badly than other people.'

'So why then?'

'Because I saw you being dragged off by the police.'

There was a silence.

'Shall I open a bottle of something?' asked Lesley. 'There's a Chablis in the fridge.'

'Brilliant. Can we drink it in your bedroom? I think my carpet days are numbered.'

When they eventually slept it was almost light, the sky a pale, smoky blue, the objects in the room clarifying, the bedspread a crumpled mass on the floor, the sheets tangled.

Four hours later the sound of someone knocking at the front door shot Lesley into wakefulness. She sat up. Darryl lay asleep beside her. Lesley lay down again, hoping that whoever it was would go away. The knocking continued. Lesley got out of bed, pulled on a negligée, made her way downstairs irritatedly and opened the front door a little way.

She did not know quite who she had been expecting but it was certainly not Jay and Susie.

'Hey towzled lady in silken gown,' said Jay, making a windscreen-wiper gesture with an enormous hand. The other was around Susie's shoulders.

'Good morning,' said Lesley.

'Oh Lesley,' burst out Susie, 'oh gloom. Mummy's absolutely furious. Jay's house isn't safe to be in and, anyway, it's full of policemen. I hoped you wouldn't mind us coming to see you. The thing is . . .' She burst into tears.

Lesley opened the door wide. 'Come in,' she said, 'I'll make milky coffee and some toast and honey.' She ushered them into the kitchen, sat Susie down and poured some milk into a saucepan.

Susie blew her nose loudly. 'The thing is . . .' she started again.

Lesley opened the cupboard to get out the honey. 'The thing is,' she finished Susie's sentence, 'that you are pregnant.' She turned to Jay. 'And you, presumably, are the father?'

Jay nodded. He gave a big grin. 'If it's a boy, we're going to call him Reefer.'

Susie broke into a watery smile. 'And if it's a girl, we're going to call her Rainbow-Lesley. Won't that be super? I mean, it'll be awfully fitting and all, because of you being my godmother, and us having used your spare room – I hope you don't mind. We wanted to keep our relationship under wraps until we'd figured out a way of telling Mummy, though it looks as though we might as well not've bothered. Also, we felt – jolly odd – as if we were somehow being watched. But after yesterday, and thinking that Jay might be in the house when the bomb went off, I couldn't bear to keep it a secret any longer.'

Lesley remembered the stormy night, when she had returned home from the Mermaid and been surprised to find Susie in the house. She had had the same sensation. She had felt that there was someone out there; that she was not alone. Lesley placed three coffees on the table and a plate of thickly-buttered toast. She opened her mouth to speak but, before she could say what she had been going to, there was more knocking on the front door.

'This, I imagine,' she remarked, going to answer it, 'will be Winifred.'

'Oh gloom,' said Susie, 'just when the toast is ready.' She grabbed a slice and hastily coated it with honey. 'Primrose too, probably.'

Lesley stopped. 'Primrose?'

'Mummy wanted me to see Primrose. She said she thought she would talk some sense into me.'

'We lit the blue touch-paper and hey presto,' said Jay.

Winifred's lipstick could have lined runways. She stalked into the house looking vehemently sensible. Primrose's hair was pulled into a charmingly disarrayed little knot. She wore a simple, naturally-dyed blackberry-coloured frock and a hand-knitted cardigan. On her feet were plaited leather Indian sandals. The two made their way, unerringly, to the kitchen. Susie had managed to gobble down her piece of toast and was reaching for another.

'Susie,' said Winifred, 'Primrose has come to talk to you. She is extremely concerned.'

'Oh Sooz,' said Primrose, who was well up on extremely concerned due to her electioneering, 'why ever didn't you confide in me? There's an absolutely wonderful place in London that everyone raves about.'

'Hey,' said Jay, interestedly, 'what's it called?'

'It's an abortion clinic,' Primrose replied coldly.

'I don't want an abortion,' said Susie, munching on her toast.

'An abortion is what you will have,' cried Winifred, unable to contain herself. 'When I think of all the nice boys I have set before you, any one of whom would have made the most perfect of husbands. And what do you do? You get pregnant by,' she looked at Jay, unable to decide on a noun that would best denote him, 'by this gentleman here . . .'

'It's not on, Susie,' said Primrose, 'this kind of thing, it's lovely in theory and we do approve awfully of it for a lot of people, one day in the future.'

'At best,' said Winifred, 'your child will be the colour of milky coffee. At worst, it could be dark chocolate.'

'I like dark chocolate,' said Susie.

'In its proper place,' said Winifred, 'I'm sure we all do, but that place is not in our grandchildren.'

There was a pause. Susie crunched steadily.

'Winifred, Primrose,' said Lesley, 'I think really the choice is Jay and Susie's.'

As one, Winifred and Primrose rounded on her.

'I suppose you knew all about this and did nothing?' hissed Winifred. 'I suppose you were covering for her the night I entertained the Paynes and their charming son, Victor, and phoned to ask where she was and the phone ostensibly got cut off?'

'Whatever Susie was doing was her business,' said Lesley, 'and Susie has always been sensible.'

'You, of all people, have no right to judge who is sensible Mummy,' said Primrose.

There was another pause then Susie suddenly stood up. 'Leave Lesley alone, both of you,' she said. Winifred and Primrose swung back to face her, startled. Susie looked Primrose straight in the eye. 'I know what you did with my sausages,' she said.

There was a stunned silence. Everyone, except for Primrose, was highly puzzled.

Susie continued. 'I know you despise me because I'm fat and I know you didn't throw your wedding bouquet at me on purpose.'

Primrose said nothing but Winifred said crossly, 'Whatever you are talking about, Susie, is irrelevant. We are discussing the suitability of your motherhood.'

Now Susie looked at Winifred. She pointed a sticky finger at Primrose. 'Why not discuss the suitability of hers? She doesn't even care what happens to her horse, let alone her children. It was me and Helen that talked about fodder and I bought the bucket. Lesley's been a brick having Cherry in her lovely garden all this time.'

'Oh,' said Primrose, who had regained some of her composure, 'everyone's getting bored with gipsydom. If you care so much about Cherry, Susie, you can have her, and the caravan; I'm sure I can't be bothered with getting rid of them.'

'Thank you,' said Susie, 'I will.'

'They can stay in the garden as long as you want, Susie,' exclaimed Lesley, overwhelmingly impressed.

'Am I to understand,' Winifred asked her daughter, 'that you are completely adamant about having this illegitimate offspring?'

'I am,' said Susie.

'In that case, I wash my hands of you. And you,' Winifred turned to Lesley, 'if you are so determined not to back me up as to the best interests of Susie, you can take responsibility for her, you can concern yourself with her – as I have had to concern myself, in loco parentis, with Primrose.'

'I should be proud to,' said Lesley.

'Hey, Momma!' said Jay. 'Mobile home!'

'You're all going to regret this a hell of a lot,' remarked Primrose.

In reply, Susie picked up her cup. 'Look Primrose,' she said, 'look Mummy: this is milky coffee, and I think it's lovely, and I'm going to live in a caravan with my man, who is lovely too, and my milky coffee baby and we'll barbecue sausages and toast marshmallows and be happy.'

'Who is this delightful woman? Tell me we'll be seeing a lot of her because I adore her already.' It was Darryl. He stood in the kitchen doorway, wearing only a pair of jeans.

'Gosh,' said Susie. 'You're the charming man at Primrose's wedding.'

'Better and better,' said Darryl.

'Susie,' said Lesley, 'allow me to introduce to you my lover, Darryl Younger. Winifred, I don't know if you have ever met Darryl?'

'Mummy!' Then Primrose's face arranged itself into a smug expression. 'It was Darryl who tried to seduce Christie Marks's younger sister at my wedding,' she informed Lesley.

'That was a long time ago and Christie Marks's sister is just an upper-class scrubber,' said Lesley. 'By the way, Primrose, have you seen the polls recently?'

With that, Winifred and Primrose departed. Lesley put more toast on. Susie sat down a little shakily.

'I think, Susie,' said Lesley, 'you should probably have a rest.'

'I'd rather go and wave at the ferry,' said Susie. 'After breakfast.'

Jay started to roll a joint. 'Let's all go wave at the ferry,' he suggested.

'Great idea,' said Darryl. 'Where's the phone, Les? Better call my agent. No point, of course, but such is habit.'

'I'm sorry you've lost your mole, Lesley,' said Susie, when Darryl had disappeared to the study.

For a moment Lesley didn't understand what Susie meant. Then, 'Why didn't you just tell me, if you were willing to inform the coalition about the manoeuvres of the Babcock campaign?' she asked.

'I wasn't sure you'd approve. I'm not sure I approve really. But I reckoned it would give us a fighting chance, that we mightn't have had otherwise, and I'm afraid I did want to get my own back because of the sausages. Oh gloom: that sounds awfully like real politics, doesn't it?'

'Susie,' said Lesley, 'I'm really not quite clear as to how sausages fit into the picture.'

But now Darryl was once more in the doorway.

'Would you believe it?' he cried. 'Bloody amazing. I've got the audition I've been hoping for. This afternoon. In London. Prospero.'

'Reefer Prospero,' said Jay. 'I like it.'

'Prospero. Gosh,' said Susie. 'We did *The Tempest* at school. Doesn't he get to say an awful lot?'

'One of the best sodding roles in the canon. Can you give me a lift, Les? I'll pick some things up from home and read my audition speeches through on the train. Ebbing Constabulary can hang on to the old jalopy for the time being.'

'Of course,' said Lesley. She forced a smile. 'Prospero,' she exclaimed. 'That's wonderful Darryl. That really is wonderful.'

'Bloody wonderful. Good news all round at the moment.'

But 'all round' had a smaller circumference than Darryl thought, even in Lesley's kitchen. Elsewhere, Winifred Took and Primrose Babcock were seething for revenge after the news of *their* morning and, even as Darryl spoke, the postman was pushing through Carmen Fitch's letterbox an unwelcome delivery which would ensure that they got it.

21

Rallying

When, after the accident involving her gallery, Carmen Fitch had exhorted Lesley not to talk to her about insurance, it was for the very good reason that, in the case of the objets d'art themselves, there wasn't any. So it was with less than cordial emotions that Carmen now opened a letter from the major exhibitors in 'Anger II' – who, in the light of Fitch's Gallery being repaired but their sculptures still not restored to their rightful position, had become suspicious and made inquiries.

It was not logical – Anna herself had nothing whatsoever to do with the letter – but, given the events of the night before; what Carmen saw as Anna's causal link with the accident; and, most of all, her artistic ungratefulness, it was scarcely surprising that she was the one Carmen alighted upon as the butt of the rage that followed her reading of the letter, which was many pages long and full of what each of the artists was experiencing. The gist of it, however, was that if the sculptures did not reappear pretty damn quick, Carmen would find herself the subject of a joint legal action.

Desperately, Carmen phoned around. The result was as before, only more so: the skip had vanished.

Carmen toyed with the idea of suggesting to the sculptors that their works were worthless, but she was the one who, with an eye to her percentage, had recommended their prices. Could she say that the sculptures had suddenly gone out of fashion and had therefore dipped in value? But would the women go for that, given the much that had been made of their art as investment, aimed at the discerning buyer?

Carmen totted up how much she could reasonably be in for, then added on what she could expect the artists to demand in recompense for psychological trauma. The overall picture was not pretty; the sum greatly exceeded what she could easily lay her hands on. Carmen puffed furiously on numerous fags and ate a bag of tomato ketchup flavoured crisps before she came up with a solution: she herself would bring some kind of legal action – she didn't know exactly what, but she had the sort of solicitor who would be able to think of one – against Susie Took. There followed a few moments' blissful speculation on what figure could be hoped for, during which Carmen regretted that she hadn't been in the Gallery at the time of the accident and suffered slight injury and extreme mental distress. Then the obvious drawbacks of this line of action occurred to her: it would take forever and the outcome would be uncertain. Carmen ate another bag of crisps – salt and vinegar this time – while searching for an alternative. Eventually, she thought of one: better by far would be to *threaten* legal action and see if Susie Took could be bullied into some kind of financial settlement.

Carmen made her way to the Took residence and pressed on the doorbell. She heard it chime inside the building but there was no answer. The only other place where she could think of looking for Susie Took was Cinderella's Bridal Gowns, which she knew was owned by Susie's mother.

Carmen stalked back down Harbour Street. The Old Fish Market Square car park was virtually empty but most of the shops were open. Jay's house was cordoned off with orange and white plastic tape but a cluster of holidaymakers stood in front of it, to be on hand to watch if anyone tried to blow it up again. The Woodcutter Inn was doing a roaring trade, perhaps because it had almost been visited by the Prime Minister, perhaps due to the reinstatement of the banner proclaiming its 'Prawns 'n' Pasta' offer.

Going into Cinderella's was like entering the interior of a meringue. Carmen's pupils ached from the sudden avalanche of white and all its permutations. She stood, blinking at an ivory silk pillow-thing, with lace surround, carried by a mannequin homunculus in a Little-Boy-Blue costume, wondering as to its purpose.

'Can I help you, Miss Fitch?' The voice appeared to doubt very much that it could.

Seated on two string-coloured canvas director's chairs were Primrose and Winifred. They each had a flowered cup of bitter orange-peel tea, which they were drinking in order to restore nerves shattered by the horrible scene they had just undergone. Both had a passing acquaintance with Carmen Fitch, due to her gallery.

'Need to see your daughter,' croaked Carmen. 'She owes me money.'

Winifred raised her eyebrows at Primrose in such a way as to indicate that, whatever this was about, they should probably hear it, because it might just possibly be useful to them. She moderated her tone a little. 'Tell us your problem, Miss Fitch.'

This Carmen, more or less, did: gesturing wildly, lighting cigarettes and dropping ash onto the carpet, allocating responsibility for the accident and its consequences to Susie but also, in the muddle of her feelings, spluttering out many of the plethora of grievances she harboured against Anna Seale.

While this was going on, Winifred exchanged almost constant glances with Primrose, indicating, by the merest of facial gestures, the direction of her thinking. Primrose replied with little nods. By the time Carmen had finished, Winifred and Primrose's minds were trotting along in perfect harmony. Fate, it seemed, had unexpectedly presented them with an unlikely ally.

How right Lesley had been when she had reckoned that, were it to come out, she would pay dearly for covering for Susie; how wrong in reassuring herself that she was inviolable because there were no skeletons in her particular closet. Certainly, Winifred might once have balked at doing the dirty, at a public level, on her own kind; but increased contact with Primrose had made Winifred more modern and, anyway, Anna Seale was not Winifred's own kind.

'Oh dear,' said Primrose, when Carmen ceased. 'What an awful shame.'

'What kind of sum are we talking about for those poor artists?' asked Winifred.

The fact that she did not blench at the amount now named made Carmen wish she had gone higher.

'I suppose,' said Winifred, 'that you are also worrying about the possibility of such a woman as Anna Seale in possession of political power? She appears so . . . undependable.'

'Gawd yes,' spluttered Carmen.

'It doesn't sound to me,' said Primrose, 'like she's thinking of anyone but herself. If I were you, I'd be wondering how I could make sure that people who saw eye to eye with me were represented by somebody less selfish. I mean, surely not everyone in your Coalition Party likes Anna?' She paused. 'And I imagine, as Anna's closest chum, you know heaps about her that they don't.'

There was a silence. Carmen contemplated a silver cardboard horseshoe in a clear plastic box, alongside a selection of garters and several packs of scented confetti.

'It *is* quite a lot of money,' said Winifred. 'Though, since Susie is my daughter, I feel, of course, as responsible as if it were I who had caused the damage. Her debt is my debt, you see – were I to assume it. But it would take several weeks to make the sum available. Perhaps not till just before the election, or even after.' She smiled at Carmen lightly and removed a piece of fluff from a green satin cummerbund.

On leaving Cinderella's Carmen didn't go to her usual drinker. She went, instead, to the Jolly Roger.

'If you're a journalist, you can fuck off,' yelled Anna.

'It's not a journalist, it's me,' said Lesley. She entered Anna's bedroom. The scene was one of utter desolation. Clothes were strewn everywhere. The room smelled musty. The curtains were drawn. Anna lay in bed in a faded, fleecy sort of garment, her face half-buried in a pillow.

'Exactly how much of this is true?' asked Lesley.

Anna raised her head a little. She was pale. Her hair was tangled. Under her eyes was pink and puffy. 'To start with,' she said, her voice somewhat muffled, 'I've never been anti-lesbian, though that's a topic that's under review at present.'

'Well Mary Janet and her Lesbian Separatists believe Carmen and they're leaving the Coalition,' said Lesley. 'Apparently what Carmen didn't say on the news, but what she is putting around, is that Susie's accident with Fitch's Gallery was a deliberate attack on lesbian self-expression, tacitly condoned by yourself.'

'Because I weighed in when Carmen pulled up in her Artmobile, quacking?'

'Presumably,' said Lesley. 'Though I cannot understand why anyone would give credence to such a preposterous claim.' She went to the window and lifted the curtain. Outside, there were two men with news cameras balanced on their shoulders, a couple of sound people with overhead microphones, wrapped in something fluffy, and several journalists. A woman Lesley recognised from an early evening discussion programme was spraying mineral water onto her face from an aerosol. She let the curtain drop.

Anna coughed. Without sitting up, she reached for her tobacco and papers. The bedside table was covered in scummy glasses.

'They don't believe it,' she said, in answer to Lesley's comment about the Lesbian Separatists. 'They just love this kind of thing, the bitches. Crises, scenes, splits, divisions, factions, walk-outs: it's all right up their street. And, in the meantime, the Government nicks the benefit off single-parents.' Anna's voice started to crack.

'The Non-Separatist Feminists are still with us,' said Lesley. 'Though the homosexuals have gone, I'm afraid, in solidarity with the Lesbian Separatists.' Anna sniffed loudly. She lit her roll-up. Lesley thought how all this solidarity, strangely, seemed to make everything so much weaker.

There was a silence.

'What about the alcoholism and the drug money?' asked Lesley. 'Those are what the media is going to be most interested in. Is it true that the Preserve The Ebbing Clifftop And Jesus Was A Black Man Party was originally funded with the proceeds of drug dealing?' She thought of the nastiness of her own, Rossetti-ish daughter, with her Kate Greenaway children. Butter wouldn't melt; and yet, how corrupt Primrose was, compared with a hard-drinking Anna or a drug-selling Jay – if Carmen was right about him.

'What I do with my own body is nobody else's fucking business.' Anna sniffed again. 'Our Party wasn't any more funded by drug money than the NHS is.'

'So it was then?'

'If you must put it that way.' Anna's voice rose. 'Why don't you bugger off, Lesley, now that you've got your answers?'

But Lesley did not budge. 'In that case,' she said, 'it is time, Anna, for you to behave like a Tory.'

'Meaning what?'

'Meaning deny absolutely everything. And the truer it is, the more they can make it stick, the louder you must deny it.'

There was a pause. Anna rubbed her hand fiercely across her nose and mouth. 'You can brazen it out, Lesley,' she said. 'I am not going outside in order to be cross-questioned by a whole load of fucking reporters. I have had it. Our numbers are so down we haven't got a snowball in hell's chance of winning the election anyway. I'm done with politics. I'm done with the clifftop. They can put a sodding missile base on it, as far as I'm concerned.'

Still, Lesley did not move. Watching Anna, it struck her how fragile the Left Wing was, compared with the Right, how spontaneously half-hearted, how easily diverted from its purpose. In-fighting was not unknown, of course, among the Tories but, when it came to public faces, loyalty was bred in the bone; valour in the face of calumny was second nature.

'For God's sake Anna,' she snapped, suddenly impatient, 'can't you put aside your self-pity for a moment? You're not the only one to have been shopped by an ex-friend. Look at all the people who have done the dirty on me – Osbert, Winifred Took, my own daughter. If you believe in something you come out fighting, and you fight until other people believe in it too.'

Anna raised her head from the pillow now. Her nose was red. Her eyes were bloodshot. They stared straight into Lesley's. 'Oh? And what exactly is it you believe in then, Lesley Sway?'

There was a frozen silence, during which Lesley realised that, apart from the need to save the clifftop, she no longer had the first notion. A tap on the door made them both jump.

Anna sat up. She ran her hands through her hair. 'If that's a reporter, you can fuck off for the moment, I'll be making a statement later,' she shouted. Then, 'I hate you, Lesley,' she whispered. 'I hate you for being so bloody intrepid.'

The door opened and Bob entered.

'Hallo Mrs Sway. Hallo Anna. No, it's not a reporter. I'm glad I've found you both together though, because I've got some rather exciting news, which I thought might cheer you up a bit. I've just been on the clifftop and I'm very pleased to be able to tell you that the first brood of lesser tit fledglings has hatched out. Two, in all, which is quite respectable, and they do look fairly healthy.'

'Hoo-bloody-ray,' said Anna. 'How right we are to continue the struggle.' Nevertheless, she pulled back the bedcovers. The phone rang. 'You get it, Lesley. I'm going to have a bath.'

'And I must be off,' said Bob. 'Others will want to know about the fledglings. I'm pretty confident I was the first to spot them though.'

Lesley went and picked up the receiver. It was Eustace.

'Thought I might find you there, Lesley,' he said. 'You've heard the gossip, of course. Bad business, very bad business. Used to happen a lot in South America.'

Lesley thought a moment. Eustace must be talking about political parties and drug money, she decided. 'Well they grow so easily there, don't they?' she said.

'D'you think so? Always assumed they grew about the same everywhere myself.'

There was a pause.

'Eustace, you are talking about the allegations against Anna, aren't you?' said Lesley.

'They're partly what I phoned about but, no, I mean your god-daughter and the black. Though you could be right, could be something to do with climate.'

'The allegations against Anna,' Lesley asked coolly: 'what did you want to say on the subject?'

'Just this, Lesley: whether they're true or not, none of us believes them.'

Lesley thought of the Lesbian Separatists, the homosexuals, the Marxists. 'I wish,' she said, 'that our left-wing colleagues were as loyal.'

'No, I heard they weren't pulling together.'

'Which means that, once again, we have the problem of numbers in terms of our support.'

'Well that's the other thing I wanted to tell you, Lesley,' said Eustace. 'Number problem solved: a chappie came round about an hour ago, said he's been hovering in the background, seeing what was what, till today, but now he wants his people to link up with us. Big meeting tomorrow. Eight o'clock. The Jolly Roger.'

'Who is it?' Anna yelled from the bathroom.

'Just a moment, Eustace.' Lesley lowered the receiver. 'It's Eustace Frogwell,' she called back. 'He says there's a man who's decided today that he wants his party to join the Coalition and that that will solve our problems.'

There was a pause. Anna appeared, wrapped in a towel.

'It's got to be Miles!' she exclaimed, excitedly. 'That really will give us a majority.'

Lesley lifted the receiver again. 'Eustace,' she asked, 'who is it?'

'Funny thing that,' he replied, 'can't remember the fellow's name. Wrote it down on the newspaper but Maud must have used it to line a whelping box.'

'Is it Miles Starey?'

'Could be,' Eustace replied, 'could be.'

But it wasn't. At eight o'clock the following evening, Frogwell presented to what remained of the Coalition, not Miles Starey's bronzed figure but William Flint's pallid one. The uproar that followed took him by surprise; there was no reason that he could see why they should not ally themselves with the British Patriotic Party – especially if they wanted to win the election.

Jack and Anna

'Earwig-oh earwig-oh earwig-oh!' Flint's army spilled into the Old Fish Market car park, where they held an impromptu rally. Flint himself stood in the door of the Jolly Roger looking, as leaders do on such occasions, too modest to take the entire credit for having caused this. Beside him, Eustace smiled and smiled. From time to time the two men shook hands or linked raised fists.

Families coming out of the Woodcutter Inn got caught up in the festive atmosphere. They bounced their toddlers' pushchairs to the rhythm of the chanting and looked pleased that it was all right to think what they thought.

Yes, this was the way to win an election. Support had grown and was visibly growing. Eustace Frogwell lost some of his Right Wing, who hadn't got the stomach for it, and all of his Left, but here was a compensatory abundance.

Drawn by the noise and the excitement, people came out of the three pubs: a gamut of opinion and all you had to do was to decide which bit you belonged in now. Back to the Mermaid for the Feminists. They burst into rival singing – sisters were doing it for themselves once again. Trouncy Lollop crossed the floor and declared her allegiance to the Marxist cause – as long as she didn't have to wear one of those dreadful hats. Rolf Watt and his followers, not to be outdone, started to bellow 'We'll

Keep The Red Flag Flying Here' – though 'keep' was perhaps not quite the word. Everyone who was, was glad to be gay. The Trots and the Anarchists sang something in translation, possibly the same song as each other, possibly not. If you wanted to save a whale you could honk your horn.

The defecting Right, as long as it made up its mind that it could stomach a four-lane dual carriageway on the Ebbing clifftop better than it could stomach being led by a newsagent, could either pop back into the Jolly Roger (where Veronica Tarrant was looking none-too-pleased with developments and wishing wishing wishing she had stuck with Tim and Primrose, in spite of the media event at the Woodcutter) or, of course, they could join New Labour. It was much of a muchness but the devil you know . . .

One or two colonely-types, seated in the dining-room of the Jolly Roger, beneath a few wall-mounted fragments of a fo'c'sle from a ship that had gone down at the end of the last century, joined in the chorus of 'Rule Britannia' issuing from outside, but subsided into humming when they spotted Veronica looking daggers and started to talk about 'Primmie and Tim' in loud voices.

'Well well well,' said Steven Toe, thinking of his forthcoming retrospective in the Sainsbury Wing; thinking of it very hard in fact.

'Well well well what?' asked Penny St John. They were going through a difficult patch.

'This is more fun than rugger,' said Rory St John.

'No it isn't,' retorted Bianca Pickle.

'I say,' said Rory, 'if you want, I'll take you for prawns and pasta.'

'I'm allergict,' said Bianca.

'Nobody's allergic to pasta.'

'Maybe it's you I'm allergict to.' She swivelled off to the kitchen.

Cornmeal porridge; not crying: now Bob Marley's dead voice exploded from a parked car, drowning out all other considerations. The British Patriotic Party broke ranks, started running, their heavy boots clomping down the streets of the little town, jumping off the sea wall, shouting 'Over here!' as if there was something that needed dealing with that they were pursuing or being pursued by. Some of them unhooked the Woodcutter Inn's banner; they paraded the length of the High Street, catcalling outside the Taj Mahal – which had closed quickly – the special offer dangled limply between them. Someone bravely spat through Olive Ford's letterbox.

I've got my information, and no one to tell it to, thought Jack Fryer, watching it all from outside the Anchor. I've got it in writing. He fingered the envelope in his pocket. He would have used the word 'irony', if it had ever been put at his disposal.

The circus moved on. People left the Square and went back to where they'd come from. A pleased media flicked fags onto the ground and hurried off to deliver copy.

In his renovated chapel, beyond the Ebb Valley, Tim Babcock, a mongrel pup – rushed down from Battersea – playing at his feet, watched it all on the television screen and debated with Dick Winters the pros and cons of now opting for an anti-racist stance. In her belfry, Primrose pressed flowers for Christmas cards. Helen helped Sorrel puff on her inhaler.

Maybe Lesley Sway or Anna could help him use what he knew, thought Jack Fryer. Crying in the bloody wilderness – they'd hammered home the Bible.

Anna and Lesley had been the first out of the Jolly Roger. News people had tried to collar them. One yelled 'Will you be entering a detoxification programme, Anna?' Another shouted, 'Mrs Sway, Mrs Sway, have you ever had any contact with Nanny Enema?' Neither woman spoke and soon there was something of more interest: the emergence of Flint and Frogwell, prompting sequins of camera flashes.

Anna and Lesley walked away from the noise, towards the silence of waves and seagulls, the dignified business of life and water. Strange, how quickly these things seemed to close a door behind them. The sky was hyacinth, thought Anna, with small splodges of white cloud: smoke from the chimneys of the city beneath the sea.

She said to Lesley, 'I remember looking up at your house on the clifftop and wondering what kind of a person you were.'

Lesley said, 'I remember looking down at Ebbing and seeing

your light, though I didn't know it was yours then.' There was a pause.

'Darryl phoned last night, late,' Lesley said. 'He's got the role he was reading for. Prospero. He's staying up in London for the time being; they're starting rehearsing almost immediately. I'm looking after his cat. The play's touring, you know – the United States and Canada – six months to a year. There wasn't much time to talk. I didn't find out whether he knows what's happened here.'

'Or cares now,' she could have added. Darryl was so excited; there were delightful people calling him to hurry up or the restaurant would be closed.

The two women descended a flight of steps onto the shingle. Except for them, the beach was deserted. Sounds from the Square and the High Street came to them muffled.

'What's going on over there?' said Anna suddenly. She pulled Lesley into a crouching position behind a breaker covered with twisted boas of bladder-wrack. Lesley looked in the direction Anna indicated. About a hundred yards away, a figure with many limbs had appeared, dragging a struggling body over the sea wall and onto the pebbles, where it was dropped and surrounded. The youths' heads were bowed in attitudes of detached interest: they could have been turning over a crab to watch it wave its claws.

Lesley gasped; she recognised one of the faces, even though he wasn't wearing his Union Jack t-shirt. Her legs became nothing. 'They're beating someone up,' she cried. 'We must get the police. We must get an ambulance.'

'You get the police. I'll go and try and stop them.'

'Anna, that's crazy. They'll just do the same to you.'

'Whoever it is needs help and medical attention. Go, Lesley. Quickly.'

The sound of a man's voice beside them wrenched Lesley's stomach. But he was saying, 'Anna's right. You go for the police, Mrs Sway. They're cowards. Anna and me'll shift them.'

He was a big man, Jack Fryer. Lesley headed off, back to the sea wall, with every bit of speed that was in her.

'We don't run at them,' said Jack to Anna. 'We just walk steadily and give them time to scatter.'

'I know what we fucking do,' snapped Anna, her fear flowing into anger, then dying almost immediately at the sight of the stricken expression that passed across Jack's face before he was able to hide it.

'Let's go then,' was all he said though, and they moved forward in silence, Anna feeling guilty and wretched, but unable to bring herself to apologise.

By the time they reached the person, he had been abandoned, unconscious, arms and legs splayed, a great starfish; his Rasta locks, soft black tentacles.

'Jay!' Anna knelt beside him. She lifted the large head onto her lap and kept it there until blue lights flashed along the High Street, until there were sirens and policemen and a stretcher.

'Anna,' said Lesley, her face white, 'the police need me for the moment.'

'I'll go in the ambulance,' said Anna.

'I'll come with you,' said Jack.

'You don't need to.'

'I'll come anyway.'

'As soon as I'm finished, I'll telephone the hospital to see how Jay is,' said Lesley. 'Susie mustn't be upset in her condition. She mustn't be told anything until we know he's going to be all right . . . Or unless she has to be.'

The identikit picture seemed to have aged. A stand, with a headline written on it in magic-marker – 'SEX STAR'S EX WAS HIV' – was visible inside the shop, not left out in case someone stole it. Plain postcards advertising secondhand mattresses, that you paid by the week to have there, were sellotaped to the window.

'You are quite sure this is the location, Mrs Sway?' asked the policeman in the hooped earring.

'Absolutely,' said Lesley. 'Yes, this is where he's living. Mr Flint told me.'

The policeman nodded at the door. One of the two uniformed ones with him knocked on it loudly. There was no answer.

'Kick it in,' said the plainclothed one.

'Police!' They yelled into the silence. Followed by Lesley, they made their way through the dark shop. One of them found a light switch. They kicked in another door at the back, that led to the flat. The stairs were lit by a single light-bulb. The walls smelled of damp. They hammered on a door at the top of the staircase. 'Police!' they shouted again. 'We're coming in.' They kicked it open and burst into the room, then stood, staring about them, incredulous.

Sacks and sacks of weedkiller.

'Isn't that what . . .?' asked Lesley.

'Yup.' The one in jeans and an earring nodded. 'Would you bloody believe it?'

At the police station Lesley asked to use the telephone. The Duty Sergeant brought her some tea and a biscuit and gave her the number of Pitsbury General.

A nurse informed her that Jay had been admitted to Intensive Care and was about to be examined. He was still unconscious. There was no news as to what kind of injury he had suffered. More would be known later.

Lesley dialled the Frogwells' number. After she had made her statement, to a polite young policewoman, she drove straight to the Frogwell Mansion.

Frogwell answered the door, looking a mixture of sheepish and defiant.

'I'm in a hurry, Eustace,' said Lesley. 'I need to get home. But I want to tell you what is going to happen. Firstly, using your South American contacts, you are going to look into the case of Lois Zimble and bring pressure for her immediate release. Secondly, I am going to call the press. You will make a statement saying that you deeply regret ever having involved yourself – and unwitting others – with the British Patriotic Party and that you now withdraw as joint leader of the Coalition and fully endorse the sole candidacy of Anna Seale.'

It was well after midnight. Jay remained unconscious but a CT scan had revealed no bleeding in the brain. Anna phoned Lesley. Susie had been asleep on Lesley's return; in the absence of further developments, they agreed that Lesley should wait until morning to tell her.

Lesley did not mention her visit to the Frogwells.

'Really, you don't have to stay here,' said Anna to Jack, sitting down again and propping her feet on a low table covered in old magazines. Pitsbury General was quiet. Behind her counter, a receptionist tapped at a computer. A man in a coat, clutching a bloody handkerchief to his fingers, had been taken to be examined. There'd been a small kerfuffle with a drunk at the reception desk, who'd slumped into a chair for a while before reeling off.

Anna looked at Jack and then away again. He was leaning back, his hands clasped behind his head, his body a diagonal. He followed her every move with his eyes. Did he know – or had he guessed? – that she knew how he felt about her? The idea had an erotic kick to it.

Anna sighed gustily. Utterly inappropriate. Things were fucked over quite enough without that. What was going on, for God's sake? It couldn't be real that they were waiting here to see if Jay would come round or not. Though, for Jay himself, it wouldn't make much difference, Anna joked to herself. She smiled, then her eyes watered.

'I don't really want to be a politician,' she said quickly, picking up a magazine and leafing through it noisily.

'What do you want to be?' asked Jack, watching her. He was imagining being allowed to comfort her, making love to her slowly, though he guessed she was probably the raucous type. He imagined tearing, rolling, thrashing and *then* making love slowly.

'A painter.' She said the word as if it were precious. 'But I'm always the first one to stick my bloody neck out. I see something that needs doing and I do it, in case nobody else does. Though I'm probably not candidate of anything any more, after the fucking mess of this evening.'

'Do you want a coffee?' asked Jack.

'Hot chocolate. Here.' Anna got some money out of her pocket.

Jack went to where the vending machines were and came back with a coffee, a hot chocolate and a bag of Maltesers. Anna sipped her drink and stuffed a handful of Maltesers into her mouth. Jack imagined the sweetness on her tongue.

'I'm a loner too,' he said.

'You talking about being a painter?'

Jack nodded.

'I'm not a loner,' said Anna. 'But I *am* independent.'

A surge of excitement ran through Jack's whole body: she knew how he felt and she was warning him about herself. *Which meant there was a point in hoping.* So long distantly admired, her character was taking on texture as they spoke. Suddenly, the letter in his pocket – his information, his written evidence – felt treacherous: Anna had made sacrifices for the clifftop; Jack had mainly just stood by and watched. That she might resent him bulling in was a risk he couldn't take. Nor, however, could he abandon his mates, see shops, caffs and bed and breakfasts close down, jobs disappear, the whole bloody environment – human and animal – killed off. If only he had been there at the beginning. If only they had been in it together. No one'd ever come in the Anchor to invite him, but neither had he gone out to join them.

Happy, unhappy, turned on, frustrated, hopeful, hopeless; initial esteem and attraction rapidly thickening into a complexity of compelling emotions and desires, Jack decided to set aside decisions for the moment. He and Anna Seale sat on, in the white, neutral, shadowless light, eating chocolates, dozing and talking until the sky woke up and this receptionist went off duty.

Eventually, a doctor came and spoke to them.

'Your friend has regained consciousness. He will be in Intensive Care for another twenty-four hours and then we should be moving him onto a ward. There doesn't appear to be any permanent damage.'

It was six a.m. Jack phoned for a taxi. Together, he and Anna walked out of Casualty and to the gates of Pitsbury General.

Shouts went up:

'There she is!'

'Anna?'

'Miss Seale, what is your reaction . . .?'

'Look this way, Anna.'

Journalists, cameras, interviewers, reporters.

It was over. They were not alone any longer.

* * *

Everything pointed to William Flint and his supporters being behind the Old Fish Market bombing. His flat had been full of the wherewithal to make explosives. A warrant was out for his arrest and for that of the youth in the Union Jack t-shirt. It now seemed likely that the bombing had, in fact, had racist motives, and was not aimed at the Prime Minister; the timing might well have been purely coincidental. Perhaps Flint and the other bombers had known about, and resented, Jay's involvement with Susie – in her statement Lesley mentioned her sense of somebody watching the house on the night of the storm when, it turned out, Susie and Jay had been there together, and Susie and Jay's feeling of being watched on other occasions. Eustace Frogwell, on finding out that he had allied himself with a group of people who had attempted to blow up, at best, a black man and, at worst, the Prime Minister, agreed that he had no choice but to do as Lesley said and stand down. To a gathered media he made a statement to that effect, adding that Anna Seale, now the Coalition's only candidate, was currently at Pitsbury General Hospital, at the bedside of that same black man who had been assaulted by members of the British Patriotic Party earlier this evening.

Anna was tired and pale, which gave her a noble aspect. She looked rather lovely – large, healthy and sensible – in the coral sunlight and the misty whiteness of the early summer's morning. Having ascertained the facts, she rose to the occasion.

It was a strong voice, earnest and full of conviction. There was honesty and humour in it. It was a voice that made you want to go where it was going.

Surely she can win without me, thought Jack, listening.

23

The Big Day

The air was mustardy with sawdust. Bonfires wafted great chocking gusts of bitter smoke into her face. There was a hot, angry smell. Singed grass sprouted across the ground in pubic tufts; scattered among it, obscenely exposed, wild flowers and plants – unsheltered now, wrong here now – roasted. Scurrying, fluttering, slithering creatures madly searched for where everything had gone.

Lesley shot up, panting, sweat running down her face. There was a knock on the door and Susie entered the room, carrying a mug and an envelope.

'A cuppa,' she said, passing it to Lesley and thumping down onto the bed. 'I didn't hear any rumblings so I thought I'd better wake you, seeing as it's the big day and all. And there's something I want to ask you.'

Lesley's heartbeat slowed. She had been deeply asleep. She was confused and groggy. Her eyes darted to the window. The light made them water but she was still able to see an almond-green haze of foliage and a sliver of sea beneath an expanse of milky-blue sky. For how much longer, though?

Susie was speaking. She was hideously awake and animated.

'. . . have it here, in the garden, if you don't mind?'

'I'm sorry, Susie?'

'The "wedding".'

'What wedding?' Lesley's fuddled mind came up with Prim-rose's reception; Darryl scattering easy charm. As if the thought had summoned him, Boots, Darryl's marmalade cat, who liked to be present when beds were unmade and still warm, now made an entrance, jumping, heavily, onto Lesley's lap.

'Me and Jay. Here. In the garden.'

It began to register. 'When, Susie?'

'Tomorrow. Sort of double celebration, if we win.'

'And if we don't?' thought Lesley. What she said was, 'Can that be done? I mean, will the vicar. . ?' She trailed off. 'I mean, I suppose it won't be a vicar.' She racked her brains, trying to recall whether she had ever known how one referred to the clergy of the Rastafarian church.

'Jay says dreadlock don't wedlock – not really. It won't be a wedding as such, more a "*wedding*".' Susie scooped two handfuls of air to make inverted commas.

Lesley decided against pursuing the topic. 'In the garden is fine,' she said. If they won, they would feel like celebrating. If not . . . it would be right for her garden to be enjoyed for the short while it would have left.

'Good oh.' Susie leapt up. Boots dug his claws in. 'Shall I put on the radio? You can get an update.'

'Thanks.'

'I nearly forgot,' said Susie, handing the envelope to Lesley. 'This came. Thought it might be a Good Luck card.' She put the radio on and left the room.

'I never told 'im as I loved 'im,' said Sally Mackerel, 'and now I never shall.'

'Ay,' said Captain Skate. There was a sound effect of crashing waves and loud seagulls, superimposed upon some quasi-classical music with lots of violins.

Lesley opened the envelope. 'Break A Leg' and a sprawling autograph. Lesley patted the card against her lips. Intermittent phone calls, feverishly rushed. Dying to know how the campaign was going. Read about it in the papers, of course, but you never knew how much to believe. Longing to get back to Ebbing for a spell of R & R before the even madder times began, but when when when? *He missed her*.

Yes, he did say that – just enough to construct magical

islands of future happiness upon; too little to believe in them really.

The music dipped.

'Ay,' repeated Captain Skate, 'thy never shall.' The seagulls got louder for a moment, then the *Ship Ahoy* theme cut in.

She was in love, realised Lesley suddenly. She had run the risk and here was the consequence. It made her feel like an invalid. If this was essentially it, there would be ages of agony to endure before she healed. If she ever did.

'It is five to nine and we go over to the news room for the news.'

'Good morning. The seaside town of Ebbing goes to the polls today, with a by-election that promises to be closely run. We now pass direct *to* Ebbing, where our reporter, Felicia Luckhart, is standing by to bring us, throughout the day, the latest on-the-ground opinion. Felicia, what *is* the atmosphere down there?'

'Hallo Mary. Yes, the atmosphere today is very varied and I feel that a lot of people have still to make up their minds as to whether to go with past loyalties or to decide their opinions based on more local issues. We have had, of course, a run-up which has been fraught with event and, although Eustace Frogwell's stand-down some weeks ago and wholehearted endorsement of his previous running-mate, Anna Seale, has put much of the original Tory component of the Coalition Party – formed to combat the clifftop road scheme – decidedly back behind Ms Seale, the past in-fighting among the Left of her party could well cause nervousness in the floating voter. Where the dice will eventually fall is hard to say.'

Lesley sipped her tea. She felt a sick fear in the pit of her stomach. A sizeable portion of the Alternative Left had now trickled back to the Coalition, but was it too late? Did the Coalition present enough of a united front for people to believe that it was capable of representing them?

'Felicia, can we now talk about Tim Babcock?'

'Yes Mary. Babcock has got to be hoping that his, at present, slight lead will carry the day and he must be worrying as to what effect the Leader of the Opposition's planned visit to Ebbing, later this morning, is going to have upon it.'

*　　*　　*

Except in the case of Veronica Tarrant, it was impossible indeed
to say how many minds were swayed by the sight of the Leader
of the Opposition who, in an egalitarian gesture, entered the Old
Fish Market Square on foot, having had them park his car at the
other end of the High Street.

Jack Fryer had taken time off for this. So, by the look of it,
had others. The Anchor was full for this time of day. The barman
had emptied the ashtrays and put out scampi-flavoured biscuits,
in the shape of fish, on the bar. Some of the waiters had got
away from the Woodcutter for ten minutes. Hortense Smith,
done up a bit, sipped a sherry. Bianca Pickle, twiddling rings,
fibre-tip cupped awkwardly in her left hand, put stars by job
ads in the London *Evening Standard*. The curtains of the Anchor
were open.

Jack harboured a dream – he couldn't bring himself to call
it a fantasy – so strong it was almost like a solid object. This
was how Jack's dream went: the Leader of the Opposition
came to the Anchor, to drink the customary pint, like they
did. While he drank his pint, he talked to the ordinary people
there, like they did. Jack told him about the clifftop. And,
once he'd done that, it wasn't Jack's responsibility any more.
Politics didn't need to concern him; there was no danger
he'd have to steal Anna's thunder – or risk her seeing it
like that.

Jack felt his dream's weight as the Leader of the Opposition,
flanked by Starey – a pair of look-alikes – paused in front of
Jay's house, inspecting the damage, asking intelligent questions;
glimpsing, perhaps, greater days ahead, when they would be
flown in by helicopter – in khakis – to inspect bigger, more
important, damage; when they wouldn't always have to be
second at national (and international) disasters.

Next, Starey and the Leader of the Opposition looked at the
menu of the Woodcutter Inn. Starey made a joke, the Leader
laughed at it. Starey made a gesture at the sky for the cameras.
The Leader looked in the same direction, judiciously. The two
men moved on.

Jack took a deep, inward breath and a sip of his pint. The
barman wiped the bar with a damp cloth, his head down,
whistling nonchalantly. Hortense Smith smoothed her skirt.

The waiters from the Woodcutter fiddled with their bow-ties. Jack cleared his throat, so that his voice was there, ready.

No one looked up until the moment, if it had been going to happen, was past. Then they saw Starey and the Leader standing outside the Jolly Roger, the Leader, momentarily, a bit crestfallen-looking – maybe because no one had bothered to attempt to blow him up, or even yell anything properly abusive. Veronica Tarrant, on the threshold, was explaining something to them – probably, judging by her hand movements, to do with the work she had had done on the building.

Back at the Caff, Jack lowered a metal net of raw chips into a vat of sizzling lard. It felt like his hopes.

He had seen feminist women, grim and assured, slamming their fists down on his formica tables. They'd take exception to anyone's assistance. Anna hadn't even wanted him in the ambulance, or at the hospital. She'd lashed out when he'd suggested how to deal with the people beating her friend up.

'Win,' Jack urged her in his head. 'Win, and I won't have to have an involvement.'

He put the radio on, caught the end of the theme tune of *Ship Ahoy*, the lunchtime edition, then the bips, followed by a stern moment of silence before the news began.

Jack cracked a couple of eggs onto the griddle, listening.

'. . . early days yet, Mary, but preliminary forecasts are suggesting that there is more grass-roots feeling than Babcock and Starey have possibly bargained for.'

What did that mean?

'Well I think, Mary, that the Ecology issue has now taken up a very much centre forum and that could tip the balance in the direction of the Coalition . . .'

Yes!

'If, and it is a big "if" . . .'

The place filled up with the lunchtime rush. There was loud chat and laughter. It got hard to hear the radio. Jack emptied chips onto plates, fried bacon and burgers, doled out baked beans, mash, sausages, the day's special, ladled custard, squirted cream.

'Felicia, what role is *personal* image having in this election?'

'Yes, Mary, that is something that we mustn't underestimate. It has to be said that Anna Seale . . .'

Jack put pasties in the microwave, drained cabbage, poured mugs of tea.

'. . . the very great advantage of being married to the previous incumbent's daughter, Primrose, who has been a tremendous asset to him in the run-up to the election, and who has shown herself to the people of Ebbing as someone deeply concerned with their affairs.'

'. . . by the fact that she would make a popular politician's wife?'

'Oh, *ab*solutely.'

'Even though her mother, Osbert Sway's widow, actually is campaign manager for Anna Seale?'

'The role of politician's widow is a complicated one, Mary . . .'

'Two egg and chips, one special, bacon sarnie, toasted cheese sarnie . . .' Jack paused. Suddenly, the radio was completely audible. The room had fallen silent. Jack looked round. Seated at one of the tables, surrounded by an entourage of reporters and news cameras, was a beautiful family: a lovely young woman, dressed in a kind of throwaway manner, cradling a perfect baby in a shawl. A handsome man. Two adorable twin girls. Two serious-faced little boys. Affecting not to notice the reaction they had inspired and looking as if they came in here, oh, simply all the time, the man and woman smiled at their offspring.

'Strawberry milkshakes all round, I'd say,' said the woman.

'. . . what we have in Ebbing is a real sense of community. And the people of Ebbing are proud of that, and secure enough in that to believe that now is the time to be forging greater links . . .' said Babcock, the whey-faced shit, yet again. Then, 'Not everyone feels the same, however.' The newscaster's voice had a smirk in it. Microsecond shot of the window of the Crab and Oyster Bar.

Anna bit into a toasted cheese sandwich. Six o'clock. A few minutes to herself then back to it. She took a swallow of Guinness. Why hadn't Jack Fryer just told them to piss off? she wondered. He hadn't given the impression of being in favour of the road, that night at the hospital. Though, now she thought about it, they hadn't discussed any of Jack's political opinions.

Maybe he was voting for Babcock. The idea got to Anna more than it should have.

Now her chest tightened. The forecasts. She watched them above the rim of her glass. Neck and neck. The Coalition was neck and neck with Babcock's Conservatives. Though would it stay that way? The newscaster pointed out – smugly, Anna thought – that the white-collar workers of Ebbing – among whom, it must not be forgotten, there was considerable support for the British Patriotic Party in the early days of the campaign – would be voting even as she spoke; their tendency, as the newscaster put it, was to be 'cautious'.

'Cautious!' Anna wanted to smash something. She wanted to seek out these 'cautious' individuals, with their gnomes and churches, and beat them up. 'Cautious?' Poisonous, ruined environment; nuclear weapons; racism; dog-eat-dog Capitalism: yes, that was playing it safe when the only alternatives were egalitarianism, peace and ecology.

Buttery sunlight floated on the small waves. Eternal dogs and children ran slowly across the blue pebbles. There were soaked lumps of driftwood. Something caught the light. Anna took a deep breath.

'If we lose, I'll just paint,' she told herself.

The cliffs were the colour of clotted cream.

'If you lose,' said another voice, 'there'll be nothing to paint any more.'

Getting up the sand from the damp floor, brushing it off the plastic chairs, where the wind-surfers had sat in their wet-suits, cleaning around in general, finding things to do that didn't need doing, Jack Fryer watched the shadows in the Caff lengthen, the sea gradually become black.

The radio spoke to a room that was empty except for him now. Didn't they ever get tired? Were they real people? Their voices never suggested they believed they were discussing something that could make anyone sad or happy. In this still time, the polling booths closed, the sea calm, Jack could imagine that there were only two people in the universe – himself and Anna Seale – and that, between them, Felicia and Mary – at mission control of the entire earth – would, at some stage of the night, decide what should become of them. Perhaps they would toss strange dice: smiles, good looks, suntans, clothes, families, education, strawberry milkshakes.

'It doesn't taste like the ones we had in Florida,' piped a precocious voice, and everyone laughed.

'That's the chemicals. Just this once, my Dove,' said Mrs Babcock. 'For Mummy and Daddy.' The children, a protective screen around the two of them, so you couldn't see them right, so you couldn't tell them you wouldn't serve them, so everyone's mouths filled with the sweet taste of strawberries when they thought of Babcocks, which made them want to let them decide the fates of nations.

'. . . yes, I think, Mary, yes, we have got a result and it will be announced in about half an hour in the Harvest Room of the Woodcutter Inn.'

The broom fell from Jack's hand. It hit the floor with a metallic sound. Grimly, he took off his apron and chucked it onto one of the tables. He walked out of the Caff and across the car park to his van. He got in.

He didn't know what time it was, though it must be late: there wasn't any traffic to speak of. Near the horizon, the ferry was a honeycomb of lights. Usually Jack would have been able to tell the hour by it, but his preoccupied mind hadn't registered whether it was on its way out or in. A bleak, green moon was rising or setting. It would be a good night for fishing, if there was anyone who fished.

The centre of Ebbing was crammed with parked cars and people. Jack squeezed the van into a bit of space, half up on some pavement. The Woodcutter Inn was surrounded by a mass of media vehicles. They looked like its respiratory equipment. There was a clot of people round the door. It didn't look like they were letting any more in. Jack's heart sank and his spirit soared – he'd tried, hadn't he?

'Here, Jack. I'll let you in round the back, if you want to see the bloody show.'

Jack experienced a wave of relief and despair. He followed his mate through an acre of kitchen. White tiles. Metal tables on wheels. Gigantic saucepans. Great stacks of white plates. Humming fridges. Through the restaurant, with its dunce-cap napkins, semi-dark, the only illumination coming from the foyer. Into the foyer, a murmuring crush of light and warmth and rectangular plastic containers of artificial plants, in beds of gravel, that people had put their fags out in.

They squeezed into the back of the Harvest Room, which had plush walls and a more hushed, less busy atmosphere. The TV lights made it hot and exaggerated every outline, made you notice shirt cuffs and collars, lips and hair colour.

At the front of the room, on a raised area, squashed beside a dusty grand piano, were the candidates and some other people. The Babcocks were holding hands. There was a woman, who appeared to be with them, in a blue twin-set and aquamarine eyeshadow. Starey was wearing a suit, but with the tie knot low on his chest, like in a menswear ad. There was a round-faced woman – Lib Dem, probably. Mrs Sway. Anna.

Crammed in the middle of them, in front of a microphone, was a grey individual with a piece of paper. He cleared his throat and the room fell silent as he started to read out the results in a garden-centre sort of voice. A wedge of adrenaline lodged itself in Jack's stomach.

A cry went up. The man continued to read but was drowned out by applause and cheering. Starey shook hands with Babcock. Mrs Babcock fell into the arms of the aquamarine woman, then she and Babcock embraced. Their supporters went wild. They let each other go and Babcock did a one-handed wave, his other resting upon his lovely wife's shoulder while she blew kisses at the audience.

Amid all the writhing and wriggling and waving, the gestures and poses, Lesley Sway and Anna Seale were a sole point of stillness. Jack's body ached for them. Second place, and close, so very close – way in front of Labour, though if Labour had been with them, the Conservatives would have been defeated. Perhaps nobody in the room but Jack noticed Anna reach out a little finger and link it with Lesley's.

Tim Babcock moved to the microphone. He started to speak but was silenced by the uproar. He stood there, smiling. Jack started to elbow forward. Eventually, Babcock quietened them.

'Primrose, thank-you,' he said, with an adoring glance back at her. Again, the crowd went wild. Jack ducked under raised arms, pushed between bodies, making space where there wasn't any.

'It's over,' his head told him. 'Now it's my responsibility.' And suddenly he saw, with crystal clarity, that he had been a fool and that, really, it had always been his responsibility.

'The result of this election shows, once and for all,' said Tim Babcock, 'that Ebbing wants the clifftop road and everything that that road can bring . . .'

Jack was at the very front of the room now. All the TV cameras were trained on Babcock at the microphone. Jack dodged round them, leapt onto the stage and shoved Babcock out of the way. He spoke into the microphone. His voice felt distant and not like part of him.

'There cannot be a road on the clifftop. The cliff won't support it.'

'What on earth is going on? Isn't there any security? Who is this man?' Babcock made a lunge for the microphone. Jack held him off it with a hand against Babcock's chest. With the other, he produced a piece of paper from his pocket.

'The cliff won't support a road,' Jack repeated. 'I've got an engineer's report here that says so. The cliff edge is noticeably crumbling. Its shape is changing – old maps show it different from how it is now. It couldn't have a bloody great road. It just wouldn't support it.'

'Why the fuck didn't you tell us that?' A voice screeched. 'Why the fuck didn't you say something sooner?' All eyes turned on Anna.

'Lies! All lies!' shouted Babcock.

Now there was a burst of mad sound, people in uniforms colliding with running journalists, reporters surging in Jack's direction.

'I'm sorry Anna,' he said, hopelessly, still into the microphone. 'I tried, but nobody listened, so I figured I must need better evidence. Then you were all arguing and, after that, I reckoned I'd be resented and I hoped it would come out right without me. But it didn't.'

24

The Wedding

The band arrived at six a.m. Not because they were early risers, but because they had spent the night driving down from Manchester. Jay's mother, who was an early riser – and who already had a great saucepan of pepperpot soup on the simmer and another, of water, coming to the boil for the crabs – let them in. She made fresh coffee and fed the musicians on banana bread and avocados. Some of them were dossed down in the sitting-room, among the other, sleeping and half-awake, bodies there when Lesley came downstairs; others had found the rugs and deckchairs and lay sunning in the garden. One, however, a woman – who'd got some kip in the van – sat talking to Jay and Susie at the kitchen table.

Lesley had presumed that Jay and Susie's 'wedding' would be a small affair, given that it was so last-minute, but word seemed to have made its way round the grapevine with quite extraordinary speed. Twenty wedding guests, at least, had shown up at the impromptu, post-election party that had erupted here the night before – including Jay's mother and several other relations. Today, around a hundred and fifty were apparently expected; among them, the gentleman who was to perform the ceremony and who Jay referred to as 'the Doctor'.

'Is he a Doctor of Philosophy or of Medicine?' Lesley had asked.

'No,' was Jay's reply.

A pot of sweet potatoes was bubbling furiously. The kitchen was full of a sensual tangle of cooking smells, combined with the summer scents of the garden and a salty dash of sea.

'Lesley,' said Jay's mother, opening the fridge and exposing bottle after bottle of Osbert's vintage champagne, 'I've got freshly-squeezed orange and I'm going to cook up some scrambled eggs shortly.'

'You don't recognise me, do you Mrs Sway?' said the woman at the table.

Hennaed hair. A pretty, rounded face. A largish curve of stomach, controlled by tight, pink, lycra shorts. Kohl round the eyes.

'Is it?' Lesley asked. 'Is it Ursula Frogwell?'

'Lesley,' burst out Susie, 'Guess what? Now we've got the caravan to live in, we're going to turn Jay's house into a recording studio, using the insurance money. We're starting our own label. I'll be doing the technical side – the sound engineer sort of stuff – and Jay's going to be in charge of the production bit. Eat Shit And Die are our first band. Jay's friends in London tracked them down for us. I'm awfully sorry but I won't be able to be your secretary any more.'

'Never mind, Susie,' said Lesley, accepting an orange juice. 'A new direction is a good idea.'

'Isn't it wonderful?' Susie continued. 'Except for you, of course, Lesley. And Ursula's going to sing at the wedding party!'

'Oh good,' said Lesley.

There was a deafening noise from the sitting-room as the television was turned on full blast. The sound was adjusted.

'Come in here, Les,' yelled Anna, who must have heard her voice.

Lesley went to join her. Some people were watching the screen with Anna. Others had pulled cushions and pillows over their heads.

'Good morning, Mrs Sway,' said Bob, standing up. 'Very pleasant evening. Very pleasant indeed. Made all the more so by the knowledge of another day of festivity ahead. Adrian and Gilda seem to be still asleep, so I think I'll just take Carrot for a quick stroll – she looks as though she needs one – and see if I can spot anything.'

'Watch, Les,' said Anna.

Lesley perched on the edge of a sofa, which seemed to contain at least one Marxist. It was a morning news programme. By now, apparently, various independently commissioned engineers had visited the Ebbing clifftop and confirmed the early findings: the cliff was not up to bearing any kind of increase in traffic. A furious member of the House of Lords was condemning the amount of public money that had been wasted on the abortive scheme. A cross shadow spokesman, with a red beard, was 'questioning how the government could realistically claim . . .'

After a while of this, Tim Babcock joined them from the studio in Pitsbury. Yes, he confirmed, the project had been shelved indefinitely, after extensive discussions on the topic with the Prime Minister the night before.

This was not strictly true. The conversation between Babcock and his Leader had lasted approximately fifteen seconds and had consisted of only one sentence: 'Make this go away, Babcock, make this go away *now*.' Extensive indeed, however, had been the furious exchanges, which Babcock saw no need to mention, between himself, Dick Winters and various branches of the Department of Transport, the topic of which was how in God's name such a fundamental detail as a geological survey had been overlooked.

The answer proved to be a simple one: a geological survey had been done, and was on record as having been done, though, someone eventually admitted, 'not terribly recently', hastily adding that, being in possession of one survey, it had been deemed wasteful of taxpayers' money to do another. 'Not terribly recently' proved to be 1842.

In the light of this, in his television interview, Babcock chose to be vague as to how out of date the 'out of date information' he referred to actually was and to lay much more emphasis upon the capriciousness of geological activity, citing as example a Northerly island that had sprung into being in a matter of hours without giving any advance warning. The sea's erosion of the Ebbing cliffs must be considered similarly unforeseeable. Having said which, and while applauding the wisdom of the

Prime Minister's decision not to continue with the road scheme, Babcock had to make it known that he himself was far from convinced by the engineers' findings. The interviewer pointed out that, to date, there were now five different reports that she herself knew of, and all of them came to the same conclusion. Babcock got a bit huffy and said that, while he was in complete accord with the Prime Minister that they should respond quickly to public concern about this matter, he believed that, if the road had still been going to be built, no one would have needed to worry about it. Later today, he would be speaking about this to a television news team from the Ebbing clifftop itself.

Lesley and Anna went out into the garden. Beyond the wall, they could see Bob, looking out to sea with his binoculars and Carrot snuffling around in the undergrowth. Meg Hughes appeared round the side of the house, carrying two sacks of mussels.

'Still here!' she exclaimed, surveying the clifftop with satisfaction. 'Still here. Until time decides otherwise!' She went into the house to deposit the shellfish in the kitchen.

Three sucking pigs were already turning on a spit above a glowing fire. Trouncy Lollop teetered across the lawn in something clingy, holding a bunch of red balloons. Rolf Watt hoisted her up so that she could tie them in the trees.

'I wonder what Steven's doing? He said he'd be here by now,' said Penny St John, who was arranging sunflowers in earthenware pots. 'He's supposed to be bringing the cake.'

'Bet I know what he's doing,' said Rory, who'd been told to put out the knives and forks.

Anna and Lesley stood in the middle of the lawn. It was hot. A perfect day for a 'wedding'.

'What I still can't understand,' said Anna, 'is who Jack Fryer reckoned he tried to talk to about the clifftop. Not me, that's for certain.'

A wave of guilt washed over Lesley. In the turmoil and excitement of the night before she hadn't really thought about it. Now, everything fell into place.

'Me,' she said bleakly.

'You? When?'

Lesley went through the occasions in her mind. 'Several

times,' she said. 'Once in the Caff – he said he had a suggestion to make, but I just told him to phone me, then I didn't really listen to his message. Then he tried to talk to me in the street . . .'

'Not your strong point.'

'I thought I was behaving like a proper politician.'

'Why didn't he try telling me, then?' wondered Anna.

'I suppose . . . Anna, I can't but feel that there was probably some emotion mixed up in it. I mean, you can be rather . . . intimidating.'

Now it was Anna's turn to experience a stab of conscience, as she thought of the night of Jay's attack: how mild Jack had been; how she had snapped at him.

Lesley turned to gaze in the direction of the river valley. Anna turned too. Emerald meadow grass. Deep blue in the shadows. Livid, juicy leaves against a mosaic of turquoise sky. The jade and agate river. 'I'm off,' she said.

'I'll give you a lift, if you like,' said Lesley.

'No, I'll walk.'

There was a pause.

'Anna . . .' said Lesley.

'Shut up, Lesley. What you're about to say is only right for good-byes. Unless good-bye is what you want to say really?' Her face filled with its quick anger.

'No,' said Lesley, 'that's not what I want to say.'

They had not noticed the sound of a rattling vehicle pulling up, squeals and exclamations, doors slamming.

'Hey,' breathed a hot voice in Lesley's ear.

Lesley jumped out of her skin. She swung round. An ancient black man, in a white trilby, held out a hand. 'My name is Doctor Orgasmo,' he said.

Anna walked down the cliff path thinking about how she could now get back to her stupid, useless, pointless art; the solitary pleasure of gleaming coils of paint; the creation of great big canvases crammed with sea and sky, snatched interactions of earth and light and water, that hardly anyone would ever see. A vision, unshared. To what end? To what purpose?

A deep sense of oppression invaded her. The odds were stacked. Though was that news? Hardly.

Anna thought of Jack Fryer. The odds were stacked. Banging your head against a brick wall got old after a while. And it was hard to believe that there wasn't someone else out there speaking for you, making sure that it all worked out okay.

Though he had made sure it worked out okay, Jack Fryer.

Seagulls floated on the warm air. Shattered waves burst into foam.

Anna tried an idea out. Herself and Jack. Nights with that strong body; that solid presence a part of her life. Lives shared but separate. For Jack, his Caff. For herself, the Crab and Oyster Bar and the cash it brought in, her messy house, weird hours and painting. Love: yes, perhaps even that – if it was big enough to fit round that type of existence.

Anna crossed the bridge over the river. The ferry was entering the harbour and people were standing on deck to have a look at Ebbing, or England, more probably. She entered the Old Fish Market Square car park. Media vans were being packed up. Men in suits, their hands in their pockets were going into the Jolly Roger for business lunches. The Woodcutter Inn had a new banner. The Anchor's curtains were closed. Anna paused. The sound of raised voices was coming from Cinderella's. She made her way over to the shop and looked in through the window, where she was amazed at what she saw: Susie's mother, Winifred Took, in discussion with Carmen, whose head kept appearing and disappearing behind a large-lipped mannequin, with painted hair, wearing a top hat.

The door was open. From Anna's position, the conversation was completely audible.

'No, I did not,' said Winifred Took. 'I recall expressing sympathy, but nothing more.'

'Sod your bloody sympathy,' rasped Carmen. 'You offered cash. We made a deal.'

'I did nothing of the kind. The very thought I find repulsive. Mrs Babcock was here and she will back me up on this.'

Anna moved away. What was all that about? she wondered. She left the Square and walked down Harbour Street. Sunlight glanced off the upper windows of the buildings. She was nearly home.

The door to Steven Toe's studio flew open as she passed it.

Anna leapt backwards just in time: an easel came crashing out, followed by two jars of paintbrushes, which shattered against the opposite wall, the brushes clinking onto the ground. Next came a clay pot. Then something framed.

'It was performance art,' cried Steven Toe's voice.

'Do you think? Do you really think I care what you do with an Ebbing scrubber? But to hear it from my own brother . . .' The rest of what Penny St John had to say was lost beneath the sound of breaking glass.

'I'm not a scrubber, I've got an interview to be receptionist in an auction house. Let me get my . . .'

But the young woman was pushed out into the street completely naked, Toe following immediately with a gallant piece of drapery. The door slammed behind him. A key turned in the lock.

Anna stood watching, an amused expression on her face. Bianca Pickle tried to wrap the flimsy bit of material around her fulsome loins, while Toe got tangled in the smock he was attempting to take off to help cover her shame.

'You'd better come into my place and I'll get you something to wear,' Anna said to Bianca.

'Ms Seale,' said Toe, noticing her now, 'that is kind of you. There seems to have been a misunderstanding.'

'Yeah, I saw it.'

Anna opened her front door, let Bianca in ahead of her and led her into the bedroom. Toe followed them into the building. From Anna's room he could hear the women's voices.

'Don't know who she thinks she's calling a scrubber,' Bianca was saying, indignantly. 'You can't tell me she's with him for his body.'

Rather than hear more, Toe pushed a door open and entered what, at first sight, appeared to be a sitting-room. At second sight, he realised it wasn't: it was a studio, filled with perhaps a dozen canvases, most of them large ones, some obviously in progress, others stacked against the walls.

The sculptor's eyes watered. He wandered from picture to picture. The sea, the cliffs, in all their moods, in every permutation of their colours: the desolate, dead, pale greys and lavenders of sulky water withholding reflection; icy green waves, seething beneath sulphur lightning; a bloody sunset over a purple ocean.

'She'll be ready in a minute,' said Anna. Then she saw Toe's expression.

'You did these?' he asked.

Anna nodded.

Toe's eyes fell upon six unstamped envelopes on a table. Unbelievingly, he read their addresses.

'And you do not have a gallery?'

Anna shook her head.

Her voice came out husky: 'I'd like to hear it, if you have any advice about my painting.'

Toe swallowed. 'There is nothing you can learn from me, my dear, nothing that anyone can teach you. If, however, you would permit me to introduce you to any, or all, of these galleries, I would consider it a very great privilege.'

The doorbell rang, which was strange because the door was open and people were just wandering in. Even the Baker's delivery boy had brought the cake – a rococo edifice of many-hued icing, marzipan flowers and dozens of cherries – straight into the kitchen.

Lesley went to answer it and found a woman standing there, her back to the house. She was medium height, slightly dumpy and wearing a floral dress with a plastic belt. She turned when she heard Lesley. The face was motherly and covered in pink powder; Lesley recognised it from the picture in the newspaper.

'Mrs Sway?'

'Nanny Enema.'

The woman smiled, cosily. 'That's my professional name. My real name is Ingrid Smithbone. I don't want to disturb you, Mrs Sway, since you obviously have some kind of family celebration happening, but there were a couple of things I wanted to say to you, if you wouldn't mind listening. One is, Osbert and me, we only had a working relationship. The other is, I read in the papers about you and the clifftop and I think it's a wonderful thing you've been doing. I'm very fond of ecology myself. I've got a bird-table in my back garden and there's a squirrel comes and feeds off it every day. Ricky, I call him. Anyway, that's all and I won't keep you any longer.'

Lesley listened in silence. Then, as the woman made to leave, she said: 'Ms Smithbone?'

'Oh, Ingrid will do, dear. Seeing as all we've got in common.'

'Ingrid, would you like to come to a "wedding"?'

Nanny Enema had just disappeared into the house when a car entered the drive at high speed. In the passenger seat was a stunning woman with thick auburn hair. The driver was Darryl.

Of course: an actress. The role of Miranda, almost certainly. Lesley took a deep breath and prepared to be dignified, prepared to rise to the occasion. For a long time she had been an actress herself, to all intents and purposes.

Darryl leapt out of the car.

'Les!' he yelled, joyfully. 'I got Susie's phone call and hot-footed it down here very first moment they'd let me.'

The woman came round to stand beside him. The two of them walked towards Lesley. Close to, the woman's appearance was even more breathtaking. Never in her life had Lesley seen eyes so large or of such a gorgeous colour. 'No, I will not be brave,' she thought. 'I simply will not be able to.'

Darryl grabbed her hand.

'Les,' he said, 'you look absolutely . . .'

'Who is your friend, Darryl?' Lesley interrupted.

The woman gave Lesley a smile that could have melted icebergs.

'This,' said Darryl, 'is Madeline Rush. Double purpose in inviting her – triple, if we count the pleasure of your presence, Maddie. Ebbing Constab still had the jalopy. Maddie here persuaded them to part with it – and no fine. Also, thought it was time you met your solicitor.'

'My solicitor!'

'Lesley,' said Madeline Rush, 'you're every bit as lovely as Darryl said you were.'

'And Madeline should know, with her eye for the ladies. Go on in and set some drinks up, Maddie, I'm going to haul Les off for five minutes.'

They walked a little way along the clifftop, in the direction of Cove. The Channel was busy. Sailing boats. Wind-surfers. A dredger. The Seaway ferry was a distant smudge of white and blue.

'Bloody beautiful, isn't it?' said Darryl. He swung round to face her. 'Listen, Les, there's something I've been wondering. This North America tour . . .'

Lesley's heart started thumping. He wanted her to continue to look after the cat. He'd like her to keep an eye on his house. He wanted her to feel free to see other people in his absence, because it was quite possible that he . . .

'. . . I was wondering if you'd consider coming with me. I missed you so sodding much while we were rehearsing.'

Rehearsing.

Standing there in the sunlight, Lesley Sway remembered reading something once that an older actor had said to a younger one who was getting worried and worked up: 'Life is not a rehearsal, don't forget. It's the opening night.'

Epilogue

Who can doubt what happened next?

Under the auspices of Doctor Orgasmo, an old jazzman, whose voice had been worn smooth by a thousand smoky nightclubs, Jay and Susie, surrounded by no real family, but many real friends, made their own, idiosyncratic vows.

Meanwhile, further along the cliff, just past the outer reaches of the lesser tit's nesting site, a group of media people set up their cameras and Tim Babcock made his way, gingerly, and with no great pleasure, along a narrow, chalky path to join them. The spot had been chosen by his PR people. It was near to the cliff edge: the sea and the sky would make for a nice contrast of colour behind the MP, as well as drawing the focus onto what would have stayed the same if the road had been allowed to happen and away from what would have been redeveloped.

'Just right here, Mr Babcock. Yes, that's lovely. Light okay? What's the problem? Sorry, Mr Babcock, if you don't mind staying there. It'll only take a minute.'

The ceremony was over. Jay's long arms closed around Susie's plump waist. Their lips came together in a loud kiss. Ursula Frogwell threw down her fag. Eat Shit And Die's electric guitars struck up a screaming chord.

'Oh no!' gasped all the birdwatchers present, assailed by the same thought.

Thank heaven the young were advanced enough to fend for themselves! Suddenly, the air was brownish with a panicked flock of lesser tits, flapping, darting and plunging in all directions.

'What on earth?' cried Tim Babcock. A mass of beaks and

feathers was coming straight at him. He stumbled backwards, sat down heavily, the bit of cliff he had landed on fell away.

'Roll the cameras,' were the last words he heard. 'For God's sake roll the fucking cameras.'

Jack Fryer was just about to lock up when the news came over the radio.

He lowered himself into a seat at one of the empty tables and remained there for some while, quite motionless, staring out to sea.

'Why shouldn't I run?' he murmured eventually. 'Why shouldn't someone like me be in parliament? This time, why not?'

A little while later he set off, on foot, to join the wedding.